Books by Richard Helms

Geary's Year
Geary's Gold
The Valentine Profile
The Amadeus Legacy
Joker Poker
Voodoo That You Do
Juicy Watusi
Wet Debt
Paid In Spades
Bobby J.
Grass Sandal
Cordite Wine
Brittle Karma
Doctor Hate
The Daedalus Deception
Six Mile Creek
Thunder Moon
Older Than Goodbye
A Kind and Savage Place
The Mojito Coast
The Unresolved Seventh
Vicar Brekonridge
Paper Walls/Glass Houses
Holy City
22 Rue Montparnasse
Bump and Run
Great White

GREAT WHITE

by

RICHARD HELMS

BLACK ARCH BOOKS

BLACK ARCH BOOKS
an imprint of
Barbadoes Hall Communications
ISBN: 979-8-9900412-3-3

For Elaine

ONE

I have always believed that neckties are a great source of relief, once taken off. Because of that, I have scrupulously structured my life in such a fashion that I'm only forced to wear a tie at weddings, funerals, and court.

On this day, I was in court, which beat the hell out of a funeral. I'd attended far too many of those recently.

I own a single suit. Just one. It's a nice one, though. Lovely bespoke wool pinstripe. Set me back about a thousand dollars, so I'm really careful when I venture abroad wearing it.

I've spent so much time over the years in the witness box that the seat now conforms to my ass, and I know all the rules. Most of my appearances involve divorce and marital rancor, with a side dish of infidelity. Today was different.

The Assistant District Attorney was a businesslike woman in black slacks, a red blouse, and a blazer. Her name was Alison Eliot. Her neon red hair was longer when we called each other by our first names and various cutesy epithets back in the day, but recently she had elected for a tight pageboy cut, probably because it saved her ten minutes in the bathroom each morning. We were kind of an item when I first hung out my shingle, but I've been happily involved with another for several years now. It was okay. Alison didn't hold a grudge.

I think.

She didn't stand as she questioned me from the prosecution bench. Hardly anyone ever stands in court. Something TV gets wrong all the time.

"Can you state your name and occupation?" she asked.

"Eamon Gold. I'm a private investigator. My office is on Jefferson Street, near Hyde Pier."

"How long have you been employed as a private investigator?"

"Twenty-six years."

"And before that?"

"I was an inspector with the San Francisco Police Department for five years, and a uniformed officer for three years prior to that. I was also an MP in the Army. Two tours."

"Do you know a man named Samuel Brownlee?"

"I do," I said.

"Do you see Mr. Brownlee in the courtroom today?"

"I do," I said.

"Can you point him out?"

I nodded toward the defense table, where Sammy sat next to his attorney. "That's him, next to Mr. Varnadore."

"How do you know Mr. Brownlee?" she asked.

"He was a client."

Now, here's the thing about testifying in court. The very worst thing you can do is go running off at the mouth. Every time I've seen a witness systematically disassembled on cross-examination, it was because they volunteered information that wasn't requested by the other side. The smartest attorneys only ask questions when they already know the answers. Their entire case is built on their narrative of the facts, and they don't want that narrative undermined by a witness who was vaccinated with a phonograph needle. The best policy is to keep all answers short, sweet, and on point. I trusted Alison not to lead me in a direction that might result in a royal butt-reaming by the defense attorney.

"What did Mr. Brownlee hire you to do?"

"He wanted me to find someone."

"Who?"

"His spouse, Rhonda Brownlee."

"Why did he want you to find her?"

"It was a marital issue. Rhonda Brownlee had left her husband and wouldn't tell him where she was."

I left out the part about all the money she spirited from their mutual bank account. I figured it would come up sooner or later anyway. I answered each of Alison's questions as succinctly as possible as I outlined the basics of the case, up to the exact moment I discovered Rhonda Brownlee's body. A couple of cops—a uniformed guy and a young police inspector named Leon Fender—waited impatiently in the back of the room to provide the details of the case after they took it over.

Alison exhausted her planned interrogation and announced to the judge that she had no more questions.

The judge turned to the defense table. "Mr. Varnadore?"

Wilson Varnadore stood an inch or two over six feet. His hair was shock white and contrasted with his onyx eyes. He had a deep Caribbean tan, far too dark for a guy who carries a caseload that would break an elephant's back. I could see from fifteen feet away that his subway tile teeth were implants, or maybe just veneers, but store-bought in any case. His suit gave my suit an inferiority complex. He wore it better too, which reminded me I needed to get back to the gym. Maybe it was the combination of his hair and dead eyes and his improbably neon dental work that had dubbed him The Great White Shark around the courthouse.

Maybe it was something else.

It was the *something else* that worried me.

Like Alison Eliot, he remained seated as he cross-examined me. "Mr. Gold, how long did you work for Mr. Brownlee?"

"A little over a week."

"Did that afford you the opportunity to know him well?"

"Absolutely not," I said.

"How so?"

"He was the client. I typically see the client twice—once when they hire me, and then when I present my findings. In the time I worked for Mr. Brownlee, I believe I was in his personal presence perhaps four hours total."

"Are you familiar with Mr. Brownlee's employment?"

I tried to think of a good euphemism for *loanshark*. Came up nearly empty.

"I believe he is…ah…self-employed," I said.

"In what capacity?"

"He provides financial assistance, typically at significantly inflated interest rates, to people who can't resort to the banks, or who have been turned down for money everywhere else."

"And you knew this when he hired you?"

"I did."

"In your brief experience with Mr. Brownlee, did you ever hear him make threats toward his wife Rhonda?"

"I heard him say he would make her pay," I said. "That was the only time."

"How did you interpret that?"

"Objection," Alison said from her table without even looking up from her legal pad. "Mr. Gold is a highly competent investigator, but he is not psychic."

"Sustained," said the judge.

Varnadore reframed the question. "Did Mr. Brownlee act in an aggressive manner when he said he would make his wife pay?"

"He said it during a telephone call. He had just discovered his wife had withdrawn a significant amount of money from their joint bank accounts. He was irritated. I wouldn't call him overtly angry."

"You discovered Rhonda Brownlee's body?" Varnadore asked.

"I did."

"And you informed Mr. Brownlee that his wife was dead?"

"I was present, with Inspector Fender, when he was informed. I suppose you could say we informed him together."

"In your busincss, you cncounter a great number of people who have experienced an emotional crisis, do you not?"

"It happens frequently," I said.

"My esteemed colleague, Assistant DA Eliot, claimed you are highly competent. Do you believe, as a consequence of your years of investigative experience, that you are skilled at reading people?"

"Better than average," I said.

"Could you describe Mr. Brownlee's behavior when you told him his wife had died?"

"He acted distraught. He sat on the sofa and wrung his hands, and he wept a little."

"And did you believe Mr. Brownlee's grief was genuine?"

Well, did I?

It was an excellent question.

TWO

A year earlier—

Jordy Pankratz looked like a cartoon bookkeeper. Something in the eyes. Even when he wasn't poring over a ledger, he squinted at everything. He resembled a cartoon mole, with dark, slicked-back hair and a scrunched face with beady eyes and a tiny mouth. His lips looked permanently pursed. He fidgeted a lot. The bruises on his face suggested he was in trouble. A highly trained detective like me can spot these little indicators.

"I'm being threatened," he said. "I need protection."

Pankratz looked like the kind of guy who'd needed protection since first grade.

"What's the nature of these threats?" I asked.

He wrung his hands and stared at the rug in my office. "I…I made a big mistake. I should have known better, but my back was against the wall. Most people in this country are one paycheck away from bankruptcy, me included. A totaled car, a hospitalization, or even temporary unpaid sick leave can push them over the edge. Bookkeepers don't make CPA salaries, Mr. Gold, and I don't make a salary at all. I freelance for companies that don't have enough cash flow to warrant a full-on accountant. I was comfortable, but not rich by any means. Not even wealthy. Then I broke my arm. Dumb bicycling accident. Clumsy people like me are foolish to even get on the damned things. Even with insurance, the out-of-pocket costs were staggering. Before I knew it, I was up to my shoulders in debt, and I couldn't figure a way out. I…I did something really stupid."

"You stole the money," I said.

"Have I told you this story before?" Pankratz asked.

"Other people have. The folks you stole the money from are after you now?"

"No. They wouldn't work that way. They'd just fire me and sue my ass off, or if they were pissed enough, they might press felony charges, but most businesses avoid that because of bad publicity. Looking back on it, it would have been better to just take my lumps with them. No. I compounded my stupidity. In my defense, my conscience wouldn't allow me to do anything else. I needed to replace the missing money."

"But you didn't have enough to do that," I said.

"No. I couldn't go to a bank. Wouldn't have mattered if I did. I had no collateral for a loan. My house is a rental, and my car might be worth a decent meal at In and Out."

"How much money are we talking about here?"

"A little south of twenty thousand dollars. I applied for a couple of credit cards I could soak to pay it off, but I was turned down. All that did was murder my credit rating. I met a guy at a bar a few months back, a fellow I knew years ago when we worked for the same company. Just a chance reunion. Wasn't planned or anything. After a few drinks, I told him about my situation."

"Let me guess. He knew a guy."

"Yeah. He knew a guy. He set up a meeting. I replaced the money."

"But now, you have to pay the guy back."

"I work with numbers, Mr. Gold. You could say I live them. I've been fascinated with sums and cyphers since I was a kid. I look at a balance book, and I can see the past and the future. I can look over your ledgers and tell you whether you'll still be in business two years from now. I look at my own situation, and I'm screwed. Unless I win the lottery, I'm never getting even with this guy."

"The vig is eating you alive."

"Vig?"

"Vigorish. The interest. Compounds by the second and never takes a holiday. You might draw within eyesight of the principle a few seconds before the heat death of the universe."

"You sound like you've run into this sort of thing before."

"I am not without experience. Does this guy have a name?"

"Sammy Brownlee."

I'd never heard of him, but that wasn't unusual for a city the size of San Francisco. There are thousands of lowlife bozos, yahoos, and loose change here I might never run into in an entire lifetime. Just because I had never heard of him didn't mean he wasn't dangerous, and the bruises on Pankratz's face told me ol' Sammy wasn't averse to paying the band for a little knuckle music to motivate delinquent payers.

"Tell me about the muscle," I said.

"The muscle?"

"The guys Brownlee sent to tune you up."

"Oh. There are two of them. Big guys. Biceps as big as footballs. One's blond. The other's bald. I heard the bald one call the other T-Bone. Probably a nickname."

"You think? Okay, Mr. Pankratz, I get the picture. I can help you, but sooner or later you're gonna have to pay this Brownlee character. I can't make the debt go away. Maybe I can keep these two guys from putting you in a hospital in the meantime."

"How can I pay the debt if I can't even pay the interest?"

I could hear the tears in his voice. The logical next question was how he could pay *me*. Work had been slow, though, and I was kind of bored, so I left that for later.

"Tell me how to contact Brownlee," I said. "I can drop by for a visit, discuss the terms of your indebtedness, but I wouldn't get my hopes up if I were you. As far as the legbreakers go, we can keep them off your back for a while, until you can dig up the scratch to get out of this mess."

"We?" He asked.

"Yeah," I said. "I'm gonna need to bring in a little help."

THREE

Sonny Malehala answered on the second ring. Even from two thousand miles across half the Pacific, he came in loud and clear. You gotta love modern technology.

"Aloha, my sensei!" he said as he answered the phone. He sounded healthy and happy. The happy part was a nice change.

I'd trained Sonny to be a private investigator after his career as a mob goon was blown when his boss got shot out from under him. Literally. He'd repaid me by winging off to Honolulu to become the security director in an adults-only all-inclusive resort in the shadow of Diamond Head. I didn't resent it a bit. The tragic love affair that drove him away from the Bay City was more than sufficient cause. I'd have probably wanted to fly as far away as possible myself.

Sonny was six and a half feet of solid beef with the brain of an English professor. He looked like an action movie hero with his shaved head and three-foot-wide shoulders. A compulsive workout addict, he hadn't been able to buy a suit off the rack since he was in the Army.

If Godzilla ever really does attack San Francisco, I want Sonny on *my* side.

"Are you busy?" I asked.

"Up to my ass in alligators, but around here we call that Monday. What's shakin'?"

"I might need some backup. Wondered whether you're up for a few nights at the Mark Hopkins."

"I always love visiting you and Heidi, but what about Delroy? Isn't he available?"

Jack Delroy was another private cop in the bay area. One of the best. I had met him when he worked for a wheelchair-bound genius named Sheldon Moon. Moon had died during the pandemic, leaving Delroy in charge of Full Moon Investigations.

"I checked. Too busy. He's a desk jockey these days. Executive type. I need an international man of action."

"You know Hawai'i doesn't constitute international, right? What's the gig?"

"Protection. Some nebbish got himself in dutch with a loanshark. Now a couple of collectors are leaving past-due notices on his face with their fists. He would like me to discourage them."

"So? Discourage them."

"Time and tide wait for no one, my eternally youthful friend," I said. "In my prime, I'd have taken them myself. My odds against two guys these days are only slightly lower than even, maybe slightly better if they're the kind of musclebound punks who grew their bulges in a gym somewhere but never touched a speedbag. I also heal slower lately. I wouldn't mind bringing someone along to provide the advantage."

"Hold tight," he said. I heard the phone hit the blotter on his desk. A few seconds later, he picked it up again.

"I checked with my assistant. Cleared the boards until Saturday. He's making my flight arrangements now. I'll text you with the deets when they're complete, but I should hit SFO sometime tomorrow."

I locked my office door and trotted down the sixteen steps from my landing to the sidewalk. Just below my office was Heidi Fluhr's art gallery. Heidi was, in no particular order, an art dealer, a classical guitarist, on the lam from German anarchists, and my solitary squeeze for the past couple of decades.

A legacy network television show I'd never heard of was filming on Jefferson Street that afternoon. The street was clogged with trailers, generators, miles of electrical cable, and several fully enclosed tents toward the Hyde Pier end. It was a common nuisance, as my office is situated within hailing distance of the pier, with a vista of the Golden Gate that Mr. Magoo would find breathtaking. I had read somewhere that Hyde Pier and Montgomery Street in San Francisco were two of the most-filmed locations in television and movies. The lords of the cinema had once again encamped at my front door.

The bell over Heidi's gallery door tinkled as I opened it. She was showing a new piece to a customer I recognized, a collector who left a bushel basket of cash in her register whenever he visited. She winked at me as I took a seat behind her desk, and she returned to the process of landing her whale.

Dependable as always, the collector bought the piece, which put Heidi in an ecstatic mood. I approved. Money always makes her amorous.

"Wanna hang out with Sonny this week?" I asked.

She squealed and hopped onto my lap, wrapping her arms around my neck. I thought I felt my pelvis snap. I winced, because *petite* is a word you'd never utter in her presence. She's nearly six feet of healthy blonde Nordic goddess, strong as a bear but soft in all the places where it really counts. She kissed me. Twice.

"I just made my nut for the next two months!" she said. "Let's celebrate! I'll close the shop and we'll take the first plane to Honolulu!"

"Not so fast. He's coming here," I said.

"Even better." She caught the look on my face and pouted. "It's work, isn't it?"

"It's work," I said. "I need backup. We should have plenty of time to hang out, though."

"Backup. That means it's dangerous."

"Maybe. Probably not. Does matter?"

"No," she said. "I suppose it doesn't. Well, we need to celebrate this sale now, and this damned film crew is murdering my walk-in business. I'm closing the gallery and you're taking me to a fantastic lunch."

"Me? You're the one who's bucks up."

"Oh, sweetie, you know it always comes up even in the bottom of the ninth. I'll make it worth your while."

Experience told me she certainly would.

FOUR

By the time Sonny's plane arrived the next day, I was tuckered out. I figured Jordy Pankratz was safe enough at work, but nighttime is when the bad guys come around, and I had already committed to protecting him. That meant a long night alone in my car outside his house.

Around midnight, Heidi parked her Miata behind me. She carried a bag around to my passenger side door. I hit the lock.

As soon as she slipped in beside me, I could smell the sandwiches in the bag.

"You heard my stomach growling all the way over at your condo?" I asked.

"Had a couple of midnight cravings," she said. "Missed you tonight. You like subs, right?"

We shared a Chuck's banh mi grinder and a couple of Cokes.

"So this is all you do?" she asked. "When does the dangerous shit start?"

"Hopefully, never," I said. "If I'm lucky, Brownlee's tough guys won't show at all tonight. Two against one is no picnic. That's why I brought this." I patted the new composite Glock on my hip. I'd finally retired my old Browning for something lighter that had been manufactured in this century. "Makes me hope even more that they stay away tonight. Discouraging these yokels is one thing. If I pull this, it becomes assault with a deadly weapon. As long as it stays in my holster, it's just intimidation. Once I yank it out, we're talking serious business."

"True about so many things," she said.

We hung out for a half hour, played a little smoochy-face, and then she drove back home. I kept up my watch on Pankratz's place until about three, when I decided even the most dedicated muscle would be strapped to their CPAPs by that hour. I took it to the barn.

I was still sleep deprived when I picked Sonny up outside SFO's baggage claim early that afternoon. The traffic guard in the pickup lane glowered at me when I hopped out of my car and popped my trunk to hoist Sonny's bag inside and took a quick second to try to give him a manly hug. It was kind of a pathetic attempt, as I could only get my arms halfway around, so I wound up kind of awkwardly patting his shoulder blades.

"Aloha!" he said as he nearly lifted me off the ground.

"Stow the Moondoggie shit," I said. "You're stateside now. And put me down!"

The right side of the car settled when he took his seat beside me. I navigated out to the highway.

"So, you're the Hawaiian Eye, now," I said. "Is Cricket as cute as she looks on TV?"

"If I had any idea what you're talking about—"

"Ever run into Magnum? Been hanging out with Rick and TC?"

"Oh. Television. Don't have a lot of time for it lately. This job is busier than I expected."

"Murder and intrigue in Waikiki?"

"Not yet, thank goodness. But the sheer volume of scams people run in hotels would blow your mind. Long cons, short cons, we got it all. And don't get me started on the whores. Sorry, sex workers. My biggest headache right now is a squatter."

"A squatter? In a hotel?"

"More like a resort phantom. We know he's sneaking into rooms and sleeping overnight, but he's always gone before housekeeping shows up."

"How would one do that?" I asked. "Purely out of curiosity, of course."

"One theory is he's stealing master keycodes from the housekeepers, but he's doing it cleverly. None of the housekeeping cards are missing. We thought he had a card reader/writer, and he was somehow copying the master keycards when housekeepers weren't looking. We changed the pass codes, but he just showed up again a couple of nights later—or, at least, evidence of his passing did."

"You'd think he'd get caught sooner or later. Nobody ever walked in on him sleeping in a room?"

"We're not the Hilton. Most people at the resort are on package deals. They show up on buses from the airport in the afternoon. Guests very seldom check in after midnight. It's so slow overnight that we only have one person at the front desk and no concierge on duty. What we can't figure out is how he knows which rooms are empty."

"Easy," I said. "Inside job. Either someone at the front desk or one of the housekeepers is in on it."

"I thought the same thing," he said. "I'm working with the IT department to put a unique tag on every individual keycard used by the staff, embedded in the master key code. If he steals the code, we'll know who he took it from. If the same stolen code keeps popping up…"

"Nothing is more inconvenient than coincidence," I said.

"So tell me about this gig."

I told him what I knew about Jordy Pankratz and Sammy Brownlee.

"I know Brownlee," Sonny said. "Not well, but I'd recognize him on the street. He's not like the old guard loansharks. Dresses upscale. Likes nice things. Looks like he should be working in some brokerage in the Transamerica Pyramid. Self-styles himself as a noble businessman savior of the financially downtrodden or some shit. Kind of a smirky douche nozzle."

"Is he dangerous?"

"If you were on an oxygen tank, I suppose he could be troublesome. I've been out of touch with the criminal element in this city since Mr. Bugliosi died, though. Things change. Brownlee might be a bigger deal now, and more dangerous."

"Pankratz described two guys—one bald and one blond. Built like weightlifters. One of them goes by T-Bone. Any idea who they might be?"

"Don't recognize the descriptions. I'll bet they're local," he said. "Brownlee doesn't have the juice to import out-of-town talent. You wouldn't do that for collecting in any case. If Mr. Bugliosi brought anyone in from Houston or Miami or Vegas, some poor bastard was taking the dirt nap. You'd be shocked how seldom that occurred. The life isn't necessarily how it's portrayed on TV. Naw. Ninety-nine percent chance these two guys are local."

"And if you haven't heard of them and I haven't heard of them—"

"They ain't shit," Sonny said. "Either noobs or really low-level thugs."

"God bless 'em," I said.

Heidi squealed and hopped on Sonny as soon as we walked through her gallery door, wrapping around him as if they'd just jumped from an airplane and he had the only chute.

"She used to greet me like that," I said.

"Abandon me for six months and I'll do it again," she said, as she dismounted. "Okay, where are we going for lunch?"

We hit a new place called Popi's Oysterette, in the Marina District. I had fish and chips. Sonny ordered a shellfish platter. Heidi chose the Dungeness crab roll and a Caesar salad, which I thought showed remarkable restraint. Heidi's appetite can strain an American Express black card. Sonny and I skipped the beer, since we would have to go to work in a few hours. Heidi ordered a bottle of Gerard Bertrand picpoul white to compensate for our integrity.

At Heidi's request, Sonny told the squatter story again, and Heidi agreed that it had to be an inside job. Just two and a half gumshoes, sitting around solving crimes and making the world safe for democracy.

After lunch, I dropped Sonny at the Mark Hopkins to check in and freshen up. He was welcome to stay at my place in the spare bedroom, but Sonny had a taste for the finer things in life, and he had given up the sweetest condo on the bay to move to Honolulu. I always offered to pay for his stay at the Hopkins when he visited. Once in a long while, I talked him into taking it, but it always found its way back to me somehow in the form of one sort of gift or another. After repeated experience, I simply indulged him when he refused my largesse.

Besides, I was still logy from the stakeout the night before. A pre-stakeout nap sounded good.

FIVE

Jordy Pankratz returned home at six-thirty that evening. Sonny and I waited for him in my car across the street. After he was inside, we paid him a visit.

I saw a shadow cross the peephole in his front door after I knocked. For a moment, I thought he was going to pretend he wasn't home. Then the deadbolt clicked as he turned it, and he opened the door.

"Mr. Gold!" His eyes riveted on Sonny. "I was afraid—"

"—we were the bad guys?" I finished. "You weren't wrong. We're just *your* bad guys. This is my partner, Sonny Malehala. I told you I'd bring him on to help."

Pankratz's hand disappeared in Sonny's paw as he shook hands. He looked back and forth at us. "Geez. I got a blond guy and a bald guy threatening me, and a pewter guy and a bald guy protecting me."

I glanced at Sonny. "Pewter?"

Sonny said, "You're getting pretty gray in there. I wasn't gonna say anything."

"Why not, man? Help a brother out. I gotta tell you, I don't see it in the mirror. What do you think? Should I dye it?"

"No, dude," Sonny said. "You do you. Age gracefully."

Pankratz's eyes bounced back and forth at us during the exchange. I could read buyer's remorse all over his face.

"Relax," I said. "It's covered. Go on inside. Enjoy a nice dinner. Watch some TV. Sonny and I will make sure nobody bothers you."

We posted ourselves in my minivan across the street. It wasn't a cool ride, but it was the most utilitarian stakeout vehicle in existence, ubiquitous and utterly unsuspicious. I had a cooler of Cokes and some cold sandwiches and a couple of bags of chips and a dozen Dunkins to keep us from passing out from starvation, and I'd tossed a pillow in the back in case we decided to take shifts. I put a Giants game on the radio. Sonny had brought his Kindle.

While this wasn't technically a stakeout, since Jordy Pankratz knew we were there, it sure felt like one.

Stakeouts are the worst. Hour after hour of tedium and clock-watching, usually without a payoff. You have to stay sharp in case the black flag goes up, and afterward it might take hours for the caffeine to wear off before you can grab enough rack time to do it all over again the next night. The only good thing about stakeouts was that I charge by the hour. It's mostly hanging out for easy money.

"I've avoided asking the obvious question," Sonny said without looking up from his book.

"And I appreciate it," I said.

"This pencil-neck Pankratz is scraping the bottom of the piggy bank. Even if we scare off the collectors, that debt isn't going away."

"We're on Band Aid patrol," I said. "Just stopping the bleeding until the medics arrive."

"If this dude can't pay Brownlee, how's he gonna pay *you?*"

"Yet to be determined."

"And, more importantly, how are you going to pay *me?*"

"Geez. I put you up at the Mark Hopkins."

"On my nickel."

"That's your choice. I offered to pay for that and your plane ticket."

"Economy Class and I aren't on speaking terms. Not a big deal, anyway. I miss you and Heidi, and I can afford to scoot across the pond anytime I want now. The hours we're stacking sitting outside this guy's house are adding up, though. Can he cover it?"

"We'll work something out," I said. "Tell you the truth, I took this gig mostly because I was kind of bored. It's been slow lately. No biggie. It happens. I was getting restless."

"What if these guys don't show up?" he said. "You plan to camp out in front of his house for the duration?"

"At some point, I'll probably arrange a face-to-face with Brownlee."

"You definitely want me along for that."

The Giants clobbered the Braves with a late-game home run rally. We ate our sandwiches. Sonny polished off an entire bag of chips and three sour cream doughnuts. We discussed the world situation, came up with no workable solutions, and concluded that humanity was screwed.

The night wore on.

Around eleven-thirty, a black Chrysler 300 cruised around the corner and parked at the curb. The illegal glass tint masked the people inside. It had super-intense headlights designed to blind you from a mile away. When they blinked out, twin spots lingered in my visual field. I tapped Sonny's arm. He put the e-book away.

"Showtime?" he asked.

"Overture. Hit the lights."

"This is it. Night of nights," he finished. He stretched a little and cracked his neck. "If I were a thug, I'd drive a car just like that."

"You *were* a thug," I said. "You drove a red Beemer."

"Guess I just had better taste than my criminal peers. Five bucks says the bald guy gets out first."

The bald guy got out first.

"I didn't take that bet," I said.

"What's the play?" he asked, as the blond guy, T-Bone, climbed from the passenger side of the Chrysler.

"Physical confrontation is the failure of negotiation," I said. "We'll reason with them."

"And if they prove impervious to reason?"

I cracked my own neck. "Then we clean their clocks and send them back to Brownlee crying with their shorts full of shit."

"I like a simple plan."

We opened our doors simultaneously and stepped out onto the street. Baldy and Blondie were two houses down on the opposite side, approaching Pankratz's porch. They were dressed in jeans and asskicker Timberline boots and black hoodies. Both wore gloves with the fingers cut off, and I harbored little doubt the gloves were weighted with lead shot. They had the confident strut of career bullies. Pankratz wasn't kidding about their biceps. They looked like tree trunks beneath the knit arms of the hoodies. As I'd expected. Musclebound.

"Yoo hoo. Oh, boys," I called out. "A minute?"

They stared at us. I think they probably spent more time on Sonny than me, but that's to be expected. He takes up twice as much space.

"The fuck you want?" Blondie asked. He had an eastern European accent.

"You're T-Bone, right?" I asked.

"How'd you know—"

"We're Mr. Pankratz's social secretaries. I'm Eamon. This is Sonny. I truly regret to inform you that Mr. Pankratz is not receiving visitors this evening. We do appreciate you dropping by, and we hope you have a safe trip home. Toodles." I waggled my fingers at them.

T-Bone glanced at Baldy. Under the radioactive light of the LED streetlamp, I could see the blood rise in Baldy's cheeks and neck.

"Look, Boomer," Baldy said. "Best thing you can do is climb back in your car and drive away yourself. You don't know who you're messing with."

I glanced at Sonny, pointed at my chest, and mouthed *Boomer?*

Sonny shrugged.

T-Bone pulled up the hem of his hoodie to show off a pistol in his belt.

"Well, that's intimidating," I said. I turned to Sonny. "Are you intimidated, Sonny?"

"Trembling," he said, as steady as an ancient boulder, at least until he drew the Colt Python I'd lent him, screwed the barrel into Baldy's ear, and yanked the pistol from his belt. It was so quick, so silent, that for a second I wasn't sure it had happened. T-Bone placed his hand on the butt of his pistol.

"Don't," Sonny said, and pointed Baldy's pistol at T-Bone. I emphasized his point with the Glock.

"Wow. They teach you that at Thug U?" I asked.

"Army Rangers," Sonny said. "We're kinda exposed here, Eamon. Can we move this along?"

"What's your name?" I asked Baldy. He looked scared now, with Sonny's revolver barrel massaging his eardrum.

"Reese," he said.

"Sonny?" I said. "Would you please choke Reese out?"

"A pleasure."

"Wait!" Reese squeaked.

At roughly the speed of light, Sonny wrapped Reese's neck in a sleeper hold. Reese struggled briefly, pissed his pants, and went limp in Sonny's arms. Sonny gently lowered him to the ground.

T-Bone watched, his face furious. He might have drawn his pistol then if I hadn't had my Glock pointed at his nose.

I pulled the pistol from T-Bone's pants and tossed it to Sonny. Sonny jacked the magazine from both Reese's and T-Bone's pistols and the rounds in the chambers. He tossed all of it into a storm drain and had the Python back up before he turned.

"Now," I said, "Technically, what Sonny and I are doing is assault with a deadly weapon. But, since you brandished first, I suppose that's a wash. So far, we're all even, though Reese down there might be a little worse for wear." I holstered my Glock. Sonny held the Python steady. "We got off on the wrong foot here, clearly. Let's start over."

I stepped toward T-Bone and extended my hand. He reflexively took it. Everyone does. Instead of clasping it, I vise-gripped his fingers with one hand and bent his thumb back with the other. He immediately went to his knees, and I stood over him.

"God, you're a dumb fuck," I said. "Recovery from a snapped thumb is lengthy and inconvenient, and the pain never really goes completely away. This is where the evening ends for you, T-Bone."

Sonny picked up Reese like a sack of flour and carried him under his arm to the Chrysler.

"I have a message for Mr. Brownlee."

"Fuck you, man," T-Bone said through clenched teeth. I put more pressure on his thumb, and he cried out in pain.

"Mr. Pankratz has every intention of paying his debt to Mr. Brownlee. It may take some time, but he'll settle up. The harassment ends here. No more tune-ups. If Pankratz tells me he's even smelled you and your buddy in the neighborhood, Sonny and I will come looking for you, and I'll show you what a gurney and a half dozen IVs feel like. Have I said anything you don't understand?"

"Eat shit and die," T-Bone growled. I put more pressure on his thumb. I worried I might actually break it.

"Okay!" he said. "All right! I'll give him the message. Let go of me, man!"

Sonny handed the field-stripped pistols back to the disheveled and chagrined thug. A few small pieces clattered to the sidewalk. T-Bone ignored them.

"I put Reese in the passenger seat and fastened his seatbelt," Sonny said. "Nothing holding you here, then?"

"This ain't over," T-Bone said, backing away. He climbed into the Chrysler and burned rubber when he turned the corner. I could hear the cheater muffler all the way out of the neighborhood.

"He's right," Sonny said. "People talk. Tonight was bad for Sammy Brownlee's business. He'll want to make that right."

"He'd better bring tougher thugs next time," I said.

SIX

Brownlee didn't bring tougher thugs.

He didn't bring any thugs at all.

The next day, shortly before noon, I sat at my desk sorting through the monthly bills. Sonny was visiting his favorite San Francisco bespoke tailor, having reminded me of the ungodly markup nice clothes carry in Hawai'i. Heidi was in her gallery downstairs. It was one of those rare, crystalline days in San Francisco, crisp and sunny with an unsullied blue sky and a breeze that kicked up whitecaps in the Golden Gate.

From my window, I could see the place on the bridge where Earleen Marley had jumped almost a year earlier, and the place below where she must have slapped the water, disappearing forever. Her body was never recovered. Not my finest moment, and it was hell on Sonny, heartbreaking enough to drive him halfway to Asia.

I heard footsteps on the stairway leading from the sidewalk to my office landing. After a couple decades in my location, I had deciphered the language of footfalls on those stairs. A man, wearing leather soles, which meant cowboy boots or fine Italian shoes. I was betting on the latter. High quality shoes suggested either a fetishist or impressive money and a fastidious nature. By the volume of the footsteps, I imagined a man not of great mass, probably wearing a suit, because shoes like that just screamed for classy rags.

The steps stopped when he reached the landing. Reading my office door. Everyone stopped to read my office door. Maybe it was because the word *discreet* was misspelled. Sometimes they stopped because they had second thoughts. Most of those were cheated wives who hadn't decided whether their scorn rose to the level of hiring a detective, and whether taking half of everything their worthless cheating bastard husbands had was worth the effort. Some changed their minds and retreated down the stairs. Men, for some reason, never retreated.

A knock on the door, and Samuel Brownlee stepped into my office. He was slightly shorter than me, and built more like a swimmer, lean and muscular. He moved with a feline confidence that suggested some dance training in his past. His salt and pepper hair was long and wavy, combed back to reveal a Prince Namor-like widow's peak and receding temples. His blue eyes danced around the room absorbing every tiny detail. His mouth seemed frozen in a smarmy used car salesman rictus that revealed expensive dental work and not a glimmer of true amusement. His hands were smooth and unmarked, his nails meticulously manicured, gleaming. The suit was everything I'd predicted. I harbored a mental image of Brownlee adoring himself in his dressing room mirror at home before stepping out.

He allowed the door to close behind him and stood in the middle of my office, apparently taking my measure. He slipped his hands into the pockets of his camel coat. One of mine was in my desk drawer, wrapped around the butt of the trusty Browning I thought I had retired.

"You're Gold," he said.

"I am," I said.

"Have a gun in that drawer?"

"I do," I said.

He slowly drew his hands from his pockets and opened his jacket. "I'm unarmed."

I placed the Browning on my desk blotter. "Makes one of us. You'll pardon my caution, Mr. Brownlee."

"So now we know each other," he said. "May I sit?"

"Please," I said. "Can I offer you some coffee?"

"Never touch it," he said. "Never developed the taste. Not trying to be rude. Just not my cuppa, you see."

His voice was cultivated and inviting. He sounded like a public radio jazz DJ, or maybe a college professor.

I let him stew. I discovered years ago that I learn more by watching and listening than I do by talking. Most people find silence uncomfortable and intimidating, and they try to fill the empty air with small talk. Sometimes they disclose interesting things.

"I've come alone for a reason," he said.

"Meaning you left your muscle recuperating in bed?"

"Those two gentlemen are no longer in my employ."

"The price of failure," I said. "Hope it wasn't something I said."

"They told me all about their confrontation with you and Sonny Malehala last night."

"You know Sonny?"

"I have eidetic imagery, Mr. Gold. Photographic memory. I never forget a name or a face. When T-Bone described Sonny, I knew exactly who he was talking about. Junius Bugliosi was an acquaintance when Sonny worked for him. I may have been harsh with those poor boys. I suspect very few people can stand up to

Sonny. On the other hand, I gave them an assignment, and they failed."

"They weren't that bad," I said. "Big doesn't mean quick. I think you hired them more for the intimidation factor. They were okay for what you wanted them to do. Sonny and I come from a different tribe."

"You know Jordy Pankratz can't pay you," he said.

"We'll burn that bridge when we get to it. What I told T-Bone last night stands. Pankratz intends to pay back every penny he owes you. Bouncing his face off people's fists isn't going to speed that up. He can't make the money he owes you if he's in traction. You want to get paid? Call off the dogs."

"How long do you intend to protect him?" Brownlee asked. The greasy smile returned, and he held his hands up, palms out. "Didn't mean to make that sound intimidating."

"Just running a cost-benefit analysis?"

"Something like that. How would you feel about a deal?"

"I may come across as a blue-collar meat and potatoes private cop," I said. "Just an ordinary joe in a rough trade. But I'm not for sale. You can't buy me off."

"I knew that the first two minutes here," he said. "And, of course, your reputation precedes you. I asked around. People believe you could be an inconvenient distraction for my business. I was thinking more of a compromise. We both get something we want."

"I'm listening," I said.

Brownlee leaned forward. "First, no more muscle. Pankratz gets the kid glove treatment."

"Acceptable. Doesn't address the central issue, though. He's already paid twice what he borrowed in vig," I said. "It's time he paid down the principle."

"I can do that."

"You conceded that quickly," I said. "I find that suspicious."

"Maybe what I want is more important than Jordy's vig payments."

"What would that be?"

"I want to hire you," Brownlee said.

SEVEN

"Plot twist," I said.

"I know," he said, beaming his searchlight smile. "Isn't life just deliciously devious? Couldn't you just pinch its cute little cheeks until the vessels break?"

I shook my head. "Okay. Shoot. How can I help you, Mr. Brownlee?"

"You can take that gun off the desk, to begin with."

"Sorry," I said. I didn't put it back in the drawer, though. I stowed it in the holster on my belt.

"I need you to find my wife. We've recently experienced a hitch in our marriage, and she left me. She's ditched her cell phone so I can't track her or phone her and she won't return any of my emails or direct messages. She's totally ghosted me."

"Are you willing to discuss why?"

"You ever see The Godfather?"

"The greatest American movie ever made?" I said. "Sure. Who hasn't?"

"Remember the scene at the end when Kay gets frozen out by Michael, and you can see the bond between them disintegrating? It was kind of like that. Rhonda married me thinking I was an investment banker. I mean, I was, and I still am, but that was just a cover. I do invest in businesses. I don't stash my loan interest money in a vault somewhere and go swimming in it like Scrooge McDuck. I keep the money moving, working, growing. It's always in play. What you call loansharking, that makes up maybe ten percent of my business, only one of my sources of capital. Everything else is legit. Usury is just the bottom rung of my empire."

"Anytime someone invokes empires, I get itchy," I said.

"I apologize. Poor phrasing. Anyway, even though the loan business is a small part of what I do, it's also the most distasteful. It's the part of my business I can't discuss with Rhonda, for a variety of reasons, not the least of which is sparing her the inconvenience of being an accomplice. What she doesn't know can't incriminate her later if it comes to that. Turns out it doesn't take much of a wedge to force people apart. I couldn't tell her about this part of my life, and it festered inside her head. She may have gotten some wrong ideas. She developed these...fantasies about who I am. Maybe she became a little paranoid. I don't know."

"There's something else," I said. "Something you're holding back."

"What makes you say that?"

"Lifelong cynicism. Everybody always holds something back. What's the rest of the story?"

For the first time since he sat down, his greasy smile faded. He blew out his cheeks and slowly exhaled.

"How confidential is this conversation?" he asked.

"Not a bit. Until money changes hands, nothing you say in this office is protected."

"And after?"

"Only a judge can force me to talk about it. Only a judge will."

"I see. Well, then. Let's continue under the stipulation that there is something else which I prefer not to divulge until you've decided to take my case. How's that?"

"I see," I said. "Your wife was feeling squeezed out in more than one aspect of your lives?"

"Perhaps," he said. "And I'd appreciate your discretion."

I pointed to the glass on my office door, which read *Eamon Gold, Discrete Investigations*. "Discretion is on the door."

"No it isn't. It's spelled wrong. That's a totally different word. That word means *separate*."

"Nitpicker. Got a deal on the painter. Let's just say I can keep a secret."

"Good. I'm here under a white flag. You and Sonny nearly put two of my guys in a hospital last night, but I came here alone, my hat in hand, willing to make a deal that could serve both our needs."

"Sonny's as trustworthy as I am, and twice as formidable. And don't kid yourself about how little your wife knows about your business. My experience is that they frequently know a great deal. If something about your work has driven her away, and there's something questionable going on, she'd have a mean weapon to use against you."

"Do you think she would?"

"That was my next question. You know her a lot better than I do."

"Wow," he said. For the first time, he had that look palookas get when they know the next uppercut will drop them onto the mat for the full count. "I really haven't thought this through entirely."

"Let's start with when she left," I said. "How long ago?"

"I've been out of town for the last week. I returned yesterday and discovered her things missing. Sometime in the last week. That's all I know."

"Did you talk with her while you were gone?"

"Several times."

"You called each time? Or did she call you?"

"I called her. What difference does it make?"

"If she's ditched her phone, she might be using a burner. If she slipped up and called you from it, we'd have the number. I don't think she'd have gotten rid of her phone before she left, so the last time you talked is probably the day she ran off. If she never called you from the burner, we have no way to trace her by phone."

"You do this sort of thing a lot?" he asked.

"I am not without experience. When was your last phone conversation?"

He checked his phone. "Three days ago."

"What time?"

"Late. Around midnight. It had been a long day."

"What did you talk about? How did she sound?" I asked.

"We were touching base, the way married people do. It wasn't a discussion or anything. Small talk. How our days went. That sort of thing. She sounded like…well, like Rhonda. She didn't sound stressed or angry or worried. If anything, I thought she might have been annoyed at me for calling so late. She's kind of a lark, sleep-wise. Hits the sheets by ten or eleven each night. Sees midnight once a year, when the big ball drops in Times Square. I probably woke her up."

"So she likely didn't leave until the next day. How much of her stuff did she take?"

"All the important things. Her luggage. Her drawers were empty. All her makeup was gone. She took the hair dryer."

"Not an abduction, then," I said. "You're describing someone bugging out. She has her own car?"

"Yes. It's still in the garage."

"Okay. She took a cab or an Uber or maybe a friend drove her off. Hell, maybe she took the BART. Is there a station near you?"

"No."

"Good. Cabs and Uber keep records. Have you filed a missing person report yet?"

"No," he said.

"That's going to look suspicious. Call her now."

"I told you. Her phone is turned off."

"It was turned off the last time you called. Call her."

He hit her connection on his phone, and then toggled the speaker. I heard the ringtone on the other end. Once. Twice. Three times. Then a robotic voice. *Your call has been forwarded to an automated…*

Brownlee thumbed the call dead.

"That's what I get every time I call," he said. "I finally stopped leaving messages."

"If she had turned off the phone, it would go directly to voicemail," I said. "The phone's turned on. It's active. The big question is whether it's with your wife."

"What do you mean?"

"I had a case where someone didn't want to be found. Instead of destroying her cell phone, she shipped it by UPS with the tracker on, and took off in the opposite direction. Threw everyone off the scent for a while until we finally ran down the phone on a big brown truck in the middle of nowhere."

"You're describing premeditation and coordination," Brownlee said. "Like she'd been planning this for a while."

"The husband is always the last to know," I said. "Except when it's the wife. Spouses keep secrets, Mr. Brownlee, whether they admit it or not. I mean, your whole situation started with keeping secrets. Case in point, is it possible your wife has become aware of your extramarital affairs?"

"It's possible," he said, after chewing it over. "I mean, yes. I've...been with other people. I've been careful, though. Discreet."

"Maybe she has as well. How social is she?"

"I get it," Brownlee said. "People keep secrets, even from those closest to them."

"Any chance she was having an affair?" I asked.

"If you'd asked me last week, I'd have said no. I'm a pretty bright guy myself, Mr. Gold. I know what comes next as well as you do. Did that premeditation and coordination involve someone else? Is Rhonda on the run with a partner or helper or companion or whatever?"

"Right now, I have an empty closet and a name. She went somewhere. Maybe she left an electronic trail—credit card purchases, hotel bills, plane tickets—that we can access. If none of that is out there, then she's really gone to ground, and that requires help. She's apparently been thinking about this for a while. If she's active socially, maybe she talked about it with her friends. They're the best place to start."

"You ever see those Real Housewives shows on television?" he asked.

"Only under duress," I said.

"She'd fit right in. Yeah. She has this clique of buddies. Classy women. Well connected. I'll put together the list and send it to you later this afternoon. I mean, you're taking the case, right?"

I thought it over.

"The interest on Jordy's loan goes away," I said. "Every penny going forward eats away at the principle. Condition one."

"I already agreed," he said.

"No more rough stuff. Ever. If he gets behind, you will discover a deep reserve of previously untapped patience."

"Done."

"You pay his outstanding balance owed to me."

"What?"

"If you hadn't been an impatient loanshark douche, he never would have had to hire me, and I wouldn't be looking for your absconded spouse. Jordy deserves a break."

"Anything else?"

"My clock starts right now. Getting Jordy off the hook is the retainer for hiring me. From here on, you get billed like anyone else."

"I expected no different."

"All right then," I said. "I'll need all your wife's checking and credit account numbers, any passwords you know, and her telephone number. Let's get cracking on that list of friends as well."

EIGHT

Sonny had plans for the evening, so Heidi and I scooted down the coast to my beach house in Montara, south of Pacifica.

I am what you'd probably refer to as real estate rich, but I came about it entirely by happenstance rather than perseverance or—even more unlikely—hard work. I bought my townhouse on Russian Hill with proceeds from an insurance settlement right before prices went stratospheric. The Montara house was part of another settlement with the private eye firm that promised me a hefty signing bonus right before the guy who hired me stroked out and nosed over into his bouillabaisse at Le Comptoir. I hadn't paid a penny out of pocket for either of them, and together they were currently worth some distance north of three million. In a gig like mine, they represented my retirement savings.

The beach house was situated several rows back from the Pacific Ocean, across the PCH, up a steep hill that affords beautiful views of the sunset over the water. It's small, only a little over a thousand square feet. I'd turned the larger portion of the family room into a woodworking shop where I crafted stringed musical instruments as a hobby. My Sjobergs cabinetmaker's bench took up a full side wall, with power tools filling another. A smaller metal workbench with a pegboard for hand tools stood in the corner.

Heidi and I lounged on the sofa. I'd fried some slices of baguette in EVOO and rubbed them with garlic cloves, and served them with prosciutto, brie, and fig jam. We sipped from bottles of a Belgian wheat ale Heidi had found at a local craft beer shop. The Biggest Movie of the Year was streaming on the screen over the fireplace. We'd missed it in the theater and wanted to catch it before the awards nominations came out. Heidi was sort of curled up under my arm and didn't act motivated to move. I was fine with that.

Before the movie, I'd planed and joined several eighth-inch thick plates of South American cocobolo wood to form the backs of a matching set of classical guitars I had agreed to build for a friend. Cocobolo, being a very oily and extremely dense wood, was a pain in the ass to work with, because it ate up sharp blades like popcorn and making a decent glue joint with conventional aliphatic resin glue was nearly impossible without soaking everything in acetone first. The payoff for all that aggravation was some of the most beautiful musical instruments you've ever seen. Brazilian rosewood might be the gold standard for guitars, but I'll take a cocobolo axe over it any day. Heidi agreed, and she was an expert on classical guitars.

In any case, I was glad to have that chore out of the way and had time to just chill with Heidi on the sofa.

"Took a new case today," I said, as I loaded up another crostino with ham and cheese and jam.

"Mr. Camel Coat?" she asked.

"You really don't miss a thing, do you?"

"It's about time you appreciated that," she said, with her barely perceptible German accent. After over a quarter century stateside, she was practically assimilated. "What's the case?"

"Runaway wife. Routine stuff. The client sent me a list of the wife's friends a couple of hours ago. I might need to brush up on my charm. There are some heavy hitters on this list."

"The Golden Gate Glitterati?" she asked.

"Queens of the Oligarchy. Living evidence that physical attraction is frequently mediated by piles of dollar signs."

"Except in our case," she said.

"True. What we have is pure…um…"

"Something," she said.

"Yes. What he have is pure something. One thing we can say with confidence, though, is that it is uncomplicated by unimaginable wealth."

"Lucky us," she said. "What's the baby detective up to tonight? I'm not complaining, you understand. I love Sonny, but I could use some *us* time."

"Funny story. Remember, a year or so back, when I was looking for Lydia Carlisle, I interviewed Maisie Blah Blah Blah Pauch?"

We called her *Maisie Blah Blah Blah Pauch* because she'd been married multiple times, and we could never remember all her married names. Sometimes, neither could she.

"Oh, yeah. The supervisor's wife."

"Supervisor's ex-wife. They're divorced. She referred me to Sonny in the first place. They went to high school together. Turns out they were kind of a thing back then. Sonny called her up the other day and they're having dinner tonight."

"Measuring Sonny for Husband Number Whatever?"

"We don't need to worry about that. Sonny's doing all right over in Hawai'i, but Maisie only marries for ungodly money or power. This is a dalliance. Having met Maisie Blah Blah Blah, though, and having successfully fended off her amorous advances—"

"Remind me to show my appreciation for that sometime," Heidi said.

"I just did. Anyway, I suspect Sonny will call in late tomorrow morning. Not that he's punching a clock or anything."

"All the better for us," Heidi said, as she snuggled up again. "This movie blows. Might grab a shower."

"Might grab one with you," I said.

"And then?"

"Maybe, in a little while, we'll grab another one."

NINE

The jangle of my telephone woke me the next morning, shortly after sunrise. Next to me, Heidi groaned, rolled over, and stuffed her head between her pillows.

"She cleaned me out!" Brownlee shouted. "The bitch emptied two of our accounts before she left."

"You just discovered this?" I asked.

"Before, I was too concerned about her whereabouts," he said. "I was worried about her. Something you said yesterday stuck in my craw, though. I hardly slept last night, and around four this morning I had a flash. The credit cards. She wouldn't have to use them if she was paying for everything with cash. I checked our bank accounts online. Two of them are down to a few dollars apiece."

"How much did she withdraw?" I asked, stifling a yawn. My breath offended me.

"Over fifty thousand, all told," he said. "The household accounts. She was in charge of them. We used them to pay contractors and repairmen and the like."

"With all due respect," I said. "Sounds like a lot less than cleaning you out."

"Well, she cleaned out those accounts. Fifty grand is a lot of disappearing money, wouldn't you say?"

"You can buy a lot of getaway for that," I said. "So maybe she isn't with a friend. Paying with cash might not be a bad thing, though. We live in a nearly cashless society now. People who pay with large amounts of paper money stand out. Folks remember them. She might be leaving a trail of transaction breadcrumbs in her wake. I'll talk it over with Sonny when we get together this morning, and we'll figure out which way to go next."

"You'd better find her before I do. If I get hold of her, I'll make her pay. You received the list I sent you?"

"Sure did. I'll call you later today, Mr. Brownlee."

By the time I arrived at the office, Rhonda Brownlee's phone had gone dark. No way to trace it. It supported my contention that she'd dumped it somewhere to throw Sam off the scent, and the battery had eventually run out of juice. Her credit card accounts remained silent.

Sonny showed up late. I wasn't surprised, and he wasn't working for me officially anyway, so I wasn't exactly in a position to grouse. To tell the truth, after the rude awakening from Brownlee, I'd rolled over and caught another hour myself.

While I waited for Sonny, I sent him a copy of the picture of Rhonda Brownlee her husband had given me. Then I cranked up my CyberShamus account, the Google-On-Steroids subscription search engine I use, and headed down a rabbit hole.

A half hour later, I'd found no trace of Rhonda Brownlee accessing any plane, train, or rental car out of town. She could have borrowed a car or bought a bus ticket with cash, I suppose, but I wasn't in the mood to complicate my investigation any further. The degree of planning she had put into her bug-out, and her husband's association with lowlifes abundant, made me wonder whether she might have found someone to create a fake passport and other papers for her. It wouldn't be the first time I'd encountered someone trying on a new life under a fresh identity.

I knew the best forgers in town. I waited until a decent hour, half past ten, and I started calling them. I had to be cagey, frame the conversation in terms of saving a damsel in distress. These guys put groceries on the table giving people second chances at life. They weren't going to just cough up the information I needed and tell me they'd provided Rhonda Brownlee with a new identity.

The first three forgers I talked to denied having done any fake ID work lately. The slow season for everyone, I suppose. I hit paydirt with the fourth, a guy who went by his dark web pseudonym Osiris.

"Eamon Gold," Osiris answered the phone. "Finally decide to get away from it all?"

"I'm pretty cool with it all right now, thanks," I said. I launched into the same spiel I'd used on the first three. Missing woman. Might be in danger. Just trying to protect her.

"What's she look like?" he said. I shot him the pic from my phone. "Okay, suppose I knew her? I mean, you don't know any more than that. Not much you can do with it, right?"

"Did she tell you her real name?"

"Presuming I know her, that's not how it works. People show up, I do the work, they give me money, and that's it. No names. I'm not into long term relationships."

"There's no way I can convince you to tell me her new name?"

"If I had ever seen this woman, I suppose you could beat it out me," he said. "I would prefer you didn't."

At some level, I had to admire his integrity. He might have been a forger, but he and I had similar standards when it came to clients. "You're telling me this woman came to you, didn't give you her real name, bought a new identity, which you provided, and then she disappeared."

"Is that what I'm saying, Gold? Maybe yes. Maybe no."

"Let's say it's yes. Do you take credit cards?"

He snorted over the phone. "Shit. Got snot on my screen. Credit cards. That's rich. Yeah. I take fuckin' credit cards. Diners Club, Discover, traveler's checks, whatever you got. I also got this twenty-foot-high advertising billboard on the Embarcadero. You seen it?"

"Cash only, then?" I said.

"Fuckin' A. Cash is the only fuckin' thing that's real, man. And some of it is kinda suspect."

"Just out of curiosity, how much would it cost if I decided to live under a new name somewhere?"

"You want ID with a paper trail, an Internet background, stuff that can be checked? Like you didn't just pop into existence five minutes ago? Thirty large."

"In cash."

"Can't live on fuckin' Green Stamps, man."

"Let's say you recognize the woman in the picture. How long would you say it's been since you've seen her?"

"Face like that? Hell, I'd probably forget everything about her in, say, three days. Maybe four. Certainly the second I hang up this phone, now that I'm getting hassled about her."

"Let's also say I never heard of you before. How would I find you? Who might refer me to you?"

"That ain't the question you want to ask, because you and a woman like the one in this picture ain't gonna run in the same circles. The guy who might refer you ain't the one who might refer her. I got a seriously impressive downline of satisfied customers."

"So what kind of guy might refer her?"

"No guy at all. You know who helps women who want to ditch their spouses and try it all over again?"

"Other women," I said.

"Bingo. I got a lot of contacts with women who run abuse shelters and shit. Sometimes I do a little work pro boner for them."

"You mean *pro bono.*"

"You get paid your way; I get paid mine. Anyway, these shelters don't just spring up like mushrooms. Someone has to foot the light bill and pay for the food service and the linen bills and shit."

"Philanthropists," I said. "I don't suppose you've had a referral lately from one of these shelters, have you?"

"Maybe," he said.

"How much to turn that into a yes?" I said.

"Use your imagination, Gold. Like the bumper sticker says, *Cash, Ass, or Grass. Nobody Rides For Free.*"

It cost me several hundred of Sam Brownlee's dollars and the promise of a free favor somewhere down the line to get the name of a shelter in the Mission District.

Osiris didn't give me the name of his contact at the shelter, but that didn't matter. Osiris had intimated that her real connection came from one of the shelter's benefactors.

I didn't even need CyberShamus to find out who it was. A simple Internet search turned up the shelter's website, with a list of the board of directors. Halfway down the page was a picture of a strikingly gorgeous woman in her forties with auburn hair and brown eyes. The bio next to the picture said her name was Phyllis Bagdasarian. Socialite wife of Armin Bagdasarian. A list of charities large enough to choke a brontosaurus.

Phyllis Bagdasarian was also the third name on the list of Rhonda's privileged clique Brownlee had sent me.

"Aha," I said to the empty office. "A clue."

Which was about the time Sonny clomped up the steps to my office and settled heavily into the chair across from me.

"You don't look rested," I said.

"My date with Maisie stretched into the morning."

"The early morning or the recent morning?"

"Like up until half an hour ago. She may still be at it for all I know. Though she be but little, she is fierce. I had to come up for air, get some work done. Who's the woman in the picture?" He held up his phone.

"Wife of our new client. We're off the hook with Jordy Pankratz. That's taken care of. We're working for Sammy Brownlee now."

"The loanshark," he said.

"Not every client is going to be Mother Theresa. Sammy's wife is missing, so he's cutting Jordy a huge break to get us to find her."

"How big a break?"

I told him. He nodded.

"Big break. And we get paid. Works for me. What do we know about the wife?"

I told him about Osiris and my research on Phyllis Bagdasarian.

"Got your walking shoes with you?" I asked.

"I prefer riding, but I'm off my workout schedule, so sure."

"If I interpreted Osiris's double-talk correctly, the ID papers Rhonda Brownlee bought cost thirty thousand. Cash. She took about fifty grand out of her household account with Sammy, leaving her with twenty large walking around money. She's paying for everything with cash to avoid leaving an electronic trail. We don't know her fake identity."

"It's a big city, Eamon," he said. "Lots of places to hide."

"This is a woman with elegantly refined tastes. She isn't going to hole up at Motel 6. You're a card-carrying member of the International Brotherhood of Hotel Dicks. I need you to hook up with your fellow security directors at the various hotels and see if they have a cash cow checked in. The folks at the front desk remember people like that. Start with your digs at the Mark Hopkins and work down the list of upscale hostelries."

"This could take a while," he said. "What's your plan for the day?"

"First, I'm going to have a discussion with Phyllis Bagdasarian."

TEN

A couple of telephone calls and some sidesteps with social coordinators led me to a lunch meeting with Phyllis Bagdasarian at the Mark Hopkins, where all the finest San Franciscans meet.

She was shorter than I expected. Like, a lot shorter. If she topped five feet, I'd be shocked. Her stiletto heels brought her to a full five-two. I nearly had to bend over to shake hands with her. Her picture on the shelter website had evidently benefited from airbrushing, but she was still in great shape for a woman poking at her second half century. She was dressed meticulously, and her hair was perfect. She'd had her nails done as recently as that hour.

"My partner is staying here," I said when I introduced myself. "Is it nice?"

"I'm slammed today, Mr. Gold," she said. "I have about a half hour to wolf down a salade nicoise and a glass of chardonnay before I pop a half dozen Altoids and hustle off to a gallery opening. How can I help you?"

I told her that Rhonda Brownlee was missing, and she celebrated with gleeful vitriol.

"Missing? I hope the bitch is dead," Phyllis Bagdasarian said. "I hope her bullet-ridden body is lying at the bottom of a mine shaft somewhere, being nibbled to bits by rats."

"I'm pretty sure she's just gone to ground somewhere," I said. "But if anything has happened to her, a statement like that about a friend might sound suspicious."

"Rhonda Brownlee isn't a friend," she said. "We know each other, and we travel in the same social circles, but we are not close. Given my druthers, if she's disappeared, she'll stay that way. No skin off my nose."

"So you didn't point her in the direction of a forger to create counterfeit ID papers?"

She burst out laughing. "Forger? Counterfeits? Fuck, honey, I wouldn't know where to start. I don't even read spy novels. I'm a romance sort of chick, but who in fuck has the time to read anyway? No. I did not refer her to a forger. It's kind of a turn-on that you think I did, though."

"If you aren't friends with Rhonda Brownlee, how would you describe your relationship?"

"You ever put two cats in a one-cat house?" she asked.

"Not a cat guy."

"Well, it was like that. We kept our distance but never let the other out of sight."

"Why? If you don't mind me asking."

"Why's it always? The woman is not to be trusted, especially with other women's husbands."

"Meaning *your* husband?"

"You know who I married, Mr. Gold?"

"I would assume it's Mr. Bagdasarian."

"And you don't know who Armin Bagdasarian is?"

I did not, and I told her so.

"He calls himself the Used Food King of California. He's in garbage, specifically restaurant scraps and the like. Industrial kitchen waste. Used grease and oil. He has contracts all over the state to pick up this shit on regular routes. He makes garden compost and biofuel and cattle feed and gods-know-what out of the stuff, and people just shove wads of money up his ass for it. He gets paid twice. The restaurants pay him to haul the shit off, and the end users buy the shit he makes out of it. He pulls it in coming and going."

"Nice gig if you can stand the smell," I said.

"Armin never gets close to it. Not anymore. He has a partner, Ruben Sahakian, who handles the day-to-day operations. Armin is the owner. He makes the biggest decisions and signs the checks. Ruben handles everything else. Armin will probably sell it all to Ruben and retire in a year or so. Armin's not an old man. He didn't pull himself up by his bootstraps, either. Family money. He grew up used to the good life. Isn't particularly interested in sweating. He's not terribly ambitious. Not interested in ruling the world or building a business dynasty. He just wants to hit fuck-the-world status, financially, yank the golden ripcord, and play golf and sail to Tahiti for the rest of his life. I rather fancy the notion myself."

"But Rhonda had designs on Armin?"

"Where did you get that idea?" she asked.

"You said Rhonda couldn't be trusted with other women's husbands. Did she put the moves on Armin?"

"She was drunk," Phyllis said, waving her fork in the air. She sipped from her wine glass and said, "But that didn't excuse it. I caught her nuzzling Armin in the butler pantry at Missy Gentry's party a few months back. Slipped her hand down his pants and fondled his junk. It pissed me off. Armin is blessed in the junk department, but this bling on my finger says I'm the only one who gets to play with it."

"That's why you wish her ill?"

"That and other things. Have you visited the shelter?"

"Drove by. Didn't go inside."

"Why not?"

"Some of the women there might take unkindly to a man of my stature wandering around off the leash."

She eyed me over the top of her glass as she sipped her wine. "A sensitive private investigator?"

"I know how to read the room."

"It's nice inside. Not the way you'd think of a shelter. It's like a big Victorian house. Everyone has their own room. Decent furnishings, no institutional stuff. Place like that is expensive. I talked Armin into backing it. Cost me a month of hummers, and I had to eat soft food for a week with TMJ, but he took the bait and he's now on the hook for half the yearly costs. So it was worth it. It's a tax write-off for him, and I get to host a lovely fundraiser every quarter, which keeps me in the social pages—such as they are, nowadays—in the *Chronicle*."

She paused to spear a slice of potato and some tuna on her plate and wolfed it down with a chardonnay chaser.

"I held a fundraiser about two months ago. Rhonda attended. Dragged her husband Sam along. He clearly didn't want to be there. She pledged fifty thousand dollars. Said she'd get it to me by the end of the week. No biggie, you know? I mean, we see each other at least once or twice a week for brunch or at the theater or the opera or whatever. I was going to run into her."

"Except you didn't," I said.

"The bitch has been ducking and dodging me ever since. Ghosted me on the phone. My calls go to voicemail. Now she's off the grid entirely. Fuck that bitch. I'm sorry if Sammy made her life tough, but would it have killed her to write a check before she vanished?"

"I suspect the fundraiser pledge was a smoke screen," I said. "Rhonda withdrew fifty thousand dollars before she took off. The pledge provided her with justification if her husband ever questioned the withdrawal. You said Sam Brownlee didn't want to be at the fundraiser. Maybe she brought him there to give her cover for taking out the money before she fled."

"And you're sure she's just in hiding?"

"Every indicator suggests, wherever she is, she's there voluntarily. I'm ninety-nine percent certain she's traveling under false documents. The guy she bought them from pointed me in the direction of your shelter. When I saw your name on the list of directors, I put two and two together, thought perhaps you had sent her."

"Why did my name stand out?"

I pulled the list up on my phone and showed it to her.

"This is a list of people who are supposedly Rhonda's friends. The guy who gave it to me referred to them as The Real Housewives."

She laughed. "I can see it. We're a vain and shallow gaggle of broads. You know that show *Company*? We're the ladies who lunch. That's our identity. Let the poor working girls slave the day away. For us, it's salade nicoise and a spa afternoon, except today it's a gallery opening, and then maybe cocktails at The House of Shields. Being part of the privileged class does not suck."

She drained her wine glass.

"Like I said, I'm in kind of a rush today. A shame, because it isn't every day a woman runs into a real private eye, especially one so easy on the eyes. For a nickel, I'd order another glass and blow off the gallery. Alas, I am shackled by my obligations, and I have promises to keep."

"And I'm out of nickels. Just a couple more questions. Someone at the shelter referred Rhonda to the forger. Who could do that?"

"Gigi Sahakian," she said. "Ruben's wife. She's a social worker, or at least she was until she met Ruben. She left the social services department to operate the shelter. Buttloads of grant money tipped the scales our way."

"She cashed in on her expertise."

"And how. She's worth it. Every penny. Being on the board, I don't get my hands dirty with the everyday stuff. I just help pay for it. Gigi knows stuff. She's been helping women get away from their hammerhead dipshit abusive partners for years. If there's a way to disappear without a trace, she would probably know it."

"Do me a favor?" I said.

"Name it," she said.

"Call Gigi Sahakian and let her know I'll be in touch. Ask her, as a special favor to the board, not to shine me on."

"Why would she do that?"

"Because I suspect she is involved with some shady people, with the best of intentions and motives, and I want her to know I don't give a shit about that. I only want to know if she referred Rhonda to a forger and why."

ELEVEN

Gigi Sahakian must have had a hundred-dollar-a-day Red Bull habit. Getting her to stand still for even a minute to talk was a chore. She was five and a half feet of raw, harried energy. Her dry brown hair was unartfully chopped short in a sort of pageboy. She didn't believe in makeup. Her face was mottled by huge sunspots, suggesting a youth spent largely at the beach. Her eyes nearly glowed from whatever stimulant coursed through her veins. One of her top front incisors was a little gray. She was in her forties, but the look in her eyes led me to believe she had seen a lifetime of misery.

I knocked on her office door. She stood at the filing cabinet, shuffling files. Throughout our conversation, she flitted about the office from table to desk. "You would be Mr. Gold. Phyllis told me you'd be by. Do you have some identification?"

Clipped, crisp, midwestern accent. She was the no-nonsense type, so I handed her my card and launched right into my reasons for shattering the sanctity of her daily routine.

"You know Rhonda Brownlee," I said.

"Yes."

"You know she's missing?"

"I know she's left her husband," she said.

"Because you helped her leave?"

She examined me more closely. "Mr. Gold, I'm very busy. In about twenty minutes, a woman will walk through that door. She's on the way from urgent care now. On the bus. The bruises and cuts on her face will be difficult to look at. Her story will be difficult to hear. It all began with a couple of people in love saying *I do*. Sometimes life doesn't play out the way we planned. Sometimes we find out the partner we thought we trusted is actually a stranger. Sometimes they turn out to be monsters. That's where we come in."

"You have a tough job," I said.

"I do, and right now I'm not doing it. Stop dancing around. Phyllis called and told me to be straight with you. Ask me what you want to ask so I can get back to work."

"Okay. You sent Rhonda Brownlcc to Osiris for a new identity, didn't you?"

"I did. I've done it for other women as well, when they could afford it."

"I don't care about that. I'm not here to bust you for fraud or forgery. I want to know why she left, and where she might have gone."

She smiled. "I don't know why you think I'd help you with that. We have no common ground. You aren't the police, so you have very little leverage beyond your charm and good looks. You're obviously working for Sam Brownlee, who wants his wife back. I advocate for Rhonda, who doesn't want to go back."

"Why?"

"Kind of personal," she said. "That's for Rhonda to reveal. My advocacy for the women who come to me includes confidentiality.

I only told you I'd sent Rhonda to the forger because you already knew. Everything else is between her and me and will stay that way."

"I have similar rules in my business."

"Then you understand why I won't answer your questions."

"How about generalities? Did she think she was in danger of some sort?"

"People don't come here because they feel safe in their own beds."

Gigi Sahakian impressed me as a smart cookie. She wanted to help her friend Rhonda, but she couldn't violate her personal code. I could appreciate that, but I also had a job to do.

"Did she know where she was going? Did she have a plan?"

"Most women don't when they come here. They do when they leave, mostly."

"Did Rhonda come here as a client?"

"We call them guests," she said. "And no. There was no need."

"Her husband was out of town for only a week."

"I believe he was."

"Forging documents isn't a speedy process," I said.

"I've heard the same."

I rolled it all over in my mind. "She waited for her husband's trip to leave, but she'd been planning it for a while. The benefit for your shelter was two months ago. She pledged fifty thousand dollars, which is exactly how much she withdrew from her accounts before she left. She knew at least two months ago that she planned to leave. But she also knew by then that her new documents would cost thirty grand, so she had to have contacted Osiris beforehand, which also means she came to you considerably earlier asking for help. She's been planning this for three months, at least. Maybe longer."

"I'm sorry," she said. "Was there a question in there somewhere?"

"I'm still composing them. One though, and it won't require you to violate anybody's confidentiality. Is there a third player in this story I don't know about yet?"

She smiled again as the front doorbell rang.

"I think you might be an exceptional detective," she said. "But I can't help you any more than I already have, and my new guest is at the door. Good luck with your search, Mr. Gold."

Sonny phoned me while I drove back to my Jefferson Street office.

"We lucked out," he said. "The security director at the Mark Hopkins is a surfer dude. I did a trade-out with him. I'm comping him a week at the resort in Waikiki to handle the legwork on this Rhonda Brownlee search. Seems all the hotel security directors are networked in this town, to keep track of the hookers and con men. He's putting the word out with the picture you sent me this morning. If she's checked in anywhere in town, they'll find her."

"Might be a dead end," I said. "It's just a hint right now, but there's a chance Rhonda went to ground with a third party we don't know yet."

"She was cheating on Sammy?"

"I'm still a little thin on details. I talked to the director of a women's shelter in the Mission District. Gigi Sahakian. She was cagey about it, but what she told me made me suspicious. I need to get a closer look at Rhonda's activities over the last several months, because it looks as if she's been planning her great escape for a while now."

"How'd they hook up?" he asked.

"One of the shelter board members. Phyllis Bagdasarian. She and Rhonda are both part of The Real Housewives. It looks like Phyllis introduced them. Her husband, Ruben, is set to take over Armin Bagdasarian's rotten food empire."

"Did you say Ruben? Ruben Sahakian?"

"Yeah. Why?"

"Ruben Sahakian's father is near the apex of the Armenian mob in this town, Eamon. Tigran Sahakian. His nickname is *Tiger*. He has a rep. One mean motherfucker. Back in the day, people shit their pants if he walked into the room unexpectedly. Real Keyzer Soze vibe. I hear he's mellowed a little over the years, but some shit stains never wash out."

"What do you hear about Ruben?"

"I only know him by name. Maybe he decided not to go down his father's path, and he's completely legit. But if Tigran Sahakian is in the picture, even along the outer margins, this case just turned a whole new shade of dark. I'd tread softly for a while, until we know he isn't involved."

"Not sure how he could be. He's about five degrees away from our client. Father of a husband of a missing woman's friend's friend? Seems like a coincidence."

"My sensei once said there are no coincidences, and the ones that violate that rule are not to be trusted. Whatever became of him?"

"Never quote me to myself. Bagdasarian is Armenian," I said. "You ever hear about him being mixed up in the Armenian underworld?"

"It's not like I kept a scorecard on me. I wasn't Mr. Bugliosi's social director."

"You know what I'm thinking," I said.

"Money laundering. Has to be. Not many better places to turn cash around than the garbage recycling business. Lots of little nooks and crannies where dirty money can disappear and pop out fresh and crispy on the other end."

"Sam Brownlee is a money launderer."

"Another coincidence."

"Which raises the question—how deep is Bagdasarian in the game? Is Ruben Sahakian his father's inside man, funneling money in and out as operations manager, or is he there to keep an eye on Bagdasarian? Bagdasarian's wife says he plans to punch out in a few years, live the high life on a mountain of money. Says he'll probably sell the business to Sahakian."

"Maybe that was the deal," Sonny said. "*We make you rich, and then you bag out and we take it all over.*"

"If that's the case, Bagdasarian would be the perfect mark. His wife says he isn't terribly ambitious."

"I still don't see the connection, Eamon," he said. "It seems like a side story. It's interesting, but how's it connected to Rhonda Brownlee running out on her husband?"

"Phyllis Bagdasarian caught Rhonda snogging Armin and measuring him for a jockstrap." I cupped my hand.

Sonny pursed his lips. "Oh," he said. "Shit's getting complicated. Bad time for me, too. I have to scoot back across the water."

"Did they ID your squatter?"

"You have a bad habit of stomping on punchlines. We think we located the phantom's accomplice. A housekeeper. They want me back at the resort to handle her interrogation and firing."

"Gonna prosecute her?"

"Naw. Bad pub. Not worth the negative press it generates. We'll scare the piss out of her, can her ass, and put out the word about her to all the other hotels. I sure hope housekeeping in Honolulu wasn't her dream career."

"And the squatter?"

"I might rough him up a little, put the fear of God in him. He'll skate, too, though. Same reason."

"This is a satisfying job?" I asked.

"It has its moments," he said. "There are dipshits everywhere, man. If you're forced to deal with them, there are worse places than paradise."

TWELVE

I still couldn't figure out who was zooming who. My head was full of stuff but lacked the connections necessary for it all to make sense. That told me I hadn't knocked on enough doors or annoyed enough people.

Gigi Sahakian had suggested there was an unknown third party in the picture, and we had already discussed Bagdasarian, so it wasn't him. Getting away would be a lot easier for Rhonda if she had an accomplice.

I had the Real Housewives list on my desk. Not interviewing every name on it felt lazy.

I have often referred to Heidi as a Nordic goddess, but if there really were such a deity, Sonya Soderquist would give her a run for the crown. She was Hitchcock's quintessential icy blonde, with aquamarine eyes that seemed to drill right through me. I could tell by the relative imbalance of her figure that she had been surgically enhanced, perhaps a present from her husband Stefan, the Scrap Metal Meister of San Francisco. Her improbable nose and immobile brow confirmed her commitment to outside help to maintain what I could only describe as her magnificent visage. She had the best legs I'd run into that week. Despite the fact she stopped time simply by walking into a room, she was neither haughty nor distant. Her voice still carried a lilt of the south Kentucky twang from her childhood as a coal miner's daughter, before people realized she was exceptional clay for molding into a model. Stefan Soderquist had come later, after others had exploited her.

"I'm looking for Rhonda Brownlee," I said.

"Well, that makes one of us, honey," Sonya said, running her finger around the rim of her martini glass. We had met at Casements on Mission Street. Since it was an Irish bar, at least thematically, I went with the flow and ordered a Samhain Old Fashioned, because a half-Irish private cop quaffing a Guinness was just a cliché. I had dressed to impress, with an open-collar pinstripe pima cotton shirt and my best tweed professor's blazer. I'd even shined my brogans.

"She could be in danger," I said.

"More likely, she's shacked up with somebody's husband."

Sonya had arrived before me. The two water-ringed napkins on the table next to her present drink suggested she had gotten a head start on me. A really big one.

"Eureka," I said. "A clue."

"Really?"

"A small one, but it begs follow-up questions. Tell me, Ms. Soderquist—"

"Please," she said. "Call me Sonya." She'd have batted her eyes if she'd had any control over them.

"All right, then, Sonya. Does Rhonda have a reputation for adultery?"

"Does sucking my husband off count?"

She watched me carefully for a reaction. I've played a lot of poker in my life. I gave her no satisfaction. Sonya Soderquist liked to play games as well, and I couldn't tell for certain whether she was telling the truth or just trying to shock me for the fun of it.

"Please. Go on," I said.

"I'm not sure I want to." Her voice was remarkably clear, without a hint of ethanol-induced slurring. Sonya could hold her liquor. "If it were anybody but Rhonda... Okay. The bitch has it coming anyway. Yeah. Rhonda's flings are kind of an open secret in our circle. She blew Stefan during a weekend group trip to Monterey."

"Without your knowledge?"

"I'm not a fucking lending library, Mr. Gold. And we're not that sort of group. We're not a bunch of swingers. At least not in any organized way. On the other hand, I'm also not the blowjob type, so maybe I should thank her. Don't get me wrong. I give a great hummer, but I don't enjoy it much. It's like mopping floors. The greatest custodian in the world doesn't hop out of bed in the morning stoked about pushing a mop all day, but nobody complains about the results."

"Close your eyes and think of England," I said.

"What?"

"There are payoffs on the back end."

She giggled. "I don't like that much either."

I smiled. She smiled back. We were becoming besties.

"You know what I mean. You don't like doing it, but being good at it is one of the things that made you the Scrap Metal Meisterfrau of San Francisco."

She raised her glass. "The way to a man's heart is not always through his gizzard. Yeah. Sure. There are payoffs. I live really, really well. Fairy-tale princess, happily ever after well. I can pull my own weight. I don't need Rhonda getting on her knees in front of Stefan like I can't, especially without asking first."

"Courtesy counts."

"So true. You get it."

"Tell me more about this circle."

"I don't even know whether that's the right word for it. Back in the day, when I was a kid, my grandma had a group of friends at her church, and they'd meet at someone's house once a week. It was supposed to be a Bible study, but mostly they sat around and ate and drank and gossiped. She called it her Circle Meeting. We're kind of like that. Social standing used to be everything in San Francisco. A few of us kept running into each other at the opera or the symphony or at the best parties, thanks entirely to our husbands' money. We just gravitated toward one another and bonded."

"The Real Housewives," I said.

"That damned TV show. I might have been born in the Appalachians, but I'm no naïve hillbilly. UK, Class of None-of-Your-Fuckin'-Business. Go Wildcats. I know the women in those shows are grotesques, and I also recognize we're exactly like them. It goes back to the whole idea of being a high-caste Brahmin, or whatever substitutes for them these days. We don't conform to other people's expectations. We are the makers of expectations. And these…are…really, really good martinis."

She giggled again.

"Was Rhonda particularly close to any of the circle women? Someone she might ask for help disappearing?"

"I don't think so." She sipped from her drink. "Wait. She did kiss Julia Wanamaker at the New Year's Eve party this past year. I mean, tongues and everything. Looked like they wanted to get a room. But it was midnight, and we were all pretty drunk already, and someone had brought along some killer weed, and there was some Ex floating around too, so I just chalked it up to getting swept up in the moment. Julia's pretty open about the revolving door on her closet anyway, so it was hard to know who was snogging who. Rhonda is not a talented drinker. She might not even remember it. I'm not aware of them hanging out together or anything, though."

"Are you aware of her fooling around with other husbands?"

"Just rumors. Not within our circle, though. I mean, yeah, I heard Phyllis Bagdasarian was pissed at Rhonda for copping a tug with Armin, but that's as far as it went. I thought that had all blown over. I don't know about Tom Wanamaker, except that I wouldn't fuck him with your pussy, so probably not."

"What's wrong with Tom?"

"He smells. Not his fault. He can't help it. Some genetic shit. Always has this fishy, garlicky scent around him. Kind of gaggy in the sweaty months. Julia should get a Purple Heart for sticking with him."

"Why does she?"

"Why do any of us, sweetie? We're the Real Housewives. We keep our great white b'wanas happy, because otherwise we'd have to find honest work."

"It's a weird dynamic," I told Heidi over dinner at a great crab place on Pier 39. "These women are like… I don't know. Barnacles. Or maybe remoras. They attach themselves to rich men and become just another status symbol, in return for security and luxury."

"It is not weird at all," she said, as she cracked open the carapace of a bright orange Dungeness to attack its innards. "It is merely archaic. And your frustration is purely American. There are only a handful of monarchies left on the European continent, and yet the peerage system of earls, dukes, barons, marquesses, and princes lives on eternal. Snagging a royal, or even a noble, is still one career path, of a kind, open to young women. Especially young women of independent wealth, since most nobles I've ever met were financial paupers. We don't have nobility in this country, unless you count the robber barons. Wealth has taken the place of blood in America. The richer you are, the more attractive you are. One might pursue a prince in Bohemia, but in the states, you want a fat investment banker. Once you hook one, you're made in the shade."

"So young, and yet so cynical," I said.

"You brought it up. And I'm not so young anymore."

"You are forever nubile in my eye."

"You should get your eyes checked," she said.

"Another interesting avenue opened. I'll interview a woman tomorrow who was seen kissing Rhonda at a party a while back. She may know who ran off with Rhonda, if she has a companion. It's probably a dead end, but the word is she's open about her dalliances and may know whether Rhonda is carrying on a side gig, relationship-wise."

"More American provinciality. Nobody is one hundred percent straight. Read fucking Kinsey, Eamon." She dipped a perfectly extracted claw into the drawn butter and slurped it up.

"Maybe the Brownlees have some sort of arrangement that Sam didn't want to tell me about. One of those open relationships. They give each other permission to pursue outside friendships. It's just one of a dozen possibilities I'm turning over in my head."

She sipped from her wine glass. "I miss Sonny already," she said.

"Duty calls," I said. "Once I clear the decks of this Brownlee affair, maybe we can wing out there for a few days."

"Deal," she said.

THIRTEEN

I found Julia Wanamaker's address online and cold-called her the next morning.

A tall, thin woman with frizzy salt and pepper hair pulled into the severest bun I'd seen in ages answered the doorbell. I handed her my card.

"Ms. Wanamaker?" I asked. I probably sounded tentative, since I had a hard time imagining the woman in the doorway cutting loose with anyone at midnight on New Year's Eve or any other time. She didn't look so certain about me either.

"No," she said in a clipped, no-nonsense voice as she scanned the card. "Ms. Wanamaker is not at home at the moment."

"Mind if I ask who—"

"I'm Jane Smith, Ms. Wanamaker's assistant."

Even her name was plain.

"May I come in?" I asked.

"Why?"

"I have some questions, and standing on the front porch is awkward."

"Why should I answer your questions? This card says you're a private investigator. Are you accusing Ms. Wanamaker of some crime? Is she a suspect?"

"Not at all," I said. "I'm trying to locate a friend of hers, and I thought she might be able to help."

"Would this friend be Rhonda Brownlee?"

"Ms. Smith, has your employer been missing for several days?" I asked.

She stared at me for so long, I thought she might have had a seizure. Finally, she sighed and said, "Perhaps you should come inside."

She stood aside and held the door open for me. I was careful to wipe my feet thoroughly on the mat. Manners maketh the man.

She led me through the house to an office. It was modern, with a chromed steel and glass-topped desk, Eames chairs, and a sofa along one wall under a postmodern mural that might have sold for the gross national product of Andorra. She gestured toward one of the chairs. She sat at the end of the sofa, at the very edge of the cushion, as if wary of sullying her boss's stuff.

"Ms. Wanamaker—Julia—left with Rhonda Brownlee. They were headed across the bridge for lunch at the Pelican Inn and a stroll through Muir Woods. Julia referred to it as a recharging expedition."

"What did she mean by that?"

"Julia Wanamaker is a very busy woman, with a back-breaking load of social obligations, which is why she needs a personal assistant. She frequently overextends herself and risks exhaustion. According to her, communing with nature rejuvenates her. She calls it recharging, as if she's soaking up energy. Like a battery."

"What day did they leave?" I asked.

"Four days ago. Monday."

"Was it common for Ms. Wanamaker's recharging expeditions to take that long?"

"Never before. Usually it's only a day trip. An outing. A day at the beach, or a drive down the coast to Monterey. Anything that gets her out of the city and in touch with nature. I assumed she would be back by that evening."

"Did she usually take a friend on these expeditions?"

"Almost never. She thought of them as opportunities for meditation, not fraternization. She wanted quiet and solitude."

"But you weren't surprised when she took Rhonda along on Monday." I didn't phrase it as a question. She struggled to find a suitable answer.

"I found it atypical," she said. "It stood out. But I was not surprised."

"Because Rhonda and your employer have become increasingly familiar of late?"

"I appreciate your obfuscation," she said. "I don't feel pressured. I can say this. If you checked Julia's social calendar, you would find Ms. Brownlee penciled in rather frequently."

"You're being a real sport about this, Ms. Smith," I said. "I know this can't be fun for you. Have you seen similar patterns in Ms. Wanamaker's social calendar in the past?"

She blushed. "I have."

"Did Ms. Wanamaker ever go off on one of her recharging expeditions with any of them?"

"She did," she said. "Please understand, Mr. Gold. I have an obligation and a duty to Julia. Under normal circumstances, I would never discuss her personal affairs—oh, I suppose I should have used a better term."

"I'm betting you were right on," I said. "When she went away with other friends, how long did she stay?"

"Only a night or two at the most. I'd get a call from Julia asking me to clear her calendar for the next day, as they were tired and had decided to get a bed and breakfast for the night. I always offered to make the reservations. She always told me they were made already, which seemed peculiar, at least the first couple of times."

"When did you catch on?" I asked.

"A couple of years ago. I'm not a naïve woman, Mr. Gold. I am, however, trustworthy. How Julia chooses to spend her time, and who she spends it with, is none of my business. I'm just here to make her path less rocky."

"She's never been gone this long before?" I said.

"Not without calling. I haven't heard a word from her since they left on Monday. Not a call or email or text."

"Try calling her now," I said.

She hit the speed dial and placed her phone on speaker. It went directly to voicemail.

"Julia," she said, after the beep, "This is Jane again. It's been four days. I'm concerned. Please call back as soon as you hear this." She clicked off. "Not the first message I've left. This feels different. I was debating consulting with Mr. Wanamaker about filing a missing person report when you rang the doorbell."

"Where is Mr. Wanamaker?"

"In New York."

"On business?"

"Everything is business for Mr. Wanamaker."

"I appreciate you being so up-front with me," I said. "I'm going to ask you to be a little more candid about the Wanamakers. Does Tom know about his wife's trips with friends?"

"Yes," she said. "And I believe he approves."

"It's that sort of marriage," I said.

"By all appearances. I am not privy to Tom and Julia's personal arrangements, but I do know that neither of them considers their wedding ring anything more than ornamental."

I showed her my list of Rhonda's friends. "You recognize these names?"

She examined the list and said, "All of them. Most of them have visited the house."

"Besides Rhonda Brownlee, has Julia ever taken one of these women on her recharging expeditions?"

"No," she said. "Only Rhonda."

"Before Rhonda, how long ago was the last time?"

She looked pained as she said, "Perhaps six months."

"I appreciate how difficult this must be, talking about your employer's personal life, but I think your suspicions are warranted. Who did Julia go off with six months ago?"

She told me.

"If I were you, I'd file that missing person report, if only for peace of mind," I said. "And give my number to the officer who takes the report. Your call went straight to voicemail, which might mean her phone is turned off."

"Or?" She looked alarmed.

"It could be dead," I said.

Gigi Sahakian was annoyed when I strode into her office at the shelter in the Mission District. I didn't care.

"You made the arrangements for Rhonda to get away," I said.

"Mr. Gold, we've already covered this," she said. "You know I did. I've admitted as much."

"Six months ago, you went on a trip with Julia Wanamaker. Where did you go?"

"I think you should leave," she said. "You have no official standing here."

"No," I said. "But I know people who do. I'm five seconds away from filing a missing person report on Rhonda Brownlee, which means police and investigations and a lot of attention paid to your personal life and this shelter. I know you went off with Julia Wanamaker six months ago, and Rhonda went off with her four days ago. They're still missing. Tell me where you went, or I'm heading straight for the police."

"I'm not saying a word until I consult with Julia." She picked up her telephone. Her call went directly to voicemail.

"It's been like that for days," I said. "As we speak, Julia's personal assistant is consulting with Tom Wanamaker in New York, and I expect she'll be calling the police herself within the hour. It's a hell of a lot better for you and the shelter if I find her first. Tell me where you went, Gigi."

She settled back in her chair, her face twisted in deliberation.

"Up the coast," she said. "Little Stinson Beach. A bed and breakfast. The Journey's Inn."

I already had my phone out. Seconds later, I had the front desk at The Journey's Inn.

"I'm a detective from San Francisco," I said. "I need to question two women who may be registered at your inn."

The woman on the other side sounded distraught. "Oh, my goodness. We don't need any trouble with the police."

"Nobody does," I said, conveniently sidestepping the fact that I wasn't in fact the police. Sometimes I stared at the ceiling late at night wondering whether an incomplete truth constituted a lie. On the other hand, Miles Davis had excelled at playing the silences. And I'd never worried a great deal about outright lying on the job anyway. Learned that from old *Rockford Files* episodes. One of my few character flaws. "The women's names are Julia Wanamaker and Rhonda Brownlee."

"I'm sorry, but I don't have anyone here by those names."

"Our information suggests they may be traveling incognito. Are you on your cell phone?"

"I am."

"Hold on. I'll shoot you a picture of one of them. They would have checked in around Monday."

I sent Rhonda's picture to the desk clerk.

"Yes," she said. "They did check in on Monday night, but not under those names. In fact, I only got the name of the other woman. I don't recall it now, but I'm sure it wasn't one of the names you mentioned."

"Please hold on." I muted the phone and turned to Gigi. "Did you send Julia Wanamaker to Osiris for fake documents?"

She nodded, sullenly.

"When?"

"Maybe six months ago. Before we went to Little Stinson."

I unmuted the phone. "Could you check that name, please?" I asked the clerk. "The one the woman used to check in?"

She put down the phone but returned a few seconds later. "Linda Arenson. That's the name she put on the guest register."

"Are they still registered there?" I asked the desk clerk.

"No," she said. "They only stayed overnight. Left after breakfast the next morning."

"Did they say where they were headed?"

"Oh, no. I don't intrude that way. We put great stock in protecting our guests' privacy."

I thanked her and stowed my phone.

"Okay," I said. "They were there, but now they're gone. And you have some explaining to do. Why did Julia want a fake ID?"

"I'm not sure I'm at liberty to divulge that."

I held up my phone. "The police are a simple speed dial away. They're probably going to be involved anyway, because as of right now my advice to Sam Brownlee is to file a missing person report. Tell me or tell them."

She chewed on a ragged thumbnail. "Julia and Tom were in a bad place. It happens sometimes in marriages. Julia has always been open about her romantic pendulum. She's one of the only true fifty-fifty bisexuals I've met. Me? I just dabble. It's a physical thing for me, a transient itch I feel like scratching every several years, nothing more. I don't experience much glamor, Mr. Gold. I spend eighty hours a week mopping up the sloppy refuse of busted lives in this place. My husband puts in at least that much time running Armin's business, and our schedules seldom dovetail. Tom Wanamaker is out of town on business a lot. Nature will find a way."

"Julia scratched your itch, in return for setting up her fake docs?"

"No. It wasn't transactional. As I told you, I referred her to Osiris before any of that happened. Julia and Tom were fighting every day and night over…something that isn't important anymore. Something Julia would prefer I don't discuss. Why do you think Tom's away on business all the time? Julia's a donor at the shelter, so she knew I do a lot of marriage work. She asked me out for drinks. We started hanging out together, when we both had openings in our schedules. She was unsatisfied and I was unsatisfied, so one night we just satisfied each other. That was all it was. She'd already purchased her documents by then. I had a chance to get away, and she suggested we drive up the coast to recharge. That's what she called it. We recharged, all right. But then we drove back to the city the next day and that was it. We barely talk about it. It was a fling. Alcohol was heavily involved. I haven't been with anyone except Ruben since."

"She squirreled away the documents until she had a chance to get away," I said.

"She must have. From what I could gather, she and Tom reconciled shortly after, resolved their differences, and everything between them was fine. She wasn't thinking of taking off anymore."

"I'm confused," I said. "Why go to Osiris to get new identities? Marriages fail all the time. Divorce is a cottage industry in this state. Not only that, but since it's a community property state, they could just cut the ties entirely and live off their settlements. What's with all the cloak and dagger—expensive cloak and dagger at that?"

"That," she said, "is something I can't discuss with you."

"We're entering the realm of confidentiality?"

"No. It's not about that. You're a smart guy, though. You can probably figure it out."

"Ms. Sahakian, is your husband laundering money through Armin Bagdasarian's business?"

Her eyes glittered. She seemed excited. "You'd have to ask him," she said, coyly, but her eyes told me he was.

"Does Armin know about it?"

"Same answer," she repeated.

"Is Tom Wanamaker involved in any way?"

"He could be, if he wanted," she said. "But probably not, for all three questions. Like they say, the wife is always the last to know. You're a detective, like you told the nice lady at The Journey's Inn. Detect."

"I'm going to the police about Rhonda Brownlee," I said. "It's time to bring them in. If she's done the deep dive, I don't have the resources to find her. They can. If they start digging, based on what you've told me, some attention might fall on your husband."

"Well, that would suck," she said.

FOURTEEN

I called Sam Brownlee after leaving the shelter and asked him to meet me at my office. I was on my computer searching for any mention of Linda Arenson, Julia Wanamaker's alias, when he climbed the sixteen steps to my landing and opened the door.

"Have you found her?" he asked. He hung his coat on the rack by the door and sat on one of the chairs facing my desk.

"I know where she went last Monday," I said. "She left that place on Tuesday. I have a lot of questions, though, and I need you to be straight with me. Does Rhonda have any history you're aware of with women?"

"Not...exactly. I mean, yes, Rhonda does have a history with women, but...Oh, my God. Did she run off with another woman?"

"That's exactly what she did," I said.

"Who?"

"Julia Wanamaker."

He held up a finger and pulled out his phone. He punched a number in his contacts. Seconds later, he said, "Tom? Sam. Have you heard from Julia since Monday?" He listened and said, "I have a guy looking for Rhonda. It looks like she and Julia went off together... I agree. I'll take care of that with Rhonda...Yeah. Call me when you get to the airport. Maybe we'll know something by then."

He stowed his phone.

"You don't appear shocked," I said. "I had an enlightening conversation with the director of the shelter in the Mission District, Gigi Sahakian. We talked about why women disappear instead of simply hiring a divorce attorney."

"Did you?" Brownlee said.

"Gigi Sahakian's father-in-law is a highly placed Armenian mobster. Her husband may be laundering Armenian mob money through Armin Bagdasarian's garbage business. You're a loanshark. Tom Wanamaker is never in town, off doing whatever he does—"

"Sales," Brownlee said.

"Another business with terrific money-laundering potential. These women are obtaining new identities for the same reason folks go into the witness protection program. They're running because they're afraid. What are they afraid of, Mr. Brownlee?"

"I couldn't tell you. And you weren't hired to pry into my business, or anyone else's for that matter."

"Here's my report then, and my recommendation. I'll write it up later today and send you a copy with my bill. Between three and five months ago, your wife approached a forger to create a new set of identification papers. That means she was planning to disappear as far back as six months ago. Julia Wanamaker had already secured similar documents several months earlier. Both women were referred to the forger by the same person. Two months ago, you attended a fundraiser for the women's shelter with your wife, who pledged fifty thousand dollars. I think this pledge was a ruse, a cover so that she could withdraw that amount from her household accounts without raising immediate attention. She used thirty thousand dollars of that money to purchase her documents, leaving her twenty thousand to get away."

"Not much," Brownlee said. "She couldn't get far with that."

"Check your other accounts," I said. "I bet there will be some small amount, less than six figures, missing from several of them. They'll look like legit expenses. Rhonda has been planning this for a while. The fifty grand was just her getaway stake. She probably has more money stashed in accounts under her new name."

"I'll check. So where did she go?"

"She and Julia Wanamaker drove to Little Stinson Beach, where they stayed at a bed and breakfast called The Journey's Inn overnight. They checked in under Julia's false identity of Linda Arenson. They checked out after breakfast the next morning and drove off."

"And you don't know where they went?"

"Not yet. Sonny had to go back to Honolulu, but before he did, he arranged for the security director at the Mark Hopkins to draw on his network of hotel security staff to keep an eye out for Rhonda. They have her picture. I can call him and tell him to have the front desks look out for a Linda Arenson as well. In the meantime, I think it's time to file a missing person report with the police."

"I agree. I was just discussing it with Tom Wanamaker. Julia's assistant called him and told him what was happening. He's already authorized her to call the police, and he's headed back to San Francisco from New York first thing tomorrow morning. Let's call the police now and make the report on Rhonda."

"Before we do," I said. "I want to revisit something I said earlier. If this disappearance is related in any way to your business and Bagdasarian's business and the Armenian mob, the police could make things uncomfortable for you."

"What are you saying?" Brownlee asked.

"Just letting you know. You're the client. You write the checks. It's my job to help you see every angle of a situation. Julia and Rhonda aren't on the run because they're in love. They're afraid of something, and they think vanishing and becoming two completely new people is preferable to remaining with their husbands and their lavish Real Housewives lives. Whatever they're afraid of is none of my business. All I'm hired to do is find them. I agree. You should call the police, but they are definitely going to be interested. They're nosey that way. You have to decide what's best for you."

"I think I know exactly what you're saying," he said. "And don't send me a bill yet. You might not be finished. Now, are you calling the cops, or should I?"

FIFTEEN

We located Julia Wanamaker almost immediately.

I was sitting at my desk later that afternoon when my telephone rang.

"This is Sean Ashford," the person on the other end said after I answered. Security director at the Mark Hopkins. "Sonny Malehala asked me to call if I got a hit on a Linda Arenson."

"Give me some good news, Sean," I said.

"We've located her."

She was at an oceanfront resort in Santa Barbara, registered under the name Linda Arenson, and had been in the spa more or less since her arrival.

"What about the other woman, Rhonda Brownlee?"

"Sorry. The desk clerk there told me Linda Arenson checked in alone."

When Brownlee and I called the police, the case was assigned to a young inspector named Leon Fender. I hadn't spoken with him face-to-face yet, but when I mentioned Julia Wanamaker, he said he'd pulled that case as well.

"They're connected," I told him. "They ran together on Monday and stayed overnight at The Journey's Inn in Stinson Beach before splitting up."

Now I called Fender again.

"Any word, Gold?" He sounded amped.

"We found Julia Wanamaker. She's at a resort in Santa Barbara, registered under the name Linda Arenson." I gave him the name and the phone number for the resort. "I'd suggest contacting their security guy. They can keep an eye on her until you can get down there."

"I can make it in about four hours," he said. "I know a detective named Lassiter in the Santa Barbara PD. I'll call on the way and let him know we're tramping on his turf."

"I'll meet you there."

The security guy at the resort in Santa Barbara wasn't a guy at all, which made me feel like a raging chauvinist. Her name was Jackie Pitino, and she was a stern, terse woman dressed in a tailored suit that nicely concealed the Glock she carried under her right arm. A southpaw. She looked like she worked out. Like, a lot. It's the hands. Dead giveaways. I called as I headed into the resort and asked if she could meet me in the lobby.

She eyed me suspiciously as I walked toward her. I was dressed casually, but I'd foregone the jeans with holes in the knees and my fraying windbreaker. I thought I looked natty. She sniffed as I drew near. I was glad I'd showered before driving down.

"You're Gold?" she asked.

"I am," I said.

"Follow me." She turned on her heel and walked briskly toward the hallway behind the front desk that contained the management offices.

"A police detective from San Francisco is on the way as well," I said to her back.

"Leon Fender. I know." She didn't even say it over her shoulder. She exuded the distinct impression that I was somehow inconveniencing her.

She opened her office door and ushered me inside. It was spartan and utilitarian. No degrees on the walls. No family pictures. Clean desktop with a blotter still in the plastic. It might as well have been a key man rental. She pointed to a chair across from her desk and planted herself in the chair facing me. She put the desk between us, not for her protection, but rather to establish dominance.

"Marines," I said. "Maybe special forces. Possibly military intelligence. Lifer. You punched out after stacking your twenty and sold your skills to the highest bidder. I bet your apartment looks a lot like this."

"I just love being reduced to a cultural stereotype," she said.

"And a film buff," I said. "*Annie Hall.*"

She didn't take the bait. "We've kept an eye on Linda Arenson since I received the call from Inspector Fender. We can't detain her, of course, and probably wouldn't anyway, since I'm not aware she's committed a crime."

"Registering under false identity?"

"We're a resort," she said. "A rather exclusive one. False identities are a dime a dozen here. And she paid in cash, so there's no fraud involved."

I told her who Linda Arenson really was, and that she was a material witness in another missing person case.

"That explains why Inspector Fender is interested, but I don't understand your involvement, Mr. Gold."

"I'm looking for the woman who's still missing."

"As is Inspector Fender."

"I convinced my client to call the police and file a missing person report. I had information Inspector Fender could use. He has resources I can use. There's mutual benefit."

The telephone on her desk rang. She answered it. "Thank you," she said. She hung up. "Inspector Fender is here. Let's go find your woman."

Leon Fender stood in the upper five-feet range. He was young, perhaps thirty or a little older. His gold shield wasn't freshly minted, but it hadn't been scuffed much yet. He was a Black man dressed in a standard-issue Men's Wearhouse off-the-rack suit that fit him surprisingly well and broken-in wingtips with rubber aftermarket soles, in which he could probably run the hundred yards in twelve seconds flat. He wore a bow tie, which I found somehow quaint, and old-fashioned horn rim glasses with wire frames under the lenses. His hair was cropped close to his head. He had a cop's eyes, constantly moving, constantly evaluating the environment. I introduced myself and Jackie Pitino in the lobby.

"Here are the ground rules," Pitino said. "Keep it quiet. No histrionics. No dragging this woman screaming out of the resort by her hands and feet. We do this surgically, and none of the other guests are inconvenienced."

"Where is she?" Fender asked.

I noticed he hadn't agreed to her terms. So did she.

"Lying by the pool," she said. "Remember what I said."

Fender and I strolled toward the pool. I could feel Pitino's eyes drilling laser holes in the back of my nice tweed jacket.

"You really planned on dragging her out of here kicking and screaming?" I asked Fender.

"Naw. She hasn't done anything illegal that I know of. That's one of the nice things about missing person beefs. Ninety percent of the time they turn up just fine." He waited several seconds and added. "She doesn't need to know that, though."

Julia Wanamaker lay on a day bed inside a clamshell cabana next to the Olympic sized pool. She wore a neon red bikini that nearly matched her hair, and a pair of sunglasses. She was decidedly well-maintained. She grinned as our party surrounded the cabana.

"Busted," she said. She held out her hands. "Slap 'em on, McDuff."

"For the record," Pitino said. "You are registered here under the name Linda Arenson?"

"Who squealed?" Julia asked. "I paid good money for that name."

"So your name is actually Julia Wanamaker?" Pitino asked.

"Well, to be completely accurate, it's Julia Longacre Stanfield Wanamaker, but why stand on formality?"

Leon Fender took over. "Ms. Wanamaker, I'm Inspector Fender with the San Francisco Police Department. Your husband has filed a missing person report on you."

"Case closed, then," she said. "I was lost, but now I'm found. Isn't that some sort of hymn? But I haven't heard anything yet from the hunky one. What about you, Sugar? Are you the bouncer?"

"Eamon Gold," I said. "I'm a private investigator. Are you all right?"

She ran her hands down her admirably preserved and meticulously augmented body. "What do you think? I think I'm pretty damned amazing. But that's not what you meant, is it? Do I look threatened or frightened? I'm snug as a bug in a rug. Could you move about a foot to the left? You're in my sun. You, the butchy hotel one. Could you ask them to send out one of those cute waiters? My margarita is evaporating."

Even with my back turned, I could feel Pitino bristle.

"Your husband is worried," Fender said.

"He called from New York City to tell you that?"

"He's on his way back to San Francisco now," Fender said. "To be perfectly honest, I'm not certain what to tell him. As far as I can see, you haven't broken any laws worth prosecuting, and I can't detain you for simply deserting your marriage."

"Problem solved, then," she said. "And I haven't deserted anything, darlin'. Just taking a little breather while the breadwinner is out of town."

"There is the matter of Rhonda Brownlee, however," Fender said. "I also have a missing person report on her, and information gathered by Gold here suggests you and Ms. Brownlee checked in to The Journey's Inn at Stinson Beach on Monday night."

"It's a lovely little place. Have you ever been there?"

"Do you know where Rhonda went when you checked out on Tuesday?" I asked.

"God. I love your voice," she said. "I could listen to it all day. Have you considered a radio career?"

"Please answer the question," Fender said. "It's a valid one, under the circumstances, though I would appreciate it if Gold would leave the questions to me." He gave me a wicked side-glance. I caught the message and clammed up.

She pouted. I think it was the first time I'd ever seen a post-menopausal woman pout.

"You're no fun. No, I don't know where she went. Sorry. She went her way. I went mine."

"So you weren't lovers," I said. Fender glared at me again.

"Oh, hell no, Sweetie," she said. "Well, not anymore. We bumped uglies once or twice, a few months back, but that was just out of boredom. Being a kept woman is not all it's cracked up to be. I was tempted, though, sharing that room in Stinson, but I stood firm. We had a different agenda."

"Making Rhonda disappear," Fender said.

"Yes."

"Why?"

"Ask her husband. He knows. I'd fill you in, but I promised Rhonda I wouldn't. You wouldn't want me to break a promise, would you?"

I thought Fender might blow a gasket. Instead, he pulled a chair away from a nearby card table and slid it next to the cabana. He sat and brushed an imaginary speck of lint from his trousers.

"Here's where we are," he said, quietly. "Right now, you're just a bored housewife on a lark. No laws have been broken. You have squandered a significant slice of police resources, but that's incidental. Legally, I have no grounds to drag you back to San Francisco"

"Is this a great country, or what?" Julia asked.

"However," Fender continued. "We don't know where Rhonda Brownlee is, and to the best of our knowledge you were the last person to see or speak to her. If something bad happens to her, we'll talk again, first because you will be my prime suspect, and second because I'll want you to know in excruciating detail the injuries you could have prevented with a single sentence. If she does anything felonious under her new identity, I'll be looking at you as an accessory. You two may have split up in Stinson Beach, but you're still joined at the hip. What happens to her blows back on you. Any questions?"

"Nope," she said. She looked at Pitino. "Oh, yeah. One question. Is that waiter fellow coming? My glass is empty, and all this threatening talk is harshing my buzz."

"I'll contact Mr. Wanamaker and inform him that his wife has been located," Fender said as we walked toward the parking lot. "Case closed."

"You must have a frustrating job," I said.

"If I had a social worker's head, maybe. I'm more like an old west tracker. I'm really only interested in finding them. Runaways and restless spouses make up eighty percent of my work. Most of them are resolved in a day or so. Nice trick with the hotel security network, by the way. I'll be cultivating a relationship with your guy at the Mark Hopkins. That's a nifty resource."

"You better hurry before he wings off to Honolulu. My sometimes partner Sonny is comping him a week at his resort."

"Any ideas on what to do next on Rhonda?" Fender asked.

"Julia Wanamaker obtained a false ID six months ago. A week later, she paid cash for a two-year old Beemer under her new identity. That's the car parked here at the resort."

"Okay."

"The desk clerk at The Journey's Inn said they arrived together, in a single car. So how is Rhonda getting around?"

"You know what I think?" Fender said.

"That the whole Stinson Beach trip was a way for Julia to teach Rhonda how to disappear?"

"Yeah."

"I think I'll drive across the bridge and canvass every used car lot I can find near Stinson Beach," I said. "Show them Rhonda's picture. See if anyone recognizes her."

"We'll split it up," he said. "It's out of my jurisdiction, so I'll need to coordinate with the locals first."

"I, on the other hand, operate under no such constraints."

"You talk funny for a private eye."

"You should hear me recite the *The Canterbury Tales* prologue in Middle English," I said. "I'll get started with the lots that start with letters A through M. If I finish before you set things up with the locals, I'll continue until you can tag in and mop up."

"You know, I typically don't like hooking up with private cops," he said. "Bunch of cowboys and undisciplined rogues."

"Rogues?" I said. "I can't recall ever being called a rogue before. I kind of like it. Remember that old TV show *The Rogues*?"

"Most of my life has been spent in this century."

"Well, you missed out then. David Niven, Charles Boyer, Gig Young. They were cool. Maybe I'll put that on my business card. *Eamon Gold, Undisciplined Rogue.*"

"Don't make me regret letting your nose under the tent of this investigation," Fender said. "I'll contact the Marin County Sheriff's Department. Maybe they can spare an investigator as well. If you find anything before I show up, give me a buzz."

SIXTEEN

I found something before he showed up.

I hit paydirt on my third shot, a place called Buzzy's Used Cars, a sun-bleached concrete block building in the middle of a shell and gravel lot just outside Red Rocks Beach. Buzzy had been dead for almost fifteen years. The lot was run by a sunburned man named Carl Lyon. He had flyaway dry frizzy gray hair, a wandering left eye, and a challenging case of Dunlop's Disease. The sodden cigar stub clenched between his teeth should have been tossed in the dumpster a day or so earlier. He wore a bolo tie and snakeskin cowboy boots and seemed to possess no awareness at all that he was a genuine American archetype.

"Yeah," he said, when I showed him Rhonda Brownlee's photo. "I remember her. Tuesday, it was. She was a walk-in."

"A walk-in?"

"Just showed up on the lot. No trade. Paid in cash. Didn't haggle. Easiest sale I made all month."

"She was motivated. She had someplace to be."

"Yeah? Where?"

"Anywhere but here. What did she buy?"

"Sweetest little Hyundai you ever saw. One owner, a little old widower who only drove it to the local strip club twice a week. He died in it."

"The strip club?"

"The car. He was in the strip club parking lot, though. We kept that to ourselves. Turns out, you have to report every goddamn fender-bender a car has ever been in, but if some geezer cacks in the front seat after a particularly stimulating lap dance, nobody gives a shit. We just hit it overnight with the ozone generator to eradicate the smell, and it was almost pristine."

"Almost," I said.

"It might get a little ripe on a really hot day, but I knocked a thousand off for the inconvenience."

"You're a real prince, Carl," I said. "Don't suppose you have a license tag number?"

"Nope. Sorry. Every car drives off the lot here with a thirty-day temp tag. I file the paperwork with the state, and they assign the tag number and send the plates."

"Have you sent that information in yet?"

"It's still in my office."

"I need the name of this woman," I said, pointing at the picture.

"You don't know it?"

"She's traveling under a fake identity. Her real name is Rhonda Brownlee. I need to know what name she's using now."

He rubbed at his badly shaven cheek. "I don't know," he said. "Sounds like invasion of privacy to me." I'd seen his avaricious expression on a thousand faces over the years.

"Fifty bucks is all you get," I said. "And you're lucky to get that. This is already a police case. A San Francisco inspector named Leon Fender will be around later if I don't get this woman's information, and he won't offer you jack shit." I pulled a couple of twenties and a ten from my pocket and held it up.

"As it happens, I'm running a special on information today," he said, snatching at the cash. "Let's step into my air-conditioned office and see if I can find those papers."

———

"She's traveling under the name Beverly Shaw," I told Fender over the phone. "She bought a Hyundai Genesis, two-door, beige." I read off the vehicle ID number and the temporary tag number. "Paid cash. I already checked. The address on her identification is fake. Doesn't exist. It's a real street, but the street numbers don't run that high."

"Good work," Fender said. "I can take it from here. I'll get the Highway Patrol on the temp tag."

"Hold on. Julia was giving Rhonda a crash course in disappearing. I bet that temp tag is already in a trash can. If I were on the lam, I'd find a wreck or an abandoned car, or maybe a car in a long-term airport lot, steal the tags, and head off into the great unknown. We know she's calling herself Beverly Shaw now, but a beige Hyundai in this country might as well be invisible."

"Even if she's paying cash everywhere she goes, we know her name now. I'll put out a BOLO on her," Fender said. "The Photoshop guys in forensics can make several pictures with various hair colors and styles. We'll distribute them to Utah, Nevada, and Arizona as well. Probably won't turn up shit, though. BOLOs on mispers are a pretty low priority. What do you do if you find her, and she isn't interested in going home? Hardly worth it to keep an eye out."

"Not my problem anymore. I think I've learned about everything I can. Your reach is a lot longer than mine. I'll file my report with Sam Brownlee and let you have at it."

"I appreciate your help, Gold. You weren't the total jerkoff I expected."

"I know you meant that in the nicest possible way," I said. "Happy hunting."

———

"Inspector Fender's handling the case now," I told Brownlee. He had asked me to present my findings at his office, which was in one of the drabber uptown high-rises. The suite was opulent, however, with rich stained hardwood walls, expensive Turkish rugs, and upscale furniture. It smelled clean. Brownlee sat imperiously behind his desk. I was positive his chair was on a raised platform, because he gave the impression of peering down at me from a court bench. "Anything I might do from this point forward would likely be stepping on his toes, redundant, or otherwise obstructive. He seems completely competent to find your wife."

"And you say she's traveling under the name Beverly Shaw?" he said, his mouth still frozen in a smarmy grin. I wondered if his teeth frequently dried out.

"That's the information the car salesman gave me." I pulled an envelope from my jacket pocket and slid it across his desk. "Maybe Julia Wanamaker knows where she's headed, and maybe she doesn't. She was teaching your wife how to disappear, after all. One of the key requirements for disappearing is that nobody knows where you are. My final report and my invoice. The invoice includes what Jordy Pankratz owed me. No rush. Anytime this month."

"I'll have my secretary cut you a check before you leave. I... I appreciate your efforts in this case, Gold. I suspect it wasn't easy to take on, given my occupation."

"Hardly gave it a second thought," I said. "Besides, it got Jordy Pankratz off the hook. If you found my work satisfactory, please tell your friends." I paused and added, "Your *legitimate* friends."

"I suppose that's fair. And I will pass the word along. Thank you."

Heidi and I celebrated my payday with a weekend at the Montara house, and a day trip to Monterey for the action on the pier, which always seemed to me no more interesting than Pier 39, just down from my office, but Heidi enjoyed the trip. She'd read *Cannery Row* again before we left, just to enhance the mood.

There was an IndyCar race at Laguna Seca Raceway, on the other side of Monterey Bay, that same weekend. Monterey was more than usually packed with fans, which made a day trip the smart choice. We lunched and strolled and shopped and visited Cannery Row where Heidi told me all about Doc and Mack and Hazel and Dora, transcribing Steinbeck with her faint German accent. After a long afternoon as tourists, we drove back to Montara and collapsed on the sofa with a bottle of malbec and a plate of butter crackers and cheese. I found the Iron and Wine station on Pandora, and we relaxed and nibbled and talked while potatoes roasted in the oven, salmon steaks marinated in the kitchen, and the charcoal ashed over in the deck grill.

"So you're on downtime again," she said.

"Something will turn up," I said. "It always does. As long as men have wandering eyes and lissome personal assistants, I'll never starve. The check from Brownlee will tide me over for a few months in any case. He's a generous tipper."

"Bless his heart," she said.

"It's hush money," I said. "But I don't care. I don't blab about my clients anyway. Except to you, that is."

"And even then, you withhold some of the facts."

"Withhold. Good word. Anyway, now I have time to finish those twin cocobolo Hauser copies for Dan Dunbar and his wife Donna. Might laminate the neck blanks and Spanish heels tomorrow. Might not. Might spend all day watching old movies on the sofa."

"And until then?"

"Grilled salmon, wine, and whoopie," I said.

She snuggled against me. "It's good to have a plan."

SEVENTEEN

The text from Rhonda Brownlee popped up on my phone on Monday.

I'd considered blowing the morning off and lazing in bed. Heidi and I had driven back to the city on Sunday night because she had to open the gallery the next morning. After our energetic weekend, she had opted to split up for the night so she could get a little sleep.

Having nothing of note looming on my social calendar, I watched television late into the night in my Russian Hill condo, the lights of the Golden Gate Bridge and Alcatraz and rugged individualists on Mount Tam twinkling in the distance through my floor-to-ceiling windows.

My bladder and my damned circadian rhythm woke me simultaneously at seven o'clock. Experience told me sleep was over for the night, so I showered, dressed, savored a breakfast of eggs, bacon, and croissants with Normandy butter and black cherry preserves, and headed toward my office around nine.

I stepped inside Heidi's gallery before trudging up the stairs to my office. The film company had moved on under the cover of darkness a couple of nights earlier, thankfully, so Jefferson Street was clear, but the gallery was empty nonetheless. Like people who've been together for a long time, we compared relative sleep quality the night before—hers was much better and longer than mine—and then we played kissyface for a minute or two before I begged off while I could still get out the door sideways.

My lack of present engagement afforded me time to finally clear my desk of the piled-up paperwork. I checked my voicemail. Sonny had left a message during the night. Just checking in. Otherwise, nothing. I made coffee and sucked on a couple of Dove dark chocolates as I waded through the administrative bother I'd allowed to accumulate. I ordered DoorDash for lunch, so I could keep working.

Around one in the afternoon, my telephone buzzed. A message. Blocked number. No name.

I hear you're looking for me.

I stared at it for several seconds. Then I typed.

Rhonda?

The little wheelie thing twirled, and a note read X is typing.

I think we should meet. I have things to explain.

I tapped out, *Where are you?*

More waiting. It was like trying to make a phone call to someone on Mars.

I'm afraid to tell you that.

I thought it over and responded *Come to my office. The police are looking for you. I'm not working for your husband anymore. My office is neutral ground.*

More waiting. *Not your office.*

Where? I tapped.

Long pause, as if she was debating whether to tell me.

Julia and Tom have a cabin on Mount Tam. Julia gave me the key and said she'd see to it Tom stayed away.

She sent the address.

Come alone, she wrote. *I'll be watching. If you don't come alone, I'll disappear again, and you'll never find me.*

I thought it over, and wrote, *The police are still looking for you. I'll come alone, but I'll have to tell them I saw you, and whatever you tell me.*

She saw the message, but the screen remained blank. Thinking it over.

I added, *Right now, you've done nothing illegal. You aren't in any trouble with the law. I'm just trying to help, but the cops have their rules. If we meet, I have to tell them afterward.*

Long pause, and then the twirly thing popped up again.

Okay. I'll wait.

After a few minutes of moral deliberation, I called Sam Brownlee. The phone rang three times and went to voicemail. Strange for midday. I left a message.

"Mr. Brownlee, this is Eamon Gold. I've received a message that might be from your wife. I'll call Inspector Fender if this turns out to be legitimate."

I stashed the phone in my pocket and headed out the door.

The beige Hyundai sat outside the isolated cabin on Mount Tam. From the front porch, I could see the spires of San Francisco and the massive Golden Gate Bridge in the distance. I wondered whether I'd seen the cabin's porch lights the previous evening from my apartment window. I checked the tag on the car. She'd stolen a set of Oregon plates somewhere and replaced the temporary tag. Clever.

Calling it a cabin was like referring to Monticello as a farmhouse. It had a cabin-like quality, with an exterior of hewn and stripped redwood logs, but was otherwise a mountain McMansion. It looked like an Alpine a-frame church, with ornate stained-glass patterns in the fully windowed front face and wings that spread both right and left. An eight-foot oaken double door sat monolith-like in the center of the front façade, at the back of a deep covered porch. I expected to be greeted by a St. Bernard when I stepped up to it.

I rang the bell and waited. A minute later, I rang it again.

She'd said she'd be watching. I surveyed the woods surrounding the house.

"Hello?" I shouted toward the trees. "I'm here. I came alone, as you asked."

Another minute passed. Something felt wrong. I parked my hand on the holstered Glock on my hip for reassurance.

"My name is Eamon Gold," I called out. "I'm here to meet Rhonda Brownlee."

Maybe I heard a twig snap in the woods. Maybe not. Just touching the Glock wasn't reassuring enough, so I pulled it and held it in both hands, pointed toward the ground.

"Rhonda?" I called out again, toward the place where I might have heard the sound. I'm a city kid. My knowledge of fieldcraft and the great outdoors ended with Cub Scouts. Every sound I heard seemed to come from everywhere.

I circled the house, looking inside the windows. Lights were on inside, but there was no smoke from the chimney, and when I peeked through the side window, I saw the fireplace cold and dark.

And I saw the slim feminine hand hanging limply over the edge of the sofa.

I rapped on the glass. The hand didn't move. It looked white and drained. I banged on the glass this time.

"Ms. Brownlee!" I shouted.

The hand remained motionless. I knew what I'd find if I broke in, but I did it anyway. I discovered the side door to the kitchen and kicked it in. The jamb splintered on the first try. I was by the sofa in seconds, but I stopped when I saw her face, or rather what remained of it. I backed up to the door again, trying to retrace my steps as I pulled my phone from my pocket to call the police.

The last thing I needed was to be taken to the woodshed by Inspector Leon Fender because I fucked up a murder scene.

EIGHTEEN

I sat in one of the rockers on the front porch of Tom and Julia Wanamaker's Mount Tam cabin, staring off into the woods. The wilderness quiet of the afternoon was shattered by four cop cruisers and their rotating blue and red lights, the tinny radio calls that echoed off the trees, and the half-dozen conversations taking place inside and out front of the house. The Marin County medical examiner's van had arrived several minutes earlier. Leon Fender showed up later, having driven across the bridge from San Francisco after alerting the local authorities.

The front door stood wide open. The interior of the house was lit like a Hollywood movie set. My mouth was dry and my skin hot. I'd seen my share of bodies over the years, and I'm a tough guy, but you never really get used to it. Some things still eat at your soul like lye.

I'd invested a lot of time looking for Rhonda Brownlee. Killing her when I was this close to making contact was just rude. Someone would take the heat for it. I figured I was as good as anyone to make that happen.

Fender stepped outside to the porch and glared at me.

"Don't look at me, Chief," I said. "I wasn't even on the case anymore."

"And you didn't call me when she contacted you. Words like obstruction are bouncing around inside my head right now."

"It was a text message. I had no idea whether it was real." I showed him the conversation on my phone. "See? I told her the police were looking for her. I told her to call you. She felt safer contacting me. I planned to call you as soon as I knew this wasn't a hoax."

"Too late for that now. I have about five minutes left to be in charge. It's not a missing person case anymore, and she didn't show up dead in my jurisdiction. This is county land, and not even my county, so the sheriff is sending one of his homicide detectives to take command. I just became third banana, and after I file my case closure report this afternoon, I'll be out entirely. So, fuck you very much, Gold. I appreciated chasing my ass with you."

"And we were such buddies yesterday," I said. "The thrill is gone."

A black Chevy Impala that might as well have had *Plainclothes Cop* painted on the side pulled up to the house. A man climbed out. He was average height, with a full gray beard. His suit was rumpled, as if he were wearing it for the fifth time that week. He might have been sixty. He might have been as old as Gandalf. He had that kind of face. He saw Fender next to me and waved.

"You the kid from San Francisco?" He walked up the steps to the porch the way General MacArthur marched onto the beach at Luzon.

"Inspector Leon Fender."

"Jack Bludis, Marin County Sheriff's Department."

They shook hands. I remained seated, mostly because the rocker was extremely comfortable. Bludis pointed at me.

"This him?"

"Yeah," Fender said. "He's the asshole."

"Hey!" I said. "I'm starting to feel unappreciated."

"I know you," Bludis said. "You were the lead on another missing wife case around here last year. Isabel Standish? Seems she turned up dead too."

"You have a good memory. My agency handled that case. Sonny Malehala was the investigator."

"Yeah. I recall. Don't suppose he's around now?" Bludis asked.

"Honolulu," I said. "Where the palm trees sway in the land of wickie-wackie."

"Geez," Bludis grunted to Fender. "Another flake. Tell me what we have here."

Fender walked him through the search for Rhonda Brownlee, including my role as the original investigator. His story ended with the interview with Julia Wanamaker in Santa Barbara. Bludis turned to me.

"She texted me about four hours ago," I said. I handed him my phone with the texts up on the screen. "Out of the blue. I'd already closed the case with her husband. He's paid me and everything. I wasn't working it anymore. I don't know how she knew I was looking for her."

"Julia Wanamaker," Fender said. "Had to be. We braced her Friday, and today Rhonda called you. You gave Julia your card, right?"

"I give everyone my card," I said. "Damn things are worthless in my pocket."

The medical examiner was a woman in her middle forties named Courtney French. Her eyes were bleary, as if she'd been awakened from a nap to take the DB call. She stepped onto the porch. She ignored Fender and me and spoke directly to Bludis.

"Blunt force head trauma," she said. "Found the weapon. Unopened bottle of champagne. Someone tried to christen her skull with it, repeatedly. No prints. No apparent other broken bones or significant bruising. She took two or three hits square in the face and probably went down on the first blow. Lividity suggests she died on the spot. Wasn't moved."

"Time of death?"

"Based on liver temp and rigor, I'd say six to eight hours ago."

"No way!" I protested.

She and Bludis stared at me.

"What Mr. Gold is clumsily attempting to explain," Bludis said, "is that he was in touch with the deceased four hours ago."

"Livers don't lie," she said. "Not in this ambient temperature."

Bludis said, "Where's her telephone?"

"We haven't found one," Fender said. "Still looking."

"She was probably using a burner," I said. "The phone in her name went dark days ago. As you can see in her texts, her number was blocked."

"Whoever texted you wasn't that woman inside the house," Courtney French said. "She'd been dead several hours at least."

"This might be nothing," I said. "When I arrived to meet Ms. Brownlee, I thought I heard a noise out in the woods. Like twigs snapping. I don't know if it means anything, but someone could have been watching me discover the body."

Bludis called one of the uniformed deputies over. "Put together a detail to canvass the woods surrounding the house. Might have been someone hiding there last night."

"Someone needs to notify the husband," Fender said.

"You know him?" Bludis asked.

"I do," I said. "I'll go with Fender to break the news."

I dropped my car at my condo, and Fender picked me up there.

"May I say how much I appreciate getting kicked off this case just as it gets interesting?" he said as I strapped in.

"Don't look at me. I didn't kill her."

"But it looks like you've been playing phone tag with the person who did."

"Yeah. I don't get that. I thought about it all the way back across the bridge."

"How do you mean?"

"Why contact me at all? Let's start with the premise that the primary agenda for any murderer is avoiding being caught."

"With you so far," he said.

"The person who killed her had to arrive at the cabin at least three hours before I was contacted, based on the M.E.'s prelim. Maybe earlier, because you don't just show up and clobber someone on the sofa. Unless she was already asleep, she must have known her killer. No sign of a struggle. They were cozy. She felt safe, right up to the instant someone caved in the back of her head and skulked away undetected."

"But not before texting you."

"Yeah. Why ruin it by texting me?" I asked. "If the killer had just driven away, it might have been days or weeks before either Tom or Julia Wanamaker arrived to find the body. Time is like air for murderers. The more time that passes after the killing, the less likely it will be solved."

"Whoever killed Rhonda wanted her to be found quickly."

"It had to be someone she knew," I said.

Fender's telephone beeped. It went to the car's Bluetooth speaker.

"Inspector Fender, this is Detective Bludis."

"Detective. I have Eamon Gold in the car with me."

He wasn't being polite. It was a warning to Bludis that a civilian was listening in. I was a cop once myself, and I know conversations between investigators are not always completely respectful, even when discussing the dead. He was telling Bludis to keep it civil.

"We found the phone," Bludis said. "It fell between the cushions on the sofa. The body kept us from seeing it before. When we bagged her, one of the techs spotted it."

"It was planted," I said. "After the killer texted me."

"No shit. You should be a detective," Bludis said. "It was a burner. The messages sent to you are on it. We've sent it to the lab for analysis, but I wouldn't get my hopes up. Probably wiped. You talk with the husband yet?"

"We're on our way," Fender said.

"Tell him I'll be down there to interview him as soon as we're finished here. Between now and then, I'll contact the cabin owners—the Wanamakers—and let them know we'll be occupying their vacation palace for a day or so. They'll need to arrange for cleanup when we leave. It'll be a mess."

"Julia Wanamaker is registered at a resort in Santa Barbara under the name Linda Arenson," Fender said. "Tom Wanamaker should be either at his home or his office in San Francisco."

"Julia gave Rhonda Brownlee the keys to the cabin?" Bludis asked.

"Yeah," I said. "Wait. No. The text said Julia gave her the keys, but we already know those texts didn't come from Rhonda."

"I'll ask Ms. Wanamaker when I talk to her. But, for now, let's say she gave Ms. Brownlee the keys. It makes sense. She was the only person we know who also had some inkling of Rhonda's whereabouts," he said. "I'll follow up with her. Keep a close eye on the husband. I'd prefer to inform him myself, but I figure, between the two of you, you'll see if he does anything hinky."

———

"I was afraid of this," Brownlee said. We were in his home. He sat on a modern leather couch in front of a tempered glass coffee table. He wore a pair of jeans, a long-sleeved sport shirt, and a pair of Bass Weejuns without socks. He looked like he'd just rolled out of bed. His face was sallow, and his eyes were bloodshot. He slurred a little when he spoke. His hands trembled as he collected his thoughts. His smarmy grin was nowhere to be found. "Somehow, I knew, deep down, that I wasn't going to see her again."

He cupped his forehead with his hand, and a few teardrops fell to the rug.

"Did she suffer?" he asked.

"I don't think so," Fender said. "It was violent, but very quick. I don't think she knew what happened."

"That's a blessing, I suppose."

"There will be an autopsy," Fender said. "They may not release the body for a week or so."

"I understand. That will give me time to make arrangements in any case. I don't really know where to start. I suppose I can just call a mortuary and hand it all over to them."

"That's probably best," Fender said. "As of today, I'm finished with this case. I'm not in the Homicide Division. The investigation going forward will be conducted by a Marin County sheriff's detective named Jack Bludis. He should contact you later today to schedule a time to talk."

Fender handed him Bludis's card, and one of his own. We talked for a while, and then Fender and I excused ourselves to leave Brownlee to his grief.

"What do you think?" Fender asked on the drive back to my condo.

"Hard to tell. He looked like he just woke up after a two-day bender. Sounded like he still had a few shots to sweat out. Six of one, half a dozen of the other. He didn't take a false step. If he did it, he's a cool one."

"I've seen cooler," Fender said. "But I agree. I didn't see anything that jumped out at me. If someone asked, I'd have to say he looked genuinely shocked and mournful."

"Someone may ask," I said. "Husband's always the prime suspect."

NINETEEN

Fender called me the next day. "I heard from Bludis. He's an okay guy, once you scrape off some of the crust. Said he knew I'd invested a lot of effort in the case and wanted to keep me in the loop as a courtesy."

"He's a prince," I said. "Any news?"

"Autopsy confirmed blunt force trauma. Initial tox screen shows alcohol and benzodiazepines in her bloodstream. So, maybe she was drugged before someone caved in her face. Might have been passed out already."

"Makes sense. No defensive wounds, and she wasn't moved from the sofa after she was murdered. We already know she was dead when I received the messages. Maybe the killer drugged her and had to wait for it to take effect."

"We'll know better when the full results come in. Julia Wanamaker was at the resort in Santa Barbara the entire time, so she's out as a suspect. She admitted giving Rhonda the key but said she didn't see her after they separated in Stinson Beach."

"Who else could have known Rhonda was at the cabin?" I asked.

"Maybe Julia told someone. Maybe Rhonda got lonely and reached out to the wrong buddy. Not my problem. It's Bludis's case now. He said he'd deal me in on the bust if it's in the city, but I'm not holding my breath. They released the body after the autopsy. Feel like crashing a funeral?"

As I mentioned, I only wear ties at weddings, funerals, and to court. I only own three ties, all in primary colors. One has contrasting diagonal stripes for days when I feel jaunty and daring.

I wore the subdued navy one to Rhonda Brownlee's funeral. I was supposed to ride with Fender, but he called me a couple of hours beforehand to let me know I was going stag. Work stuff. It happens. Heidi offered to be my wingwoman. I told her not to worry. I was more curious than grief-stricken.

And I was on a mission.

It promised to be a big funeral. Rhonda's social network was wide and diverse. My job was to focus on The Housewives, see if any of them behaved strangely or acted out of character.

It was a lousy day to do anything. An atmospheric river loomed over the Pacific, threatening to dump a foot or more of water on central and northern California over the next couple of days. The skies were gray and roiling. Spits of cold rain misted in bands as the outer edges of the storm approached. The wind periodically whipped through the cemetery, swirling dead leaves and bending flowers over the sides of bronze chalices at some gravesites.

I surveyed the crowd and found Julia Wanamaker, Phyllis Bagdasarian, Sonya Soderquist, and Gigi Sahakian huddled together under the largest mortuary tent I'd ever seen. I kept my distance and watched. The three Housewives were dressed as if lunching with Truman Capote at La Côte Basque. Gigi was in a simple dark skirt and navy blouse.

"One of these is not like the others," I said to myself. Then I reminded myself that Gigi had arranged for fake IDs for at least two of the women at the cemetery that day and might have done so for the others as well. I suspected the Housewives liked to keep Gigi Sahakian close at hand. She might have been their only link to the ordinary world.

Sam Brownlee sat in a folding chair on the front row, at the head of the casket. He leaned forward, his hands clasped, staring at the fluorescent green plastic turf under the chairs. People tried to talk to him, but he didn't answer beyond nods or the occasional thanks. He looked broken up inside.

Sonya Soderquist recognized me and pointed me out to the other Housewives.

"Busted," I said. I'd lost my status as observer. Nothing to do but jump right in and be social.

"Mr. Gold," Sonya said as I walked up to the group. "How surprising to see you here."

"Just paying my respects," I said.

"I heard you found her body," Phyllis said.

"That's right," I said. "Felt like I should be here today. Maybe, if I'd gotten to her quicker…"

Julia patted my arm. "Don't blame yourself. You had no idea where she was, after all. Have you selected a seat yet?"

"I don't rate," I said. "Figured I'd stand in the back with the idly curious."

"I won't hear of it," Julia said. "You will accompany us. You'll save me some embarrassment. As usual, Tom is out of pocket and unable to escort me. As soon as I was located and safe, it was back to the salt mines. Besides, we never had a chance to chat in Santa Barbara."

She dragged me to the second row, on the other side of the aisle from Brownlee. Sonya and Phyllis tagged along. Gigi stayed behind. A few seconds later, I saw her talking to a man I didn't recognize, but whose features suggested western Asia. Probably her husband, Ruben.

Phyllis placed her hand on my arm and leaned in close, speaking softly. "Mr. Gold. About our conversation the other day. The awful things I said. I do hope you know I would never have wished any real harm on Rhonda."

"Oh, you don't have to worry about me," I said, patting her hand. "I'm not even on the case anymore. The fellow you really need to worry about is Detective Bludis in Marin County. He has all my notes, and there's probably something in there about our conversation. Don't worry, though. He's a nice man. Very understanding. I'm sure he'll recognize in a flash that you were just mouthing off."

Her eyes looked briefly frantic, but she regained control in an instant. Icy.

I felt a hand on my shoulder. It felt heavy. I turned in my seat. It was the man I'd seen talking to Gigi.

"A second?" he asked.

I excused myself. The man started walking away from the tent. I followed him. When we were far enough away that we couldn't be heard, he turned to me. He was an inch or so shorter than me, hardly enough to mention, but built like a college wrestler, thick and beefy. He had that confident look people get when they think they're such a badass nobody would dare piss in their grits. His calm voice suggested he preferred intimidation to confrontation. I was cool with that.

"You'd be Ruben Sahakian," I said.

"You've been checking up on me, Gold?" he asked.

"Nope. You aren't really on my radar. Well, you weren't. Now…"

"You asked my wife if my father was laundering cash through Armin's business."

"She told you that?"

"We don't keep secrets from one another. Look. I'm as busted up as anybody that Rhonda's dead. Of all these Barbies my wife associates with, she seemed the most human. The most down-to-earth. And Sammy's not a bad sort himself. He's taking this whole thing hard."

"Very empathetic of you," I said.

"But here's the thing. She's dead. You're not looking for her anymore. So, any curiosity you might have had about my father's business seems irrelevant now. Wouldn't you say?"

"You're mostly right," I said. "I'm not looking for her. I found her. Nobody's paying me to look into anything at the moment. Your problem isn't with me. This is a murder investigation now. Your issue is with the police. The way Rhonda took off, she was scared of something. Someone. I know she was intimate with Bagdasarian in some way, and you run Bagdasarian's business. Maybe she heard or saw something. Maybe you found out. Maybe none of this is true, and I was chasing up a blind alley. In my business, you don't learn things unless you ask questions. Sometimes you just lob stuff up against the wall to see if it sticks. If I do it, you can bet Detective Bludis will as well."

"We can handle the police," he said. "We have nothing to hide. It doesn't suit my father's purposes to have some private cop poking around, though. I'm trying to keep this friendly. Just passing the word along. I'm no threat to you in any case. I'm not my father."

"Oh, I bet you're a lot more like him than you prefer to admit," I said.

"Are you deliberately provoking me?"

"Are you deliberately intimidating me? I get your message, Ruben. Loud and clear. Let's leave it at this. You see me walking your way on the street? Cross to the other side. I'll do the same for you."

His eyes surveyed me from head to toe, as if looking for a barcode. "I asked around about you, you know."

"Nine out of ten blondes recommend me."

"People say you're okay. They say you're trustworthy."

"Brave, clean, and reverent, too. Well, not so reverent."

He shook his head. "I might ask my dad to zip you just for being a smartass. Folks say you're fair. You don't jump to conclusions. You can keep a secret."

"I am a Discrete Investigator. Want one of my cards?"

"So, no more questions about my father's business, and we'll take different sides of the street from now on. Have I missed anything?"

"I think we understand one another," I said. "And good luck with the cops."

"Speaking of which," Ruben said, pointing toward the tent. "What in hell is that?"

A line of three police cruisers wove their way through the cemetery toward the tent, their lights flashing but the sirens muted out of respect. Leading them was a black Impala I recognized immediately.

Ruben Sahakian and I trotted back to the tent just as the cortege stopped in the middle of the asphalt driveway. Jack Bludis and Leon Fender hopped out of the black lead car, and the cruiser cops joined them next to the tent. Fender pointed at Brownlee.

"That's him," he said.

Brownlee stared at the ground as Bludis stood next to his chair.

"Samuel Brownlee," Bludis said. "I'm Detective Jack Bludis of the Marin County Sheriff's Department. You are under arrest for the murder of Rhonda Brownlee. You have the right to remain silent…"

Sahakian and I watched in silence as Bludis read the Miranda rights and the uniformed cops cuffed Brownlee, who looked as if he were sleepwalking as they led him back to the cruiser.

I made my way to Bludis and Fender. "This is why you couldn't make it?" I asked Fender.

"We found a critical piece of evidence this morning," Fender said. "Had to follow up on it."

"How'd he do it?" I asked. "Because I'm not feeling the logistics."

"What you feel isn't important," Bludis said. "You were a big help with this case, and I appreciate your contribution, but that's over now. I don't see how we're obligated to share evidence with you."

"Let it go," Fender told me. "What we have is strong. It's solid. I expect you'll be a witness at the trial. You'll see it then."

TWENTY

One year later…

"…And did you believe Mr. Brownlee's grief was genuine?" Wilson Varnadore asked me from the defense table.

Well, did I?

It was an excellent question.

I looked at the man sitting next to Varnadore. I had a hard time seeing the dashing, devil-may-care loanshark who'd hired me. Brownlee's substantial holdings and his shady business dealings, and the fact he owned a King Air and possessed a pilot's license, made him a flight risk, so he'd spent the last year on a no-bond hold in the county lockup.

I recalled the moment Fender and I told Brownlee we'd found Rhonda's body. I tried to read him and came up with nothing but mixed messages. Relief. Shock. Fear. Loss. Anger. I remembered the dejected man leaning forward in his folding funeral home chair staring at the ground, unable to look up at his wife's casket. I didn't remember guilt. What did it look like? Whatever it was, I didn't recognize it in Sam Brownlee's face when he learned he'd been widowed or later at the funeral. I didn't see it in the broken thing sitting next to Varnadore now.

"Yeah," I said, after a pause that felt like hours. "I think it was genuine. It looked real to me."

"Based on?"

"I was a cop. I had to make my share of death notifications. After a while, you see patterns. He acted pretty typical."

"In all of the death notifications you've made in your career, did you ever see someone react genuinely who later turned out to be the killer?"

"Objection!" Alison Eliot cried out from the prosecution table. "Irrelevant."

"The witness has already testified to his experience making death notifications," Varnadore said. "He testified that he was able to recognize patterns as a result. The prosecution did not object to his qualifications. Why would they object to his observations based on those qualifications?"

"Overruled," the judge said.

"I'll repeat the question," Varnadore said. "In all of the death notifications you've made in your career, did you ever see someone react genuinely who later turned out to be the killer?"

"No," I said. "Not when they behaved like Mr. Brownlee."

"No further questions," Varnadore said.

"Redirect?" the judge asked Alison.

"No, Your Honor," Alison said. "The State has no further questions for this witness."

She glared at me as she said it.

I was excused by the judge, and I made my way to the rear of the courtroom. Almost immediately, Leon Fender buttonholed me and directed me into the hallway.

"What in hell was that?" he asked, without even saying hello.

"Congratulations on the promotion," I said. "I heard you finally made the Homicide Squad."

"Fuck that, Gold. That's something else you owe me for. I was totally cool with Missing Persons. Half my cases turned out happy. Now it's bodies for breakfast, lunch, and dinner and more tragedy than you can fit in a moving van. And I got to deal with yokels like you trying to torpedo our case on the stand."

"I didn't torpedo anything," I said. "I answered the questions honestly. You were in the room with me when we informed Brownlee. You saw the same thing I did."

"Maybe I did, and maybe I didn't. That doesn't change the fact that he was *there*, man. He was at the cabin, right in the death window. That's a fact."

I'd heard a lot of facts over the last couple of days. The tox report showed high levels of alcohol and benzodiazepines in her blood. Taken together, the combination could be readily fatal. It would certainly incapacitate you. An empty wine bottle in the trashcan at the cabin showed no evidence of the drug, but there was a trace in the single wine glass next to the sofa where I'd found Rhonda's body. Bludis wasn't fooled. The telephone messages sent to me trumped everything else. His conclusion was simple—somebody drugged Rhonda with wine laced with benzos, waited for her to pass out, caved in her skull with a champagne bottle, and then messaged me to come find her. Only problem was that Rhonda was already dead by then. The killer was just a little too efficient.

Then came the damning evidence the day before. The first thing Detective Bludis did, with Fender's assistance as his San Francisco liaison, was check Sam Brownlee's phone history, including the location logs. The phone revealed multiple unanswered outbound calls to Rhonda's family plan cellphone, but no incoming calls from either that phone or the burner found stashed under Rhonda's body at the cabin. The location logs showed his phone was at Brownlee's home through the entire time Rhonda could have died.

Then Fender discovered that Brownlee drove a Cadillac CT-5. That model had OnStar. After a long discussion with a judge, that could have gone either way, Bludis secured a warrant for Brownlee's OnStar records that led to the discovery that broke the case. While Brownlee's cellphone had remained in his home for the entire day and evening leading up to the discovery of Rhonda's body, his car had not. The GPS tracking showed it traveling across the bridge and directly to the cabin on Mount Tam, arriving roughly five hours before I received the first text from Rhonda's burner phone. The car returned to San Francisco immediately after the messages ended. By the time I showed up to find Rhonda's body, the Caddy was already parked and cooling in Brownlee's garage. Traffic cams on the Golden Gate Bridge confirmed that the Caddy had crossed into Marin County that morning and had returned a half hour after the text messages. The cams couldn't see the driver because of glare off the illegal windshield tint, but it looked terrible for Brownlee regardless.

It was damning evidence. My impressions of Brownlee's mental state were probably nothing in comparison. Unless he had a ringer on the jury, he was probably going down. I said as much to Fender.

"What did you want me to do on the stand?" I said. "Lie? I gotta tell you, Leon, I still don't see all the pieces fitting. How did Brownlee find out Rhonda was at the cabin? All the calls on his phone up to the time of death are accounted for. There were no emails or messages on his computer giving him her whereabouts. Why kill her in the first place? Jealousy? She wasn't seeing anybody, the way he was. She was just trying to get away. What was she afraid of, and how did that get her killed?"

"You're making it too complicated," Fender said. "Reasonable people do reasonable things and irrational people do whatever shit they do. Sometimes the real motive just doesn't make sense."

"Do you see Brownlee as irrational?" I asked.

"Well, he's been tenderizing in the county lockup for a year, so..."

"I mean back then. When we told him his wife was dead. Was he irrational then?"

"I think he knew we were coming and had time to prepare."

"Which suggests rationality and planning. I get the car evidence. It's strong. He can't account for that time except with his cellphone records."

"Which are easily explained."

"Which are easily explained. I agree. Leave the phone at home to establish your location and take the car. Who thinks about OnStar tracking your location? There are a hundred ways to screw up every time you commit a murder, and this looks like his. That's why I'm confused. How he did it is easy. I just can't figure out *why*."

"Good thing it's not your responsibility then," Fender said. "I like you as a person, Gold, but if you burn my case, I will drag you to the depths of hell and leave you there without a roadmap."

I had nothing else to do, and I'd been excused, so I hung out in the courtroom and watched the rest of the day's testimony. Normally, I find criminal court drier than melba toast, and nowhere near as tasty. I had some skin in this case, though, and I wanted to see how it turned out. I also took off my tie and stuffed it in my jacket pocket. I was just one anonymous soul among the masses now.

The rest of the day consisted of evidence by the prosecution explaining the technology used to track Brownlee's car. A GPS engineer from Cal Tech explained the process by which the car was tracked, and how the data was stored and accessed.

Interestingly, Wilson Varnadore didn't try to impeach any of the witnesses or question their findings. It looked as if he was willing to stipulate that Brownlee's car had driven to the cabin and back on the day Rhonda died, but that left the question of whether Brownlee was in it.

In fact, the only question he asked each witness was, "Is your tracking technology able to detect who is driving the car when it's moving?"

Each of them told the court it did not have that capability. As soon as they said that, Varnadore ended the cross-examination. He knew what he was doing, sowing seeds of doubt with the jury.

The judge gaveled the session into recess around four in the afternoon. I watched the deputies apply the cuffs and manacles to Brownlee, who stood silently and motionless as they did. His head hung almost to his chest. He hadn't said a word all day. He looked as defeated as I'd ever seen a man.

I'd already made plans to meet with Heidi for dinner and maybe some canoodling later. I was hustling toward the elevator to the parking garage in a state of anticipatory reverie when someone called me from behind. I turned and found Wilson Varnadore, the Great White Shark, striding in my direction, his hand extended like an inveterate politician.

"Mr. Gold," he said. "A minute of your time?"

"I'm not sure we should be talking," I said. "I'm a witness for the prosecution."

"And a fine job you did for them today," he said, beaming his hundred-thousand-watt smile. "But you've been dismissed, and I for one have no plans to recall you. After today, I have a feeling you're on Alison's shitlist, so I'd say we're free to discuss pretty much anything we want. Quick question. I know you've done work for attorneys in this town."

"A few."

He stopped at one of the empty conference rooms scattered about the criminal courts for exactly this purpose. He opened the door, peeked inside, and said, "Please. Just a minute or two. Might be five." He grinned again. Who could resist?

Reluctantly, I stepped inside the conference room. There was a small desk and a sofa. To his credit, Varnadore went directly to the sofa, instead of trying to establish dominance by taking the desk. A point in his favor. I wasn't letting my shields down yet though. I sat on the sofa as well.

"I am in need of the services of a detective like you," he said.

"You want to hire me," I clarified.

"I do. Do you know Libby Cordelia Hackney?"

"We've never met," I said. "But I know who she is. Every private cop in San Francisco knows. Maybe every one in California."

"I'm representing her."

"Okay." I let it hang there. I wanted more information.

"Her trial is scheduled three months from now. I would prefer to have her exonerated by then."

"You're presuming she's not guilty," I said. "Popular opinion holds otherwise."

"Especially among the private investigator set?"

"There may be some special antipathy among our crowd. Libby Hackney gave us all a black eye."

"Allegedly," Varnadore said.

"Look," I said. "Everyone thinks private eyes are a bunch of cowboys. We have rules, though. Some are hard and fast. One of the biggest is we don't kill our clients. Hard to get paid that way. Libby was hired to gather evidence of business fraud, and then she slept with the guy she was tailing. Then she killed her client in a scheme to keep the guy. I'm sure you've heard the story. It was in all the papers."

"You've already decided she did it, then," Varnadore said.

"If I were still cop, I'd have cuffed her and stuffed her myself and not lost a minute of sleep over it. If you're defending Hackney and want me to work the case, I'd have to claim mixed feelings about it. Yeah. I think she did it."

"The stories in the paper didn't include the most important details, because the police didn't divulge them. I've come across some interesting items in discovery that shed a completely different light on Libby's case. I think she's being framed."

"And I should care—why?"

"Because you know how it feels. You think Sam Brownlee is being framed, don't you?"

"What makes you think that?"

"Your testimony on the stand today, for one thing. You have a reputation for having a soft spot for underdogs. You like to take on cases in which someone is being treated unfairly."

"I have a low tolerance for boredom," I said.

"Libby Hackney is being railroaded," Varnadore said. "Every bit as much as you believe Brownlee is being railroaded."

"Prove it."

"You first. Let me hire you. For one day. One day only. I'll pay double your hourly rate. You look over the stuff I have on the case and talk to Libby. That's all I ask. If you still aren't convinced, walk away."

"One day," I said.

"I'll sweeten it for you. You and I both believe Sam Brownlee is innocent."

"I'm not convinced," I said. "But I have strong doubts."

"He's going to be convicted, Mr. Gold. That's a given, now. I've already told him it's a lost cause, but this is only the first round. I plan to appeal on a number of grounds, most of which will likely be denied, because that's how things work in this business. What I really need is exculpatory evidence, enough to warrant a new trial, which is where *you* come in. I'll try to get Brownlee some soft time in the interim. Whether you take the Hackney case or not, I'd like to hire you to help clear Sam Brownlee as well. I'd prefer to have you on both."

TWENTY-ONE

I took the job, of course. I always knew I would. I just wanted Varnadore to give me a good reason. Brownlee closed the deal.

I picked Heidi up at her gallery and we strolled across Hyde Pier to the twinkling lights of Pier 39. We ate at a French place overlooking boulders in the bay on which sea lions lounged and occasionally honked and roared at passing tourists. There was a particularly large number of them basking alongside the pier. We smelled them before we heard them as we strolled. No biggie. After a decade or two, you get used to it.

"Picked up a new gig at court today," I said.

"Where all the finest criminals hang out," she said.

"Working for Wilson Varnadore," I said.

"Case in point. The Great White Shark? What's the gig?"

"Remember I told you about Libby Cordelia Hackney?"

"Vaguely," she said. "Something about murder."

"She came up kind of like me. A uniformed cop at SFPD, but she never earned her gold shield. She started working for Sheldon Moon," I said. "When Moon died, she quit. Hung out her own shingle. Specializes in divorce cases. She likes to run the honeypot routine."

"The conversation has already meandered into an area with which I am unfamiliar." She sipped from her glass and waited for me to explain.

"It's old spycraft shit, with a twist. In the classic honeypot scheme, a slinky female spy seduces some poor schlub with high security clearance and a lot to lose, then blackmails him into betraying his country. Libby put a different spin on it. The wife hires Libby to find out if the husband is cheating. So, Libby approaches him at a bar, puts the moves on him, and if he takes the bait, she reports to the wife that he's definitely receptive to knocking off a little on the side. Infuriated, the wife doesn't mind shelling out for hours and hours and hours of surveillance as Libby follows hubby around, even if he isn't actually cheating."

"Sounds a little unethical," Heidi said.

"It's in the gray area. People seldom act out of character, especially if they don't think anybody's watching. She only continued surveillance if the husband took her up on her advances, indicating willingness to engage in voluntary adultery. If she'd told every wife the husband was probably cheating, even if he rejected her outright, that would be truly unethical. What she was doing was only shady."

"I remember the story now," she said. "She was hired to investigate some business dispute, and she killed her client."

"Allegedly."

"Varnadore wants you to work the case?"

"Her trial starts in three months. Somehow, Libby has convinced Varnadore that she's innocent. He says he found something on discovery that sealed the deal. He wants me to talk to her and look over what he has in the files."

"Toward what end?"

"Like I said, he thinks she's being framed. Like Ned Racine in *Body Heat*, but in reverse. He thinks Bobby Sladen is lying on an exotic beach somewhere sipping a mai tai, surrounded by alluring and adoring wahinis. He wants me to prove it."

"How do you feel about it?"

"Libby Hackney made life tough for a lot of private cops in this city. She really pissed in the well. She cast a shadow on the entire profession. I'm trying to be objective, but it isn't easy. I'll meet with her at the jail tomorrow, try to get a feel for her. It's a one-day gig. If I feel anything hinky, I'm free to walk away when I go off the clock tomorrow. There's more, though."

"What?"

"Varnadore's representing Sam Brownlee."

"Whom you believe to have been framed."

"*Believe* is a strong word. I have suspicions. Some pieces don't fit. Varnadore's already lost the initial trial. Brownlee's getting convicted. Varnadore wants me to work the appeal, try to find evidence that will trigger a new trial and get Brownlee off the hook."

"You can do the one without doing the other," she said.

"True enough," I said.

"But, being you…"

"Yeah," I said.

TWENTY-TWO

I started at Varnadore's office. He and his partners occupied ten thousand square feet of office space on the tenth floor of a building around the corner from the Bryant Street Hall of Justice. Large brass letters inset into the wall as I exited the elevators proclaimed I had successfully accessed the lair of Varnadore, Skakel, and Abernethy, Attorneys at Law. The entire space was like a carnival sideshow mirror house of glass-enclosed offices with breathtaking views of the bay. I had a decent view from my desk as well, but this one kicked mine to the curb.

"Mr. Gold," the receptionist said, before I even introduced myself. "Mr. Varnadore told me to expect you this morning."

"He does not lack for confidence," I said.

"You got that right," she said. "He's arranged for you to use a spare office while you review the Hackney documents. Please follow me."

She led me down a crystal canyon of offices toward a separate hallway and opened an office door for me. I was a little disappointed. No floor-to-ceiling window with a view of the bay. Just a drab little conference room. A three-inch thick legal folder lay on the table.

"Can I get you anything?" she asked. "Coffee? Tea? Soft drink?"

"A fistful of amphetamines," I said. "Legal files put me into a coma. Tell you what. It was such a lovely day, I walked here. A Diet Coke would be nice."

"I'll alert Mr. Varnadore you've arrived," she said. "And I'll be right back with your Diet Coke."

"Couldn't resist, then?" Varnadore asked when he walked into the room. He was in his own environs, seemingly a place where he could kick back a little, but he still dressed like he was arguing a landmark case before the Supreme Court.

"I'm approaching this with a bushel basket of healthy skepticism," I said. "Want to walk me through the high points?"

"Sure," he said. "I need to be somewhere else in about a half hour, but I have time to review the case. The murder victim, Arlen Drake, was a self-made millionaire who built his fortune on small businesses. Like, really small. Automatic car washes. Vending machines. Food trucks. If it could be capitalized for under a hundred thousand dollars, he was in. Most of his empire was built north of the city in backwaters like Corte Madera and Larkspur and San Rafael."

"But he lived in the city," I said.

"He did, and he was murdered here, which is why it was investigated by the SFPD. About thirty years ago, Drake won a podunk Petaluma radio station in an all-night poker marathon. He had no idea what to do with it, so he found someone who did. He hired a station manager named Simms, whose previous call letters had been sold out from under him, and he turned the whole operation over to him."

"What kind of radio station?"

"The kind you never heard of. Not much to talk about. It's a five-thousand-watt daytime flashlight. The signal becomes scratchy and undependable by the time it nears Santa Rosa, only a few dozen miles away. It's a real small-time operation. This guy, Simms, convinced Drake that automation was the best way to go. They subscribe to syndicated music shows from around the country, so they can get by with a single ad salesman. The station is only on the air from sunrise to sunset. Simms laid off all the staff except the licensed engineer who kept the place running, the ad salesman who made it pay, and the on-air board tech who punched buttons and twisted dials in a small dark room and read *Hustler* all day long. The latter, as it turned out, was Simms' eighteen-year-old son, unfortunately named Tim."

"Tim Simms. Bet he got beat up on the school playground a lot."

"He's the station manager now. His dad died eight years after Drake won the station. By then, Tim already knew everything there was to know about the place. The station has permanent residence at the bottom of the Arbitron ratings every quarter, but it still makes money because the overhead is peanuts."

"It's always about the P and L statements, isn't it? So how does all this figure in with Drake's murder?"

"About a year and a half ago, Drake sold half the station to a man named Bobby Sladen. Actually, it was fifty-one percent."

"Okay."

"Tim Simms introduced Sladen to Arlen Drake."

"Aha," I said.

"What?"

"Just seemed like the right thing to say. Go on."

"Simms managed the syndication subscriptions. He paid the electricity bills and the maintenance bills. He paid the rent for the offices the station leased. He cut the paychecks Drake signed. He read the trade magazines and followed the station sales all over the country. Thirty years at fifteen-thirty on the AM dial had made Tim an unchallenged expert on the low-budget broadcast business. It was all he had ever done. He knew, within a few thousand dollars, what an appraiser would say the station was worth. It wasn't much. When he heard Bobby Sladen's offer, he nearly fell off his barstool. When Sladen offered him a ten percent finder's fee for brokering the deal with Drake, he thought his ship had come in."

"I can imagine. How much was the offer?"

"One-point-five million. Half up front for controlling ownership, and the rest due six months later."

"So Simms was looking at a payday north of a hundred fifty grand."

"He never saw a penny of it. Six months passed. Then seven. Eight. A year. Each month, when Drake approached Sladen about completing the sale, there was a new excuse."

"Did any of them check out?"

"Nobody looked into it, at first. After a year, Drake decided it was time to get lawyers involved. One of the senior partners in his hired firm advised him that while the contract was valid, Drake's continuing leeway given to Sladen weakened his case. He suggested hiring a private detective to gather clear evidence that Sladen was engaged in fraud."

"And it was his great misfortune to hire Libby Cordelia Hackney."

"Maybe yes. Maybe no. I want you to interview Libby and get her side of the story. I can tell you, she isn't proud of it. Some of it makes her sound guilty as hell."

"Maybe because she is?"

"I'd ask you to set aside your professional prejudices regarding her tactics and techniques, at least for the duration of this assignment. However, even as her attorney, I'd agree that she made some terrible decisions. She told Drake she was keeping an eye on Sladen, trying to find out why he was shining Drake on. She kept Drake abreast of her observations, and she kept a relatively tidy case file, up to about a month before Drake was murdered."

"I know some of this from the newspaper reports," I said. "Even as she was working for Drake, she started banging Bobby Sladen."

He opened the file to the section on Sladen, which included a picture of him.

"I already said she isn't proud of what she did. She followed Bobby Sladen for two nights and finally cozied up to him at a bar inside a North Beach restaurant. This is Sladen."

He was tall, lean, and athletic, with sandy blond hair, piercing blue eyes, and a million-dollar grin. He sported a fashionable and masculine three-day growth of beard. "Yeah. I saw this picture in the paper. I showed it to Heidi when Libby was first charged, and she pronounced him *yummy*."

"Five days after the last note in Libby's file, Drake's housekeeper arrived for her weekly cleaning at his San Francisco house and discovered Arlen Drake bent over the back of a chair in his living room, his hands bound behind him with duct tape, and a bullet hole in the back of his head. Nine-millimeter. Ballistics matched the bullet to a pistol registered to Drake, found on the floor in the living room. It had apparently come from an open drawer in Drake's bedside table. Forensics turned up no prints on the gun, but Drake's prints were on the bullets in the magazine and the chamber. Few random unaccounted-for prints were discovered inside or outside the house. The locks hadn't been jimmied, and no windows were broken or unlocked. The front door was locked when the housekeeper arrived. No money or other valuables had been stolen. Other than the bullet wound in the head, there were no signs of a struggle. It was a true locked-room murder with no obvious motive."

"Who was the lead investigator on the case at SFPD?" I asked, flipping through the file.

"A detective named Spears."

I looked up. "Dexter Spears?"

"I believe that's correct."

"Well, fuck a duck."

"What's the matter?"

"Spears and I have a history."

My first partner when I earned my gold shield was a veteran named Frank Raymond. I broke for the private sector. Frank broke bad. He sold his soul to the wrong people, and he died for it. Before he did, though, he was paired with rookie inspector Dexter Spears, a nepo baby political appointee whose early career was tarnished when Frank's crooked dealings were exposed. Spears always blamed me for some reason.

But I wasn't about to tell The Great White Shark about that. I hadn't even told Heidi about it.

I said, "Dexter Spears has some redeeming qualities. His mother likes him, and he's reputedly fond of small animals. I've heard he's a fantastic dancer. Unfortunately, as detectives go, he's sort of useless. The moke who graduates last in their class at med school is still called *Doctor.* Dexter's that kind of cop."

"You don't like him,"

"To be fair, he isn't fond of me either. You know the inspector who testified in Brownlee's trial?"

"Leon Fender?"

"Yeah. He was in Missing Persons when we first met. Collaring Brownlee put him on the fast track to Major Crimes, in the Homicide Division. He drew Dexter Spears as his partner. That means he's also investigating Drake's murder. So how do I get in touch with this Bobby Sladen guy?"

"You don't, at least right now. That's the problem. Five months after the murder, Bobby Sladen disappeared. A neighbor noted that the grass in his front yard was high, and notified the HOA, who first taped a notice on Bobby's door. A week later, they sent a representative to knock on the door. The mailbox out front overflowed with mail. Finally, one of the neighbors called the police to request a wellness check, in case something had happened to Bobby. The police discovered the house empty. Bobby hadn't been home for some time. Nobody had. The cops estimated he had been gone at least four weeks."

"That's not encouraging."

"The Missing Persons detective assigned to the case recognized Bobby Sladen's name from newspaper accounts of the investigation. Because Bobby owed Drake half the price for the radio station, he had been a prime suspect, but he had an ironclad alibi, having been verifiably in Vegas with some poker buddies when the murder happened. Even so, Missing Persons contacted Detective Spears, who suggested that they have forensics screen the house again. Want to guess whose prints they found?"

"Libby Hackney's?"

"Cops and private eyes have to register their fingerprints. It took the AFIS system about fifteen seconds to match the prints found in Bobby Sladen's house with Libby's records. Look, I gotta boogie. I just dropped by to thank you for keeping an open mind. Take your time with the file. Try to put aside your preconceived notions about the case. Ms. Pringle at the front desk can arrange for you to visit Libby at the jail, though I suspect you're familiar with all the processes there already."

"I've dropped by once or twice," I said.

"I'm sure you have. There's a legal pad and some pens in the desk if you want to make any notes."

"Copier?" I asked.

He shook his head. "Not with this file. There are portions in there that I do not need Alison Eliot to find out about. One of the beauties of discovery. She has to give me everything she has. I can hold a few cards up my sleeve. If you find anything you need clarified, just put a sticky note on the page and make a note of it. I'll be happy to answer any questions you have when you're finished."

"Anything else?"

"The file is a summary. There are boxes of materials in our document storage room. Typical District Attorney's office bullshit. Swamp us with tons of garbage so we waste time sifting through it for the sweet stuff. They think I won't call for a continuance to analyze the data or the judges will get tired of giving extensions. They don't know me very well. They don't know I've gotten every judge in this town laid, some twice, and we're talking the high-priced spread. The judges give me substantial leeway. In any case, think of the file as a synopsis, or Cliff's Notes on the case. Anything you want to know more about, we have it stored. I have a half dozen first year associates poring over the discovery dump as we speak, so more information is in the pipeline."

Ms. Pringle returned with my Diet Coke and slid a paper plate with a couple of doughnuts on it on the desk as well. *Easy to look at* had probably been one of the boxes on her employment interview. Maintaining appearances in a high-caliber law firm appeared to be a priority. I quickly discovered she was sharp as a tack as well. She was tall and lithe and redheaded, and I am not ashamed to admit I took more than a look or two when she was in the room. I may be in a long term committed something-ship, but I am not dead.

"An appreciative client brought in ten dozen," she said. "There're more if you want them. In the staff lounge."

"I'm not staff."

"Today, you're on the payroll. You're staff." She winked at me and closed the door.

This stuff happens to me a lot. Go figure.

Hackney was in an interview room uptown two hours after her prints were identified. Suddenly, Dexter Spears became interested in her, since it was related to Drake's murder. He and Fender both conducted the interview with Hackney. The transcript was included in the file.

HACKNEY: Sure. I've been there. Are you telling me Bobby's missing?

INS. SPEARS: How did you come to be at the Sladen house?

HACKNEY: Hold on. Hold on. Wait a minute. Has something happened to Bobby?

INS. SPEARS: How do you know Mr. Sladen?

HACKNEY: I'm not saying shit until you tell me what's going on. I was a cop, you know. I know how this shit works. Has something happened to Bobby?

INS. FENDER: His house is unoccupied. It appears he hasn't been there in weeks. Nobody has seen him. You keep calling Mr. Sladen Bobby. You're familiar?

HACKNEY: Yeah. I know him. It's a long story, and I don't look so good in it, if you know what I mean, so if Bobby's missing, maybe I need to have a lawyer up in here.

INS. FENDER: Are you asking for an attorney? You were a cop. You probably still dream Miranda, so you know your rights backward. You want an attorney, Ms. Hackney? You aren't under arrest, after all.

HACKNEY: (after eight seconds of silence) No. Not yet. So he's really missing, huh? I just thought he'd ghosted me.

INS. SPEARS: Ghosted?

HACKNEY: You know. Like ignoring my texts and emails. I can show you on my phone.

(Forty-seven second silence while HACKNEY showed INS. SPEARS and INS. FENDER her telephone)

INS. SPEARS: So your last contact with Bobby Sladen was five weeks ago. That was the last time he texted you. Is that correct?"

HACKNEY: Yes. He last texted me on the thirteenth of last month.

INS. SPEARS: Can you tell me how your fingerprints were left in the Sladen house?

(Eleven seconds of silence)

HACKNEY: I'm not proud of this. Let me say that right up front. I been to church. I confessed about this shit. Okay. I've been sleeping with Bobby Sladen. Check his sheets. I bet my DNA is all over them.

INS. FENDER: When did your affair with Mr. Sladen begin?

HACKNEY: Maybe five months ago. Arlen Drake hired me to follow him before he died. You know how I work.

INS. SPEARS: How's that?

HACKNEY: You know. I put the moves on a husband to see if he's willing to cheat.

INS. SPEARS: Sounds tawdry.

HACKNEY: Well, girl's gotta make a living, you know? And I don't actually fuck 'em. At least, not usually. It's not like I'm some hooker. And this was kind of an unusual case, since it wasn't about cheating. Mr. Drake wanted to know if Bobby was planning to defraud him out of half the cost of his radio station. But I got my methods, and they work for me, so you dance with the one what brung you, I suppose. I tracked him for a couple of days and finally caught him in a bar. I sidled up to him, and he bought me a drink. We took it from there.

INS. SPEARS: You slept with him then?

HACKNEY: Hell, no, man. Weren't you listening? I admit I thought about it, though. Have you seen a picture of the guy? They had to mop down my bar stool after I left. I got him talking about his work, and Bobby bragged about cutting this deal to buy a radio station. Said he was only a few days away from putting the money together to close. At one point he said he was embarrassed that he'd let it go so long. Said he planned to call the owner the next day and clear things up. He seemed on the up and up. So, I finished the job for Mr. Drake, collected my paycheck, and forgot about the case until I saw on the news he'd been murdered.

INS. SPEARS: How did you…um…reconnect with Bobby Sladen?

HACKNEY: After the funeral.

INS. FENDER: Arlen Drake's funeral?

HACKNEY: He was a client, and a recent one at that. I just thought it would be a nice gesture to show up.

INS. FENDER: Were you worried that Bobby Sladen might recognize you?

HACKNEY: I wear a disguise when I'm working. Different hair, different makeup, and I don't wear my eyeglasses on the job. Contacts. Hell. It worked for Clark Kent, right?

INS. SPEARS: You met Sladen at the funeral?

HACKNEY: At the reception afterward. I just wanted to offer my condolences. I shook his hand, but he didn't let go while we talked. Tell you the truth, it was a little awkward. He said he had some people he needed to visit, but he wanted to talk some more with me later, and he asked me to hang out.

INS. FENDER: What did you do?

HACKNEY: I hung out. Fuck, man, did you not hear me describe him? This guy wetted me up just putting the moves on me in a bar. Fuck yeah, I hung out. I'm not proud of it now, especially after he ghosted me, Mr. Wham-Bam-Thank-You-Ma'am. Fuck that loser. I hope he's coyote shit at the bottom of a canyon now. Wait. That didn't come out the way I intended. Let's just say I'm kind of pissed at him for ignoring me, but if something's really happened to him…you know.

INS. SPEARS: You said you'd been sleeping with Bobby Sladen. When did that begin?

HACKNEY: Exact date? Let me check my phone. He texted me a sweet note the next morning. Hold on. Yeah. The fifteenth. See the text on the sixteenth?

INS. FENDER: The night of Arlen Drake's funeral?

HACKNEY: It's tacky, right? I thought so at the time. *"This is really tacky,"* I told myself, right before I balled his brains out. I know that sounds awful, but you want the truth, right? I don't regret it. He did not disappoint.

INS. FENDER: How often did you meet?

HACKNEY: Couple of times a week. We had to be careful, you know. I mean, the police were investigating Drake's murder, and they suspected Bobby at the time, and I'd worked for Drake, so we had to keep it on the down low. It looked hinky. We discussed taking a trip together to get away from all the prying eyes as soon as the case was over, and then he dropped off the radar.

INS. FENDER: Ms. Hackney, I'm going to give you an opportunity to reconsider your testimony today. We found a burner phone in Mr. Sladen's bedroom side table. There are messages on there, from you, predating the murder of Arlen Drake. Let's start over. When did you first sleep with Bobby Sladen?

(Sixteen seconds of silence)

HACKNEY: You know what? I think I'd like that lawyer now.

TWENTY-THREE

Libby Cordelia Hackney tried to x-ray me with her eyes.

I met her in an interview room at the jail. The interview rooms were just cells that had the bunks removed and a stainless-steel table screwed to the floor, with a couple of swing-out chairs attached to the table. There was nothing to throw or rip out of the wall or use as a weapon. It was uncomfortable as hell, but it was the only place available to interview her.

Hackney was about five-six. She walked with an athletic spring. Her eyes were constantly in motion, assessing her environment. Her hair was thick and bushy and curly, and fell over her shoulders. Being incarcerated, she didn't wear makeup, but her cheeks were rosy enough without rouge. Jail seemed to agree with her. Some people hear the steel door clang shut and go to a dark place so deep inside themselves they didn't even know it was there, and they never come out. Some try to be the swinging dick on the block. Others try to make themselves invisible and hide for the duration.

Libby Hackney looked like she was on vacation at Club Med. She was initially suspicious when the deputy walked her into the room. She must have recognized my face, because she sneered when she saw me.

"Speed date?" she asked.

I handed her my card.

"I know who you are." She dropped the card on the table. "Sorry I don't look my best. I was gonna get a mani-pedi and a hot oil treatment, but the line at the beauty parlor upstairs was fuckin' ungodly."

"I've been hired by Wilson Varnadore," I said.

She faked a shudder. "I know he's the best, but have you ever looked in his fuckin' eyes, Gold? Like the last thing Quint ever saw. Gives me the fuckin' shivers. I shouldn't say anything. I'm lucky to have him. Coulda wound up with some kid straight out of law school floggin' a hundred cases a day as a public defender."

"How did you wind up with Varnadore?"

"Luck of the draw, man. He was in arraignment court when they read the charges. The judge is a hardass who probably wrote the Gideon decision a million years ago. He didn't think the rookies in the PD office were able to give me the attention I deserved. He picked Varnadore out of the crowd of attorneys in the back and assigned him the case. Shark's getting paid the state per diem by the Administrative Office of the Courts. I got a huge discount on the high-priced spread."

"You're indigent?"

"Bobby Sladen's face and donkey cock weren't his only attractions," she said. "He had some serious money. I was one parking ticket away from giving handies in truck stops at ten bucks a pop. Now they say I might have gotten rid of him? Why? I sure as shit would have married him first at least, for the money. You're a hot shit private dick. You tell me how this story makes sense."

"It makes sense if he set you up to take the fall for Arlen Drake's murder," I said.

"Now you're talkin'. Geez, I'd fuck a cactus for a cigarette."

"Can't help you," I said.

"Fuckin' boy scout. Okay, so what do you want to know?"

"Why you lied to Inspectors Fender and Spears, for starters," I said.

"I'm no bimbo, Gold. My brain works as good as anybody else's. Soon as I heard Bobby was missing, I knew why I hadn't heard from him in weeks. I thought he'd ghosted me, had enough fun. Figured he had run into someone he liked better. No skin off my nose. Plenty of fish in the sea. Then I got hauled into Third Degree Central, and I knew shit had gone off the rails. Right away, I knew he had set me up. Telling the cops I was sleeping with him before Drake was murdered only made me look more guilty and involved."

"I work for your attorney," I said. "You tell me something, it's like telling him. Same privilege. So tell me the story the way it really happened."

"I don't want you to get the wrong idea," she said.

"My opinion of you is unimportant. I'm not introducing you to my parents. I'm trying to keep you out of Chowchilla. What happened?"

"Yeah. Okay. I started sleeping with him about a week after Drake hired me. It was a shitty thing to do. My head was in a weird place though, because I had recently broken up with a guy I'd been dating for almost a year, and Bobby was just so fuckin' gorgeous. I mean, that's not typical in my business. Half the guys I'm hired to tail look like Ernest Borgnine. So I hit Bobby up in a bar a second time. He remembered me. We got a room. Bada bing, bada boom. It was fun, and he certainly tickled all my lady parts the right way. I was deeply in lust with that hunk."

I waited for her to tell me more. She seemed like the type who felt obligated to fill the silent spaces.

"First morning I woke up with him, I realized I was playing with fire. It was stupid, but it was done. Story of my life. Damage control is my brand. I told him we needed to get burners. I had no desire to get my ticket lifted just for getting laid, so we couldn't leave a traceable paper trail."

"Where are the burners?"

"They found his in his bedside table. Mine's at the bottom of the bay halfway to Alcatraz. We didn't use them after Drake died. No real reason to."

"You really hooked up with him at the funeral?"

"Fuck, man. We slept together the night *before* the funeral. He got a suite at the Ritz. I helped him mess it up. Don't look at me like that. I already told you it's fucked up. I do not look good in this story at all. The son of a bitch set me up but good."

"He was playing poker in Vegas when Drake was murdered. His three partners confirmed his alibi, as did the casino video. Where were you?"

"In bed. All day. Fuckin' excruciating menstrual cramps. I took a handful of Midol and a couple of Xanax and zoned out on Judge Judy all afternoon. Didn't even hear about the murder until the next day."

"How?"

"Bobby called me, on the burner. If you have his phone, it'll be recorded there. Said he'd been trying to reach me all night long. He could have been at my bedside with a bullhorn, and I wouldn't have heard him. Once I passed out, I was dead to the world until the next morning."

"How did he sound when he finally reached you?"

"Tired," she said. "Not frantic. Not worried. Dulled out. Numb. I didn't think much about it at the time. You've done death notifications before. You know how people sometimes shut down after that initial shock. He told me Drake was shot with his own pistol. Son of a bitch had the balls to ask me where I was the day before."

"Did you know he had a pistol?"

"Drake? I'd never seen it, but Bobby told me about it. Told me where he kept it. Did it in a text. I thought it was strange, but then I forgot about it. Soon as Inspector Fender told me they'd found his burner, I knew Bobby had zoomed me. After the funeral, we both agreed to destroy the phones. I knew I didn't kill Drake, and he had a Texas Hold 'Em alibi, so we agreed that neither of us needed evidence of our affair lying around. We were in the clear, right? I tossed my phone into the bay off the Red Line ferry. He kept his to set me up. When the police found it, there was the message telling me exactly where to find the gun in his house."

"So, here's the thing," I said. "You're right about Bobby's alibi. It's ironclad. Let's assume you didn't kill Drake—"

"I didn't," she said.

"Then who did? The motive was personal. Someone held a grudge against him. They went in with an agenda. They taped his hands behind him, bent him over a chair, and splattered the carpet with his brain. This doesn't look like a crime of passion or opportunity. This was an execution. Think it through. How would you pull it off?"

"Two people," she said. "It's risky to try to duct tape his hands behind him otherwise. You'd have to holster the pistol or put it down. It gives Drake a chance to escape or grab the pistol."

"No sign of a struggle, so he complied," I said. "Maybe he thought it was a robbery. Probably figured they'd take what they wanted and leave."

"Until they bent him over the chair," she said.

"One person could do it," I said. "It wouldn't be easy, but once he allowed his hands to be taped, anyone could have killed him."

"Fucker Bobby set me up to take the heat. He planned to kill Drake all along. I happened along as a convenient patsy. He played me, setting me up with the telephone messages. He hired someone to visit Drake while he was grazing at the Bellagio buffet and I was flyin' high on benzos. These confederates found the pistol, right where Bobby told them it would be, bound Drake's hands, acted as if they planned to rob the place, and parked one in the back of Drake's head. Wiped down the gun, dropped it on the carpet, and waltzed out the door. Bobby boinked me for a few more weeks to establish our relationship and make me look guilty as shit, and then disappeared with his accomplice, leaving me holding the bag."

"I can see it," I said. "Let's say that's how it happened."

"Fucker probably even has video of us together," she said. "Just in case."

"That does raise an interesting question," I said.

"Video of me and Bobby?"

"No. The accomplice. I see three possibilities. First, Bobby and the shooter ran off together. Second, Bobby—being a psychopath—killed the shooter and ran off on his own. Third…"

"The shooter's still around," she said. "Hiding in plain sight."

TWENTY-FOUR

While I was at the jail, I decided to kill two birds with one stone. When the deputies escorted Libby back to her cell, I asked to speak with Sam Brownlee. He and Libby shared an attorney, and I worked for that attorney, so nobody gave me any shit.

I tried to see the devil-may-care loanshark in the hairy lump the deputies deposited in front of me. Couldn't find him anywhere. Gone was the hundred-thousand-watt smile. His hair hadn't been cut in jail, and hung limp, three inches of silver at the roots. His skin was dry and pale, and his eyes were dull. He stared at me and sighed.

"Gold," he said.

"How're they treating you?" I asked.

"What do you want?"

"I'm working with Varnadore. Another case, but the carrot is that I get to work your appeal."

"Why?" he asked.

"Word on the street is you're taking the fall for Rhonda. The conviction's in the bag. Alison Eliot's already shopping for a celebration outfit and a bottle of Veuve Clicquot. Some people think you might not have done it."

"I didn't," he said.

"I'm on your side, Sam. But a lot of this story doesn't make sense. The biggest problem is your car."

"Which one?" he asked. "I own four cars."

"You know which one. The Caddy. The one that somehow found its way to Mount Tam without you. I've read Fender's report on the case in Varnadore's files. I want to hear your end of it from your own mouth."

"Why?"

"I like Fender, but I don't know him well enough to trust him. He's partnered with an inspector I wouldn't assign to find a lost contact lens. Sometimes people acquire bad habits in the wrong company. I want to know if there are any substantial discrepancies between what he wrote and your story."

"Okay," he said. He sat silently for almost a minute, composing his thoughts. "I was up really late the night before. Heartburn. Drank too much wine at dinner. Fact is, I'd been drinking too much all week since Rhonda disappeared. Emptied the bottle and tried to go to bed just before midnight. My stomach attacked me around one, and I wasn't getting to sleep anyway, wondering where Rhonda might be. Moved to the home theater, curled up on a loveseat, and watched TV until almost sunrise."

"You were alone?"

His face screwed into a scowl. "Yes, Gold. I was alone, at least after midnight. I'm no poster child for monogamy, but I wasn't fucking anyone when I hired you, and I haven't since. I sure wasn't going to have anyone around for a sleepover with my wife missing. How in fuck would that look?"

"Who were you with the night before?"

"My personal assistant, Laura Hope. She dropped by mid-evening with some papers that needed to be signed. I hadn't been to the office since Rhonda disappeared, and Laura was tending to the big stuff. Some things needed my signature, though. She hung around for a glass of wine and then went home around nine-thirty that night."

"The medical examiner said Rhonda died around ten in the morning."

"By then, I was dead to the world. Around sunrise, I gave up and took one of Rhonda's Ambien tablets. That finally knocked me out, for about nine hours. I woke around three in the afternoon, not long before you and Inspector Fender arrived."

"And your Caddy was in the garage when you woke up?" I asked.

"Hell. I don't know. You've been to my place. The garage is down the hill from the house. Anyone could go in or out without me knowing. I didn't go anywhere between the time I woke and the time you and Fender showed up to tell me Rhonda was dead. I never checked the garage."

"According to your OnStar data, the Caddy left your garage around eight in the morning, more or less the same time it left each morning you took it to work. It drove directly to the cabin on Mount Tam, arriving shortly before nine, and remained there for a little over four hours, leaving five minutes after my text session with Rhonda, or whoever sent them. We know now that Rhonda was long dead by then. Three hours dead, according to the autopsy."

"I was out cold the entire time," he said. "Anybody could have taken my car and returned it before I even woke up."

"Anybody?" I asked. "What kind of lock is on your garage?"

"Push button code pad," he said. "But the electronic garage door openers in the cars override it. If you have either the opener remote control or the code, you can get in."

"But you'd need the keys to start the car."

"Yes."

"Where were your keys when you were asleep?"

"On my dresser, with my wallet. I put them there when I dressed for bed."

"Your doors were locked, and the security system was armed?"

"The doors were locked. I forgot to arm the security system."

"Who else knows the combination for your garage?" I asked.

"Rhonda did, obviously. My assistant, Laura. That's it."

"Do you keep a spare garage remote in the house?"

"Sure," he said. "We hung it on a hook in the mud room, along with spare key fobs. Saved time opening the garage in the rain."

"I wonder whether they're there now."

"You're welcome to look. Varnadore can get you inside the house. He has my keys. You'd better check soon, though. The trial costs have eaten away at my savings. I'll have to put the house up for sale to pay for the appeal."

"Where was Laura Hope on the day Rhonda died?" I asked.

"I have no idea."

"Don't take this the wrong way, but were you sleeping with her?"

"Not anymore. We had a fling a couple of years ago. Before I hired her. My previous assistant was offered a job with one of the television studios in Los Angeles as a staff writer. I had an opening. Even though Laura and I had stopped seeing each other, I thought she would be a good fit for the position. I tend to be attracted to bright, talented people."

"You were able to put the sex stuff behind you?"

"Mostly," he said. "There were some moments of tension."

For a brief instant, I caught a glimpse of his trademark smirk.

"So how long before Rhonda died did you sleep with Laura?"

"It wasn't like that. I mean, yeah, we hooked up a couple of times after I hired her, but the affair part of it was over. Every once in a long while, we'd both get horny at the same time, and it was on like Donkey Kong. Just an office quickie. Then it was over, and we got back to business. Really. Ninety-nine percent of our time together was work-related."

"So answer the question."

"I don't remember the dates. Maybe a month before. Six weeks, tops. Perhaps six months before that. I think it was just twice after she came to work for me."

"And Laura Hope had your garage code?"

"She had everything. My garage code, my security system code, my Netflix password. I trusted her. Still do, if you're suggesting she had anything to do with the killing."

"I'm not accusing her," I said.

"Good."

"Yet," I added. "I need to talk to her. Does she still work for you?"

"Not exactly. Soon as I was arrested and denied bond, I had Varnadore set up a severance package for her. Sweet one. It's disbursed monthly. She's set for at least another year. I hoped this would all be behind me by now, and we could get back to work. No such luck. It wasn't her fault she was out of a job."

"Unless it was," I said.

TWENTY-FIVE

"That shit about sleeping straight through the murder?" Leon Fender said. "Sure, Brownlee tried to sell it to me."

I'd called Fender and invited him to lunch. He was naturally suspicious, so I put his mind at ease and confirmed his worst fears about my invitation by telling him I wanted to pump him about the Brownlee case. I offered to make the medicine go down easier with some Hayz hot dogs.

"If he was under the influence of alcohol and Ambien, he might sleep through a six-point-five quake, let alone someone opening his garage and driving off in the Caddy," I said.

"He can't prove any of that happened. His only alibi for the time his car was missing and his wife was murdered was he was *asleep?*"

"I've already identified one other person who had access to his garage and car during that time."

"Laura Hope. The assistant. Don't look at me like that. You think we're numbskulls, Gold? We know how to ask questions too. Laura Hope is alibied. You'll find it in the discovery files."

"Don't forget that Rhonda knew the garage code and had a key fob for the Cadillac," I said.

"Right. She hitched a ride across the bridge, took the Caddy out of her own garage, drove it back across the bridge to Mount Tam, killed herself, texted you a couple of hours later, then drove the car back to San Francisco, parked it in her garage, and hitched back to her own murder site. I want to see Varnadore try to sell that to a jury."

"You don't have to be snarky about it," I said.

"I don't know why the fuck I'm even discussing this case with you."

"Maybe you have the same doubts I do, but you can't state them openly because you're in the belly of the beast."

"The beast?"

"The big blue blob. You're part of the cophouse machinery at Eight-Fifty Bryant Street. You made your bones busting Sam Brownlee. You can't raise your hand at the back of the room now and say you think you made a mistake."

He had just taken a bite of his dog. He looked at it as if he regretted even rolling out of bed that morning, and he put it back on his plate.

"Some of the story doesn't fit," he said quietly. "That's between you and me and this fuckin' Chicago dog. That doesn't mean it isn't true. Sometimes you draw a weak case. The pieces fit badly, but somebody has to ride the bolt, so you go with the best possible case you can build. That's why we have juries, Gold. If I fucked up, they can correct it."

"That's what you're counting on with Brownlee? That the jury will see something you couldn't tell them directly?"

"Like you did on the stand the other day? You practically told them you thought Brownlee didn't do it."

"And you only thought it," I said. "Which one of us stacked the most burn time on that one?"

"Check the discovery files," he said. "We interviewed Laura Hope the day after I discovered the Caddy had been driven to Marin County. See if you can find a hole in her story. I'll admit it. I got a woody myself when I first heard she knew the code to the garage. She's covered, though. You'll see."

"What's not in the murder book?" I asked.

"What do you mean?"

"I had a gold shield once. I know some stuff doesn't make it into the book. Discovery only gives me what you wrote down. It doesn't tell me what you're carrying around inside your head."

He looked down at the half of a Chicago dog still on his plate. "Shit. I was looking forward to this, too. Seems I've lost my appetite."

He put on his jacket and turned to leave, but stopped before he reached the door. He stared out at the street for a few seconds and then returned to the table. He leaned in close, because the place was crowded, and he didn't want to make a scene.

"Fuck you, Gold. Fuck you twice. Sideways. Are you insinuating I'm a dirty cop, or lazy like Spears? Are you suggesting I cut corners? I record every goddamn thought I have on a case. Read the fuckin' murder book. Every word. Show me where I held anything back."

"I can't," I said. "It isn't there. Sit down. Please. I think, whether you want to admit it or not, we're on the same side here."

He glared at me, grabbed the rest of his dog, and stamped out the door.

We sat in Varnadore's fishbowl office. It was post time somewhere, so he'd broken out the Macallan and the crystal glasses. I took it neat, because I'm not one of those rocks barbarians. We sat in his leather and chrome mid-century modern furniture and gazed out over the bay as we discussed the day's discoveries.

"I'll track down Laura Hope tomorrow," I said. "And I want to talk to Julia Wanamaker as well. Rhonda didn't send those texts, but whoever did knew the cabin belonged to the Wanamakers. Unless Julia showed Rhonda where she hid the keys, she might have known Rhonda was holing up at the cabin."

"Interesting. As I recall, she had an alibi," Varnadore said.

"Maybe she told someone else Rhonda was there, and they don't have an alibi. Whoever messaged me from Rhonda's phone knew I was looking for her. That narrows the list of suspects."

"All excellent work," he said. "I would like to remind you, however, that we are focused on the appeal in Brownlee's case. We still need to keep Libby from being convicted in the first place. I don't want to tell you your business, but I hired you to work on the Hackney trial. The Brownlee case was just an incentive."

"I hear you," I said. "Finding Bobby Sladen is the priority there. Without him, she's toast."

TWENTY-SIX

Varnadore was right. Libby Hackney was my priority, which meant finding Bobby Sladen—or whatever had happened to him.

I returned to my office, cranked up CyberShamus on my computer, and did a deep dive on Robert Earl Sladen, thirty-nine, recently dropped out of sight.

It occurred to me that, simply by being in the wind, Bobby cast a little shade on the state's case against Libby. At the very least, it constituted reasonable doubt unless someone came up with any concrete evidence that Libby had dispatched him to improve her chances with the jury. I hadn't seen any so far. What I saw looked like a classic frame-up.

Bobby was a widower who had married well. This much I knew already. Katrina Sladen came from money—the old, musty kind that probably originated in one sin or another but had been sanitized by the passage of time and the limitations of human memory.

On the surface, one might have thought Bobby targeted Katrina for her wealth, until reminded that they had first hooked up in high school, when such considerations aren't terribly important. Maybe Bobby was initially attracted to her for other reasons, but with maturity recognized the potential for an easy life and exploited the already-burgeoning relationship.

When Katrina Sladen died after a brief and completely unsuspicious illness at age thirty-one, Bobby inherited most of her assets, which he burned through as quickly as was humanly possible. He was already in troublesome financial waters when he offered to buy Arlen Drake's radio station.

Varnadore's files included the murder book from the police. Spears and Fender—mostly Fender—had assembled a reasonably competent history on Bobby Sladen. It was workmanlike and informative, but mostly bounced off the atmosphere of his life. It was the starting point.

They'd run Bobby's financials, which weren't much to write home about. After wasting the inheritance from Katrina, save for a few million in trust money he couldn't touch, and bouncing from career to career, Bobby hadn't accumulated much personal wealth. All of his jobs had paid well. Some had paid excellently. Bobby always seemed to ping-pong between boom and bust.

There weren't a lot of people to interview. Before Drake's murder, Bobby hadn't worked in almost three months. I suppose I could have braced his poker buddies, see if maybe they had conspired to alibi him, but there was no point given the casino video that backed Bobby's alibi. I did want to talk to them, if only to be complete, but I didn't expect to learn much.

I started with Bobby's most recent employer and moved backward from there. Unless he was decaying in the trunk of a scrapyard Monte Carlo somewhere, Bobby needed help to disappear. His social contacts—at least those noted in the murder book—were surprisingly scarce. Maybe he developed a relationship with someone at work who helped him kill Drake.

Bobby's most recent job had been with Psylastics Engineering, a manufacturing firm located across the Bay Bridge in Alameda. CyberShamus told me they built fire detection systems and carbon monoxide sniffers. The owner was named Shad Cole.

"Unusual name," I said, as I sat across from Cole in his office later that afternoon. The company was housed in two connected Quonset huts in an industrial park I remembered all too well from a horrible night when I turned my back and walked away from a doomed old friend who thought he had lured me there to die.

Time had healed those wounds.

Mostly.

Shad Cole was in his early fifties, but in surprisingly good shape for his age. Washboard stomach, and arms that strained at the elastic cotton of his company tee shirt. He took care of himself. While shabby outside, Psylastics Engineering was clean-room spotless inside. I could tell Shad Cole took pride in his business.

"I'm a local boy. My parents were genuine Haight Ashbury hippies," he said. "My given name is SunShadow Electrolux Cole. People beat me up in school a lot less when I called myself Shad. How can I help you, Mr. Gold?"

"Wanted to ask you a few questions about Bobby Sladen."

He scowled.

"Aha," I said. "A clue."

"You know how one rotten apple can spoil a bushel?"

"One of my mother's favorite sayings," I said. "She was usually referring to my friends. Bobby was a rotten apple?"

"He was an odd sock. He didn't fit in at all. Never assimilated into the zeitgeist of Psylastics Engineering."

"How could he not?" I said, looking around at the sterile surroundings.

"Right! You see it. I hired him because a friend asked me. Said Bobby was a good outside salesman, and he was. He produced. It was when he was inside that he became a problem."

"There were issues with the other employees?"

"Bobby likes to dip his wick, if you know what I mean," Cole said. "I'm a straight arrow, Mr. Gold. *Mens sana et corpore sano*, all the way. Never cheat on my taxes or my wife. A clean conscience never killed anybody, and the truth is easier to remember. I don't put up with a lot of hanky-panky on the job, and I sure don't need any drama under my roof. Bobby Sladen never met a stranger. He really knew how to close deals, which was the only reason I put up with him as long as I did. He could also charm the panties off a mannequin, which was where the problems kicked in."

"How long did he work here?" I asked.

"A little over a year. Good year for the business, too. If I were a lesser person, if I were only concerned with the bottom line, he'd probably still be here."

"What happened?"

"A woman in the billing department. Angela Friday. Sweet person. Widowed. Afghanistan. Terrible thing. One of those IEDs. Losing her husband had her on the ropes. Took her almost two years to get her feet back under her. I take care of my people, Mr. Gold. We have a decent employee assistance program here, helped her a lot, and I made sure everyone was patient with her as she recovered. She was almost herself again when Bobby Sladen waltzed in and pasted a bullseye on her back."

"How do you mean?"

"I think he decided right off he was going to have Angela come hell or high water. He zeroed in on her. Worked the angle that they were both widowed. Complimented her every chance he got.

Brought her little presents—you know, stuff that looks innocent. Coffee. Little packets of Scottish shortbread. Some chocolate truffles. He was real cagey about it. Didn't come on like some lounge lizard. First he got her to like him. I didn't think much about it at first. I respect my employees and try to help them when I can, but I don't count any of them among my close friends. Makes it too hard if you have to let someone go."

"So what happened with Angela Friday?"

"I don't know the details. None of my business. But I hear they got it on, real heavy. For maybe a month or two. Then, all of sudden, he broke it off. It was like she fell off a cliff. Backslid all the way to where she was after her husband died. Bobby Sladen broke that woman's heart, scooped up the shards, and fed 'em to her. Been almost a year now, and she's still not right."

"Can I speak with Angela?" I asked.

"Sure," he said. "If you're gonna talk about Bobby, though, you better take in a box of tissues."

Angela Friday was an attractive woman in her middle thirties. She had one of those pear-shaped bodies, narrow in the shoulders and wide in the hips, but not so much that she looked like a light bulb. Her hair was short and curly. Her face was moon-like, round and plump in the cheeks.

Shad Cole had arranged for us to use a conference room for the interview, so we wouldn't be disturbed.

"I don't want to upset you," I said. "But this might be a difficult conversation. I'm looking for Bobby Sladen."

"Oh," she said. She had a west Texas accent. "I read in the newspaper that he was missing. Why do you want to find him?"

"You know about his business partner's murder?"

"Yes," she said. "It was terrible."

"A private investigator was charged."

"Libby something," she said. "I heard about that too."

"I'm working for her attorney. There is strong evidence suggesting Libby didn't commit the murder. Bobby makes a great alternate suspect, especially since he's nowhere to be found."

"I could see it," she said. "I reckon Bobby is capable of just about anything. If he did it, I hope you find him. He deserves whatever he has coming. I wouldn't mind gettin' a couple of kicks in myself. With my pointy boots."

She picked a tissue from the box on the table in front of her and dabbed at her eye.

"I need to ask you some personal questions," I said. "I already know you and Bobby had an affair."

"Yes," she said. "I'm not proud of it."

"From what I've heard, he could be a persuasive fellow."

"Persistent is more like it. You know I'm widowed."

"Mr. Cole told me."

"It was a long road back. At the end of it, a charming, drop-dead gorgeous man paid me special attention. He was a widower. We shared an experience most people can't understand. For the first time in years, I felt…seen. Happy again. I thought, maybe, that was my reward for hanging in there and rebuilding my life. Like, the universe was giving me a big ol' attagirl. Here's the cherry on your sundae, Angie!" She swiped at a tear on her cheek. "Some reward."

"Is it your impression that he seduced you?" I asked.

"Oh, hell no. If anything, he kept his distance. He'd get only so close, and then back away. I practically had to drag him into my bed. Later, one of my girlfriends told me that's the way con artists work. They want you to think it's all your idea. After almost three years of a dry spell and all the shit I went through during it, I was like a starving woman at an all-you-can-eat buffet. I was kind of a wild child before I got married. I know a lot of stuff. I think I surprised him."

"And you kept seeing him?"

"We had to keep it quiet, because of work. He didn't want me calling him too frequently."

"How did it end?"

"Bobby met me at my apartment one night. Told me he'd discovered his business partner had hired a private investigator to dig up dirt on him. He said we needed to cool it, to protect my reputation. Breaking things off for my benefit. I took it hard. It came out of the blue. I always knew we weren't permanent. I figured from the start it was a temporary thing, but I wasn't ready for the party to be over."

"I don't want to upset you any more than I already have," I said. "But he was sleeping with that private investigator."

"I know. It was in the news. Why do you think I'm so fucking bitter? That was Bobby in a nutshell. Self-serving son of a bitch."

"Have the police interviewed you about the murder?"

"Of Bobby's partner?"

"Yes."

"Not a word," she said. "Never heard from them."

"Don't take this the wrong way," I said. "But can you account for your whereabouts on the night of the murder?"

Her eyes grew wide. "I don't even know when it was. I have no idea where I was or what I was doing. Why? You aren't accusing me of—"

"I'm not accusing anybody," I said. "That's not my job. But, like I said, I work for Libby Hackney's defense attorney. Part of any good defense is instilling reasonable doubt in the jury. One way to do that is give them someone else to look at. You were sleeping with Bobby within weeks of the murder. You were intimate with Bobby at a time when he couldn't have killed Drake. That means, if he was responsible, he had to convince someone else to do it. Someone he felt particularly close to and trusted to get the job done. It wasn't my intent, and I'm sorry to inconvenience you, but I have a feeling Mr. Varnadore is going to want the jury to hear your story."

"Why?" she said, grabbing at another tissue.

"We already think he set up one woman to be charged in this murder. Why not set up two to muddy the waters even more?"

"I'm sorry I agreed to talk to you now," she said.

"I don't blame you," I said. "And I apologize. If I were you, though, I'd figure out where I was the day Arlen Drake was murdered. Reasonable doubt, remember?"

TWENTY-SEVEN

"This just raises more questions," Varnadore said.

"That's how it works sometimes," I told him. "Puzzle pieces are just puzzle pieces until they fit together."

"Bobby dumped his paramour Angela because he had found someone new and exciting to play with in Libby Hackney, whom he knew was hired to get dirt on him for Arlen. Bobby knew where Arlen kept his gun and told Libby where it was. That doesn't change the fact that he was playing poker several hundred miles away when Arlen Drake was murdered. If Bobby is our angle for reasonable doubt, he still needed an accomplice, which points right to Libby again."

"Angela might still come up with an alibi," I said. "She knew Drake and Sladen were partners in the station. Considering how close she was to Bobby, and how much press Drake's murder generated, it's hard to imagine she couldn't recall where she was when the murder took place. It's like not remembering where you were on Nine-Eleven. Drake's murder should have been important enough to burn the memory into her brain, if only because of the association with Bobby Sladen."

"Some people are absent-minded," Varnadore said.

"There's another thing. Bobby had already purchased fifty-one percent of the radio station when he worked at Psylastics and was sleeping with Angela Friday."

"And?"

"Why was he working there? He had two steady income streams, one from the trust fund he inherited from his wife and the other from the station. Why sell widgets for Psylastics?"

"Some people can't sit around counting money," Varnadore said. "They get antsy."

"Or maybe, even with two incomes, he was cash strapped. We know he kept shining Drake on about paying the remainder of the contract on the station. Maybe his money was being siphoned off by something."

"Like what?"

"Debt, maybe. He ran through the liquid part of his inheritance in less than five years. Wonder where it went. Bobby strikes me as the reckless type. Maybe he owes money to people who only give extensions at the cost of a fingertip, the kind of people who can make you disappear if they want. Bears looking into."

"What's next?"

"I'm going to give this Angela Friday thing a few more kicks, check her out on CyberShamus, but this was only the first ex-employer I've interviewed about Bobby. For all I know, he has a string of scorned girlfriends out there lined up for a chance to turn his life to shit. We may wind up presenting the jury with a bushel basket of motivation, opportunity, and reasonable doubt."

"I fired Bobby Sladen because he stole from me," Greg Avery said.

Avery owned Morphectics Software, a Silicon Valley tech firm. Perhaps the word *firm* was ambitious. The entire company occupied two storefront offices in a cheap strip mall in East Palo Alto, with a laundromat on one side and a *carniciera* on the other. Avery sported what might have been the last mullet in civilized California. He looked like a guy who spent most of his life sitting in a dark room, pudgy and pale. The half-gallon Big Gulp on his desk completed the tech nerd stereotype.

"We're sort of a clearing house," he said. "We don't actually generate any code or write any games or anything. Every year, hundreds of software companies go broke. People who depend on their software for gaming, business, writing, database management, or whatever can no longer access it for updates or reloads. We buy the software and stockpile it—mostly digital, in servers back in the storage room. We also have a storage facility filled with programs on CDs and DVDs, but the demand for those isn't as great anymore. We have almost sixty-seven terabytes of obsolete software on file. People who can't find it anywhere else can buy it from us."

"There's a living in that?"

"Pretty good one, if you keep the overhead low. Most of the process is automated anyway—online payments and downloads don't require a strong skinware presence."

"Skinware?"

"Human operators. The computers handle ninety-five percent of our business, and I just sit back and watch the orders on my desktop. I'm mostly here to keep the servers running and in good shape, and to handle the paperwork."

"What was Bobby Sladen here for?" I asked.

"We have to acquire software titles in order to sell them. He had two jobs. The first was to make the deals for the obsolete or discontinued software. He was good at that. Real good. Smooth talker. Great at glad-handing. Tell you the truth, I don't like people all that much, and I'm not comfortable negotiating shit. He was a good match in that department. I never had any complaints about his acquisition deals."

"But you said he stole from you?" I asked.

"That was the other end of his job. He came into my office about six months after starting work. Said he'd had a brainstorm the night before. Wanted to run a new opportunity by me."

"A can't-miss, get-rich-quick scheme?"

"Not at all. It sounded plausible at first. He said he'd met a woman whose kids were home-schooled. She was part of a collective of homeschoolers, and said their biggest complaint was the lack of comprehensive curriculum software that wasn't full of loony-toon right-wing evangelical garbage, like Jesus riding dinosaurs and shit. You should see some of the bizarro world systems some homeschool parents are buying. I won't even stock 'em. Anyway, Bobby told me he asked the woman if these collectives of homeschooling parents were common, and she told him they were all over the place. Turns out kids need socialization as well as education, so parents organize group activities and even sometimes group instruction for them."

"Bobby wanted to turn the parent groups into a revenue stream," I said.

"Made sense to me. Hell, it's all electrons anyway. Unlimited inventory. The more people depending on it, the better. We've stocked self-directed, objective, scientifically developed educational software that would be perfect, ready to download. The second part of Bobby's job was to contact these home-school parent groups and sell them the programs."

"How'd that work out for you?"

"Very nicely, at first. Have you ever met Bobby Sladen?"

"No," I said.

"Looks like a TV star. Most of these parent groups are comprised of mothers in their thirties and forties. They went gaga over him. He walked into the room and they practically threw checks at him wrapped in their underwear. It was fuckin' Chippendales with soccer moms. For a while, I thought Bobby was going to turn me into the next fuckin' Jeff Bezos, he was moving so much product."

"And then?"

"Then I found out he was skimming off the top. I don't understand the technical details, but my accountant looked at the books while prepping our taxes and discovered the numbers didn't add up. He did a deep dive into the company's financial records. Bobby had ripped us off for almost a hundred thousand dollars. Fuckin' idiot. As much as we were pulling in, I'd have given him that as a bonus and shook his hand while I did it. In fact, that's what I told him when I fired him. *Enjoy the bonus, asshole.* I put the word out on his ass to every other digital company in Silicon Valley, too. Motherfucker."

Carl Jepson said, "Yeah. I saw on the news his partner in that radio station up in Petaluma was murdered. I always figured he did it." Jepson was a stout man, barrel-chested and thick-wristed. He looked every bit like the former lower-tier NASCAR driver he had been before hanging up his helmet and opening a string of high-end car lots.

"Why?" I asked.

"Something's off in that man's head. He ain't right. I hired him as a floor salesman at my dealership five minutes after he walked into the office. Handed him a pen and told him to sell it to me. Next thing I knew, it was like we'd known each other forever. I broke out the good hootch and we toasted his hiring. That's Bobby Sladen. From stranger to best buddy in five seconds flat. That's his gift. He's a smooth one, all right. Might even say slick."

"How'd he do on the job?"

"Great. Outstanding, even. Salesman of the month three months running. He had a talent for scoping out the looky-loos on the lot and avoiding them. It was like he could smell a serious buyer as soon as they drove in off the highway. He moved a lot of cars for me. Wish I had ten of him, if they came without the faults."

"What kind of faults?"

"The boy loves to chase skirts. Mostly the wrong ones. I think he's got some kind of forbidden fruit fetish."

"I don't follow," I said.

"I can understand a woman wanting to get it on with Bobby. He's pretty good-looking. I've seen him in the gym shower after playing squash, and he's got nothing to be ashamed of. If I was hung like him, I'd walk around with a sandwich board announcing it."

"Women like him."

"You can say that again. I heard on the news he even got it on with that private investigator his partner hired to follow him. The one charged with killing him. Is that some balls, or what? Anyway,

Bobby doesn't strike me as the forward-looking sort. He doesn't think things through. Possible consequences don't have much impact on him. He just does what he wants and lets other people clean up the mess he leaves behind. He might have the gift of gab, but sometimes his dick writes checks his mouth can't cash."

"With anyone in particular?"

"I got a complaint about him from a customer. Said Bobby sold his wife a car straight off the truck. All the bells and whistles. I mean, this piece of iron was loaded. It probably had some gizmo that would tickle her clit while she tooled down the interstate, I don't know. He gave her a great deal. Tremendous deal. I signed off on it, because Bobby told me this woman was in a club or something, and if we really took care of her, she'd send all her trophy wife friends our way. He didn't tell me she'd offered him a hummer in his office if he dropped the price."

"The cad," I said.

"She did her sword-swallowing act, he cut the deal, she took the car home. Her husband asked how she got such a great price, and she told him she blew the salesman. It's one of those marriages. He called and bawled me out over the telephone."

"Because his wife blew Bobby?"

"Because he knew his wife and he thought we should have cut a lot more off the price."

"Ah," I said. "It *is* one of those marriages."

"Anyway, it was the most expensive blowjob Bobby ever got. I withheld his commission for lying to me about the circle of friends who'd stampede the dealership if I signed off on the deal, and for not telling me why he was really dropping the price."

"How'd he take it?"

"How do you think?" Jepson said. "He quit on the spot. I pulled his application from HR and looked over it again. Seems pulling up stakes at a moment's notice is kind of his style. Guy who'd treat me like that? Sure. He'd kill his business partner. Better yet, he'd have someone else do it for him. He's not much for getting his hands dirty."

"He fucked my wife," Barry Charles said at Garbinger Aircraft. "The bastard could sell the shit out of an airplane, but some things you just can't overlook. You say he's missing? Best news I heard all day."

"How do you sell an airplane?" I said. "People just kick the tires, or what?"

"It ain't like buying a car," he said. "Takes a while. Lots of boxes to check. Test rides. Mechanical inspections. From first phone call to closing handshake might take months. Somehow, Bobby Sladen found a way to turn it into weeks."

"Does he fly?" I asked.

"Steadiest stick I ever saw. Told me once he trained in T-38s in the Air Force but never saw action as a fighter pilot. He was as good as anyone I ever met, though. Cool and collected, like he had ice water in his veins. Nothing rattles him."

I made two notes. First, I needed to see Bobby Sladen's military records. The second was more concise and possibly explained his sudden disappearance: *Can fly an airplane.*

Might explain why he didn't show up on any transportation manifests after he disappeared.

"And…your wife?" I asked.

"My second wife," he said. "I suppose you could call her a trophy wife. She's younger than I am. Fuck, son, she's younger than my oldest daughter. I hear people talking and laughing behind my back, but they ain't sinkin' their drill into any twenty-somethin' later tonight, so fuck 'em. I'm old enough I don't have to give a shit what people think anymore. What they don't blame on cantankerousness, they'll lay off on senility."

"Bobby did some drill sinking of his own," I said.

"Boy's lucky I didn't have my shotgun when I found out. Fired his ass on the spot. I'll put up with a lot of shit but thumpin' my wife's out of bounds. I put too much work into stealing her from her last husband to let some matinee idol-lookin' saddle tramp waltz in and rustle her out of my corral."

I left him one of my cards.

Had a feeling he might need it someday.

TWENTY-EIGHT

I was in my office the next morning arranging my interview schedule for the day when Fender trudged up the sixteen steps and through my door.

"Inspector," I said. "Offer you some coffee?"

"No thanks." He sat in the chair across from me. "I don't like how we left things."

"Did you bring flowers?" I asked. "When you make up, you're supposed to bring flowers."

"Fuck you."

"That's how we ended things yesterday," I said. "I'm not certain this relationship can be saved."

"Gimme the real four-one-one on Spears."

"You're lashed to the mast of a sinking ship," I said.

"Guy doesn't want to make waves when he's the newest gold shield on the floor," I said. "But I've seen things. Stuff that bothers me."

"Dexter Spears's uncle has a lot of pull at City Hall. Don't cross him if you enjoy working for the SFPD. He also has a nasty temper, and he likes to get even. As long as you're in his hip pocket, you're as protected as he is. Get on his bad side, though, and you'll be working the late show in vice."

Fender shuddered.

"Maybe it's nothing," he said. "You'll find it buried deep in the financials in the discovery files, but you need to know what you're looking for. It doesn't just pop right out at you. Sladen is cagey. Sneaky. He's not into big gestures or leaving massive heaps of evidence in his wake. There are periodic withdrawals from his primary bank account. Cash. Always twenty grand. Usually about once a month."

"A lot of walking around money," I said. "I think we're on the same wavelength. I was wondering yesterday why Bobby was working at Psylastics after he bought into the radio station. He kept shining Drake on about closing the second half of their deal. Maybe it was because he had a hitch in his cashflow giddyup."

"Because he was paying money to someone else," Fender said. "Someone he couldn't shine on."

"What if he borrowed the money he used to pay Drake for the first half?" I said. "Figured he'd run one scam or another to pay it back and then borrow the second half, but his plans fell through. Now he's on the hook to both his lender and Drake, and he's barely making ends meet so he takes a side gig at Psylastics. I'd like to take another look at that contract Bobby had with Drake."

"Why?"

"What happens if Drake dies? Does Bobby then pay the estate for the rest of the station?"

"I can answer that," Fender said. "When Drake died, according to the contract, the station went entirely to Bobby Sladen. They took out an insurance policy to cover it."

"And you have *Libby* in jail facing trial for Drake's murder?" I asked.

"Bobby was gambling in Vegas when Drake died," Fender said. "That's a fact. I figured he was good for it from day one but try proving it. When we discovered he was banging Libby Hackney, and her alibi sucked balls, Spears wasn't interested at first, but the next day he wanted to drag her in, sweat her, and get her to give up Bobby. He thinks she was righteously stand-up and refused to roll over on her boyfriend because they are in it together. I tend to disagree. I think she doesn't know jack shit."

"Varnadore and I discussed that last night," I said. "Bobby didn't kill Drake himself. Just doesn't work. But his former employers, people who knew him, all believed he was fully capable of talking someone else into doing it for him. Most of them think he did."

"But not Libby Hackney," Fender said.

"I don't think so. It doesn't resonate for me. There's a player here we don't know yet."

"Maybe I can help with that, but you never heard a word from me."

"Ooh. Sounds juicy."

"You know Libby Hackney was a cop."

"I do."

"I can't believe I'm telling you this. She applied for promotion to inspector. Has college, which you know helps. It looked like a strong application. Then it just went up in smoke. Scuttlebutt in the locker room says someone on one of the higher floors wanted a little more from her than her resume, if you catch my drift. She turned him down. The position went to someone else, and she left the force to join Sheldon Moon's outfit as a detective trainee."

"It's an old story." I knew. I'd lived it.

"Well, there's more. Yeah. I found the evidence on Hackney, but it was Spears who ramrodded it down the D.A.'s throat. I told him it was weak. He insisted. He's been spending a lot of time in conference with Chief Metterling lately. Metterling is the guy who supposedly put the moves on Hackney. Maybe it's nothing."

"Maybe it's something."

"I just know Spears didn't give a rip about Hackney when I first brought him evidence that she'd been with Bobby. It was only later, after a couple of summonses to the tenth floor, that he went all gung-ho on her."

"At the very least, Varnadore can use it as a smoke screen. Thanks. Worth looking at. Here's something. Did you know Bobby was a licensed pilot?"

"Followed up on it. Checked all the local airfields. No unaccounted-for planes took off within the several days after he disappeared. It's in discovery."

"He could have gone to ground until things cooled off and then flew away."

"Or he could have hitched a ride with a buddy. Maybe even the accomplice who shot Drake. Too many moving parts, Gold. Maybe he flew off into oblivion. Maybe he didn't. So far, all we can find says he didn't."

"Maybe it's like Rhonda Brownlee. Bobby has a spare identity he's using to hide in plain sight."

"That would just complicate the shit out of my day."

"I'll keep looking. I'm right, though? You don't buy Libby for the killing either?"

"I never said that, and you never heard it. Let's say I have concerns."

"But you aren't allowed to voice them?"

"I'm a grown-ass man," Fender said. "I can say anything I want. Just have to be willing to take the shit that comes with it."

"Goes with being a grown-ass man," I said.

TWENTY-NINE

I figured it was time I took a look at the radio station at the center of the whole Drake case. I drove across the bridge and up the highway to Petaluma. I hadn't been there in years. Like most places, it had grown.

Drake's radio station consisted of a waiting room, two offices, and a studio sardined into a small storefront on a busy four-lane strip dotted with fast food franchises, hardware stores, used car lots, and a couple of titty bars. The walls were 1970s printed luan paneling. The waiting area seats were folding metal chairs. The magazines in a rack between them touted the release of a now five-year-old car, and equally obsolete invitations to vacation in lovely Ukraine.

The front desk was deserted. The two office doors were closed. A heavy urban beat shook the door to the studio. Through a glass window next to it, I saw a pudgy kid in his early twenties leaned back in an office chair in front of the broadcast console. He was reading a magazine and picking his nose. I rapped on the glass, and he nearly hit the ceiling jumping out of his chair.

"The hell, man!" he shouted when he opened the door. He had greasy rusty red hair hanging almost to his shoulders, and a straggly beard that looked like he'd glued spider webs to his chin. He wore a faded Run DMC tee shirt and ratty jeans. A shower wouldn't have killed him. The volume from the speakers jumped a hundred decibels, becoming a physical thing that pushed me back a foot or two. "You scared the piss out of me!"

"Looking for the manager," I yelled over the din.

The kid pointed at the office door farthest from the studio and closed the door. He pulled a curtain across the window.

I knocked on the office door. Nobody answered. I knocked on the other office door. Same response. I rapped on the studio window again.

"What?" the kid growled when he opened the door. "I'm workin' here, man!"

I pointed to the office doors. "Nobody answered."

"Then they're not here, are they? Sheesh."

"Any idea when Mr. Simms will return?"

"I didn't fuckin' know he was gone," the kid said. "Wait. There he is."

A man walked through the front door with a couple of wrapped submarine sandwiches in his hand. He saw the kid and tossed him one. The kid caught it and closed the studio door in a sweeping motion.

"Help you?" the man said as he unlocked his office door. He was on the short side, maybe five-eight, and soft, the way people get when they sit in a radio studio ten hours a day for thirty years. He was balding and at least had the self-respect not to attempt a comb-over. His nose was bulbous and heavily veined. I suspected John Barleycorn was a beneficiary in his will.

"Are you Tim Simms?" I asked.

"Sure am. What can I do for you?" He had the sort of voice you've heard give the time and temperature a million times.

I followed him into this office. Like the waiting room, it was covered in cheap paneling. The furniture was utilitarian but inexpensive stuff probably bought on clearance from Office Depot. A case on a far wall contained several Little League championship trophies. Concert posters covered one entire wall. Simms sat behind his desk and unwrapped his sandwich.

"Sorry to be rude," he said. "I have an appointment across town in an hour and a half, and this is my only chance to eat today. What can I do for you?"

I slid my card onto his desk. He read it without picking it up.

"Private detective, eh?" he said. "This have something to do with Arlen Drake?"

"I work for Libby Hackney's attorney," I said. "Tying up loose ends."

"I'm a loose end?"

"Not really. I'm more interested in the station itself. It's the reason Drake was murdered, after all."

"Hell of a thing." He took a bite of the sandwich, chewed, and swallowed. "Can you imagine being killed over this shithole? Don't get me wrong, Mr.—" He glanced at the card again. "—Gold. I mean, this is the only place I've worked all my adult life, but look around you. It's a fuckin' dump. Die over this place? No thanks. What happened to Arlen was a shame, a real shame, but what made it worse was what a waste it was."

"Were you here?"

"You mean, do I have an alibi? Sure. We've been between ad salesmen for a spell. Bobby was supposed to pick up the slack, but he's been kind of scarce for several months. I was out updating an account over at Western Auto. They've always been one of our biggest advertisers. That and the Safeway. Hell of a thing. I learned about it over the radio, even before the police came calling."

"Or maybe they dropped by and the guy in the studio didn't hear them."

"It's possible. You heard it out there. That idiot kid I hired to run the board will be deaf before he gets his cherry busted. We changed to an urban contemporary format about a year before Arlen died. Mostly rap and hip hop. Chasing the trends, you know. We don't actually originate any programming except for the commercials, which I record in the studio at night when we're off the air. Everything is syndicated, the music, the news, everything. So, Jeff was probably in there with the volume jacked to eleven and never heard or saw a thing."

"Jeff?"

"The kid. Jeff Lineberger. We have a part-timer who runs the board on the weekends, but Jeff's our only full-time jock right now. He's kind of dumb, but so was I at his age. He's dependable, and he does whatever I tell him, unless it entails keeping an eye on the place."

"You always keep the front door unlocked when nobody is here except the kid?"

"Have to. Fire regulations. If the business is open, the door is unlocked. I tell Jeff to keep an eye on things. Sometimes he does. Sometimes he doesn't."

"Tell me about Bobby Sladen," I said.

"Not that much to tell. You know my dad worked for Arlen Drake?"

"I read it in the reports."

"You could say this shithole station is the family business. Dad put me on the control board when I was younger than Jeff Lineberger. He worshipped Arlen. Dad had just been let go from a station in Sonoma after fifteen years, and Arlen snapped him up on the spot. I don't think he missed a single paycheck on that deal. After Dad died, Arlen promoted me to station manager, but left me on the board during the week. Taught me everything there is to know about running a low-watt radio station without losing your shirt. I don't worship Arlen like my dad did, but I owe him everything I have, and I'm grateful to him. I'd favor Arlen over Bobby Sladen any day, so my opinion of Bobby might be tainted."

"Understood."

"I thought Bobby was up to no good. I'm not a worldly man, Mr. Gold. When you're tethered to a radio station the way I am, there isn't time to see much else out there. I suppose I could hire someone to take some of the load off, especially now that Jeff's running the board. But someone has to sell the airtime and write up the traffic sheets and maintain the transmitter logs. Right now, it's just me, Jeff, and Doug Petrie."

"Who's that?"

"Our first-class radiotelephone engineer. Every broadcast station has to have one. Doug's been with Arlen for twenty years. Stays mostly out at the transmitter shack. Keeps his mobile home there, so he's available at a moment's notice if we go off the air. With only three of us on staff right now, and only two here in the station regularly, it's kind of tight. I may be overly protective of this station, as shitty as it is—pour a couple of beers in me and I call it KRAP—but it is my livelihood, and Bobby just set me off wrong."

"How do you mean?"

"The boy just wasn't right. He reminded me—did you ever see that movie *The Music Man?* Like that. Trouble right here in River City. Bobby come swinging in here like a house afire, tossing around big plans and promises and money like he was some kind of Rockefeller. It all just felt wrong. Who gets that excited over a station with a signal that might make it to the county line?"

"But you introduced Bobby to Drake."

"I did, and I regret it to this very day. Met Bobby on the golf course. Pure chance. A foursome was short, and he was available. We got to talking about our work, and he had a ton of questions in the clubhouse afterward about the station—how much programming cost, our ad revenue, stuff like that. I thought he was just curious until he came right out and asked whether Arlen might be interested in selling out."

"He offered you a ten percent finder's fee."

"Yeah. I never saw a penny of that. Only made me more wary of him."

"Did you discuss your suspicions with Drake?"

"They weren't suspicions, really," he said. "Just a bad feeling. Maybe I was just scared Bobby would take over, bring in all his own people, and squeeze me out, like what happened to my dad back in the day before he came here. Getting fired is a given in this business, but it's never happened to me, and I'm not anxious to experience it. Something felt wrong. I didn't mention it to Arlen. Didn't get a chance to, really, before he was killed."

"Why?"

"He was hardly ever here. Arlen was getting old. He was ready to retire, move to Palm Springs, and take it easy for the rest of his life. I read somewhere that the happiest two days in a man's life are when he buys a boat and when he sells it. Reckon the same goes for radio stations. He'd divested almost everything else, cashing out on all his businesses. Only the station remained. The day Bobby waltzed into Arlen's life might have been the happiest he'd known since the day he was handed the keys to this place."

"And then Bobby stonewalled him."

"Took the wind out of Arlen's sails, I can tell you that. I think he was already ninety percent shut of the place anyway, but as the months wore on and Bobby didn't close the deal, Arlen became more and more distant. Maybe he saw his golden days in the sun in Palm Springs being eaten up waiting to seal the deal that wouldn't end. He came in less and less. I called him a week or so before he was murdered about some damn thing or another. He told me to run it by Bobby, that he had other things on his mind. Gotta tell you, Mr. Gold, I knew the man for forty years and I never heard him that low."

"Did Bobby discuss any of his plans for the station with you?"

"Not really. He liked to talk. I don't think he liked rap and hip hop all that much. He talked about switching to a sports talk format once. Another time he said he might go all-news. I don't think he knew shit about radio or the business."

"Why would he buy a station then?"

"Run it right, keep the overhead low, and a place like this is a little goldmine. You have to hire the right ad salesperson and know which syndicators deliver the biggest bang for the lowest buck, but once you establish your regular advertising accounts, it mostly runs itself and produces a tidy profit each year. I should know. I handle the books along with everything else. A radio station is a great investment, if you have the right people to run it."

"Arlen Drake is dead. According to the contract, the station belongs to Bobby Sladen now."

"And he's missing," Simms said. "Damned inconvenient. I need his ass to show up in the next four weeks to sign the quarterly tax forms."

"What happens if he never shows up?"

"Beats the hell out of me. That's up to the lawyers. I reckon they'll find some distant relative somewhere to inherit it. Not my problem. I'll just keep this place chugging along until he either returns or someone shuts the bastard down."

Simms gave me directions to the transmitter shack a couple of miles away. I had always assumed radio stations were located in the same place as their antenna towers. Silly me.

The shack was a concrete block building with a steel door a bazooka couldn't penetrate. Heavy coaxial cables snaked from the back of the building, under a chain-link fence that surrounded the tower, and finally into the tower itself.

The door to the shack was open. An ozone smell rolled from it. I peeked inside. The entire space might have been ten feet square, dominated by a machine that looked like something out of Dr. Frankenstein's lab, with orange glowing vacuum tubes and dials and switches galore. The side wall was a workbench littered with electronic components. Standing at the workbench was a man in cutoff jean shorts, a cutoff sweatshirt, and boots with thick rubber soles. His belly protruded from under the cropped sweatshirt. His hair hung stringy and limp, partly from sweat and mostly from neglect. I smelled him before I saw him.

"Hello," I said.

He whirled around. He was in his late fifties or early sixties. He had a full beard, neck and all, sprayed through with graying strands, and his teeth hadn't seen a dentist in decades. His eyes were bloodshot.

"Don't move!" he said.

I held up my hands. "Got me, Sheriff. What now?"

"Step outside the door."

I complied. He followed me outside.

"I don't know what kind of shoes you have on, and there are eleventy-seven ways to die inside that shack. High voltage. That goddamn transmitter was built by fuckin' Marconi. Keeping it running is like maintaining someone on life support. There's always a live wire exposed somewheres. I know what to avoid, but the wrong move in there could put you in the ground. What in hell are you doing out here anyway?"

"You're Doug Petrie?" I asked.

"Yeah. You ain't servin' papers, are you?"

I handed him my card. He squinted at it.

"I'm working for the attorney representing Libby Hackney, who was arrested for killing Arlen Drake. Since the whole case revolves around this radio station, I figured it would be a good idea to learn everything I can about it."

"All right."

He walked toward a single-wide trailer parked about fifty yards from the fence surrounding the tower. Instead of going inside, he uncoiled a plastic garden hose screwed into a water faucet rising from the artesian well beside the trailer and pulled the hose around the back. I followed.

"Nice garden," I said, as he began to spray down a twenty-by-thirty-foot patch of tilled earth lined with tomato, string bean, pepper, and cucumber plants. Sunlight created a dozen rainbows in the scattered mist.

"I like to watch things grow," he said. "Food tastes better when it comes from your own hand. Now what's the deal with you again? You're investigating the murder? I thought the police had that handled."

"I'm working for the defense. How long have you worked for the station, Mr. Petrie?"

"Call me Doug. Everyone does. Been a long time. Twenty years, I reckon. Got my First Class Radiotelephone license in the Navy. My nickname there was Sparks. Every radio tech in the Navy is called Sparks. Go figure. Once't I bounced with my twenty and a pension, I decided something from the Navy should pay off for me. I still had my license. I've always been handy with electronics. Comes natural to me. Got into the radio engineering business and never looked back. This is my third station. The other two didn't last so long."

"Why's that?"

"What difference does it make? They both gone under anyway. One has had three different call letters since I left. Ever' time a new owner comes in, they want to clean house. I figured when I came here that it would last maybe a year, but somehow the place just keeps chuggin' along year after year. That's Tim Simms. I don't know how he does it, but I'm glad he does, because I don't cotton to pulling up stakes again. I reckon the station will go to dead air one day, and they'll find my body in the trailer. That's my plan, anyway. Just no time soon."

"So you knew Arlen Drake well?"

"Not really. Saw him mebbe once a year. Arlen hardly never come out this way. He let Tim run ever'thing, and he mostly stayed back in San Francisco counting his money. Nothin' against him. The few times I saw Arlen, he seemed like a decent enough type."

"How about Bobby Sladen?"

"The man who's buying the station? What about him?"

"He's missing, for one thing."

"I don't know nothin' about that," Petrie said.

"What do you know about Sladen?"

"Nothin', boss. Never met the man. Tim told me about him. Said he was kind of slick. I don't think Tim likes the idea of working for Sladen."

"Any particular reason?"

"Tim's a good man. Has a good head on his shoulders. He knows more about low-budget broadcasting than anyone in the business. Now this Sladen character waltzes in with a buttload of cash, knowing jack shit about radio, and he wants to toss everything on its head. I don't think Tim is happy about that. You think Bobby Sladen killed Arlen?"

"Why do you ask?"

"Bobby's missing, you say. Tim told me the police already arrested a woman for the murder. You also say you're working for the woman's attorney, which means you're trying to get her off. If she didn't do it, then someone else had to. You're trying to pin Arlen's murder on Bobby Sladen."

"If I can find him," I said. "I know he didn't do it personally, because his alibi is solid. But he could have hired someone else to kill Arlen. I won't know if I can't find him."

"You keep looking, then," Petrie said. "Anything that keeps this station running works for me, and right now he owns the whole thing.

On the way back to my office, I stopped by the jail and asked to meet with Libby Hackney.

"Bring me any smokes?" she asked as she plopped down on the metal chair across from me in the interview room.

I slid a pack of Winstons across the table. I'd stopped at a convenience store on the way into the city and bought them for her.

"Big fuckin' spender. Don't forget to expense these out to the Shark, okay?"

"Tell me about Metterling," I said.

"Motherfucker," she said. "Please tell me he's dead. Bonus points if he died screaming. I'll blow you for the video."

"He's alive," I said.

"Another item I'll add to my list of proofs there ain't no God. What about the motherfucker?"

"That was my question. You don't like him."

"Demonstrating the observational skills that made you the World's Greatest Detective?"

"You're confusing me with another guy down in Los Angeles. What about Metterling?"

She chewed on a thumbnail and stared at the sealed pack of Winstons as if they held the secret to immortality.

"What did you want to be when you were a kid, Gold?"

"Wide receiver for the Forty-Niners."

"What happened?"

"Jerry Rice was faster than me and had better hands, along with a few hundred other guys. Metterling."

"I always wanted to be a cop. I watched fuckin' T.J. Hooker on reruns when I was a kid and said that shit was for me. I wanted to spend my life riding on car hoods and busting scumbags. I was such a fuckin' straight arrow. The day they pinned a badge on my tit at the academy graduation was one of the proudest of my life. And I was fuckin' ambitious, man. I was gonna shoot through the ranks like a missile and make inspector before anyone in my class. Almost did it, too."

"What happened?"

"You make as much noise as I did, climbing the ranks, people notice. You know why the honeypot trap works so well for me?"

"Why?"

"I don't look like much right now but give me an hour to prep and the right warpaint, and I'll knock your socks off. Nature gave me an axe that won't quit, and I know how to wail it. Guys take one look and get happy pants. Like shooting fish in a barrel."

"Okay."

"It's a double-edged sword. I can work it to my advantage, but I can't turn it off. People on the higher floors at Eight-Fifty Bryant noticed my work, but they also noticed *me*. Some of them, anyway. One in particular."

"Metterling."

"Fuckin' Captain of Major Crimes. My prospective *capo di tutti capi*. I took the exam and put in my application like a hundred other street pukes. I came off watch one day, and there was a message to report to Metterling's office. I wanted to make a good impression, so I showered and did my hair nice and put on a little makeup and dressed in my civvies before I hit the elevator. It wasn't sexy or anything. White blouse, gray slacks, blazer. Businesslike. You know. Dress for the job you want and all that shit."

"How'd Metterling respond?"

"Like I'd walked off the floor of fuckin' Victoria's Secret. I mean, he didn't stick his hand down my shirt when I walked through the door, but the message was clear. He offered me a drink. What the fuck? I was off duty. I drink. Why not? He said he'd had his eye on me since the academy. I was impressed, exactly the way he expected me to be. He said the department valued diversity and inclusion, and if I made the inspector rank, I'd be a good fit."

"So far, so good," I said.

"Context and inflection are important. As soon as he said it, he put his hand on my leg, and I suspected what my promotion depended on," she said. "Then he put my hand on his crotch, and I knew it. He didn't summon me to his office to tell me I had the promotion. He wanted me to know I had to earn it. Fuck him. I thought I already had."

"He pressed the issue?"

"He was too smart for that. I found out later he's done this with at least three other women candidates. Sometimes we all meet for drinks and plot his grisly murder. Maybe I shouldn't say shit like that in here. I thought about it. Not the murder, but the other thing. I considered snorkeling his fat ass for my gold shield. Hell, I've done worse. A half hour in and out, stash it in the rancid memory lockbox, and move on. I'm not proud of it, but that gold shield represented more than a job to me. It was the culmination of a childhood dream. I'd earned the fucker, and Metterling pissed all over it by implying I might get it if I showed him a good time. In the end, I decided the price was too high. I told him to ram it. Told him if I ever heard again that he'd propositioned a recruit, I'd burn his fuckin' dreams to the ground. I turned in my badge and gun the same day."

"There's talk," I said. "Can't tell you who's talking. The lead inspector on your case wasn't interested in you as a suspect at first. Then he reported your association with the case to his superior."

"Metterling," she said.

"Next thing, you're in the slam and facing murder charges. Your alibi sucks, sure, but that and the fact you were sleeping with Bobby Sladen are all they have on you. That is literally their entire case. There's no evidence that you were ever on Drake's property, or that you were involved in any way with his killing. I'll see Varnadore later today. Don't want to get your hopes up, but you might be out of here before you finish that pack of cigarettes."

"Better hurry," she said. "I got a wicked nicotine jones."

"Perfect," Varnadore said. "That's exactly what I need."

"You can't let it track back to Fender," I said. "I promised."

"Don't need to," he said. "Libby's civil service jacket is public record. It will show her career trajectory clearly blasted out of the sky within days of applying for inspector. I'll visit her later today to draft an affidavit outlining Metterling's misconduct to present to the police commissioner and the D.A., along with a brief outlining exactly how flimsy the evidence against her is. I think I can make the case that her arrest and charges were...premature."

"She's already told me her first job the minute she's back on the street will be to get statements from the other candidates Metterling hosed," I said. "She was willing to suck it up and put him in the rearview until she was popped into the concrete block hotel. Now she's on a mission from God. I woke up this morning and gave thanks my name isn't Metterling."

"I'll make a few calls. I anticipate a surprise retirement announcement from Eight-Fifty Bryant within days," Varnadore said. "This doesn't prove someone else killed Arlen Drake, but it's almost as good. The D.A.'s office will need a video of her blowing the top of Drake's head off before they'll consider charging her again."

"There's still the matter of Bobby Sladen," I said.

"Not my problem if I get Libby off the hook," he said.

"The cops are going to put Libby in a fishbowl until Bobby turns up."

"I'll see to it there's no harassment. You've done excellent work, Gold. You can expect an impressive bonus on top of your bill."

"Work's not done yet," I said. "There's still Brownlee. And I want to find Bobby Sladen."

"You have the green light on Brownlee. Go get 'em, Tiger. I'm not paying for Bobby, though."

"Sure you are," I said. "That bonus, remember?"

THIRTY

Switching gears from finding Bobby Sladen back to the murder of Rhonda Brownlee required me to return to my Brownlee notes and read them all over again. It had been nearly a year since the murder, and my memory needed refreshing.

I was reviewing my case file when Libby Cordelia Hackney stomped up the stairs to my office and paused for perhaps a nanosecond to read the glass on my office door before barging through it.

She cleaned up nicely. The dry flyaway hair in jail was now a mass of soft curls that framed her expertly made-up face. She wore stylish glasses and jeans with Timberland boots, and a Nickelback tee shirt under a Lands End flannel with the sleeves rolled up.

"Nickelback?" I asked.

"Fuck you, Gold. I like Nickelback. Your door's spelled wrong."

"Different strokes for different folks. Varnadore got you sprung? I didn't read about it in the newspapers."

"And you won't. The police don't like their dirty laundry aired in public. I was quietly liberated from my cell before sunrise this morning. It was like the fucking walk of shame. Varnadore sent a car to pick me up. I've spent most of the day repairing the damage."

"A day well spent, from the looks of it."

"Thank you. Which means I gotta thank you twice, I suppose. The Shark told me you went to him with the shit on Metterling. Varnadore had a couple of drinks with the commissioner, who, it turns out, has received several reports similar to mine. They brainstormed some solutions. Metterling's on his way out."

"Happy to help," I said.

"There was some talk about making it right for me and the other women by offering us reinstatement and a fast track to inspector, but I don't think it'll go anywhere. The city would rather write a fat check and forget the whole shitshow. Varnadore's already negotiating the numbers. So, I'll get paid, at least. Impressively."

"As will Varnadore when he takes his cut. Turns out taking the AOC money for defending you paid off for him."

"Lawyers always get paid. So, you wanna help me find Bobby Sladen and fuck him up?"

I shook my head. "Sorry. It's tempting, but I'm already working another case for Varnadore."

"You're no fun." She pouted.

"Job's a job. Bobby is decidedly on my radar, but I'm being paid for another gig. Until I wrap it up, it's a priority. You have some idea where he might be?"

"I had a lot of time to think about it in jail. Bobby's a psychopath, but he's also a little narcissistic. He likes to be admired. He tells a lot of stories with him as the heroic central character. He's also kind of hyperactive, so while I was trying to snooze after we messed up the duvet, he would run off at the mouth. I realized the third night I banged him that he was full of shit. Every story contradicted another. He had himself in two or three places at the same time. I figured out real quick he was bullshitting me, like he bullshits everyone else."

"But you kept seeing him."

"We've covered this, Gold." She held her hands a foot apart.

"Verily, thou exaggerates," I said.

"Not by much. Guys think women can't be horndogs too. I love a good ol' rumble in the sheets as much as anyone, and I'm kind of a size queen."

"Duly noted," I said.

"Bobby Sladen is a psychopath and a narcissist and very possibly a murderer, but he also knows his way around. He gave me the kind of tingles that had me coming back for more. Easily one of my top three fucks. I'm ashamed to say that, since he also landed my ass in a concrete box. Guess I went a little cock blind there."

"The course of true love never did run smooth."

"True lust, maybe. Anyway, he spouted a lot of bullshit, which I knew was bullshit, but I politely kept that to myself. A couple of things he talked about were consistent, though. He never contradicted himself about his wife."

"The dead one? Katrina?"

"Yeah. Everything he said about her was consistent. You know she came from money."

"It's in the files."

"There's a trust fund he can't crack. It provides him with a subsistence income for life. Part of the prenup. The money is deposited directly into Bobby's account each month."

"Let me guess. Twenty thousand dollars."

"How did you know?"

"Fender told me, sort of. He pulled Bobby's financials. Bobby withdraws twenty thousand dollars a month from his primary account. Almost regular as clockwork. Takes it all out in cash."

"Why?"

"I think he owes somebody a lot of money he can't pay back. The vig is soaking him dry. I think he borrowed the money to buy into Arlen Drake's radio station, but something ate into his cashflow, and he couldn't pay back the lender and he couldn't pay Arlen to finalize the deal. He was turning over every penny of his trust fund payout each month just to stay afloat. So he found a way to get both off his back. If Arlen died, his insurance paid the remainder of the station cost to his estate and Bobby took possession. Bobby found a patsy to kill Drake while he was playing cards with his poker buddies, providing him with an ironclad alibi. With Drake dead, Bobby could sell the station and get clear with the lender. It's a loss, but it's also a fresh start."

"That doesn't flush, Gold. I mean, it looks good on the surface, but it doesn't explain why Bobby disappeared. And, I gotta tell you, I'm not completely sold on him as the killer anyway."

"For real, Libby?"

"Don't look at me that way. I agree with you, right up to the point of the murder. Bobby borrowed the money for the down payment for the station. He couldn't pay it back because the income from his trust fund only covered the vig and he needed the station income to eat and put a roof over his head. Arlen was murdered, but not necessarily by Bobby. Bobby knows, once the estate is settled, he'll own the station. In the interim, he can't sell it because it's still in probate, and he's falling farther and farther behind to whoever lent him the money in the first place. So he makes a deal with the lender. It's a fuckin' bust-out. He signs over the station to the lender in a post-dated contract in return for keeping his skin. They keep a close eye on Bobby until the estate closes. Like, under guard in a basement somewhere. Soon as everything settles, the lenders show up at the register of deeds with the contract, take possession of the station, and give Bobby the heave-ho."

"The *big* heave-ho?" I asked.

"Maybe, but probably not. Loansharks don't kill people, mostly. Maybe they'll just turn him loose with empty pockets, no radio station, and a suggestion to make better decisions next time around."

"In your story, who killed Drake?"

"Maybe the guys he borrowed from. Maybe someone else. I'm not eliminating anyone. Doesn't change the fact that I'm gonna kick Bobby Sladen's balls into the base of his skull the minute I see him. Nobody puts Libby Hackney in a box."

"In the meantime, think about this," I said. "If Bobby isn't being held pending the settlement of Drake's estate, as you suggest, and he isn't decomposing under a highway bridge, he needs to keep making the monthly payments even while he's in hiding. As far as I know, his bank accounts aren't frozen. When does the next trust fund check drop?"

She slipped a handful of her business cards onto my desk. "Do me a favor, Gold. If you get swamped, shuffle a little business my way. Gotta boogie. There's an asshole out there who needs finding."

Sam Brownlee didn't look much better this time than he had the last time I visited him in jail.

"Any word?" he asked. It was barely more than a whisper, but it echoed off the concrete block walls and the stainless-steel furniture as if we were conversing in a crypt.

"Not yet. I have some questions about your loansharking business."

"What does that have to do with Rhonda?"

"It's the reason she ran off, remember? She became an entirely different person because something about your business scared the shit out of her. It's time to come clean with me, Sam."

"About what? I told you everything when I hired you."

"That's not how I recall it. You said there were things you preferred not to discuss until I took the case. So I took the case, and you never ponied up with the whole truth. I already know you were sleeping with Laura Hope, however infrequently. I know Rhonda got around a little herself. She was seen at a party with her hand down Armin Bagdasarian's pants, and I know she had a liaison with Sonya Soderquist's husband in Monterey."

"I know about all of that," he said. "She didn't keep any of it secret. In fact, I think she enjoyed tossing it in my face. I wouldn't call it a storybook marriage, unless the book is *Anna Karenina*." He tried to flash the million-watt smile but only managed a smirk.

"Who else did she shack up with?" I asked.

"The thing with Soderquist was nothing," he said. "Phyllis Bagdasarian told me she saw Rhonda grabbing Armin's junk. I could have told her a lot more, but I…" he stopped.

"You were dependent on Armin Bagdasarian. He invested in your loansharking business, didn't he?"

"You're making quite a leap, Gold."

"Not so much. Part of the police investigation included running your financials. You're robbing Peter to pay Paul. Everything you own except for your house is leveraged to the studs to pay for everything else. You have twenty plates spinning on twenty sticks at any given time, and it's all you can do to keep them from falling."

"Until I wound up here," he said. "Now they're all smashed on the floor. What can I say? It isn't easy keeping up with the Dow Joneses."

"You needed regular cash injections to keep it all humming along. Since the foundation of all your businesses was usury, investing in you might have been seen as a growth opportunity. Bagdasarian showed up at just the right time."

"Him and his manager."

"Ruben Sahakian. And there it is. You know who Ruben is, right?"

"You think I'm an idiot? Sure I know. Everybody knows Tigran Sahakian."

"And you didn't think it curious that Tigran's kid shows up on your doorstep offering to capitalize your loan business?"

"I knew what I was getting into."

"I asked Gigi Sahakian last year whether her husband was laundering Daddy's dirty cash through Bagdasarian's waste rendering business. She danced around the question, but implied that he was, and that Bagdasarian knew about it. I asked whether Tom Wanamaker was involved, but I didn't ask about *you*. Wanna bet coming to you was Ruben's idea, not Armin's?"

"The thought crossed my mind."

"And if it was Ruben's money, then it was also Tigran's money."

He shrugged and said, "I can't exactly go down to the local savings and loan, Gold. Fuck, man. I was loansharking! The shit I did would make Shylock flinch. I'm not clean either, you know. What did I care if some dirty money rolled my way?"

"Well, here's the problem. Bringing Tigran Sahakian into the picture complicates things a lot. So far, we've been talking about a bunch of nouveau-riche bon vivants living the high life on someone else's nickel. You're a tight-knit pack of jackals, playing grab-ass with each other's spouses and pretending like it's all good fun. Then, suddenly, some of the spouses buy new identities and try to disappear. I want to know what they were running from."

"I can't tell you. If I knew, I would, but I don't."

"I know Rhonda was fooling around with Armin Bagdasarian and Stefan Soderquist. Who else?"

"For God's sake, man," Brownlee said. "The woman's dead."

"And someone killed her. Hiding infidelity makes a great motive."

He sighed. "I suspect she might have been hooking up with Ruben."

"Not Tom Wanamaker?"

"Fuck no. I don't even think Julia shags his stinky ass anymore. Ruben, though. Yeah. I think. I never caught them, and Rhonda never told me anything, but I saw the way they looked at each other, and how they talked together when they were away from the crowd."

"She told you about the others?"

"We weren't faithful, but we were honest," he said.

"How thoroughly modern."

"I suppose."

"And, yet, if she was knocking boots with Ruben Sahakian, she never told you. Instead, she bought a new identity and bugged out."

"What are you saying?" Brownlee asked.

"Maybe she wasn't running away from *you,*" I said.

THIRTY-ONE

I had enough questions whirling around inside my head to keep me busy, but just before the jailer led Brownlee away, I stopped him.

"One more thing," I said. "Nothing to do with your case. Something else I'm working on. Suppose a guy wanted to borrow a significant amount of money, say, somewhere in the low seven-figure range. The vig's twenty large a month. Is that the kind of deal you could handle?"

Brownlee chuckled. "Right now, I have to budget a week out just to buy a candy bar. I couldn't handle shit."

"But back in the day. How big a note could you carry?"

The jailer looked impatient. "This gonna take long?" he asked.

"Just a minute or so," I said. "How about it, Sam?"

"No. I wouldn't loan that much. I was good for fifty, maybe a hundred grand. Anything else I had to get approval for."

"From Ruben Sahakian?"

"From Armin, but yeah. The final nod probably came from Ruben."

"But never anything near a million."

"Fuck, no. Too big a risk, at least for a small-time operator like me."

"So who could stake a guy with, say, two million dollars?" I asked.

"You gotta deal with some heavy hitters. Tigran Sahakian might do it directly. JuneBug, back in the day, but he's dead now. Some wildcat tech billionaires over in Silicon Valley would do it on a lark. Those fuckers wipe their asses with Franklins. What's this about?"

"A guy I'm looking for bought half a radio station with the promise to buy the other half in six months. He's making monthly payments of twenty grand in cash to someone, so I think we can rule out the tech billionaires. I think he's treading water."

"So follow him and find out who he hands the cash to."

"That's the problem. He's in the wind. To follow him, we have to find him first. Thought I might work it from the other end, find out who might lend him the money in the first place."

"It's a short list. Tigran, Boyd Demarest, Marcus Dallie, maybe Vassily Palyenko."

"Shit. You're just reciting the Most Wanted posters from the post office," I said.

"I said it was a short list," he said. "People who can lend seven figures are seldom upright citizens. Tell you what. I'll get a message to Ruben, tell him you're trying to find evidence to get me sprung. I'll ask him to help you out. Maybe he can ask Tigran for you. If Tigran didn't lend your guy the money, he'll probably know who did."

"The last time Ruben Sahakian and I talked, we agreed to stay on opposite sides of the street."

"Always a wise strategy when dealing with the Armenian mob," Brownlee said.

I phoned Libby from my car.

"Is this someone with good news or money?" she asked before even saying hello. I could hear that she was in her car also. She must have glanced at the phone quickly. "Oh, it's you, Gold."

"Maybe I can help with the good news part," I said.

"Hit me."

"I met with one of Varnadore's clients in jail. He's a loanshark."

"Sammy Brownlee," she said.

"That was quick."

"My IQ is four times my bra size, asshole. Everyone knows about the Brownlee case, and he's the only loanshark I know in the can who can afford Varnadore. What about Brownlee?"

"We're working on the assumption Bobby Sladen has gone to ground because he can't pay back the loan he took out to buy Drake's radio station. I asked Brownlee who would back a nearly two million dollar play like that."

"And?"

"It's a short list. Tigran Sahakian, Boyd Demarest, Marcus Dallie, maybe Vassily Palyenko."

"Jesus. I wouldn't want to piss off any of those guys even with John Wick backing me up. Why's it never easy, Gold?"

"Here's the thing. The Sahakian connection might be a link between our two cases. I'm on the way to have a talk with Tigran's boy Ruben about my case. Brownlee said he'd ask Ruben to help with yours as well."

"So you'll ask Ruben whether his daddy staked Bobby's loan for the station?"

"Professional courtesy, since I'll be there anyway."

"And once we know that?"

"Brings us one step closer to Bobby. Either Bobby is under lock and key, or he's dead, or he's just keeping a really low profile. Neither of the first two helps us. If it's the last one, he's going to keep making the payments just to avoid becoming one of the first two. Arlen Drake's murder is still an open investigation. All we really care about is finding Bobby."

"Speak for yourself. I want to bruise him up a little."

"Living well is the best revenge, Libby."

"Fuck that shit. I prefer bloody knuckles and teeth in the gutter."

"The more we talk, the more I see why the DA found you such an attractive defendant. If we know where Bobby will make his next payoff drop, we can let Leon Fender know. The kind of people we're talking about? You don't want to take them on with a half-baked plan and an attitude. We turn it over to Fender and let the cops pick him up."

"Sounds kind of pussy to me," she said, after a few seconds.

"How long did you work for Sheldon Moon?" I asked.

"Six months before he caught the plague and died."

"How many field cases did you work in that time?"

"A half dozen. Mostly backing up Jack Delroy. I had to pack some supervised hours before I earned my ticket. Why do you ask?"

"You never earned your gold shield. You were a good street cop, but there's a difference between patrol and investigations. You have instincts, but you are so raw. Someone like Delroy or Moon might have been able to throttle you back a little."

"Or you?"

"You could do worse. So far, your private eye highlights have involved sleeping with the guy you're staking out, the murder of your client, and spending weeks in jail on a homicide beef. I am not encouraged by your career trajectory."

"So what? We work different sides of the street, Gold. You're the old guard. You have rules and codes and shit you have to follow. You do things your way, and I'll do them mine."

"Let's leave it here, then," I said. "You do your thing. If you find yourself in over your head, and I suspect that will be a weekly occurrence for you, give me a ring. Sometimes we all need backup."

"Yeah," she said. I waited for the snark. Instead, she said, "Thanks for covering Sahakian for me. I'll work on Demarest and Dallie somehow."

"What about Palyenko?"

"I wouldn't dial up that animal with *your* finger. If he has Bobby tied up in a basement somewhere, Palyenko can keep him. Serves the bastard right. Besides, if we strike out with the other three, we'll already know it's him."

I couldn't argue with her logic.

THIRTY-TWO

Phyllis Bagdasarian had told me her husband hardly ever ventured near his used food business. As soon as I parked in the gravel lot outside, I understood why. I was surprised the EPA hadn't declared it a supersite.

I was glad I hadn't dressed in any really nice clothes, because after this visit I'd probably have to burn what I was wearing.

Bagdasarian's plant was inside a hundred thousand square foot prefab steel building in an industrial ghetto south of the city. While I was there, three different trucks backed up to the loading docks in the rear to offload the detritus from a hundred restaurants across the bay area. None of it smelled fresh. I missed my COVID mask.

Ruben Sahakian stood at the front desk chatting with the receptionist when I walked into the main office. His face darkened when he saw me. I think he flexed a little..

"Thanks for seeing me," I said. I extended my hand. He stared at it as if he couldn't decide whether it was a booby trap or an olive branch. Finally, he took it in a half-hearted grasp.

"Sam Brownlee is a friend," he said. He glanced quickly at the receptionist. The message was clear. She wasn't completely read in on all of her boss's dealings. "How's he doing?"

"Holding up," I said. "He's looked better."

"I can imagine. Why don't we go to my office? More private there. Pamela, please hold my calls."

Sahakian's office was drab and spartan.

"You don't spend a lot of time here," I said.

"Would you?" he asked. "The last thing I ever expected was to wind up as a garbage man. This place smells like the ass end of Hell. It's even worse in the back, where we keep the fermentation tanks. Look, Gold. I think we got off on the wrong foot at Rhonda's funeral. Then the cops came to arrest Sam, and there was no chance to…well, I'm sorry if I came on too strong with you. It was an emotional time."

"I can understand completely. Especially given the special nature of your relationship with Rhonda." I waited to see if I had struck a nerve.

He raised his eyebrows. He nodded once or twice.

"I wondered whether she told Sam. That's what he meant when he requested that I answer all your questions?"

"It's a start," I lied.

"He's not angry with me?"

"Sam? I don't think it was that sort of marriage, Mr. Sahakian. Unless you killed her, that is."

"Please. Call me Ruben. And I didn't kill her. I can account for my time that day."

"Nice to know. In any case, he has a lot more on his mind than his wife's dalliances."

"I can imagine. What can I tell you?"

"I already know about your business arrangement with Brownlee," I said. "It's an extension of your arrangement here with Armin Bagdasarian. Diversification, you might call it. You take a big pile of dirty money and turn it into a little pile of clean money. A little clean money invested in a high-profit, low-risk endeavor like loansharking can become a big pile of money again in no time. No judgment, you understand."

"Of course," he said. "And it was obvious you figured all of this out last year, based on the questions you asked my wife."

"Spur of the moment thing. Occurred to me literally a second before I asked her. I probably could have been more diplomatic. Did she know about your affair with Rhonda Brownlee?"

"No."

"Are you certain?"

He paused. "No," he said. "Not certain. Confident. Why do you ask?"

"Someone killed Rhonda. Someone drove Sam Brownlee's car to the cabin before Rhonda died and stayed there until hours afterward. Your wife Gigi arranged for Rhonda and Julia Wanamaker to obtain fake identities, as she has for other women in the past. She knew where Rhonda and Julia went in Stinson Beach."

"Because Gigi had a brief fling with Julia there," Ruben said. "I'm saving you the discomfort of informing me. I already know. I'm a Stanford man, Mr. Gold. I can see where this is going. Yes, Gigi and Julia have been close friends for years. Some years closer than others. Julia and Tom donate a great deal of money to the shelter. I strongly support my wife's work. Using my father's connections, I helped her locate the forgers she uses to generate the new identities. Gigi and I have visited Tom and Julia's cabin on Mount Tam. Several times, in fact."

"If Gigi discovered you and Rhonda were having an affair?" I asked, leaving the rest of the question in the air between us.

"I can imagine your next question," he said. "Where was Gigi when Rhonda was murdered in Julia's cabin?"

"All right then. Where was she?"

He aged ten years before my eyes. "I don't know," he said. "I have no idea."

Ruben excused himself a few seconds later. He didn't give a reason. He just said, "Stay here," and left the room.

When he returned minutes later, he was more buoyant. His eyes were bright. He sniffed a couple of times before he sat down.

"Where were we?" he asked.

"Did you just snort a line, Ruben?"

"Uh, yeah. You want some? I figured you were on duty—"

"That's cops, and no, I don't want some. Kinda interested in why you did, though."

He held up his hands and squinted at me. "I got a problem, man."

"One might infer."

"You try hanging out in this place twenty hours a week. It smells like someone shit and puked in an abattoir. Armin and Phyllis are out sunning and fucking on their cabin cruiser in the bay, while I'm here day in and day out waiting for my sinuses to collapse from the stink. Sometimes I just gotta stuff something else up there to get through the day. Now, it's possible my wife is a murderer. Yeah, I did a fuckin' line. Maybe I'll run down the hall and do another one, because you are harshing the shit out of my buzz right now."

"Let's take five," I said. "Talk about something else."

"What?"

"You ever heard the name Bobby Sladen?"

"No. Who's Bobby Sladen?"

"A guy in another case. Different situation. He borrowed three-quarters of a million to buy half a radio station, but he couldn't come up with the money to buy the rest of it, and he's paying someone twenty large a month. Thought it might be you or your dad."

"Tiger doesn't trust me with taking on that sort of obligation yet. Working my way up to it using Sam. Or I was."

"While you were putting it to his wife?"

"You said no judgments."

"You call your dad *Tiger?*"

"Everyone calls him Tiger. Tigran. Tiger."

"Would Tiger take on that loan?"

"I didn't say *you* could call him Tiger," Ruben said, his eyes glittering. I had a feeling he'd done more than one line in his absence. He reached out and slapped my thigh. "I'm fuckin' with you, Gold. I mean, whatever you think of me is probably abso-fuckin'-lutely true. I could have you killed with a phone call, you know."

"You could try. Others have failed."

"Aw, fuck it. I won't, because, for some reason, I like you. But I could. You should never forget that."

"Sounds like the foundation for a beautiful long-term friendship," I said.

"So what? You want me to ask Tiger if he's taking regular vig from this guy—what's his name?"

"Bobby Sladen."

Ruben scribbled something on his desk blotter with a Mont Blanc pen and reached for the telephone. Seconds later, he said, "Ruben. Want to ask Tiger something."

He drummed his desktop with the fingers of his free hand.

"On hold," he said. "No respect."

"Family," I said.

"I know. Right? Oh! Hi, Crystal…Yeah, Ruben…Is he…Yeah. Sure." More drumming. Ruben rolled his eyes and pantomimed shooting himself in the temple. He must have been reading my mind.

Finally, he got through. "Tiger?...Quick question…Did we make a three-quarter million loan to a guy named…" He checked the desk blotter. "…Bobby Sladen?"

He listened, and said, "I'm doing a favor for Sam Brownlee, might help him get out of the joint…Yeah…Hold a sec."

He covered the mouthpiece with his palm.

"Who you working for?" he asked.

"Sam's attorney. Wilson Varnadore," I said.

Ruben uncovered the mouthpiece. "Great White," he said. "Yeah. Hold on."

He covered the mouthpiece again.

"He never heard of Sladen, but he and Varnadore are occasional golf partners. Wants to know if you want him to put the word out, find out who gave him the loan."

"He'd do that?"

"Sam Brownlee made us a lot of money, Gold. If he's cleared, he can make more. Tiger's a pragmatic man."

"Sure, then. I'd appreciate it."

"You'll owe him, you know. Or, rather, The Shark will."

"Considering Varnadore's hourly rates, I think everyone will come out of this in the black," I said.

Ruben asked his father to check out the source of Sladen's loan, and to get back with him. After he hung up the phone, his face grew somber again.

"Scoring points with my dad, I may have lost my focus."

"Gigi," I said. "We really need to know where she was the day Rhonda died."

"And if her alibi doesn't float?" He shook his head. "Fuck it. We'll burn that bridge when we get to it. I'll ask."

"Let me," I said. "I'm being paid for it."

In the year since Rhonda's funeral, Gigi Sahakian had grown her hair out. It fell past her shoulders, pulled back with a pink scrunchie. Her attitude toward me hadn't improved. She grimaced when I appeared in the doorway to her office.

"Mr. Gold," she said. "It's been a while."

"I last saw you at Rhonda's funeral," I said.

She shuddered. "How horrible. The police barged in and arrested Sam. So shocking. Rhonda would have been appalled. I felt so sorry for her, to go out on such a terrible note."

"As I recall, you were still angry at her at the time for welshing on the fifty-thousand-dollar donation."

"What are you saying?"

"I'm working for Wilson Varnadore, Sam Brownlee's attorney," I said. "Mr. Varnadore and I are following up on Brownlee's claims that he was framed for his wife's murder."

"You mean you think you've discovered a way to instill just enough reasonable doubt to hang the jury?" she asked. "I've spent a hefty chunk of my life in courtrooms. I know how the game is played—most often to a woman's disadvantage."

"I can imagine you've seen your share of tragedy in courtrooms over the years."

"What do you want?"

"Tying up loose ends. Filling in blanks. Dotting the 'I's."

"Blowing smoke up my ass," she said. "You're nowhere near as artful as you think. Please ask your questions. I'm busy."

"Do you recall your whereabouts on the day Rhonda Brownlee died?"

"I'm sure I was here. I'm here every day."

"Do you keep some kind of log that shows when you're here and when you aren't?"

"I don't punch a clock, if that's what you mean. I'm salaried. I'm here when I'm needed here, which has been twenty-four-seven since the pandemic lifted. A lot of women found out more than they wanted to know about their partners during quarantine."

"An appointment book, then, or perhaps you documented contact with one of your clients—"

"Guests." She corrected automatically.

"Guests then. Maybe a counseling note or an intake report that shows you were here."

"Am I a suspect now?" she asked. "This doesn't sound like filling in the blanks. You already said you and Varnadore think Sam Brownlee is innocent. Are you trying to put me in his place?"

"Not if you can verify your whereabouts. I'm not talking about me, now. If we can demonstrate that Sam couldn't have killed his wife, the police are going to do some checking up on their own. It's better if I can tell them up front that you're in the clear. Better for you, better for the shelter. You do want to avoid bad publicity."

"Why me? What makes me such an attractive alternative?"

"A confluence of circumstance. You knew for months that Rhonda was going to run. You helped both Rhonda and Julia buy new identities. You knew they went to The Journey's Inn, and you knew how to get to Tom and Julia Wanamaker's cabin where Rhonda died. You'd had an affair with Julia, however brief. Seeing her so close to Rhonda stirred something in you, perhaps homicidal resentment."

"Oh, please!" She laughed. "You were doing fine right up until the melodramatic flourish at the end."

"You had a better chance of knowing where Rhonda was than anyone else. And you had motive."

"You mean I knew Ruben was putting it to Rhonda."

Sometimes, my eyebrows raise on their own accord, no matter how hard I try to control them.

"Yeah. I knew about it," she said.

"How'd you find out?" I asked.

"How else? Julia. One thing about the Real Housewives. These bitches can't keep secrets for shit. And, for some reason, they all want to dump their shit on me."

"One of those faces," I said. "You knew Rhonda stayed at the cabin when Julia took off for Santa Barbara, because Julia outlined her plans before they left. Rhonda was sleeping with your husband, and with your occasional squeeze Julia, and now they were running off together, using papers you arranged for them, to live the high life on the Mexican Riviera or wherever while you languish, chained to this shelter like Prometheus to his eternal rock."

"You're reading way too much into this," she said.

"It all goes away with an ironclad alibi," I said. "In any case, I'm not here to bust your chops. I really am clearing up loose ends, and you're a big one. Inconsistencies are someone else's problem to deal with. Varnadore has enough already to establish reasonable doubt. If I were you, I'd anticipate a subpoena soon. And, if Brownlee is released, that alibi will come in handy when the police come calling."

"I'll keep that in mind. Now, if you don't mind, I have a thousand tasks—"

"Why did Rhonda run away?" I asked. "She's dead now. Nobody can touch her. What was she so afraid of that she felt the necessity to change her entire identity, empty a couple of bank accounts, and disappear?"

She chewed on her lower lip. "Same answer as last time," she said. "You'd have to ask her."

"A little late."

"Yes. But I'm not responsible for that. Mr. Gold, I see a thousand women in distress every year, from all social strata and all walks of life. If I allowed myself to become emotionally entangled with their tragedies, I'd have stuck the loud end of a pistol in my mouth years ago. Being in my business requires a certain level of detachment."

"Business," I said.

"Yes. Non-profit, to be sure, but we still maintain a balanced budget each year. We take in money not from sales but from donations and grants. Everything we take in, we spend on consumables and shelter upkeep, salaries for the staff, insurance on the property, and incidentals. So, while we don't manufacture or distribute a product or make a profit, we are a business, and our books always balance."

"But Rhonda Brownlee wasn't a guest at the shelter. She was your friend. Do you avoid uncomfortable entanglements with your friends as well, Ms. Sahakian?"

"She was sleeping with my husband," Gigi said. "Rhonda wasn't a friend. She was a rival. I'd have paid for her new identity myself if it got her a million miles from Ruben. I didn't care why she was running. I was just glad to get rid of her."

"Not helping," I said. "If I were you, I'd figure out where I was the day Rhonda died. The police may be curious down the road."

THIRTY-THREE

Heidi had scrounged tickets to the touring company of *Mean Girls*. I'm not a musical theater kind of guy, but Tina Fey makes me laugh, and I felt the need to immerse myself in something saccharine before plunging back into the distasteful lives of Sam Brownlee and his sybarite circle of friends.

I'm enough of an old stick-in-the-mud to treat a night at the theater like a special event, with a suit and everything—but no tie. Ties were still for weddings, funerals, and court only. The theater no longer rated. It was also an opportunity to show Heidi a classy evening on the town.

I took her to dinner at Chapeau. We shared the escargot app because we are at heart banal tourists. Being, in addition, an eloquent troglodyte, I ordered the filet with duck fat potatoes and creamed spinach. Heidi indulged in the cassoulet, which came in a tureen only slightly smaller than the Roman Colosseum when it was flooded to stage naval battles. We split a full bottle of Pierre Ravaut Cotes de Nuits-Villages, because I was feeling spendy, and we were close enough to stumble to the theater if necessary.

"How's the case going?" Heidi asked, the candlelight from the table centerpiece flickering in her aqua eyes.

"Cases," I said.

"Thought you were finished with Polly or Dolly or whatever her name is."

"Libby. Got her out of jail, but the real killer is still out there somewhere, awaiting apprehension."

"Killer. Sounds like a job for the police. Or O.J."

"Leon Fender's on it."

"What's he like?"

"Good cop. Thorough investigator. I think he has the right stuff. Only problem is he's tethered to Dexter Spears."

"Why doesn't he just shoot himself now and avoid years of torment?"

The waiter, ever attentive, raised an eyebrow as he freshened her glass.

"You don't know who Dexter Spears is, do you?" I asked.

I'd never told her about Frank Raymond and how he walked into a fatal trap I'd set for Dexter Spears, proving my entire case theory wrong. I'd been convinced Spears was the dirty cop. I'd never imagined it was really my own former partner, and that he'd shown up with the intent to kill me. It was one of my luckiest days. Frank wasn't so fortunate.

Some shit you keep locked away. Life runs more smoothly that way.

"I know you. If you don't like this Shears fellow, he's obviously a bad character."

"Spears, and he's not so much bad as he is lazy and privileged."

"Brown-noser?"

"Nephew of the guy who browns noses," I said.

"A nepo baby." She sipped at the wine. "Can we survive another bottle?"

"Depends on whether you plan to get to the theater before the second act."

"It's early yet. So, reading between the lines, your guy with the right stuff, Fender, might make better headway in the case if he weren't paired with lazy and privileged Dexter Spears."

"I think he might have solved it already without Spears. Arresting Libby put them two weeks behind on the case. Time for detectives is everything. The longer a case sits, the worse your chance of solving it. Spears is a political animal. Libby didn't leave the SFPD under the friendliest terms. The chief of detectives, a horndog bozo named Metterling, had a hard-on for her, in both connotations. First he wanted her. After she quit, he wanted her head on a pike. Dexter was wired right into Metterling's office. Between them and their limp-dick attempt to frame Libby, they probably blew any chance of finding the real killer."

"But they did not factor in *you,*" she said.

"It's Libby's case. As part of the settlement with the department, she kept her ticket. Damn thing is practically bulletproof now. She's got private eye tenure. Hell, I don't even rate that. The guy she was sleeping with when Arlen Drake was murdered has gone missing. He owes somebody a lot of money. She thinks she might be able to run him to ground. I'm just providing support services, finding information for her on the fly."

"You're going to adopt her, you know," Heidi said, without a trace of jealousy.

"Adopt her?" I sliced off a perfectly seared sliver of the filet, speared a mushroom, and allowed them to melt in my mouth.

"Like Sonny. I've been with you too long, Gold. You're an easy read. You're slowing down."

"Am not," I said, reaching for my wine glass. "I'm just more intentional these days."

"You can fight bad guys till the cows come home, but you can't fight the calendar. Don't kid yourself. There's no ugly portrait in your attic, my love. Your life lives on your face. Having someone younger, faster, maybe tougher around for backup is not a bad idea. Besides, I think you like Libby. I think you see something in her, like you did with Sonny."

"She tossed away her shot at a gold shield, rather than submit to a scumbag chief detective. She walked away from the job because of her principles."

"So did you."

"She'd be a handful, being so rough around the edges," I said. "Street smart, but way too cocky."

"I recall a young cocky detective a few decades ago who put a guy in the hospital for trying to steal my bank bag. That guy had some brass balls."

"She can't quote Rabelais," I said.

"Rabelais is *so* overrated," she said. "And, after a while, kind of tedious. So, are you taking Libby under your wing?"

"We'll see how things work out."

"Because, before you do, she and I need to meet. You don't adopt a baby detective without bringing her home to Mama first."

THIRTY-FOUR

I planned to track down and interview Laura Hope, Sam Brownlee's personal assistant, the next morning. I had just booted my computer when Leon Fender stomped up my steps and into my office.

He wasn't happy.

Behind his glasses, his eyes looked bloodshot, like he'd spent all night poring over witness statements. In a bar.

"Inspector," I said.

"Fuck you, man." He slumped into one of the chairs in front of my desk and hung his arms over the back. "Metterling's on the way out."

"Varnadore informed me. If it helps, your name never came up in the conversation."

"Shit, man. It didn't need to. You think people in this town don't talk? Cops, especially? Everyone knows the story about Hackney and Metterling. She wasn't shy about it when she left. They also know you've been cooperating with my investigations. These people are detectives, Gold. They're every bit as smart as you, most of them smarter."

"Debatable."

"They can figure shit out. I'm getting the stink-eye around the shop."

"Metterling's a scumbag," I said. "If you were responsible for him getting the boot, you should get a medal, but in fact you didn't tell me anything that was substantive anyway. Libby told me the entire story, which I relayed to the Shark, who talked things over with the commissioner and the chief. At the very worst, you put the idea in my head. And remember, I'm a pretty smart cookie too. I know how to make inferential guesses."

"You make a decent living as a private cop?"

"Ebbs and flows," I said. "Mostly flows the last several years. I'm usually bucks-up. My IRA is fully vested, but I'm not in the mood to yank the ripcord yet. And forget whatever you're thinking. You're good and I don't need competition. Besides, I might be taking on someone soon anyway."

"Hackney?"

"Why do you say that?"

"Just a hunch. And I like a regular paycheck anyway. Okay. When I started up your fuckin' stairs, I was primed to ream you out for putting me under the heat lamp at Eight-Fifty Bryant. You're right, though. Metterling was a dipshit of the first order. He didn't just harass the women recruits. He's also a racist douchebag. People talk. I heard things he said at my promotion review. I've harbored some disgusting violent fantasies about that dude lately. So I'm glad he's gone. You might not be, though."

"Why?"

"Seniority, dude. Shit doesn't always flow downhill."

"Don't say it," I said.

"Dexter Spears is in line for Metterling's office."

"The best laid plans," I said.

"Gang aft fuckin' agley," he finished. "On the upside, I won't have him as my senior partner anymore. On the other hand, now I have to trudge upstairs to kiss his ass."

"Captain of Major Crimes is a political office," I said. "Spears is a political animal. They're substituting one *apparatchik* for another."

"So you better have some good fuckin' news for me, Gold. I am fresh out of disappointment and am bordering on irritation."

"Varnadore is convinced Brownlee is going down for his wife's murder," I said. "But he plans to appeal, obviously. Taking the hit on the initial trial gives him time to prep for the appeals."

"And gives you time to dig up fresh dirt for reasonable doubt."

"I think we might be ahead of schedule. If anyone with the police had some concerns about Brownlee's guilt, they'd profit from talking with a woman named Gigi Sahakian."

"Why?"

"Because she arranged for Rhonda Brownlee to buy the new identity. Gigi's husband Ruben Sahakian—"

"*Tiger's* son?"

"Am I the only person in San Francisco who didn't know this?" I asked.

"So he is Tiger Sahakian's son?"

"Yeah."

"Oh, I'm hating the shit out of this already. Okay, give me all of it."

"Ruben Sahakian was having an affair with Rhonda Brownlee at the time she disappeared. Gigi Sahakian knew about it. She arranged for Rhonda to obtain phony papers partly to get rid of her. Rhonda wasn't only sleeping with Ruben Sahakian, she was also having a walk on the wild side with Julia Wanamaker."

"You got a lot of circumstance here, Gold."

"Enough to establish motive. But there's more. I braced Gigi yesterday at the women's shelter she runs. She couldn't account for her whereabouts on the day Rhonda was killed."

"Okay."

"Gigi also had a fling with Julia Wanamaker, a couple of years ago. She knew about the Journey's Inn in Stinson Beach, and she knew about the Mount Tam cabin, because Julia had taken her to both of them. Julia told Gigi about her plans to leave Rhonda at the cabin and split for Santa Barbara, so Gigi knew Rhonda was up there alone. What better opportunity to take Rhonda out of the picture entirely? And now she can't account for her time that day? Who doesn't know what they were doing the day their husband's paramour was murdered?"

"It's a good story," Fender said. "Not good enough for the DA yet."

"But it's good enough to sway a jury. Juries are made up of people who watch way too much TV. They expect a surprise revelation in the third act. Gigi just gave Varnadore everything he needs. It occurs to me that this is the sort of thing the SFPD would want to be on top of. Nothing is more embarrassing than getting caught flat-footed in court."

"Excellent!" Wilson Varnadore said, displaying what I thought for an instant was a double row of ivory-white teeth. I blinked and tried to remember the last time I'd had a full night of sleep. "We may not have to take Brownlee's case to appeal after all. I think I can establish reasonable doubt with this."

We were in his fishbowl office overlooking downtown. He'd poured two fingers of Macallan for me to sip on while I outlined what I had learned.

"There are a few hitches in the story," I said. "Brownlee's Caddy being the biggest. I still need to figure out who drove it to the cabin."

"The devil's in the details."

"I plan to interview Laura Hope, Brownlee's former personal assistant. She knew the access code for Brownlee's garage pad, and she knew Brownlee kept spare key fobs on a hanger in the kitchen. She knew almost everything about him, and I mean everything."

"They were sleeping together?"

"According to Brownlee, a whole lot before she went to work for him, and once in a blue moon after that. Twice in the six months leading up to Rhonda's murder."

"Jealousy as a motive?" he asked.

"You've seen Jack Bludis's murder book. She alibied out. She was at a brunch meeting in San Francisco around the time Rhonda died. Had the credit card receipt to prove it. Hard to impeach a time-stamped image from American Express. I don't see her as a suspect. Someone took that car out, though, and it sure as hell wasn't Rhonda. Sam Brownlee still maintains he was out cold from sleeping pills. The only other person we know who had access was Laura Hope."

"Or maybe Sam or Rhonda shared the keypad code with someone else. A neighbor, perhaps."

"Somebody shared it with somebody," I said. "I already asked Brownlee. He denied giving it to anybody but Laura. I don't know whether Rhonda shared it with anyone else. The only other person to ask is Laura Hope."

"On another matter," Varnadore said, "I've heard from Libby."

"She's working for you too?"

"Hardly. She's still a client, though. I understand she's on the warpath, searching for Bobby Sladen."

"She asked me to pitch in with her, but I'm tied up with this Brownlee case."

"I worry about her, Gold. She has good instincts, but she's like a Great Dane puppy. I think they forgot to install her fear button. She's likely to get herself into trouble."

"My girlfriend Heidi thinks I should take her under my wing," I said. "Teach her the ropes the right way. She doesn't have to learn everything through trial and error—mostly error."

"No," Varnadore said. "I'd consider it a personal favor if you'd keep an eye on her. Don't let it interfere with the Brownlee case. We're back in the courtroom on Tuesday. The more noise I can throw at the jury, the better, and you're digging up some juicy tidbits. If Libby gets in over her head, though, I can live with less ammo in the courtroom. This Bobby Sladen character might be missing for a reason other than personal choice. Somebody might not like Libby poking around."

"If she calls, I'll help out," I said.

THIRTY-FIVE

I was halfway to Laura Hope's condo when my telephone rang. The Bluetooth screen on the dash said it was a blocked ID. Probably someone tracking me down to talk about my extended car warranty, but in my profession, it seldom pays to send a call to voicemail.

"Gold," a voice said on the other end when I answered. Ruben Sahakian.

"Mr. Sahakian," I said.

"My wife got a call from a cop named Fender," he said. "You have anything to do with that?"

"I cannot tell a lie," I said. "Especially to guys who can make me disappear with a single phone call. Gigi couldn't pin down her whereabouts the day Rhonda was murdered. When I left her, she said she'd check her records. I passed it along to Fender. I'm kind of surprised he followed up on it so quickly."

"Why?"

"They have their guy. He's already on trial. She knew about you and Rhonda, by the way. The whole thing. That isn't good for her."

"I can't believe it," he said. "You'd have to show me solid evidence that she did it for me to cave on this one. We don't have a perfect marriage—hell, who in my business does?—but I think we know one another well enough. I can't see her doing it."

"Not for me to decide," I said. "I just shake the trees and gather the fruit that falls. If she alibis out, nobody would be happier than me. If she doesn't…" I let the rest hang.

"Got something for you," he said. "That Bobby Sladen thing. Tiger asked around. You want to talk to Boyd Demarest."

"Why am I not surprised?" I said.

"How so?"

"Demarest is exactly the kind of Aryan Brotherhood ratshit who ruins my day just by waking up each morning. Remember when all the gangs were just ethnic?"

"Hey, white's sort of ethnic," Ruben said. "And is that a crack? Tiger and I are Armenian."

"Right now, you're almost on my side," I said. "I would never risk that by insulting you."

"Douchebag."

"You could snort a line if it will make you feel better."

"Remember what I told you, Gold. One phone call."

"Thanks for the tip, Ruben. And thank your father for me. I hope Gigi's cleared right away."

"Tiger's gonna want more than a thank-you," Ruben said. "But he appreciates the gesture."

As soon as I hung up on Ruben Sahakian, I hit the speed dial for Libby Hackney.

She answered, and we both simultaneously said, *"Boyd Demarest!"*

A second later, we both said, *"Shit."*

"How'd you find out?" she asked.

"Ruben Sahakian."

"Tiger's boy?"

I sighed. "Yes. His wife is a person of interest in the Brownlee case."

"And he cooperated with you?"

"I suspect they enjoy a strange and unique relationship."

"She's strange and he's unique. Old joke," she said.

"Where'd you get the name?" I asked.

"I called him."

"Just like that?"

"We had four possibilities, and you were going after Sahakian. Marcus Dallie told me to ram it. Demarest was the next name down the list. Told him I was Bobby Sladen's girlfriend. Said if that didn't mean anything, to hang up. He didn't hang up."

"Did he confirm lending Sladen the money?" I asked.

"He wants a meeting. I told him I wanted to bring backup. So, you wanna back me up?"

"Did Jack Delroy already turn you down?"

"Yeah. What about it?"

I hung up on her.

My phone rang five seconds later.

"We got cut off," she said.

"Sure we did," I said.

I hung up again.

My phone rang.

"I can do this all day," I said.

"It would be easier to say yes," she said.

"Heidi says I'm going to adopt you," I said.

"Who's Heidi? And why do I need adopting?"

"We'll discuss it later. When's the meet?"

"This afternoon. Four-thirty."

"Where?"

"I'll text you the address. You're coming, right?"

"I have a couple of wits to interview for Varnadore. I should be finished by then. You sure you want to do this? I'd recommend you call Inspector Fender first. We both came up with this loanshark angle together. He's already read into it."

"I want to be there," she said. "I want to look in Bobby's eyes when we finally run him to ground, and I want him to know I was the one who put his face in the dirt."

"Sounds fun. Backup's nice, too."

"That's why I'm calling you. If I trot in there with an SFPD inspector, nobody's gonna talk to me at all. You at least have some street cred."

"Some?"

"More than me. So. Are you in?"

I thought it over.

"I'll call you when I'm done with the interviews," I said.

THIRTY-SIX

When Brownlee said he'd taken care of Laura Hope, he wasn't kidding. Her condo was a few blocks from mine, in a building I'd coveted for some time. Being out of a job hadn't affected her standard of living at all, at least outwardly.

She answered the door within seconds of my ring. She was taller than average, but still only came up to my collarbone. Her hair was long and straight and silky brown. It fell below her shoulders. Her face was pale and freckled. She had a nice smile. Nice everything. I handed her my card and explained I was working for Varnadore on behalf of Sam Brownlee. She invited me inside immediately.

"How is Sam?" she asked. "I haven't seen him in months. On the television, he looks haggard." She had a cultivated voice. Seven Sisters accent. Professional. The kind of voice you associate with money and 1930s movie actresses.

"You haven't attended the trial?" I asked.

"Appearances. Sam's idea. He wants to protect me from the fallout."

"Sounds like he's taking the fall for you," I said. I pushed it with a little smile that suggested I was only half-joking.

"Is this going to be *that* sort of conversation?" she asked.

"Just clearing away the loose ends," I said. "I understand the police talked with you, and you established a concrete alibi, so I don't think you have to worry."

"I was at brunch with Mitzi Coltrane and Barbara Lanziger. I gave the police the receipt for the bill."

"Yes. Inspector Fender told me. I'm more interested in your visit with Sam Brownlee the night before."

That rocked her. "I…the night before?" she asked.

"You dropped by Brownlee's house to have some papers signed. That was between seven-thirty and eight o'clock. You drank a glass of wine and left around nine-thirty. Is that correct?"

"Why, yes. Now that I recall it, I did drop by that evening. Sam hadn't been by his office in days, because he was caught up in Rhonda's disappearance. Some papers piled up and needed signatures."

"And you slept with him as well?"

"No!" She almost squealed it. The Seven Sisters accent vanished. "Oh, my God, no. Not that night. Did Sam say we slept together?"

"You did have an affair with him, though." I didn't state it as a question.

"That's been over for…well a long time."

"Not entirely over."

I had her hooked. She was convinced I knew everything about her. Once they think they have nothing to hide, the lips loosen really quickly.

"How recently had you slept together before Rhonda disappeared?"

"It wasn't like that. Tawdry hotels and such. After I came to work with Sam, we had sex maybe three times. Once was here in my condo, but the others were in his office. Both times we were working late. We just got frisky and said nobody would care if we took another lap around the park. Quickies, both of them. The last time was a few weeks before Rhonda died. Before that, months."

"That was a satisfactory arrangement for you?"

"Not at all."

"Really?" I said.

"It was impulsive and irresponsible. I would have preferred not to have sex with Sam at all, if it was all pointless and empty. We broke up in the first place because I knew he'd never leave Rhonda, and I didn't want to waste my time on a dead-end love affair. Neither did I savor becoming one of those tacky homewreckers. I was a little surprised when Sam called to offer me an assistant position. He reassured me that I came to mind when the position opened because of my previous administrative experience. Said he was out of town a lot. He needed somebody he trusted running the company in his absence."

"Did he say why he was out of town a lot?"

"Didn't have to. I made his travel plans. I already knew. That was my role, Mr. Gold. I was supposed to anticipate what Sam needed almost before he knew it himself. I was privy to all his business dealings."

"Including loansharking?"

"I kept the books on that end of the business. Yes. Usury was a primary foundation of Sam's legitimate businesses."

"Along with infusions of cash from the Armenian mob."

"Mr. Gold, you may represent Sam Brownlee, but there are some matters I believe even he would prefer to remain confidential."

"He's already told me he was taking in money from Tiger Sahakian by way of Armin Bagdasarian. That's how he funded the loans. We both know those loans were never going to be paid off.

The vig was guaranteed lifetime income. Free, clean money. Inspector Fender knows about this as well. We aren't telling stories out of school here. I just wanted to make sure you were in the loop."

"Why?"

"Curiosity, mostly. Because I don't know, and I've discovered that stuff I don't know often comes back to bite me on the—" I stopped and smiled. "But I'm getting off topic. You knew about the money laundering for Tiger Sahakian?"

She nodded. "Yes," she said, quietly. "I warned Sam about it."

"How so?"

"He told me he had an opportunity to expand the lending business. An angel had shown up with a lot of cash to invest."

"An angel," I said. "He used that term?"

"I recall it specifically. I recognized immediately that he was falling in with gangsters. I suppose, by then, I'd become less sensitized to the idea of shady dealings. Even so, I couldn't see this sort of deal ending well for Sam. He was starstruck, though. Had dollar signs in his eyes. He told me once that he learned years ago never to let an opportunity pass by. Said you'll miss every shot you don't take. He took his shot."

"You were in love with him," I said.

She smiled. "Does it matter, Mr. Gold? Some stories are not intended to end happily."

"You knew the combination for Brownlee's garage."

"Yes."

"And the code to his security system?"

"Yes. I also know his bank card PIN and his computer passwords. Since Rhonda died before him, I'm now the executor of his estate. I told you. Sam trusted me to run the business in his absence."

"How did Rhonda feel about you being so close to her husband?"

"We never discussed it. To tell you the truth, she was seldom around."

"Convenient."

"Not at all. It was obvious Sam still had…feelings. He didn't consider our relationship to be in the past."

"It wasn't, at least three times after he hired you."

"I've already explained that. In any case, Rhonda's frequent absences only increased the pressure on me to spend more time with Sam."

"You explained that you had sex with Sam two weeks before Rhonda died. Impulse or not, that's a razor's edge, timewise. One might infer you were in an active affair with Brownlee at the time his wife was murdered."

"I'm sure, as a private investigator, you see your share of infidelity," she said. "Not all of it is conspiratorial. Sometimes, things just happen."

"When you visited Brownlee on the night before the murder, did you happen to notice whether the spare garage door opener and key fobs were on their hooks in the kitchen?"

"That's a detail I wouldn't normally notice, Mr. Gold."

"But you are aware he kept them there?"

"Of course. I simply don't know if they were there that night."

"Do you know why Rhonda ran away?" I asked.

"Not a clue. As I said, we didn't have a great deal of contact. I spent most of my time with Sam at his office. I believe she preferred it that way."

"Because she knew about your affair with Sam?"

"I don't know what she knew. I do know Rhonda wasn't faithful herself, but I can't say whether it mattered in their marriage. Sam and Rhonda acted…independently of one another."

"Brownlee has been in jail for almost a year, awaiting trial. You haven't found employment since he was arrested."

"I'm still ostensibly working for Sam. I receive a monthly subsistence check that covers all my expenses and then some. It's sort of a retainer. Sam believes he is going to be exonerated, and he'll need me to help get him back up to speed when he's released. He doesn't want me poached by some other company."

"Waiting with a candle in the window," I said. "Now that Rhonda's out of the way, I suppose that will make things between you and Sam easier."

I could almost see the gooseflesh rise on her forearm.

"How do you mean?" she asked.

"No need to sneak around. You said you broke it off with Brownlee because he'd never leave his wife. That obstacle's out of the way."

"I can only imagine the types of people you encounter in your line of work," she said. "I suppose, after a while, you cynically look for the most unsavory motives in everyone."

"That's probably it," I said. "Have you shared the garage keypad codes with anyone, ever? That's the real loose end I needed to cover today, not that the conversation hasn't been scintillating."

"Sam wouldn't keep me as his trusted personal assistant if I got blabby with his personal information. I have never shared any of it with anyone. Would you like to hook me up to a lie detector?"

"Never use them. Between you and me, they're wrong about three quarters of the time. You know what I do trust, though?"

What's that?"

"Human nature."

THIRTY-SEVEN

I'd parked my car illegally in the basement deck at Laura Hope's condo. I wasn't worried. The clergy placard I stuck in the back window worked about ninety-eight percent of the time. I kept a Roman collar and a black tee shirt in the glove compartment for tight pinches.

I sat in my car and processed the conversation with Laura. She fancied herself a master of verbal swordplay and leaned far too heavily on her gold-plated education and pseudo-sophistication. She was a phony, but that didn't necessarily mean anything except that I couldn't trust a word she said.

The important thing was she had provided another sliver of reasonable doubt. Nothing I'd found so far was a smoking gun that would spring Brownlee with a handshake and an apology from the SFPD and the DA. That's not how things ever worked. It was obvious to me, though, that after taking on the investigation when Jack Bludis retired, Dexter Spears hadn't done his due diligence. Once Laura Hope established her alibi—brunching with friends—he'd stopped looking into her. Leon Fender had good reason to be uncomfortable with the progress of the case against Sam Brownlee. Spears had taken a lot of shortcuts.

I dialed Fender. He answered on the second ring.

"What'cha got, Gold?" he asked.

"You need to do a deeper dive on Laura Hope," I said.

"She alibied out. Couldn't have done it. End of story."

"She slept with Brownlee only a few days before Rhonda died. She had a more intense affair with him, a year or so before, and broke it off because—get this—he was never going to leave his wife."

"Motive," Fender said.

"Opportunity as well. She could have gotten the Caddy out of Brownlee's garage while he was out cold on Ambien and wine and handed it off to a confederate."

"That doesn't make a shred of sense, Gold. Why frame her boyfriend if her goal was to kill the wife so she could have him herself?"

I thought for a bit.

"Gold? You still there?"

"What if that was the mistake?" I said. "What if taking the Caddy was the fatal error?"

"Did you get any sleep last night?"

"Brownlee had four cars in the garage. Only one was a Cadillac with OnStar. Hear me out. Laura wants to get Rhonda out of the way so she can have Brownlee for herself. We found Julia Wanamaker in Santa Barbara. Maybe Brownlee figured out Rhonda was at the Wanamaker's cabin, somehow, and he told Laura. Laura employs an accomplice. Neither can use their own cars, and Brownlee has four for the taking. Laura gives the confederate the garage keypad code, or maybe she goes there herself before sunrise to take the car. She was there the night before. Who knows? Maybe she slipped something to Brownlee to put him out for twelve hours while she took the car. She hands the car off to her confederate, who drives to Mount Tam and kills Rhonda while Laura is enjoying her avocado toast at brunch."

"Still doesn't wash," Fender said. "We can skip the unknown subject and just say Brownlee and Laura Hope conspired to kill Rhonda so they could be together. We don't need hocus pocus to sell that to a jury."

"No," I said. "You don't. You don't even need Laura Hope, do you?"

"You like this guy Brownlee," Fender said.

"Yeah. If you discount the fact that he's a criminal, he's an okay guy."

"He is kind of charming. Bet he could be pretty convincing, given the opportunity."

"You mean, when a cop comes to inform him his wife is dead?"

"You know what?" Fender said. "I think you need to have a talk with your employer."

After he hung up, I sat in the car and ran through every interview and piece of evidence I'd run across since going to work for Wilson Varnadore. I tumbled them all around inside my head, looking for the inconsistencies and the foul balls. The more I thought, the more I dreaded what I believed would be my ultimate conclusion. When it arrived, I felt like a complete tool.

I don't think Wilson Varnadore appreciated it when I barged past his assistant straight into his office.

"Tell me you don't know he's guilty," I said.

"Brownlee?" Varnadore said, without taking a beat. "Why on earth would I do that?"

"There's a reason people need defense attorneys, and you're the high-priced spread. The higher the billables, the faster the dance. You didn't hire me to prove Brownlee innocent."

"Dear God, no," Varnadore said. "I only wanted to get him acquitted. Double jeopardy, Mr. Gold. It's a beautiful concept. Throw in enough reasonable doubt, muddy the waters, hopelessly confuse a juror or two, and Brownlee will walk out of the courthouse a free man."

"A free man who killed his wife."

"That's conjecture."

"It's the only answer that works. Brownlee really had me fooled. He's quite the con artist. I've run it over and over in my mind. I've come up with a dozen scenarios that explain how his car wound up at the Mount Tam cabin. Only one of them holds water."

"He drove it there," Varnadore said. "I came to the same conclusion weeks ago, after my ninth or tenth tour through the murder book."

"But you hired me—"

"To establish reasonable doubt, as I said. And you've done a marvelous job. Do you know the one question I never, ever ask a client?"

"What?"

"*Did you do it?* Knowing the answer really isn't necessary for me to do my job, and it can be a genuine burden. I'm a defense attorney, Gold. One of the best. Ninety-five percent of my clients are guilty as sin. They don't come to me to prove their innocence. They come to me to minimize the damage to their cushy lives and phony-baloney careers. Did Sam Brownlee drive his Cadillac to Mount

Tam to murder his wife? All the evidence says he did. Do I know it for certain? No."

"Because you never asked."

"And he never offered. Regardless, I intend to use the information you've brought to great advantage in securing his freedom. I am in your debt, except that I'm not any longer. By now, the postman should have delivered your check, including the healthy bonus I mentioned, to your mailbox."

"The bonus was hush money," I said.

"Not at all. I deeply appreciated your contributions. In any case, hush money is unnecessary. I would remind you that any communications between us or with my client are covered under attorney-client privilege. You can't even be compelled to testify to them in court."

"Now I know why they call you The Great White Shark," I said. "Good job. You tied me up like a Christmas roast."

"And this is where I find out whether your reputation for discretion is deserved. I believe our business is concluded; wouldn't you say?"

"And how," I said.

"He did it," I told Fender on the telephone as I drove back to my office.

"Brownlee?"

"Yeah. I can't prove it, but he did it. I really hate being lied to."

"Are we talking about Brownlee or Varnadore?"

"Both. And I've already said everything I'm allowed to. I'm even on fucking record testifying that I thought Brownlee was genuinely shocked to find out his wife was dead."

"I was there, remember? He almost fooled me as well. I surmise from your distress that Varnadore intends to use all the stuff you dug up to introduce reasonable doubt. He wants to hang the jury and take his chances that the DA won't refile."

"You're a smart cop."

"Answered without answering. Varnadore really does have you bound up."

"You could say that."

"We have means and opportunity. We're still lacking motive. Why would he kill his wife?"

"At first, I thought it was because of Laura Hope. She was adamant that Brownlee would never leave Rhonda, though. She broke up with him over it. I didn't get the vibe that Laura was more than just a convenient and familiar occasional hump. She's in love with him, which was her motive for the murder, but the timeline just doesn't add up, and as you said, using the Caddy would only implicate Brownlee, ruining her motive. None of it added up until I just accepted that Brownlee did it."

"So it wasn't a love triangle," Fender said.

"Rhonda didn't just leave. She purchased an entirely new identity. People do that when they're scared. Terrified."

"What were she scared of?"

"Whatever it was, it probably got her killed," I said.

"Which means Brownlee's part of it," Fender said.

I thought for a moment. "Julia Wanamaker also purchased a fake identity from Osiris, a few months before Rhonda Brownlee did. I may pay her a visit, but I want to talk to Brownlee first."

THIRTY-EIGHT

"Can we make this quick?" Brownlee asked after the jail attendant left us alone in the interview room. "Lunch is in a half hour. It's Swill Day. Extra chunky. I don't want to miss out."

"I know you did it," I said, shooting him the scowl I reserve for street mimes and door-to-door evangelists.

He shrugged. "Did what?"

"Killed your wife. It's the only explanation that holds water."

"Certainly, you don't expect me to confess," he said. "That would be foolish, considering I'm innocent."

"I'm hung up on the *why,*" I said. "Rhonda was terrified of something, frightened enough to buy a new identity, steal thousands of dollars from your personal accounts, and try to establish a new life elsewhere."

"It really hurt my feelings, you know? I gave her everything."

"I keep going back to our first conversation," I told him. "You compared your marriage to Michael and Kay Corleone in The Godfather. The implication was that the pressures of your criminal enterprises had driven a wedge between you and your wife. You also intimated activities that you couldn't talk about."

"Well, I'm sure not going to talk about them now."

"I don't think you planned to kill her when you hired me. That decision came later."

"You're barking up the wrong tree, Gold."

"I don't think so. I bet you really took Ambien after you killed her, just to have it in your bloodstream in case anyone tested."

"It's a fairy tale, man."

"I asked someone the wrong question. Or maybe the right one, but the wrong one for them. I think you knew all along why your wife ran away."

"Thinking and proving are two different things," he said. "If you could prove I did it, you wouldn't be here badgering me. I think I'm done with you, Gold. Varnadore already told me he's cut you loose. Gave you a hefty bonus on top of it. Why don't you go spend it on a nice holiday with that art dealer girlfriend of yours."

He must have seen the color rise in my face.

"What?" he asked. "You think I didn't check you out? I don't hire a custodian at my office without a thorough background check. I did a deep dive on you, as soon as you and Sonny kicked my guys' asses. Sonny I knew. You, I had to research. I liked what I found, or I wouldn't have hired you. Her name's Heidi, right?"

"Are you trying to intimidate me?" I asked.

"No. Hell, I'm grateful for all you've done, Gold. Because of you, I'm probably getting sprung in a few days. I'll be back in business in a matter of weeks, hauling in all those bushels of cash I love so much. Reasonable doubt. I love that phrase. I owe you, man. I mean it. But you're dead wrong about me and Rhonda."

"I don't think so," I said.

"Too bad about that double jeopardy thing, then. That's a real bitch. Was there anything else? Because I need to get in line for the swill."

After a quick fast-food lunch, I drove to Julia Wanamaker's house. I didn't call first, because I didn't want her to disappear again.

Even before I rang the doorbell, I smelled the cannabis. The aroma worked its way through the jamb. I waited. After a minute, I hit the bell again. I could hear people moving around inside, and I had all afternoon.

The door opened. A woman peered outside through rose-colored eyes and the weed odor intensified.

"Why, Ms. Smith," I said. "You've changed."

She had. Jane Smith, Julia's assistant, had blossomed since my investigation the previous year. She'd done something stylish with her hair and had paid better attention to her makeup. She wore a lace pool coverup over a bikini that revealed curves I had completely missed—or ignored—at our last meeting.

"I'm sorry," she said. "I don't know what you're talking about."

I handed her my card. She squinted at it, and I recalled she had worn glasses a year earlier. The card apparently refreshed her memory.

"Oh," she said. "I…uh…"

"Hey, Smitty!" a man called from inside the house. "Who is it?"

She looked back over her shoulder as a heavyset man wearing swim trunks padded toward the door. His torso was shaped like a flattened basketball, his chest covered with a mat of curly graying hair. His legs, in contrast to his body, were spindly and hairless below the knee. He was more or less every woman's dream, if they had pervasive daddy issues. He joined Jane Smith in the doorway.

"Help you?" he asked.

And then I smelled it. A curious combination of sardines and garlic that cut through the weed and made me want to back up a step or two. It wasn't revolting as much as unpleasant and unexpected. I'm a tough guy, though. I stood my ground.

Jane Smith handed him my card.

"Ah," he said. "Gold. I know who you are, but we've never met. Tom Wanamaker."

He held out his hand. His eyes were slitted and bloodshot. I shook with him and tried to remember if I had wipes in the glove compartment.

"I don't mean to intrude," I said. "I'm actually looking for your wife."

"Is she missing again?" he asked. "I hadn't noticed."

"Just following up on the Brownlee case. Loose ends. She isn't around, then?"

"Not for several months," he said. "There have been some…changes since last year. Adjustments."

Jane's hand slipped to her side. She reached back and caressed the side of Wanamaker's thigh. I suppressed my gag reflex.

"My wife left me," he said. "Or maybe I threw her out. The memory is still a little hazy. A lot of alcohol was involved. Hey, this is kind of awkward, talking here on the stoop. Why don't you come inside?"

Minutes later, we sat in the living room. Wanamaker had thrown on a seersucker pool robe. A baggie of weed sat open on the coffee table, alongside an impressive hand-blown glass bong. The combination of the weed stench and Wanamaker's unfortunate genetic predisposition produced a head-spinning cloud in the room.

Jane Smith didn't seem to notice, and I was pretty sure Wanamaker had lost the ability to smell himself decades ago.

"I finally got fed up with her theatrics," Wanamaker said. "Never marry a crazy woman, Gold. They're a wild ride, but the cost always exceeds the benefits. After that affair with Rhonda, and after Sam was arrested and charged, I'd had enough. I'm a businessman. I have a reputation. I don't need to be connected with murders and missing person cases. I cancelled an important meeting in New York to dash back across the country because my wife was missing, except she was just on another lark. I told Julia that if she wanted to live under another name, fine with me. She could use the one she was born with."

"And she left shortly after?"

"The next day. I didn't kick her out, but I didn't stop her leaving, either."

I waggled a couple of fingers at Wanamaker and Jane Smith.

"You look cozy. Did…this begin before or after Julia left?"

"Not that it's any of your business, but it was afterward," Jane said.

"Well…" Wanamaker said, cocking his head to one side. Jane punched his side with her elbow and shit-grinned.

"It's not important," I said. "Idle curiosity. Any idea where I can locate Julia?"

"Sure," Wanamaker said. "She's at the cabin. Been there for several months."

"The cabin where Rhonda was murdered?"

"Oh, yeah. You've been there. I almost forgot you found her."

Given the blue haze in the room, I was surprised he could remember his name.

"I'm surprised she'd want to live there, given what happened," I said.

"We gutted it and remodeled after the murder. Soon as the police released it to us. Neither of us wanted to walk in there and think, *Oh, right there is where someone caved Rhonda's head in.*"

"Understandable."

"You wouldn't recognize the inside now. Took it right down to the logs and rearranged the floorplan. Still looks the same on the exterior, but inside it's brand new. Right after we finished, Julia and I had our big split. She said she was going to ask for the cabin in the settlement. I signed it over to her outright."

"Generous," I said.

"Expeditious. She was gonna get it anyway. Julia always gets what she wants. This isn't a rancorous divorce. We're both getting what we want. We might even come out of it as distant friends."

I was halfway out the door before I thought of something else.

"Mr. Wanamaker, when Julia was missing with Rhonda Brownlee last year, Sam called you to ask if you'd talked with Julia, right?"

"I was in New York. I remember it clearly. I called Smitty here right after the call and asked her to file a missing person report."

"By chance, did you mention to Brownlee that they might be at the cabin?"

"Sure I did. He asked me whether they might be off together. It made sense. I suggested they could have just taken a jaunt up to Mount Tam for a few days. I recall it distinctly."

"Thanks," I said. "I'll leave you to your…whatever, now."

THIRTY-NINE

I still had the cabin address in my car GPS, but I didn't need it. The route I'd taken to discover Rhonda Brownlee's body was imprinted on my brain.

I parked in the small gravel lot beside the cabin, next to a metallic blue Beemer, and knocked on the front door. Nothing. I checked the knob. Locked.

I felt the hood of the Beemer. Cold.

Maybe Julia was inside, asleep, and hadn't heard my knock. Maybe she was hiding from me, hoping I'd just give up and drive away. Or, maybe, she was off on a nature hike.

"Looking for me?" a woman said behind me. She walked around the side of the house. For a moment, I didn't connect her with the voluptuous bikini-clad Real Housewife in Santa Barbara a year earlier. She wore a dirty tee shirt and cut-off jeans, with thick cotton socks and sneakers. Her hair was pulled up and stuffed under a woven straw gardening hat. Her face was well-scrubbed and makeup-free. "I know you from somewhere."

The voice was unmistakable.

I handed her my card. "We met last year in Santa Barbara. I was with Inspector Fender of the SFPD."

"Oh, yeah. The hunky silverback with the sexy voice. I remember you. Sorry about being such a mess. I was working in my vegetable garden down the hill out back, and I wasn't expecting a gentleman caller. Please, come inside. I have the air conditioner running."

She led me around to the back door, which opened into the kitchen. She poured me a glass of iced tea.

"Hope you like it southern style," she said.

"What's southern style?"

"That's where you pour in sugar until the spirit voices of your besainted grandmothers say *Enough, child.* Then you pour in a little more. It's an acquired taste. Careful. It'll eat the enamel off your teeth if you let it."

I tasted the tea. I could feel my blood sugar surge.

"I'm tying up some loose ends in the Brownlee murder case," I told her.

"I can't wait to hear all about it," she said. "First, though, I am a sweaty, filthy mess. I must smell like Seabiscuit after the Kentucky Derby. I'm gonna grab a quick shower and get in some clean clothes, and then we can have our talk."

"You aren't going to run away, are you?" I asked.

"Why bother? You'd just chase me down again. You seem to be good at it. Don't suppose you'd like to scrub my back? No. I can tell by your expression you wouldn't. Pity."

———

Fifteen minutes later, she was back on the sofa, with her own glass of tea. Her carmine hair was still damp and slicked back. She'd changed into jeans and an oxford cloth shirt she'd left unbuttoned halfway up and knotted under her breasts. She was barefoot, and despite having retreated to the wilds of Mount Tam, I could tell she religiously kept her mani-pedi appointments. Without makeup, she looked fresh and glowing.

"Now," she said. "Where were we?"

"I only have a few questions, if you don't mind."

"Mind? I'm all ears, honey. I don't get a lot of visitors up here. Talk my ears off if you like."

"Six months before Rhonda Brownlee was murdered, you purchased false identity papers from a man referred to you by Gigi Sahakian," I said.

"I still have them," she said. "That nice police detective didn't take them from me, because he said I wasn't using them for illicit purposes."

"Why did you buy the papers?"

"Oh, I don't know." She twirled a damp ringlet of hair around her index finger. "Romantic whimsy, maybe. Have you never fantasized about running away, Mr. Gold?"

"Never had a lot to run away from," I said. "I'm content with my situation."

"Lucky you. Some of us aren't so fortunate. Try being chained to a man who smells like a garbage scow."

"You never noticed it before you were married?"

"He had like a hundred dollar a day Paco Rabanne habit. That was bad enough, but I told myself I could live with it. Turns out I couldn't. Thank God he spent most of his time on the road. He asked me to come with him a few times, but I always found something more important to do. Can you imagine being cooped up in an airplane with him for five hours?"

"Jane Smith doesn't seem to mind," I said.

"Poor thing lost her sense of smell when she caught COVID. Never came back. There were times I envied her. So Janie's getting it on with Tom?"

"You didn't know?"

"Tom and I communicate through attorneys these days. We're not bitter, you understand. It's just tidier that way."

"He stated as much."

"Such a dear, but I haven't been able to get within four feet of his cock for years. If Janie wants it, more power to her. I'm set one way or the other."

"You said you and Rhonda didn't have an affair. Gigi Sahakian believes otherwise."

"Well, maybe it was a *little* affair. Like, two or three times over a year or so. Hardly worth mentioning. I think Rhonda was willing to give a lot of new stuff a try once she saw a chance to get away from…" She stopped and sipped her tea.

"Yes?"

"I was going to say she saw a chance to get away from Sam."

"That's what I wanted to talk to you about. Rhonda's motive for leaving her husband and assuming a new identity."

"I see. At this point, we are entering the realm of conjecture."

"You don't know?"

"I know lots," she said. "Maybe just not what you want to know."

"Why did Rhonda want to get away from Sam?"

"She was scared."

"Why?"

"I don't know. She never came out and told me. I assumed it was the usual—covert abuse, pummeling with pillowcases full of oranges, that sort of thing. I never saw a bruise on her, and believe me, I checked, but some forms of abuse don't show on the outside. You know Sam. You know what he's like. He's as slippery as a greased pig and twice as fast on his feet. He's the kind of guy who makes a woman dress up in costumes and then he degrades them."

"Rhonda told you he did that?"

"No. He's just the type. I don't like Sam. You know Rhonda's story?"

"Some of it."

"Came from dirt. I mean, literal dirt. Never lived in a house that didn't have wheels attached until she was eighteen. She grew up in one of those parts of the country where a virgin is a girl who can outrun her brothers and uncles. She had a gift, though. She could sing. Voice like an angel. I know. She's sung for me. Got a scholarship to a small state school, got her degree, and came west to find a job in music. Did some backup work with a few acts. That's how she met Brownlee."

"And that was it for her singing career?"

"Sam Brownlee has some strange traditional ideas about the role of women," she said. "He has to be the breadwinner. It was a source of pride, or maybe the idea of not being able to provide for all their needs was shameful to him. I don't know. The idea of his wife working was…well, he didn't like it. He told Rhonda that she should embrace the idea of a life of leisure. He introduced her to Phyllis Bagdasarian, who introduced her to the other Housewives."

"That's when you met her."

"Yup. I knew right away she was a bad fit. She and Gigi Sahakian were the odd socks in the club, but Gigi really never has been completely inducted. Phyllis pushed Rhonda through like there was a deadline."

"Armin Bagdasarian is in business with Sam Brownlee," I said.

"No shit. You know about Rhonda and Armin, right? The party?"

"She groped him."

"That's a polite way to put it. I was there. Hell, we all were. Rhonda was drunk. Champagne cocktails. People excused her later because she was kind of cross-eyed, but the fact is she gave Armin a handie because Sam told her to."

Ah! I thought. *A clue.*

"You know this to be true?"

"Rhonda told me herself. We had a lot of time to talk while we were shacked up in Stinson Beach. Fact is, talking was all she wanted to do, dammit. Sam was in a bit of a money crunch. Rhonda mentioned it to Gigi."

"Why?"

"Fuck, Gold. I don't know. Everyone tells Gigi everything. She's like a safe deposit box where we can stuff away all the shit we can't keep to ourselves but don't want anyone else to know. She's like a fucking priest. She'll take shit to the grave. At least that's what we thought. You want to hear this or not?"

"Go on."

"Rhonda told Gigi that Sam was in a crunch. Next thing you know, Armin approaches Sam with financial backing."

"Reason suggests that Gigi is not as discreet as she pretends," I said.

"I'm putting a lot of unconnected pieces together with this story," she said. "I've had a lot of time to think about it, living up here alone. Like I said, some of it is conjecture, but the facts so far are just the way Rhonda told me. Yeah. I think maybe Gigi told Ruben, and Ruben convinced Armin to invest in Sam's business. I hear all the other wives talk. I know a thing or two about subtext, and the internet's a real thing. I know Ruben's working for both Armin and for his father. I watch TV. *Ozark*. I know how money laundering works. No biggie. Nobody in the top two percent is totally clean. That hill you climb to get to the top is a pile of bones. Anyway, the party where Rhonda fondled Armin's balls was the next weekend. That's what everybody knows about. Not everyone knows that she was with him again a few hours later, and she did a hell of a lot more than jerk him off."

"And she did this because Sam told her to?"

"It was part of the deal. Something Armin insists on. Some kind of fucked-up loyalty test. Deep down, he's kind of a sick fuck. Sam said they were going down the chute unless he could find some cash fast. Armin—by way of Ruben—offered the cash, with a hitch. Sam told Rhonda they were ruined if she didn't rock Armin's world. The psychopath pimped out his own fuckin' wife."

FORTY

"She told you about Ruben Sahakian?" I asked.

"Another tribute from Sam," Julia said. "Armin bragged to his buddy Ruben about how Rhonda turned him inside out. Ruben wanted a taste. Sam got her liquored up one night at a pool party and talked her into it. Between you and me, Rhonda was a little flighty anyway. She'd have probably done it on a dare if she were in the right mood."

"Ruben thought it was her idea. He said he didn't know whether Sam knew about him and Rhonda."

"Maybe. I don't know. Rhonda didn't say. She did tell me Sam pushed her into it, though. She also said their standard of living improved dramatically afterward. I put two and two together. I knew what Sam did. I figured the money had to come from somewhere. Rhonda was finally rolling in in it. All it cost her was her dignity. Like the rest of us."

"But why run?"

"Why not, Gold? She was surrounded by people with souls so shallow they'd dry up in the sun before noon. She was getting passed around like a fatty at a Dead concert. She concluded that her value to Sam was transactional, especially after he hired his girlfriend as his assistant. He's a piece of work, Sam."

"She knew about Sam and Laura Hope?"

"She fuckin' caught them in the act. She was feeling cozy and domestic and dropped by Sam's office with some takeout chicken parm one night when he was working late, just to surprise him. Hopped off the elevator just in time to hear Laura in Sam's office ordering him to—and I quote—*give me that dick*. Rhonda handed the parm to some homeless guy and called Ruben on her cell. Hey, she had permission, right? Sauce for the gander and all that. From the way she told it, she boinked him the first time just to throw it in Sam's face. Turns out she dug it. Big time. Kept coming back for more. Fucking Ruben Sahakian served a multitude of purposes."

"Gigi knew about Rhonda and Ruben."

"Gigi knows everything. I don't think she gives a shit. Between you and me, I believe she'd slip a stiletto between Ruben's ribs if she didn't know his dad would make her death the stuff of legend. Ruben's generous in a kind of passive aggressive way. He gives, often generously, but he expects something in return. In Gigi's case, it's loyalty and keeping the secrets. And let me tell you, Gigi knows a lot of secrets."

"What does she have against Ruben?"

"Besides the fact he's nailed every one of the Housewives at least once?"

I raised an eyebrow.

"Yes!" she said. "Me too. The boy's kind of persistent. And kinda worth the wait. Gigi has a different world view. She's a crusader, a Madonna. She wants to buy the world a fuckin' Coke and teach it to fuckin' sing. She doesn't have time to lie back and stick her feet in the air every time Ruben goes into rut. Ruben plows buttloads of money into the shelter through Armin's recycling business to keep Gigi happy. Deep down, he cares about her, I suppose, but they're more like fuckbuddies than spouses. Friends with very occasional benefits. Gigi puts up with the screwing around, because it frees her up to save the world, but that doesn't mean she isn't jealous and resentful about it."

"It's a mink-lined mousetrap."

"Same for all of us Housewives, stud. The only one of us who's done shit with our lives is Gigi, and she isn't really a member anyway."

"Another reason for resentment. She gets to revolve around the outer orbit of the Housewives but is never really included. But it doesn't wash."

"What?"

"Running away. Yeah, Rhonda was exploited, sure. Sam turned their wedding certificate into a sublet agreement. By your account, though, there was a lot more money coming in, and she was enjoying her affair with Ruben. She wasn't sneaking around, because Sam had encouraged her to make Ruben happy in the first place. Her situation was distasteful, perhaps, but not intolerable. Why buy an entirely new identity and try to run away? And why was she murdered? I don't see the motive yet."

"You know why I moved up here to the cabin?" she asked.

"No."

"To get away from all that shit. After a while, it's hard to figure out who's zooming who this week. Escaping and becoming someone else completely can be highly attractive. At the bottom of it all, though, is greed. Rhonda was tossed around to grease the skids for Sam's business dealings with Armin and Ruben, which are decidedly dirty. It's like the fucking Sopranos. Everybody's working an angle. Rhonda got caught up on one of them."

"Whose angle?"

"I don't know a lot here, okay? She was keeping something locked up deep inside, something she wouldn't talk about. And she never did. But it has something to do with Ruben and Tigran Sahakian. That's all I know. That's all she would say."

"She saw something or heard something, and it scared the shit out of her," I said. "She told Sam. Sam knew which side his bread was buttered on. He was so deep into Tiger Sahakian's pockets that he couldn't risk cutting off his cash flow. The financial reports assembled by the police indicate Sam was leveraged up to the Windsor knot in his necktie. Everything but his house was tied up paying for something else. He was walking a tightrope. Rhonda knew something that endangered the entire house of cards, and now she was in the wind."

"You think Sam killed her after all?"

"I know he did. Now I also know why. The same reason he pimped out his wife. He owed a debt to Tiger Sahakian he could never repay, just like one of the poor schmucks he lent money to. When Rhonda told him whatever it was she had discovered, he could have protected her. He could have told her never to tell anyone else, forever. He could have done a lot of things. Instead, he told Ruben. Ruben told Tiger and Tiger ordered Ruben to take care of it. Ruben relayed the message to Sam: *'If you insist in being part of the problem, you will also be part of the solution.'* He could protect his wife, or he could be stand-up and take the loss like a man. Then came the big order. "This is your problem. You find the solution."

"Tiger Sahakian ordered Sam Brownlee to kill his own wife?"

"It's the motive I've been looking for. Not infidelity. Not anger over being abandoned. He did it to save his own skin. He gave in to every demand I made of him when he hired me. It cost him a big chunk of change. He didn't care. Money was nothing at that point, when he was already staring down the barrel of a gun."

"You think he hired you to find Rhonda so he could kill her?"

"I'm beginning to."

"That's fuckin' monstrous."

"It's survival. He was desperate to find Rhonda so he could solve Tiger's problem. Once I discovered she had run away with you, it was only a couple of steps to finding out she was here in your cabin. He called your husband the minute I told him you were also missing. They talked several times before you were located in Santa Barbara. I already asked. Tom suggested he look at the cabin."

"Fucker. I take back everything nice I said about the stinker."

"I'd already told Sam the model of car Rhonda bought. When he saw the same model parked at the cabin, he knew he had her. The way I see it, he showed up here and projected a conciliatory tone. *Please come home. All is forgiven.* He asked for her forgiveness, and they sealed the deal with the bottle of wine he brought, which he adulterated with benzos. After she passed out, he smashed her skull with the champagne bottle, messaged me with her burner, wiped it down, stashed it between the sofa cushions, and drove back to the city. There, he took a couple of Ambien to shore up his alibi, and he waited for me and Inspector Fender to ring his doorbell with terrible news."

"I'm not a detective," she said. "But I think you're still missing an important detail."

"What was it that Rhonda found out? What did she see or hear that was so terrifying she felt the need to disappear completely to save herself?"

Julia nibbled at a thumbnail. "She never told me. I can't help you, Mr. Gold. Except…"

"Yes?"

"If you want to know a secret, you go to the keeper of secrets. Maybe she told Gigi."

FORTY-ONE

I had probed Gigi Sahakian about her husband's business once before, and it had resulting in a veiled threat from Ruben at Rhonda's funeral.

I already knew Gigi sometimes unethically passed information she had received confidentially to her husband. As soon as Rhonda confided in her that Sam's finances were perilously imbalanced, Armin showed up as his savior. That convinced me that Armin Bagdasarian was as dirty as Ruben. I had assumed that Armin was another one of Tiger Sahakian's marks, an unintentional money laundering front for the Armenian mob. It never occurred to me that he might be in just as deep as Ruben.

Ruben wasn't exploiting Armin's business. They were partners. The only reason Ruben would continue to work there was if he had skin in the game.

Gigi Sahakian already disliked me. She made that clear every time we met. On the other hand, she hadn't rejected the notion of Ruben laundering money through Armin's business outright. She'd been coy about it. Julia suggested Gigi resented her husband. Maybe it was for more than his serial philandering. Maybe she felt as trapped as Sam or Rhonda Brownlee. She knew too much to simply walk away, and if she dropped Ruben Sahakian, she'd also lose the largest slice of contributions to her shelter—the thing in her life toward which she had demonstrated her greatest loyalty.

If I pressed her, and if Rhonda had divulged her secret, Gigi might tell me what it was, just to spite her husband. I was also certain she would turn right around and tell Ruben what I knew, and he'd make that phone call he'd warned me about.

What could Rhonda have learned that was so terrifying? There were only so many options. Murder came to mind. Perhaps she overheard Ruben telling someone about killing a guy. Maybe she saw a killing but didn't tell anyone. Or, maybe someone knew what she had learned and had threatened her into silence.

I called Leon Fender.

"What'cha got, Gold?"

"I have a motive for Brownlee killing his wife," I said.

"Shoot."

"She was sleeping with Ruben Sahakian, partly to cuck her husband and partly because Brownlee wanted her to for business purposes. Basically, he pimped her out, but she kind of got into it. She started putting together her bug-out kit about five months before she was murdered. I think she saw or heard something that scared her to death, and she told Gigi Sahakian about it."

"Why?"

"According to my source, Gigi's like a pin cushion for trauma. Everybody wants to stick some in. Rhonda thought she could tell Gigi anything. I've already discovered that Gigi passes some private information along to Ruben when it's mutually beneficial. She likes to play both sides of the street. Sam Brownlee's entire business hinged on keeping Ruben and Tiger Sahakian happy. Rhonda had knowledge that threatened the Sahakians. I think Ruben Sahakian ordered Brownlee to kill his wife."

There was a long silence on the other end.

"It works," he said. "Only one problem. We don't know what Rhonda knew. If we can figure out what she discovered about Ruben and his dad, we're there."

"I was thinking about that. Rhonda decided to run about eighteen months ago. I figure you have some sort of relationship with the SFPD gang division?"

"We don't call it that."

"Whatever. You know someone who keeps tabs on organized crime, right?"

"Suppose I do?"

"I fucked up in a big way," I said. "I trusted Varnadore and I believed Brownlee. Maybe I'm slowing up. I should have been more suspicious, but I was too busy patting myself on the back for getting a client off the hook to realize Brownlee was taking me for a ride. Rhonda Brownlee was killed for a reason, and I think it was because she knew something that threatened Ruben and Tiger Sahakian."

"Why are you telling me all of this?"

"The welcome mat at the Sahakian house doesn't apply to me anymore. I think Rhonda told Gigi Sahakian her secret. If I put the screws to Gigi one more time, she's going to have Tiger bring in a guy from Houston. If a cop shows up, though…"

"What makes you think she'll talk to me?"

"Just a hunch. My source suggests she isn't entirely happy with the arrangement between her and her husband. She's afraid he might bring home something you can't cure with a shot of penicillin. She almost admitted to me that Ruben was funneling dirty money through Armin Bagdasarian's biofuel plant, and I know

Brownlee was taking money from Tiger as well. A lot of it. Maybe a wife can't be compelled to testify against her husband, but I don't think she'd take a lot of convincing to do it voluntarily. She's kind of done with the guy, except for his checkbook."

"And?"

"Here's what I'm thinking. Contact your buddies in organized crime. Find out if there was some sudden disappearance within Tiger Sahakian's Armenian gang, or any other suspicious activity between eighteen and twenty months ago. A sore thumb kind of situation. Something that doesn't feel right. Something unsolved."

"What then?"

"See if you can connect it directly to Ruben Sahakian or Armin Bagdasarian in any way. Telephone records, bank deposits, whatever. Some kind of link. Rhonda made a sudden decision eighteen months ago, which suggests that's when she learned whatever she learned."

"This is kind of a longshot, Gold," Fender said.

"I know. The nice thing is, when the longshots hit, they pay off big. One more thing. I'm backing up Libby Hackney on a visit to Boyd Demarest this afternoon. If I should disappear, he'd be a good place to start."

"I don't work missing persons anymore," he said. "I'll ring you back after I talk with OC."

FORTY-TWO

Boyd Demarest ran his debatable criminal empire from a former sanctuary in a closed church he'd purchased for a song with meth money a year after he walked out of the pen.

A busted-in member of the Aryan Brotherhood and a confirmed white supremacist and Christian nationalist, Demarest had channeled the skills he had learned running a Blockbuster franchise before his conviction into building a minor crank cartel that owned roughly forty square blocks near the southern border of the county. His customer base was bikers and migrant workers and truck drivers and lot lizards and just about anyone who could beg, borrow, or steal the few bucks a hit of shatter costs these days. Careful demographic targeting of the most desperate margins of society had yielded a bounty crop of cash for his organization.

Recognizing the value of diversification, Demarest had invested his illicit drug money into every cash-based legitimate business he could gobble up for pennies. He also ran several illicit video gambling operations and a string of Asian rub-and-tugs scattered around the city.

First and foremost, however, Boyd Demarest considered himself a Soldier for Christ and Caucasians. He had discovered cheap military-looking tunics in a business uniform catalog and had decided that his organization—being ideally paramilitary in nature—would demonstrate its identity by adopting a common dress. He'd gotten the idea after seeing a couple of Guardian Angels on a subway in New York City. Nobody told him the Bloods and Crips came up with the idea way ahead of him. He designed several cloth badges with vaguely disguised white pride symbols, lightning bolts and skulls and eagles and such, which he handed out to each recruit along with a set of tunics, one for each day of the week.

Demarest's gang was made up of military dropouts, former cons, wannabe cops who couldn't pass the physical or the psych tests, rabid ammosexuals, flat earthers, Dominionist zealots, unreconstructed Confederates, and any other variety of square pegs whose psychotic world views made perfect sense to them while alienating anyone with two brain cells to rub together. They were mostly pasty thugs with grudges against society in general, and especially against anyone who thought they were smarter or better, which was almost everyone. The greatest benefactors of Boyd Demarest's criminal enterprises were the tattoo parlors south of the Mission District and STD clinics all across the county.

The stained-glass windows inside the church were occluded by alternating immense Nazi and Klan flags that hung vertically, obscuring images of the Beatitudes and Acts of the Apostles with swastikas and the Rosy Cross. Between the windows were sconces shaped like torches, topped with LED bulbs that flickered yellow and red simulated flames.

Someone with blacksmithing skills in Demarest's brotherhood had constructed an iron throne similar to one he'd seen on television in the joint and had placed it where the altar had previously stood in the sanctuary. The church was small. It probably had seated four hundred people in its prime. Even so, with the sanctuary decked out in fascist and racist symbols and Demarest sitting on his ridiculous status symbol, elevated imperiously over the main floor, wearing his banana republic uniform, and despite the fact that I was surrounded by more firepower than Butch and Sundance in Bolivia, I almost snickered.

"Impressive," I said. "That chair looks uncomfortable, though."

"It is." Demarest had one of those rumbling South Georgia accents that dared you to piss him off, half redneck and half chewing tobacco. "The trick is not minding that it's uncomfortable."

He was shorter than I expected, maybe five-ten. His head was shaven and waxed to a gleam. He wore sunglasses indoors, which was intended to intimidate but mostly looked pretentious. I kept that opinion to myself. The way he filled out his uniform, he'd stayed in shape after walking away from the weights in the prison yard. He had twin lightning bolt tattoos on either side of his bull neck, which stood for SS. I wondered whether he had a swastika tattooed on the back of his head. He looked the type.

He nodded toward Libby at my side. "You the girlfriend?"

"Libby Hackney," she said. "I think you and I are both looking for Bobby Sladen."

"You know where Bobby is?" Demarest asked.

"We were hoping you do," I said. "He's a suspect in a murder case. He tried to frame Libby for it. She's understandably upset."

"Don't go killin' him," Demarest said. "Bastard owes me a shit-ton of money."

"Three quarters of a million and change?" I asked.

"You know a lot," Demarest said.

"Did he come to you for another three-quarters?"

"Yeah. Several months back. I hope you haven't been snoopin' around my business, mister."

I handed him my card. He glanced at it, and then held it at arm's length, trying to make out the print.

"They make those shades with bifocals now," I said.

"Getting' fuckin' old," Demarest said, as he stuffed the card in his pocket.

"Lot of that going around," I said.

"So you're Gold. Nice to finally put a face on the name. I heard of you." He pointed at Libby. "You, I never heard of. You say Bobby tried to frame you? This about the murder of that radio station guy?"

"Yeah," Libby said. "We think Bobby killed his partner when you wouldn't come up with the second half of the radio station purchase price. They had an insurance policy that paid off Bobby's debt if anything happened to Drake."

"So Bobby killed Drake for the insurance money. And you say he's on the run?"

"We're looking for him," Libby said. "Nobody's seen him for weeks. Here's the thing, though. Bobby couldn't have done it himself. His alibi is rock solid. That means he had a confederate, someone who did the actual shooting."

"And you think he used one of my guys?" Demarest said.

"He used someone," I said. "The murder scene was clean. It had the mark of a pro, someone who's been killing people for a while, and knows how." I emphasized the word *pro*, stroking Demarest's ego, and hoped he wasn't smart enough to see through it. I was pretty certain he wasn't, but people surprise you.

He smirked and nodded. "I got some guys who could pull it off, sure. But they didn't. I can see why you'd think so. You think I made a deal with Bobby when he ran into financial straits. You believe I knew about this insurance policy, and when Bobby realized I wasn't going to give him another big bag of money to bail his ass out, he figured his best option was to get out from under the whole damn thing. You think I offered him a couple of my guys to do the job and give Bobby a solid gold alibi, and in return, when the insurance money came in, he'd sign the whole damn station over to me and walk away clean."

"Wow," I said. "That story's a lot better than mine. Let's go with that one."

"Except it never happened," Demarest said. "Yeah. I lent Bobby Sladen the money for fifty-one percent of that piece of shit flashlight radio station. And, yes, he came to me six months later asking for money to pay for the rest of it. I refused. I never intended to lend the entire amount. This was a bust-out deal from the start. Bobby's a fuckin' sucker. Nothin' but a mark. I got a buyer over in Utah ready to sign a check for the station whenever Bobby runs out of money and signs the station over to me. Radio preacher. One of them prosperity gospel types."

"But Bobby's not around now to sign it over," I said. "He hasn't shown up to pay the vig on the loan in months. You're getting nervous."

"I got people keeping an eye out for him."

"That's why you agreed to see us so quickly," Libby said. "You want to find Bobby as badly as we do."

"He owes me north of a million now. That's a piece of change," he said. "Someone's got to be accountable for that. Bobby has a regular drop. Same day every month. He said he had some sort of trust fund that pays twenty large every month. When he gets paid, he brings it to the drop."

"Where's the drop?" I asked.

"Fuck that shit, Gold. I don't know you that good. If we get to a point where you absolutely need to know, I'll tell you then. So, Bobby was supposed to make the drop a little over a week ago. No show. Hasn't been seen since. Yeah, I got feelers out, looking for him myself. Then, I get a call today from some chick who says she's his girlfriend. I thought maybe Bobby was sending you to negotiate for him. Maybe offering you as collateral until he could come up with my money. Wouldn't be the first time. So, I agreed to see you right away. Now it turns out you know about as much as I do. You're no good to me, so maybe it's time for you to go."

"Finder's fee," Libby said.

"What the fuck?" Demarest said.

"I'm gonna make Bobby wish his daddy jerked off in a gym sock the night he was conceived. He owes you a million? Bobby owes me a pound of flesh for what he did. What's it worth if I deliver him to you?"

"Libby," I said. "Maybe not the time—"

Demarest cut me off. "Wait. You can do that?"

"I'm gonna run him to ground," Libby said. "After I take my share out of his hide, what do I care what you do to him?"

"Hold on," I told her. "This isn't the way. If you don't deliver Bobby to the police, you'll be a suspect the rest of your life. Maybe they can't touch you, but they can sure talk about you. Your credibility will always be in question."

"I don't care what you do to his ass after he signs the papers giving me the station," Demarest said. "I'm not interested in anything but the money. Slam his ass in a cell so hard he leaves a grease spot on the back wall, for all I care. You bring Bobby to me, your cut will be…oh…five percent."

"Not much of a cut," Libby said.

"Libby—"

"Okay. Seven percent. That's as high as I go. That's seventy grand. You could do a lot worse. You bring Bobby here, he signs the papers, and then you can dump him in the bay if you like."

FORTY-THREE

"Thanks, Gold," Libby said as we walked toward our cars. "I can take it from here."

"Hold on," I said. "Let's talk about this."

"Nothing to talk about, Scout. You heard him. Seventy thousand. I can take the rest of the year off."

"No, you can't. Think this over carefully. Take it through all the hurdles. Let's say you find Sladen, and you take him to Demarest, and he signs over the station. The paper's probably worthless. The radio station's tied up in probate, at least Arlen Drake's forty-nine percent of it, and Bobby can't profit from killing Drake by taking the insurance money. Even if they settle Drake's estate, the station will be evidence in the trial, and who knows how long that will go on? Finally, even if we find Sladen, we have jack shit until we identify his shooter. Bobby has an alibi nobody could crack. So just finding him won't solve that."

"When we find Bobby, I'll kick the fucker's name out of him."

"Okay. You have a plan. So far, so good. But until then, let's concentrate on the *where* part. How do you propose finding him?"

"I told you. Shit-For-Brains never shut up in bed. He bragged about his fucking car while he was inside me for Crissake. Talk talk

talk. I listened. He mentioned some things. People. No names, but they're leads. The hard part is separating the real stuff from the bullshit. It was mostly bullshit. I'm gonna hit some of the bars where he used to hang out tonight, see if any of his party buddies have any idea where he's gone. Maybe he's contacted some of them while he's been underground."

"He would do that?"

"Fucker can't stand to be alone. Not for long. Some kind of abandonment issues or some shit. I don't know. I just know he needs to get out among people once in a while or he'll claw his face off."

"Be careful. And remember what I said. If you even suspect you're in over your head, call me. You're dealing with Boyd Demarest now."

"Sure, Pops," she said. "You wanna remind me of my curfew too?"

My telephone rang on the way back to Jefferson Street. Leon Fender.

"You got some kind of crystal ball stuffed up your ass?" Fender asked.

"That would explain a lot of things. Why do you ask?"

"Soon as I mentioned Tiger Sahakian and the time frame to Organized Crime, they invited me to lunch."

"Aw. They're sweet on you."

"More like I might have something they've been looking for, for a long time. Turns out I did. There was a big shakeup in Tiger's organization about nineteen months ago. Happens in every gang in town, every several years. Entropy and all that. Everyone's happy as long as the money keeps rolling in, until someone decides they want to be happier than everyone else. This is one of those zero sum game situations. It isn't enough that someone has to win. Someone else also has to lose."

"Paradigm shifts are seldom a tidy affair," I said.

"And how. OC didn't share the particulars, and this wasn't one of those *you-show-me-yours* scenarios anyway. They are extremely interested in a man named Goren Zornakyan. Goes by Gary Zorn. Or, at least, he did. He hasn't been seen since…"

"Eighteen months ago," I finished.

"Nineteen, but who's counting? The hot money says he was chummed into the bay."

"That would explain the proliferation of sea lions near Pier 39."

"Jesus. So, apparently Tiger Sahakian got this gargantuan bug up his butt about Gary Zorn a couple of years back. Zorn was ambitious. He noticed that Tiger will never see eighty again and he could imagine a future in which a power vacuum emerged. He was positioning himself to jump as soon as the opening occurred."

"What happened?"

"Tiger didn't die, and he didn't retire. Gary Zorn became impatient. He got careless. He pulled something stupid, and he got busted."

"OC turned him?"

"Worse. DOJ. The FBI. They jumped at the opportunity to turn him into their personal elf on the shelf inside Tiger's organization. They ran him for a couple of years, during which he provided some decent intel. Dumb fuck imagined once he got Tiger out of the way, the feds would cut him loose and he could take over."

"And then he disappeared."

"Like he'd never been there at all. His apartment looked like the cleaning woman had just left. All his clothes were on hangers or in drawers. Same for his toiletries. Everything in the fridge still fresher than the sell-by date. It looked like he would walk in from work any minute and mix a martini before dinner."

"He was nabbed somewhere else."

"No shit. He could have disappeared a dozen ways. Some of them voluntary."

"Someone told him Tiger was coming for him, and he bugged out."

"There are worse reasons, I hear," Fender said.

"But you're not in that camp."

"I think this guy was compost before we even met."

Several seconds later, he said, "Gold? You there? You didn't get hit by a bus or anything?"

"Compost," I said. "Holy shit. Compost. I think I know what happened to Gary Zorn. We really need to talk to Gigi Sahakian."

I told Fender I'd meet him at the women's shelter and explain everything there.

He arrived five minutes before me. He was waiting in the drive when I showed up, his hands in his pants pockets, his service weapon visible in the holster on his hip. I stopped and rolled down my window.

"She's not here," he said. "Hasn't been here in two days."

"Do they know where she is?"

"No. She called in yesterday, though. A check-in."

"Even on the run, she can't let this place go," I said.

"You think she's on the run?"

"I think she knows a lot more than she should, and she knows someone else knows she knows it. She's smart and resourceful. Yeah. I think she bugged out."

He walked around the car and opened the passenger door. After sitting, he said, "So you want to tell me what the fuck this is all about?"

"Hold on," I said. I found Osiris in my phone contacts and hit the speed dial.

"Lose my number," he said when he answered.

"Hold on. This is important. Someone's life might be in danger."

"Who?"

"Your feeder at the woman's shelter."

"Gigi?" he said, and immediately cursed. "Fuck you, Gold. You tricked me."

"I didn't do any such thing. I've known she refers women to you for over a year. I'm also playing fair with you now. I have a cop in the car. Say hello to Inspector Fender."

"Hi, there," Fender said.

I added, "I haven't told him who you are, and I won't, unless a judge orders it. We cool?"

A long silence. "Don't much like talking to cops."

"On the phone or at the station. Makes no nevermind to me," Fender said. "I don't need to know who you are. I do need you to answer some questions. And remember, Gold knows who you are. We can come to you, if you like."

"No," he said. "For real? Gigi's in trouble?"

"On several levels," I said. "You know who her father-in-law is."

"Sure. I don't need no trouble with Tiger Sahakian."

"You aren't even part of the conversation," I said. "Just need to know if Gigi bought a set of ID papers from you."

"You're askin' a lot, Gold."

"You've known me for how long?"

"Long enough. Not sure I want to know you anymore, though."

"Fair enough. I've always shot straight with you, though. Right?"

"Straight enough."

"Believe me. I wouldn't ask if it weren't important. Gigi may have learned something that could get her killed. If she's gone missing, and it looks like she has, it may be because she knows someone is coming for her. We need to find her before someone else does."

"I got your phone number. Let me think about it for a few minutes. I'll text you."

He clicked off without saying goodbye.

"If he doesn't text you back, we're going looking for that boy."

"Good luck. If he doesn't text me back, we'll never see him again. You think he doesn't have his own bug-out papers ready to go? Bet he's already cut himself an Amex black card with a million-dollar limit."

"So what the fuck is going on anyway? Why do you need Gigi so bad?" Fender asked.

"I thought Armin Bagdasarian was one of Tiger's marks. Now I know he and Ruben Sahakian are partners. In fact, Armin might pull a little more weight in Tiger's organization, because Ruben is stuck dealing with the business day in and day out. He kind of resents Armin taking it easy. You know what the business is, right?"

"Something about biofuels."

"Ethanol and biodiesel. Also cattle and chicken feed, some nitrates, and raw materials for the fertilizer industry. It's all recycled food. Armin's platoon of drivers runs a circuit picking up used fryer oil and food garbage all around the county. That's refined to make biodiesel fuel. The real stinky part of the business is the ethanol and nitrates side. When I was at the refinery, I saw three trucks roll up in a half hour, full to the brim with restaurant food waste. The waste food is conveyed from the dock into huge steel fermentation vats. Add a little water, a little heat, a little time, and Mother Nature spits out two hundred-proof rocket fuel. After draining off the ethanol, the only thing left in the tank is sludge. It all dissolves into a gloppy mess that's dried and applied to other uses. The byproducts sell for almost as much as the fuels."

"Okay. With you so far."

"Soon as you said Gary Zorn was compost before we even met, I thought about the Bagdasarian plant. I think Ruben and Armin got rid of Gary Zorn by tossing him into one of the ethanol tanks. It's all about decomp and fermentation anyway, so no smell to worry about. Everything in that plant smells like death already. When the process was done, you couldn't tell Gary shit from restaurant shit in the sludge. Right now, Gary could be in a few dozen bags of chicken feed down at the FCX."

Fender shuddered. "I can see it. And you're saying Rhonda found out about it, somehow, and that's why she acquired a new identity and ran away."

"She was sleeping with Ruben Sahakian at the time. Julia Wanamaker says she was scared about something, and if she talked to anyone about it, it would have been Gigi."

"Even though she was fucking Gigi's husband."

"She didn't know that Gigi knew about that. And she was desperate. She told Gigi what Ruben and Armin had done. Maybe Gigi knew about it already. Maybe she didn't. When I showed up again asking questions a few weeks back, I opened a lot of expired cans of worms. People are asking questions about Rhonda Brownlee again, just as everyone was certain Sam was going to die looking at concrete block prison walls. Maybe Tiger and Ruben are behind Wilson Varnadore's attempts to establish reasonable doubt with Brownlee's case, and maybe they aren't. Maybe they'd be just as happy if Brownlee took the fall, as long as they weren't implicated. Once in prison, it would be easy to have him shanked, and the secret would die with him. Now that it looks like he might get off the hook…"

"Everybody's head is on a block. If Brownlee is acquitted due to reasonable doubt, they know the police are going to look for another perpetrator."

"And Gigi knows stuff she shouldn't know," I said.

"Makes her a liability."

"The good news is she phoned the shelter yesterday. She was alive then."

"Probably in hiding," he said. "If Sahakian's holding her somewhere, I don't think they'd let her contact the outside world. That's not how abductions work."

"I agree. She's in the wind. We just need to hope Osiris is in a cooperative mood."

My telephone vibrated. A message. Osiris.

"Speak of the devil," I said. "We are looking for a woman named Samantha Derby." I forwarded the message to him.

"I'll put out a BOLO on her," Fender said.

"Me, too," I said. I found Sean Ashford's number at the Mark Hopkins on my phone and punched it.

"Eamon Gold," he said when he answered. "Haven't heard from you in a while. How's Sonny?"

"Tall, wide, tanned, and handsome," I said. "He's flourishing in Waikiki."

"That's a nice resort he has. Had a great time surfing out there, and Sonny comped me a freakin' suite. Told him I'll return the favor any time he visits."

"Was wondering if I can access your network of hotel security officers again," I said. "Same deal. Woman may be checked in under a fake ID."

"Sure. Not a problem. Working that search with you last year gave us some ideas for better overall coordination. We shoot requests like this back and forth several times a week now. It's really made my job easier."

"We're looking for a woman traveling under the name Samantha Derby. I'll send along the particulars and a picture in a few minutes. If anyone sees her, they should contact either me or Inspector Leon Fender at the SFPD."

"Is this woman dangerous?" he asked.

"Only to herself," I said.

FORTY-FOUR

Fender said he had to get back to the office. He ordered me to stay in touch under pain of death. I think he meant it.

I decided to take one more shot at Brownlee in the jail. I arrived and asked to meet with him. The clerk at the front desk checked a notepad.

"I'm sorry, Mr. Gold. You're on the list."

"Happens more frequently than you might think," I said. "Which list is it this time? Most Dashing Detective in Town?"

"The do-not-visit list. The inmates here are allowed some degree of control over who visits and who doesn't. Prisoner Brownlee has put you on the no-go list."

"Has he, now?" I said. "Well, that's interesting."

I phoned Wilson Varnadore from my car.

"You had Brownlee put me on a do-not-visit list at the jail?"

"Do you think I shouldn't have? You visited him and accused him of murder after I terminated your employment. Can you give me a good reason why you should be allowed to speak with him again?"

"Oh, I don't know. Perhaps because he killed his fucking wife and might just get away with it."

"You have just described the specific purpose for which he hired me. I don't know whether he killed her or not. I don't care. My job is to see to it that he isn't railroaded by a justice system that only wants a pound of flesh from someone, regardless of true guilt."

"Did you read that off the back of your business card?"

He dropped the call without saying goodbye.

I wasn't good company for Heidi that evening. I was sullen and quiet at dinner and stared at the screen while we watched TV and sipped wine afterward. I fiddled at the workbench on a new project, but I couldn't focus on the moment, which is a bad idea when you're working with razor-sharp tools, so I abandoned it and sulked on the sofa some more.

"You're no fun tonight," Heidi said around nine o'clock. She has a penchant for brutal honesty.

"Somewhere out there, a woman is on the run because her husband and father-in-law stuffed a snitch into a compost fermenter."

"Hate it when that happens. But kudos for being environmentally conscious. Would it help to talk it through?"

"I think Fender and I have everything sorted. Only thing we're missing is a witness who can confirm it. I tried to talk to Brownlee at the jail today. Varnadore told him to deny visits."

"Or maybe it's the other way around," she said.

"How so?"

"What if Brownlee doesn't want to talk to you because you have it all sorted out, as you say. Perhaps he's under pressure from outside to stay quiet."

"Like the Finch case last year," I said. "The one where her husband threatened her if she answered any more questions from me."

"I don't remember the particulars," she said. "But you should consider that perhaps this wasn't Varnadore's idea."

"That would be bad," I said. "It means the guys who are pulling his strings know Fender and I are onto them, and they're heavy hitters. There's more, though. The feds are involved."

"Which ones? There are so many letters."

"FBI. Maybe the DOJ. These guys are on the radar of some people way up the food chain in DC. I expect to hear from them any time now. Fender triggered them when he poked the Organized Crime Unit at SFPD about disappearances and murders eighteen months ago. They've been putting pressure on the OCU to find something they can follow up on, even though everybody knows who killed the guy. We just need evidence. I don't think Brownlee was involved in that murder, but he knows about it. It's why he killed his wife. She found out, and the killers considered her expendable. They had Brownlee by the balls. Probably gave him an ultimatum. Buy off the sword or bear it."

"Did you just quote the medieval weregild laws from Germany?"

"I've picked up a fact or two over the years. They told Brownlee he could remove his wife as a liability, or they'd just take him off the gameboard instead, and probably still kill her as well. They put him in a box with only one survivable exit. That's why he hired me in the first place. He was desperate to find his wife before the guys decided to cut their losses by killing both of them."

"And now your prime witness has run away."

"Probably the smartest move. The people she has the goods on don't fool around. They like to leave examples in their wakes. She'd know, too, being married to one of them. I think this case just became too big for me. Time to punch out and leave it to the guys who can issue subpoenas and drag people into small dark rooms for interrogations. I'm not getting paid anymore anyway."

"But you still have unanswered questions."

"Everybody dies with those," I said. "Most people can live with it."

"Most people are not you."

"Fender's read into the whole story. He can take it from here."

"That's why you've been so buoyant and ebullient all evening? Because Fender will wrap up the case you basically solved?"

"Never said I liked it," I said. "Man's got to know what he can do and what he can't."

"I have never seen the thing that you couldn't do," she said.

"Maybe we're there now," I said.

FORTY-FIVE

The feds arrived at my office bright and early the next morning.

Too bad for them I slept in.

Being newly unemployed and largely unplugged from my own investigation, I decided to turn off the alarm and let nature have its way with me.

I woke around nine-thirty, cooked a huge country breakfast, and dropped Heidi off at her condo. It was the day each week she closed the gallery and lavished on herself in a fancy day spa. For some reason, despite the fact she would be parading around naked as a jaybird and sans makeup all day, she said she needed time to pull herself together before showing up in public. Go figure.

I stopped on the way in and grabbed a half dozen Dunkins. I was newly unemployed and might need the sugar to get through the day.

I found the FBI calling card stuck in my door. Agent Angela Diaz. A note on the back in feminine cursive. *Sorry we missed you. We need to talk. Call me.*

After making some coffee, I called her. She answered after the second ring.

"Mr. Gold?"

"At your service."

"Are you in your office?"

"I am."

"Stay there. I'll be there in fifteen minutes."

"Cool beans."

I set the telephone on the desktop and tried the coffee, which had cooled to precisely the correct temperature while I was talking. After a couple of sips, I called Fender.

"Getting rousted by the FBI," I said. "Angela Diaz. Know her?"

"She's tough, but she's good," he said. "I've been talking with her ever since the OCU guys contacted the Feds with our findings. She's on our side."

"Good to know. Any news on Gigi Sahakian?"

"Nothing yet."

"My hotel security network's on the lookout for her. If she's checked in anywhere between here and San Diego under her alias, we'll hear about it. Beyond that, it looks like I'm out of it."

"Maybe not after your discussion with Agent Diaz."

"Do you know something I don't?"

"Plenty. It's possible your role in this case isn't finished yet."

"Time will tell," I said.

FBI Agent Angela Diaz arrived exactly fifteen minutes after her call. I commended her punctuality when she walked through the door.

"Your door is misspelled," she said.

"It's a Japanese *kintsugi.* Perfection is to be found in imperfection."

She rolled her eyes. She was in the middle five-foot range, with reddish-brown hair she kept cut close to her head. Quick to dry and easy to take care of. Late thirties. Her suit was tailored, unlike most FBI agents I'd encountered, and it showed off a form carefully crafted during hours of *krav maga* or Brazilian *jiu jitsu* classes. Her face seemed frozen in a grim no-nonsense rictus. She looked like every fed I'd ever met. They focus on making a no-nonsense first impression.

"You're working alone?" I asked. "In my experience, you people travel in packs."

"We have a task force assembling downtown in the police headquarters. Some of the agents are still in transit."

"I could have waited. In the spirit of conviviality, I brought doughnuts."

She stared at me for precisely seven seconds. "I need all your files on Ruben and Tigran Sahakian."

"Easily done. I have none."

"What? I thought you were investigating the disappearance of Gary Zorn."

"Nope. That's a side deal. I was working for Wilson Varnadore, who is defending Sam Brownlee for the murder of his wife. Ruben and Tiger showed up as part of that investigation."

"I need all your files on Brownlee, then."

"Privileged. If it were any other case, I'd happily hand them over. But when Varnadore terminated me, he made it clear that everything we had discussed, which is almost everything in the case, is considered privileged communication. There was a time when every FBI agent was a lawyer or had at least attended law school. Is that the case with you, Agent Diaz?"

"Yes."

"Then you know even a judge can't crack attorney-client privilege, and all my communications with Brownlee were part of those communications, as I was working under Varnadore's aegis."

"Well, that's a problem."

"Except one," I said. "I visited Brownlee in jail after Varnadore handed me my pink slip."

"The content of that conversation?"

"I told him I'd finally concluded he killed his wife, and now I think I know why. The good part is that none of it is privileged. Sure I can't get you some coffee? It's kind of a long story."

Once she had a doughnut or two inside her, Agent Diaz became a lot more personable. I outlined my hypothesis that Tiger and Ruben Sahakian killed Gary Zorn when they found out he was snitching for the feds, and they disposed of the body in a composting chamber at Armin Bagdasarian's plant. I described how Rhonda Brownlee was spite-fucking Ruben after discovering her husband playing hide the pickle with his assistant Laura Hope, and outlined my belief that somehow, during the affair with Ruben, Rhonda found out what happened to Gary Zorn. Now she knew way too much to live.

"I think Sam Brownlee killed his wife because Ruben and Tiger told him to. It was a test of loyalty, and it removed a troublesome witness in the process. They had a mortgage on Brownlee's dreams.

They told him he could kill her, or he could join her among the recently deceased. It was all or nothing. He was either with 'em or ag'in 'em. His choice."

"He could have come to the police, or the FBI," Diaz said.

"Brownlee's a psychopath. A high-functioning one, to be sure, but like every other psychopath in the world he's only truly interested in Numero Uno. To save his skin, he'd kill a dozen Rhondas. So, that's what I think happened. There are no files, but everything I've told you came from conversations that took place after Varnadore showed me the door."

Okay. I lied a little. Sue me.

"And, now, Ruben Sahakian's wife Gigi is missing," she said.

"I think Rhonda told her everything before she ran away," I said. "She's the keeper of secrets, and Ruben knows it. She secured fake docs from a forger I know. I just hope she got away before Ruben could take her out of the picture as well."

"How well do you know Ruben Sahakian?" she asked.

"Not well. We've met on a couple of occasions. The first time he threatened to stuff me in an oil drum. The second was more cordial, but he also snorted a gram of coke and still said he could have me killed with a single phone call. It's that sort of relationship."

"His wife is missing. You're a private detective. Perhaps you could approach him about looking for Gigi."

I was reaching for a maple glazed doughnut. I pulled my hand back. "Scaring up some business," I said. "Seems plausible enough, if I were the ambulance-chasing type."

"Which you aren't."

"But Ruben doesn't know that. You want me to wear a wire and maybe get Ruben to say something offhand that could put a noose around his neck."

"Inspector Fender told me you were smarter than the average private cop."

"Cuter, too."

"Matter of taste."

"You're trying to talk me into putting my life on the line for your investigation. The least you could do is butter me up a little."

"Are you going to help us, Mr. Gold?" she asked.

I thought about it and picked up the maple doughnut. "Sure," I said. "Why not?"

FORTY-SIX

I found Ruben Sahakian at Armin Bagdasarian's rendering plant. He looked irritated when he walked around the corner to the front desk after being paged by the receptionist.

"Gold," he said. "You wasted a trip out here."

"I'm not here on business," I said. "Can we talk?"

I gestured down the hall, toward his office. He huffed a couple of times, but eventually nodded.

"Come on back," he said, glancing again at the receptionist. There were parts of his life he didn't want her to know, and I was one of them.

The office was as bare as the last time I'd visited.

"What is it?" he asked as soon as he closed the door.

"I know we didn't get off on the completely right foot," I said. "That's probably my fault. I just heard that your wife's missing. I wanted to drop by and offer my sympathies."

"Sympathies? Curious word."

"Probably the wrong one. Condolences didn't sound appropriate. Fact is, in situations like this, I seldom know exactly what to say. You ever feel that way?"

"And how do you know she's missing?"

"A guy with the SFPD. Leon Fender. He tried to visit her at the shelter, and they said she hasn't shown up in days. He tried calling her, but her phone went to voicemail. Just like Rhonda Brownlee last year."

"What do you want, Gold?"

"Like I said, we got off to a bad start, you and me. I'd like to try to make that up to you. If you'd like, I can help look for Gigi."

The color rose in his neck and cheeks. "Jesus, Gold. My wife's missing and you're angling for a paycheck?"

"Nope," I said. "Totally gratis. You don't have to pay a dime. I just want to help. You know. To clear the air between us. Between you and me, I like Gigi. We've had several conversations over the last year, and I want to make sure she's okay. After what happened to Rhonda…"

"What about Rhonda?"

"Nothing. Shouldn't have even mentioned it. I know you and she were a thing. Don't want to draw parallels. Two completely different situations. I mean, would you believe it? I actually suspected at one point that Gigi killed Rhonda. Sounds dumb now."

"It always did."

"Well, spousal jealousy and scorn are a thing, you know. Gigi once told me she arranged for Rhonda's traveling papers as much to get her out of your bed as any other reason, including friendship. She was motivated to keep you. That's devotion there. Most wives would have hired a divorce attorney on the spot. Gigi just shipped the competition out of the picture."

"Rhonda wasn't competition. Rhonda was just…a thing."

"Oh, she was more than that. Brownlee told me. She was a tribute. He encouraged her to sleep with you, in return for backing his loanshark enterprise. He referred to you and your father as his angels. You know that term from show business?"

"No."

"It refers to money that appears at just the right time out of the blue. Like a gift from angels. You and your father saved Brownlee's bacon. He wanted to make sure you knew he appreciated it."

"He did," Ruben said. "Just supports what I said. Rhonda was nothing, really. A dalliance."

"That dalliance went on for a long time. Months, as I recall. No judgments here. I'm on your side, remember? I want to find Gigi as much as you do. To do that, I need to know everything I can find out, so long as it doesn't stomp on your toes, business-wise. When did you start sleeping with Rhonda?"

"Almost two years ago. Maybe a year before she was killed."

"So, off and on for—what? Eleven months? A year?"

"Yeah. About that long. What does that matter?"

"Just getting the timeline straight. How frequently did you and Rhonda hook up?"

"Is that important?"

"I'm trying to figure out when Gigi discovered you were cheating with Rhonda. She never told me."

"Maybe once a week. Sometimes twice. Sometimes not at all. It wasn't a regular thing."

"Rhonda approached Gigi about fake ID papers six months after you started sleeping with her. That's probably when she found out about the affair. She told me she wanted Rhonda out of the way. Either Rhonda confessed, or Gigi found out another way."

I held up a finger and pulled out my phone. Seconds later, I had Osiris on the line.

"This number will be deactivated tomorrow," he said. "I'm makin' tracks, man. Whaddayawant?"

"That last thing I asked you about. When did you do the job?"

"Fuck, man, I don't know. Eighteen months, two years ago. About the same time I did the Wanamaker papers. Gigi asked me to make her one too. Swear to God, Gold, I'm in the wind. You fucked me up but good. Rot in hell, douchebag."

He cut off the call.

"She knew eighteen months ago," I told Ruben. "Right about the time Rhonda approached her."

"She never said a word," Ruben said.

"She had a lot of time to make plans to run away. For all we know, she made the arrangements a year ago or longer. We could be following a very cold trail. Hey, does the name Gary Zorn mean anything to you?"

He had been staring at the floor. His head snapped up; his eyes were wide.

"What?"

"The police found a slip of paper with the name Gary Zorn among Rhonda's effects at the cabin. In her purse. Mean anything to you? I looked online and couldn't find a listing for anyone by that name anywhere. Strange, huh?"

"Yeah. Strange."

I shrugged. "Probably nothing. The way the paper was folded and carefully stowed in a zippered pocket of her purse, the police thought it might mean something. Maybe he's one of Gigi's and Rhonda's mutual friends. For all we know, he might be able to tell us where Gigi's gone. I can keep looking for him if you want."

"No," Ruben said. His face had suddenly gone stony. "No. That's all right. I don't need your help, Gold. In fact, I might just file a missing person report with the police myself, let the professionals handle this."

"Wow," I said. "That stings."

"I appreciate you dropping by." He didn't extend his hand. "But I can take care of this from here."

A half hour later, I was in the temporary task force meeting room at Eight-Fifty Bryant Street. Leon Fender sat next to me. The freshly appointed Chief Inspector, Dexter Spears, sat at the head of the table. Next to him sat Agent Diaz and her partner, a husky, ruddy-cheeked man hovering around forty, named Lawrence Schultheis. Spears kept trying to kill me from across the room with his eye lasers.

We had just finished listening to the tape recording of my meeting with Ruben.

"He knows the name Gary Zorn," I said. "I did check. Goren Zornakyan is listed with an address and phone number. Even has a Facebook page. Gary Zorn doesn't exist anywhere, because Zornakyan never legally changed his identity. It was his gang bust-in name. The only way Ruben would have recognized the name and gotten so rattled was because he knew how Zorn disappeared."

"And now he suspects his wife knows everything Rhonda knew, including what happened to Zorn," Fender said. "We'd better find Gigi before he does. We already know he isn't beyond wife-killing."

"When it's someone else's wife," I argued. "Would he be so eager to park one between Gigi's eyes if he finds her?"

"We're not going to take that chance," Agent Diaz said. "Right now, our priority is locating Gigi Sahakian. She may be the only person who can tell us exactly what happened to Zorn."

The meeting broke up a few minutes later, with each agent and detective scurrying off to cover their specific assignment for the afternoon. I chatted with Fender and felt Agent Diaz's hand on my shoulder.

"Thanks, Gold," she said. "You didn't have to do that."

"But you can take it from here," I finished. "I'm pretty good at subtext."

"Good," she said. "The FBI appreciates your cooperation."

"Do you still give out those cool Junior G-Man pins? I always wanted one when I was a kid."

"How about an official letter of commendation?"

"Signed by J. Edgar Hoover himself?"

"Flake," she said. She squeezed my shoulder almost hard enough to snap my rotator cuff and walked out of the room.

"So ends my brief career with the Federal Bureau of Investigation," I told Fender. "Gonna look swell on my resume."

"I'm out of the loop as well. The feds always tell you when they walk in the door that they're here to cooperate and assist. Next thing you know, you read about the bust in the *Chronicle*. Doesn't matter. Soon as I show up at my desk downstairs, someone will throw a fresh murder book at me."

"Let's go grab a beer instead," I said. "Blow off the rest of the day."

"Can't. Crime never sleeps," he said.

"I read that once on a Two-Gun Terry bubblegum card."

"She's right," he said. "You are a flake."

We were interrupted by a flurry of activity in the temp office quarters set up outside the meeting room. The rumble of multiple conversations increased in volume, and people started running around, grabbing jackets and stowing pistols and cell phones. It looked like all hands on deck.

"Something's up," Fender said.

Agent Diaz stepped inside the conference room.

"Gigi Sahakian," she said. "It isn't good."

FORTY-SEVEN

We were in the car with Agents Diaz and Schultheis. They sat in front. Fender and I sat in the rear.

"SFPD patrol came across a lone car in the Baylands Nature Preserve parking lot in East Palo Alto. The Byxbee Park lot was closed for repairs, so nobody should have been on the premises. He realized as soon as he parked behind it that something was wrong. The driver's side window was open, and Gigi was slumped in the front seat. Two behind the ear. Small caliber. She's been dead since sometime early last night."

"Professional hit," I said. "And she knew the hitter."

"How so?" Schultheis asked.

"High temp yesterday was in the middle fifties. No reason to have the driver window open unless she was talking to someone. That suggests she knew the guy who killed her. Maybe it was someone she thought she could trust, and he gave her the twenty-two-caliber kiss-off. Any cameras in the parking lot?"

"We have the locals checking now," Diaz said.

I felt Fender bristle next to me at the word *locals*.

"I would have sworn Ruben thought Gigi was still alive," I said.

"Maybe he did," Fender said. "He might not know she was on a hit list. Tiger could have kept that from him, to give him plausible deniability."

"We have an officer on the way to pick Ruben up, bring him to the scene," Diaz said. "We'll check out how badly he loses his shit when he sees what happened to his wife."

The Byxbee Park car lot was a sea of flashing red and blue lights when we arrived. Everybody wanted in on what promised to be front-page headlines the next day. I saw Dexter Spears wading through the cars to get to the taped-off crime scene.

"Your boss is here," I told Fender.

"He must be expecting news cameras."

Spears spotted us and changed direction, striding in his loose-limbed scarecrow lope toward us. He ignored me completely.

"You got here quick," he said to Fender.

"We rode with Agent Diaz. I didn't have to retrieve my plainclothes car."

"Well, you can ride back with me. What a clusterfuck," Spears said, surveying the growing circus. The ME van drove around the corner to join the throng. "No point in sticking around. We're fuckin' dingleberries on this case. The FBI is running the whole show and freezing us out, but who do you think the papers will blame if we don't solve this one in the next six hours?"

"If it's all the same to you," Fender said, "I'd like to stick around for a bit, as the liaison between SFPD and the FBI."

"It isn't all the same to me," Spears said. "This isn't the only murder in town today, and somebody's going to expect the SFPD to solve at least *some* of them."

Spears looked around the crowd again, his hands on his hips. Finally, he shook his head.

"You're right," he said. "Someone needs to keep the lines open with the feds. Shit. I hate these guys. Headed back to the barn. The FBI might control this case, but you're the SFPD investigative presence here. Make yourself useful, early and often. Carry on."

He walked away without saying goodbye. Fender and I stood at the periphery of the crime scene tape and watched the A team do their thing.

"Make myself useful," Fender repeated. "Great advice."

Agent Diaz joined us a few minutes later. "The popular opinion agrees with you, Gold. Professional hit. Probably an out-of-towner, already back in his living room in Vegas or Houston or Miami sipping a cold one and watching reruns of *The Golden Girls*. We'll run the ballistics anyway, but it will come up zilch. These guys don't leave tracks."

"Tiger Sahakian's cleaning up loose ends," I said. "I don't think Ruben knew about this one. She died last night, and I'd swear he believed earlier today that she was still alive. Brownlee might have conned me, but Ruben isn't that slick."

"We'll have a hard time pinning it on Tiger as well," Diaz said. "I don't think we'll ever identify the shooter, and even if we did, I bet Tiger has six or seven layers of protection separating them. Any case we made would be circumstantial."

I said, "Maybe we can play the fact that Daddy kept Ruben out of the loop. Hit him hard with what we have, let him know he's on the hook for the Gary Zorn murder, and that his father just had his wife killed to cover it up. Maybe he'll roll over."

"Too risky," Diaz said. "We're not ready to run with that yet. Still gathering evidence." She pointed toward the car. "Including the new stuff we still have to process."

"He already knows we found Zorn's name," I said. "That was the plan after all. Name drop Zorn and see if he flinched. Boy, did he. He probably already suspects you're circling the camp, waiting to pounce. Don't tell him everything. Just enough to make him wonder what the rest of his life in orange coveralls would feel like."

A SFPD patrol car with flashing lights and wailing siren wended its way through the parking lot toward the taped-off murder scene. Before it stopped the passenger side door flung open and Ruben Sahakian jumped out on a dead run. Two officers stopped him at the edge of the tape. Agent Diaz marched up to him.

After introducing herself, she said, "We can't allow you on the other side of the tape. It might contaminate the scene."

Sahakian's eyes were red, rimmed with tears. He looked over Diaz's shoulders at the car, where the body was partly concealed with a tarp and the ME stood outside the door with one of the paramedics, collecting the necessary samples and data.

"What happened?" he asked.

"We're still figuring all that out," Diaz said. "You can stand here if you want, but I can tell you from experience that nothing interesting is going to happen for a long time. We have a tent set up over there, with coffee and some pastries. Would you be more comfortable there?"

"You're sure it's Gigi? That's not her car."

"It is Gigi," Agent Diaz said. "And that is her car. More specifically, it's registered to Samantha Derby, the identity your wife bought from the forger you introduced her to. She purchased the car under that identity with cash only a couple of weeks ago. Do you have any idea why she might have been here? Was she meeting somebody in particular?"

"Gigi's been missing for several days. It isn't common, but she has occasionally just taken off for no discernible reason. I didn't think much about it until Gold showed up at my office this morning and said the police had been to the shelter looking for her. I've been trying to call her all afternoon. Then this officer showed up and…" He stopped, as if the words simply wouldn't come.

Ruben turned around and saw me for the first time.

"Gold," he said. "What in hell are you doing here?"

"I was in a meeting with Inspector Fender when the call came in," I said. It was technically true. I didn't mention it was a meeting with the FBI, and that it was about *him.* He didn't need to know that. "With Gigi missing, I had a bad feeling, so I came with him on the run. I'm sorry, Ruben. Really. I'd have liked to help you find her alive."

One of the CS techs stood at the open passenger side door of Gigi's car and raised his hand. "Agent Diaz! You should look at this."

Diaz trotted around to the passenger side, where the tech showed her Gigi's purse which had been sitting in the footwell on the passenger side of the car. Gigi pulled a sheet of paper out of a zippered pouch inside, read it, then had the tech secure it inside a clear evidence baggie. She walked back over.

"Mr. Sahakian," she said, "We need to talk."

FORTY-EIGHT

Sam Brownlee looked chipper and confident, sitting at the defense table on the last day of his murder trial.

The evidence had all been presented. The final arguments had been made, and the attorneys had completed their summary addresses. The case was in the hands of the jury now.

Anticipating a fortunate turn in his circumstances, Brownlee had finally visited the prison barber. He wore the suit in which he had been arrested at his wife's funeral a year earlier. It hung loose on his slightly emaciated frame, but it was more dignified than a prison jumper.

Wilson Varnadore sat at his side, reviewing notes on another case as they waited out the jury deliberation. The bailiff had announced a half hour earlier that the jury had reached a verdict. It had taken five hours. Not speedy, but not terribly long either. Those verdicts were the hardest to predict.

I sat in the back of the gallery. I didn't wear a tie. I had a great view, though.

Around a half hour after I arrived, the judge entered from her chambers. She directed the bailiff to reseat the jury. Alison Eliot sat somberly at the prosecution table, her assistant fidgeting at her side.

The jury filed in. They didn't look happy. They didn't look sad. They didn't look like anything at all. Twelve poker faces.

"Has the jury reached a verdict?" the judge asked.

The forewoman stood. "We have."

"Hand the forms to the bailiff."

The forewoman complied, and the bailiff delivered the papers to the judge, who glanced at them before asking, "In the matter of Samuel Brownlee, regarding the charge of murder in the first degree, what is your verdict?"

The forewoman quietly replied, "We find the defendant, Samuel Brownlee, not guilty."

Brownlee showed emotion for the first time since entering the courtroom. He stood at the defense table and raised his fists in the air. Then he turned and grabbed Wilson Varnadore's hand, shaking it furiously. I didn't hear it, but I could lip read Varnadore's words. Reasonable doubt.

Reporters covering the trial deserted the courtroom to make their various deadlines with the surprise verdict. After a year in jail and rampant speculation regarding his guilt, Sam Brownlee would walk out of the court a free man. That was front page news.

Brownlee continued celebrating at the front of the courtroom. He turned and saw me sitting at the back, and pointed at me, grinning broadly. I shot him with my finger, mostly because the deputies downstairs had made me leave my pistol in the trunk of my car. He'd played me, and now he was gloating about it.

I grinned back.

I knew the game was only in the top of the ninth.

The doors to the courtroom opened, and Agents Diaz and Schultheis walked into the room, followed by three sheriff's deputies. They strode straight up the center aisle, through the swinging door and handed a folded slip of paper to Brownlee.

"Samuel Brownlee, Agent Angela Diaz of the FBI. This is Agent Lawrence Schultheis. You are under arrest as an accessory in the murder of Goran Zornakyan."

"Wait!" Brownlee croaked. "What is this?"

"Let me see that," Varnadore asked. Brownlee handed him the papers. Varnadore glanced over them.

"You gotta take care of this," Brownlee told him.

"This is a federal grand jury indictment," he said. "I'm afraid you'll have to comply, Sam. Listen to me. You know the drill. Don't say a word to anybody. Not a single word. I'll see you shortly."

The deputies led Brownlee off, followed by Agents Diaz and Schultheis. He protested all the way. I watched from my seat in the back of the gallery. Varnadore noticed me there as Brownlee was taken back to jail.

"You had something to do with this," he said to me.

I held my thumb and forefinger about half an inch apart. "Maybe a little bit."

"I hope you didn't violate our confidential privilege," he said. "I could make that very expensive for you."

"The FBI has been investigating the murder of Gary Zorn for almost a year and a half. That was long before we even met. My contribution to the arrest arose from information I learned *after* you terminated me. I can't say I'm disappointed with the outcome, though."

He gathered his papers and stowed them in his briefcase.

"It wouldn't be ethical for me to agree with you," he said. "But I will admit there are times when I question whether I'm on the side of the angels. I truly believe in Gideon, Gold. Every man who stands in the dock is due the very best defense available to him, and I'm the very best defender I know. I play my part in the process, and I play it superbly. Kind of wreaks havoc with sleep sometimes."

"I weep for you," I said. "But only a tear or two. In months without an 'R'."

"You're a singular person, you know that?"

I didn't say anything.

"I may call on you again," he said.

"I may not answer."

Having essentially cracked the Gary Zorn murder case for the FBI, I was invited to join Leon Fender in the observation closet behind the one-way mirror that Sam Brownlee now stared at glumly.

Agent Diaz walked into the interrogation room, carrying a thick folder, and sat across from Brownlee. She opened the folder and read silently for the next fifteen minutes as Brownlee stewed and fidgeted. Finally, she closed the file and placed her hand on top of it.

"We know you murdered your wife," she said.

"Jury just said otherwise."

"Doesn't matter. We aren't charging you with that anyway."

There was a knock on the door. Wilson Varnadore walked in and sat next to Brownlee, who was now visibly shaken.

"I was under the impression the interview wouldn't begin before I arrived," he said.

"He's been read his rights. I'm allowed to say anything I want in this room," Diaz said. "He's allowed to clam up if he pleases. If he chooses otherwise…" She shrugged.

"Did you tell her anything?" Varnadore asked Brownlee.

"Only what everyone knows. The jury found me innocent."

"They found you not guilty," Diaz said. "There's a difference, and it isn't just semantic. Mr. Varnadore, I was just explaining to your client that we know he murdered Rhonda Brownlee, regardless of what the jury said. We know you did it, and you know you did it, and we know why you did it. You were forced by Ruben and Tigran Sahakian to kill her because she found out they had murdered a federal informant named Goran Zornakyan, who went by the name Gary Zorn."

When he heard the name *Gary Zorn*, Brownlee went pale.

"Bingo," I said, behind the glass.

"Don't say a thing," Varnadore warned Brownlee.

"Gary Zorn played both sides of the fence," Diaz continued. "He coveted the power Tigran Sahakian wielded, and knew it was only a matter of time before there was a vacuum at the top of the Armenian mob in the bay area. He planned to be sucked up into it. He tried to establish his own power base, clumsily, and he got clobbered by the FBI, who turned him. Zorn became a rat. We allowed him to continue his criminal operations in return for a constant flow of information from inside the Armenian organization in San Francisco. Gary fucked up. Tigran found out about him. He and Ruben Sahakian murdered Gary Zorn and stuffed him inside a compost fermentation tank at Armin Bagdasarian's biofuel plant."

"I haven't heard a word connecting this to my client," Varnadore challenged.

"I was getting there. Ruben Sahakian funded Sam Brownlee's loansharking enterprises through Bagdasarian's business. Brownlee was leveraged to the eyeballs, practically tits-up before Ruben came along. Brownlee's wife was having an affair with Ruben Sahakian. She was in the wrong place at the wrong time and overheard the wrong conversation. She heard Ruben talk to his father about stuffing Zorn into the tank, and he knew exactly what it meant. She went to her husband to ask for help. He owed the Sahakians far too much, though. Sam here told Ruben what he had learned, and assured the Sahakians that he could control his wife. Rhonda didn't want to be controlled. She wanted help. When Sam betrayed her trust, she disappeared, and she became a liability. The order came down from Tigran Sahakian. *Find her and shut her up for good.* Brownlee hired a local private investigator to locate his wife, and then he murdered her. We know every bit of this to be true."

"Absurd," Varnadore said. "I can poke a dozen holes in that story."

Diaz opened the file to a photo of a handwritten piece of paper. She showed it to Brownlee.

"Is this your wife's handwriting?" she asked.

"Don't answer that," Varnadore told him.

"Not necessary," Diaz said. "We've already found other samples of Rhonda's handwriting. This is a match. Her fingerprints are on the paper. It's genuine. It's a handwritten account, produced by Rhonda Brownlee, dated about a week before she disappeared last year. It tells the entire story, including how Sam Brownlee refused to support his wife when she came to him for help, choosing instead to align with his financial backers. She describes the discussion between Tigran and Ruben Sahakian in minute detail. This is a holographic smoking gun, as admissible in court as first-hand testimony. Still staying quiet, Mr. Brownlee?"

"Say nothing," Varnadore warned. "None of this has any bearing on you. None of this implicates you in the murder of this Gary Zorn in any way."

"Except it does. As soon as Rhonda reported the conversation to Sam, he came into possession of evidence of a murder. Not reporting murders by his business associates to the police made him an accessory. Withholding it after his wife's murder is obstruction. We can tack on other stuff as we come up with it."

"It's a thin case," Varnadore said. "Try harder."

"Oh, I have more," Diaz said. "A lot more. For instance, there's—"

"Deal," Brownlee said.

"Shut up, Sam," Varnadore said.

"I know how things work," Brownlee said. "He who squeals deals. Right?"

"Yes," Diaz said. "However—"

He said. "Get me immunity, and I'll tell you all of it. Put me in witness protection. I'll hand over both Tiger and his asshole kid. I'm a small fish. You want the Great White Whale, right?"

"Sam!" Varnadore warned again.

"They *know*, Wilson," Sam said. "They fuckin' know everything. The only way out now is to deal."

"I've counseled you to remain silent," Varnadore told Brownlee. "If you choose to disregard my counsel, whatever happens is not my responsibility."

"What a champ," I said, behind the glass.

Fender snickered. "This is my favorite part. When they crumble."

"It *is* fun," I said. "Shame there's no popcorn."

Inside the room, Agent Diaz tapped her fingers on the case file. "I'll be back in five," she said. She left the room. Seconds later, she walked into the observation room and joined us at the mirror.

"Say nothing," Varnadore told Brownlee. "Not a word. They're still recording in here. Here's what's going to happen. Agent Diaz will return in five minutes with a deal. It will be attractive. You do not have to take it. I can make this go away, Sam. At the very worst, we can get the DA to drop the accessory charges and get a reduced sentence on obstruction. With a little luck, we can get you off entirely."

"Reduced sentence," he said. "If I roll over on Tiger—"

"Shut the fuck up, Sam!" Varnadore whispered coarsely. "For Christ's sake, are you a complete idiot?"

"No," he said. "I'm not. If I go to prison for one day, just one hour, Tiger will have someone there to kill me. I'm a fuckin' dead man walking here, Wilson. I only have one way out. New start with a new name. Hell, everyone else has been doing it the last year. Why not me?"

"Calm down. We have multiple options."

"Name three. You don't know these people. They threatened to kill me, and they meant it. I didn't know a damned thing, and they told me if I didn't—"

"Quiet! Damn it, Sam. You are making it extremely hard to defend you. Everything you say is on the record. Just shut your fucking mouth and let me handle things."

Inside the observation room, Diaz said, "If I leave them in there long enough, Brownlee's gonna confess to the Lindbergh kidnapping."

"Naw," I said. "He was in Berlin that day, springing Adolph Hitler from prison."

Diaz looked at Fender. "You've done good work on this one."

"Thanks," Fender said.

"I helped," I said.

"Yeah, but you don't wear a badge, and I suspect it's for a good reason. Inspector Fender, have you considered a career with the FBI?"

"Could solve a lot of problems," I said.

"Yeah. It could," Fender said. "You're on the level, Agent Diaz?"

"Call me Angela. Yeah. You have a college degree, right?"

"UCLA."

"State school. Okay. Whatever. Apply. I'll put in a good word for you. Hang tough, team. Going in for the kill."

A few seconds later, she sat across from Varnadore and Brownlee.

She said, "If the information's good, we can offer immunity on the accessory charge, but he has to cop a plea on obstruction. He'll serve the sentence in a Club Fed, probably Allenwood. Tiger's not sneaking anybody in there."

"Witness protection?" he said.

"Gee, here's the thing on that, Sam. That paper I showed you? The one Rhonda wrote? We found it in Gigi Sahakian's purse, after she was murdered. Rhonda gave it to her for safekeeping when she ran, in case anything happened to her. Gigi realized it could be her insurance policy as well. Turns out, not so much. Whoever killed her didn't know she had it and just left it behind. Ruben figured out right away that his father had Gigi killed, and he's really, really pissed about it. Like you said. He who squeals deals. Only thing is,

Ruben squealed first. He gets witness relocation. He already rolled over on his dad and on you. A few other people as well, including Armin Bagdasarian and the guy who probably parked two behind his wife's ear. Ruben's turning into a virtual fountain of information."

"Fuck," Varnadore said. "Here it comes."

"So, the deal is what I offered. Give us what we need. No accessory beef, and you do maybe two years in a cushy country club on obstruction. After that, where you go and what you do is up to you."

"And if I don't cooperate?" Brownlee said.

"You go down on both and stack your considerable time at a Supermax. We'll probably pile a few other charges on as well, just to give Tiger plenty of time to send his regards."

"They'll find me after I'm released."

"Not if you're agile and quick. We'll work out a way to give you a head start."

"They're going to fuck you," Varnadore said.

"Two years," Brownlee said. "Tiger's an old man. He could be dead by then, and Ruben's no threat if he's keeping his head down and running a Quickie Mart in Peoria. I could walk away clean."

Agent Diaz stood. "I'll let you talk it over."

"I'll take it," Brownlee said.

Varnadore put his hand on Brownlee's arm. "Sam, one last time—"

"Stop it, Wilson. I'm doing this. I'll take the deal. Two years is two years I wouldn't get in a regular prison. We'll deal with the rest later. Bring in the papers and I'll sign."

Diaz pulled the agreement papers from the file and placed them in front of Brownlee. Then she turned to the mirror and winked.

FORTY-NINE

Heidi made a killing of her own at a single artist showing that sold out, and she insisted we celebrate our combined victories with a night on the town. I scored an eight-thirty table at House of Prime Rib on Van Ness. We arrived an hour early so we could relax in the cocktail lounge. I had an Old Fashioned. Heidi ordered a healthy pour of Parducci True Grit cabernet. She told the bartender to leave the cork out, as the evening was only beginning, and the wine needed to breathe.

"So it's over?" she asked.

"As far as I'm concerned. It's time to spend a little bit of Varnadore's bonus money. We could wing out to the islands for a few days. Sonny will comp us a suite. We can lie on the beach and eat at Trader Vic's."

"I like that idea. Except Trader Vic's has been closed for years, darling."

"Can't be. I saw it on an episode of *Hawaiian Eye* the other night on that channel that sells catheters and walk-in tubs."

"First, I'm worried that you're watching that channel. Second, maybe check out a show that was made in this century."

"Tell me about this artist who made you rich today."

"She's promising. A recent graduate of SCAD. Works in sort of a mixed media. Oil and acrylics."

"Savannah's a whole country away," I said. "How'd she wind up here?"

"Same way a lot of people do. Followed her heart."

"Hope she finds it. People leave those lying around here all the time. I heard a song about it."

"Guy she hooked up with in Savannah was from the city. She decided she had a better chance of making it here than in Georgia."

"They're still together?"

"Oh, yes. Very happy. He sculpts. She paints. They fuck. A lot, according to her. It's mostly what she talks about, at least to me."

"Ah, fair youth. Over in an instant, but the pain remains for a lifetime."

"Kind of cynical," she said. "And speaking of youth, what's up with Libby?"

"You remembered her name this time."

"Are you taking her on?"

"I don't think that's up to me." I signaled to the waiter for another Old Fashioned. "I've let her know I'm available if she gets her ass stuck in a crack. She's wildly independent, though. She might call. She might try to tough it out herself. I'd just hate to be Bobby Sladen if she ever catches up with him."

"And what about the loanshark?"

"His best chance is if the old man dies before he gets out of jail. Ruben Sahakian is in an FBI safe house somewhere, because surely by now Tigran has heard that his son's rolling over on him. Brownlee's in protective custody as well. It's basically solitary."

"But no blowback on you?"

"None that I can think of. Ruben knows I never heard about Gary Zorn before the FBI showed up. He knows they were wired in for months before we even met. He's going into the relocation program in any case. Those people keep a very low profile. Practically invisible. Nobody will ever hear from him again. Once he's out of jail, Sam Brownlee will buy a new identity and disappear, he hopes. He'll probably be selling junk desert land to chump retirees out of a trailer in the Mojave in three years. Everyone else I pissed off is dead or not much of a threat. For once, I think I dodged all the shrapnel."

"So, still spry and nimble after all these years." She held up her glass. I clinked and we sipped.

"I have my moments." I smiled at her over my glass.

"Want to demonstrate later?" she asked.

"I'll consider it a command performance."

I was in my office the next afternoon, waiting for the telephone to ring or for someone to trudge up the sixteen steps to my landing. I'd already paid the bills and completed my case reports on Sam Brownlee and Wilson Varnadore. I'd vacuumed and dusted my office, wiped down the windows with Windex, and cleaned the top of my desk. I was considering cleaning my pistols, just to relieve the boredom, even though I'd just done it the weekend before. I had the stereo on a local oldies channel I noticed I'd been listening to more and more lately. Heidi was busy in the gallery, rehanging the standing collection after the showing the day before.

It was a dull, dishwater day. It had been overcast since the previous evening. The water of the bay was choppy in a westerly wind that whistled under the bridge. The sea lions had deserted the pier temporarily. I wondered what they knew. I recalled animals had acted strangely just before the Loma Prieta quake in 1989. We were kind of overdue for a big tremblor. I really needed to keep myself occupied, or thoughts like this would make me kind of loopy.

My telephone buzzed. Libby Cordelia Hackney. I wondered for a second why I'd put in all three names as I answered the call.

"Eamon Gold, Discreet Investigations," I said.

"Really, Gold?"

"A woman recently told me I had a radio announcer voice. You aren't impressed?"

"Who listens to the damn radio?"

"An apropos question, considering your current case. Are you in trouble?"

"No. But I could use some help anyway. You ever heard of a guy named Doug Petrie?"

"An engineer or some shit. Worked for Arlen Drake for a couple of decades. One of the three."

"Three?"

"Tim Simms said the radio station was run by only three people. He handles all the administrative bother. Some kid named Lineberger works the board during the daylight hours. Petrie lives at the transmitter in a single-wide in case anything breaks there. He keeps everything running."

"You ever meet Petrie?"

"Once. For about ten minutes, while you were in jail. I was just trying to figure out how the whole radio station worked. Why?"

"I might have something. Don't want to talk about it on the phone. You at your office?"

"Sure. Not planning on going out."

"Be there in an hour."

She hung up without saying goodbye. I opened my laptop and called up my notes on the Libby Hackney investigation. It was something to do while I waited. After a few minutes, I called Leon Fender.

"You still have the Arlen Drake investigation?" I asked.

"It's in review, now that our prime suspect was sprung."

"You know those charges were going nowhere. What's in review about it?"

"Well, because Metterling was involved, it's a hot potato. On the one hand, a man is dead and we don't have anyone in custody. On the other hand, it was the current lieutenant of homicide who blew the case in the first place. It's a black mark on his record. I think he'd prefer that it just dried up from neglect and disappeared."

"Fuckin' Spears," I said.

"He alone makes that FBI agent's suggestion attractive."

"You considering it?"

"Giving it some thought. If I join, do I have to wear one of those ugly suits?"

"I believe the ugly suits are optional. The wingtips as well. You're stuck with a tie, though, which puts me one up on you."

"Are you calling for a reason, or are you just bored?"

"A little of both. Wanted to catch you up on a few things and make a suggestion. Libby Hackney is on the warpath, looking for Bobby Sladen. It's part revenge, but she's also convinced that Bobby was behind Arlen Drake's murder, and he tried to frame her for it."

"I would very dearly like to talk with Mr. Sladen myself," Fender said.

"I don't know what's happening, but Libby's on the way to my office right now. She's got a bug up her butt about a guy named Doug Petrie. He's an engineer. Works for the radio station Bobby was buying from Arlen Drake. I interviewed him a few weeks back, didn't get any weird vibes from him other than the fact he's a burnout who lives in a trailer next to a radio shack. He said he hadn't met Sladen yet, though. He also called me *boss*. What do you make of that?"

"He's done time. Road crews call the gun bulls *boss*."

"He was either being cagey or he wasn't in the loop on the sale. Now Libby thinks he might be connected somehow. I'll know more when she gets here. You might want to start digging into Petrie, though."

"On her recommendation?"

"On mine. I can't explain it, but after looking over my own notes, I just have a feeling she's on to something. I don't know what it is, yet. I like her instincts, Leon. I think she has the right stuff, but she's rough as a cob. If she's getting a tingle from this Petrie guy, I think it's worth following up."

"I'll pull up his records," Fender said. "If she tells you anything germane to the case, you need to forward it along as well. Got me?"

"On speed dial."

FIFTY

I was still waiting for Libby when Fender called back.

"I hate it when you're right," he said.

"Petrie?"

"He has a record. Before his Navy hitch. South Carolina."

"I didn't think the Navy took recruits with felony beefs."

"They give you one. If you have two you can't sign up. The nature of the felony is kinda germane as well."

"Charges?"

"Petrie was busted for cannabis distribution. He was driving a Chevy with six bricks of Mexican ditchweed in the trunk. This was back in the eighties, in the middle of Nancy Reagan's Just Say No bullshit and the heyday of the war on drugs. Paraquat and all that shit."

"Those were uncool times."

"And how. Klan judges who had been sitting on the bench since Reconstruction wanted to make examples out of hippies, even if by the eighties there weren't more than a couple hundred hardcore flower children left. Petrie copped to simple possession and did six months on a road gang. Had a few shit jobs once he got out, but the prison record hung over him. Finally he wandered into a recruiting station in Charleston and they gave him a haircut and a uniform."

"He said he got into radio while in the Navy."

"We're waiting on his military record, but I did pull his first-class ticket from the FCC, and the dates are right. His employment record says he's been with Drake's station for almost twenty years. Before that he did a few short stints at other stations."

"Any legal problems?"

"Clean and green since he punched out of the Navy. No warrants, no beefs, not even a parking ticket. This boy likes to fly under the radar. I hate to say it, Gold, but other than the prison record, my dick's not getting hard over this one. What does Hackney have on him?"

"Don't know. She's on the way here now."

"I appreciate you dropping this in my lap anyway. We haven't had any luck tracking Sladen down, and any tip is progress. Call me if Hackney has something useful."

I was thinking about lunch when Libby clomped up my stairs and walked into my office without knocking.

"My feet are killing me," she said.

"Hungry? I was about to head out for a bite."

"Famished. Skipped breakfast this morning."

We hit The Codmother on Beach Street for fish and chips. Since nobody was keeping tabs on me, I ordered a beer. She stared at me as I soaked the fries with malt vinegar.

"Ketchup's not good enough for you?" she asked.

"Not here. Tell me about Doug Petrie."

"I've been schlepping my ass from bar to bar for days. I'm so sick of ginger ale."

"Ginger ale?"

"Looks like scotch and soda. If I drank at every place I visited, they'd have to snatch my liver out when I croak and beat it to death."

"Any luck?"

"Like I told you, Bobby can't stand being alone. Sooner or later, he has to come out of hiding just to get his social jones satisfied. I have a couple of pictures of him. Showed them around wherever I went. A lot of people recognized him, but none of them had seen him in weeks. Ran across another couple of women he slept with as well. Those were interesting conversations, but not productive. Then I hit this place in East Petaluma called Pancho's. Bartender recognized Bobby right off thc bat. Turns out the asshole owes him money."

"For what?"

"Football bar bet. Goes back to the Super Bowl a year ago. Hundred measly bucks, but this guy holds a grudge. He's been pestering Bobby to pay up for months, right up until the last time he walked into the bar."

"The bartender makes a better suspect than Petrie so far. So how did he come into the picture?"

"This same bartender said, the last time Bobby came into the bar, this Petrie guy was with him."

I shook my head. "Petrie told me he never met Sladen."

"Everybody lies, Gold."

"Yeah. The bartender knew Petrie?"

"Petrie's lived in those parts for twenty years. He was a regular at this place in East Petaluma a few years back, but then he stopped coming in. The bartender was kind of surprised to see him. He'd heard Petrie took the pledge."

"Petrie lied. That's something. The real question is *why*."

"That's not all. This bartender, his name's Alan White. Nice fellow. Kind of cute. Rad tats. Might go back and hit him up."

"Focus."

"Anyway, he said Bobby and Petrie sat together, but they didn't look very happy. They argued about something."

"Could Alan overhear the conversation?"

"No. Too loud. There was a lot of finger-pointing and fist pounding on the table, though. Petrie was hot. Bobby kept trying to calm him down, but eventually Petrie drained his bottle and stomped out the door."

"When was this?"

"About a week after Arlen Drake was murdered. Alan remembered because there was a big Final Four game playing on the TV, and Bobby and Petrie ignored it entirely. I checked the dates."

"All right," I said. "I think you might be on to something, especially because I asked Petrie directly about Bobby, and he claimed they never met. Sounds like they knew each other pretty well. I had Leon Fender run his background."

"Is he dirty?"

"Not at all, unless you count a felony weed beef from four decades ago. He's squeaky clean ever since. Honorable discharge from the Navy, and no legal issues whatsoever afterward. On paper, he doesn't play."

"Half the people stacking time in prison had no criminal history before they were popped. Crimes of passion, embezzling, assault. People snap, Gold."

"Well," I said. "At the very least, we know Petrie lied to me about knowing Bobby. He needs to account for that. Maybe he also knows where we can find him." I started writing an email. "I told Fender I'd keep him in the loop. Let me update him, and you and I can take a ride up to Petaluma."

We pulled off the highway onto the dusty dirt road that led to the radio station tower and Doug Petrie's dilapidated single-wide. He was outside the mobile home, watering his garden. In the time since I'd last visited, the corn had grown another couple of feet, and the tomatoes were beginning to ripen. He had earbuds in and didn't hear us drive up. When he shut off the hose, he turned and saw us standing by the car.

"He'p ya?" he said. He squinted a little and then recognized me. "Oh. The detective fella. Who's she?"

"Another detective," I said, without giving her name. If Petrie knew Bobby, he might also know about Bobby and Libby. No need to complicate the situation. "Can we talk?"

"Sure," he said. "Lemme put this hose away first."

He rolled the hose onto a reel attached to a wooden post next to the garden and pointed toward the trailer.

"AC's on," he said. "It's more comfortable in there."

We followed him inside the trailer, where I was once again surprised to find it well-kept inside. The place was clean and smelled of cleansers and disinfectant. The furniture was relatively new and in good shape.

"Get ya somethin' to drink?" he asked. "Got Coke, some iced tea, and a fresh-half gallon of Simply Lemonade."

"Nothing harder?" I asked.

"I don't drink alcohol, Mr.…Damn, I forgot your name."

"Gold," I said.

"I quit drinking a few years back, Mr. Gold. Was in a program for a while, but it's been a bit since I attended. Haven't really felt the urge. If I don't got it, I can't drink it, so I don't buy it."

"Curious," Libby said. "Alan White said you were in his bar a few months back."

"Alan who?" Petrie said.

"A bartender. Pancho's in East Petaluma. He says you used to be a regular."

"Oh, Alan. Been a while. Knew who you meant once you said Pancho's. He's right. I was a regular. Not anymore. You been checkin' up on me?"

"We're still looking for Bobby Sladen," I said. "Don't suppose you've seen him around?"

"Like I told you, mister, I never met the man."

"Alan White says differently," Libby said. "He says you and Bobby were in his bar together during the NCAA Final Four this year. That was only a week after Arlen Drake was murdered. He says you had quite the discussion. It became a little loud, and then you stomped out. What were you arguing about?"

Petrie stood and walked to the refrigerator.

"Sure you don't want a drink?" he asked.

"Answer the question," I said. "We know you lied about knowing Bobby Sladen. The police know as well. I told them just before we drove up here."

"Now why would you go and do something like that?" Petrie said, as he pulled a shotgun from the space between the refrigerator and the wall. I grabbed for my Glock, but he was on me before I could pull it and he slammed the stock into the side of my head.

It wasn't hard enough to take me out, but I saw stars and couldn't think for enough seconds for him to yank the pistol from my holster and stow it in the refrigerator freezer.

He rotated the shotgun and pointed it at Libby.

"Hand over your gun," he said.

"Don't have one," she said, holding her jacket open to show him.

"Your ankle," he said.

She pulled up her pants legs to show him she wasn't armed. He opened a drawer and tossed Libby a roll of black duct tape.

"Arlen Drake's hands were bound with black duct tape," I said, shaking my head to clear the cobwebs.

"Don't mean nothin'," Petrie said. "You can buy this shit in any hardware store in the country. Here, lady, you tape his wrists behind him."

"Not a chance," Libby said.

"It's that or a load of double-aught in your ear. You choose." He leveled the shotgun at her.

"You killed Arlen Drake," I said, as Libby reluctantly wrapped the tape around my wrists behind my back, glaring at Petrie all the time.

"Naw, but I was there."

"Where's Bobby Sladen?" I asked.

"Oh, he's somewhere abouts. Yeah. I was in that bar with him. He was trying to cheat me. That's why I run off the way I did. Okay, lady, you're next. Turn around."

Libby resisted, but Petrie was surprisingly strong and agile for his age. He bent her forcefully over the back of his living room chair as she struggled. When she didn't cooperate, he slapped her across the right ear. She screamed then, as a trickle of blood dripped down her earlobe.

"You broke my fuckin' eardrum!" she shouted at him as he wrapped the tape around her wrists.

"I promise it'll only hurt for a few minutes," Petrie said, hefting the shotgun. "Busted eardrum is the least of your worries."

"You and Jeff Lineberger," I said.

"What's that?" Petrie asked.

"It was you and Jeff Lineberger. Tim Simms said Lineberger was hired only a few months before Drake was murdered, but after Sladen bought half the station. Bobby played poker while you and Lineberger took Drake out. You bent him over the chair in his apartment exactly the same way you did with Libby, wrapped his wrists in duct tape, and then Lineberger planted one in the back of his head while you watched."

"Think you're smart," Petrie said. "All my life, people been acting like they're smarter than me. Well, who's smart now?"

"Arlen Drake's death triggered the insurance policy that would have allowed Bobby to own the entire station. What did he promise you and Jeff in return for killing Drake?"

"More than he could scratch up," Petrie said. "That's why we were fighting in that bar. He promised both of us a hundred thousand bonus for getting him the entire station. Then he could only come up with twenty. And we had to split it."

"The missing payment to Boyd Demarest," I told Libby. She nodded. "Bobby was robbing Peter to pay Paul."

"Don't know nobody named Peter or Paul, but he was ripping the shit off of us. I spent my whole life scrapin' around for some kind of security. A hundred grand could set me up for life, considering I don't have all that long left anyway, and my expenses are kind of minimal." He gestured around the trailer with the barrel of the shotgun.

"Bobby isn't going to let you live," I said. "He's a stone-cold psychopath killer. Sooner or later, he'll turn you and Jeff against one another, let you take each other out, and he'll resurface with the entire station ready to hand over to Boyd Demarest."

"You keep saying names I never heard," Petrie said. "I don't know no Peter or Paul, and I don't know anyone named Demarest."

"You don't want to," I said. "Boyd Demarest turns five guys into shark chum every day before lunch. He's backing Bobby's play on the radio station, and he's kind of pissed that Bobby missed the payments for the last several months. When Bobby pops back up, sooner or later, there's going to be hell to pay. You can get ahead of all of it now, by turning yourself in, taking the heat for being an accomplice, and laying it all out on Sladen. You could make a hell of a deal, Petrie."

Petrie opened the refrigerator and took out a can of Diet Coke. He popped the tab and took a long swig.

"It's attractive," he said. "And I'd roll over on Bobby in a second after the way he treated me."

"Do it," Libby said. "You'll sleep better at night."

"If only I could," he said. "After that argument that night, Bobby tried to smooth things over. He came here. He talked a big game, but he'd burned me long enough, and I wasn't in the mood. Then he threatened me. Shouldn't ought to have done that."

I turned to Libby. "Bobby's dead."

"I figured that out already, Gold."

"Yeah," Petrie said, as he sat on the sofa, the shotgun lying across his lap. He sipped at the soda. "I didn't take much to being threatened. We fought. He was good. Not good enough. I pushed him across the kitchen, drove the side of his head right into the corner of that cabinet over there. The head injury probably woulda killed him, but I was in a hurry to finish the job. Used that black tape there. Wrapped it around his nose and mouth and waited. Didn't take long. Coulda shot him, I suppose, but we'd already made enough of a mess, and I like to keep things tidy."

"Where's Bobby?" I asked. "What did you do with the body?"

"The garden," Libby said.

"Right," I said. "The garden."

"Thinkin' about putting in a stand of winter cabbage. Dead guys make great fertilizer," Petrie said. "Found that out a few years back."

"A few *years?*" I said. "How many bodies do you have buried in that garden, Petrie?"

"Enough. Two more, in a few hours. Gonna wait until dark, on account of I gotta kill you outside, behind the radio shack. Don't want to mess up my crib."

"It's not going to work," I said. "The SFPD detective investigating Drake's murder knows all about you. I called him as soon as she told me you'd been seen with Sladen, and I had him run a background check on you. He has your entire life story on his desk right now."

"Bullshit."

"You were busted for cannabis possession in South Carolina. Six bricks. The judge sent you to a road crew for six months. One month for each brick. You ask me, you got off light for the time and place."

Petrie plopped onto a chair across from us. He kept the barrel of the shotgun pointed directly at my chest.

"Well, fuck, then. I'm sure as shit not getting the hundred grand Bobby promised me. No real reason to hang out here after I plant you two. Reckon I'm gonna have to kill Jeff after he gets off the air as well, since he can put the finger on me if your cop fella catches up with him."

"My car has a GPS tracker," I said. "If I go missing, Inspector Fender will know in five minutes where I went today. You don't only have to get rid of us; you have to ditch the car as well. Think you can do that without leaving any of yourself behind? A hair, an eyelash, a gob of spit, some dry skin? DNA labs today can pin your ass to the wall with a flake of dandruff. The way I see it, Doug, you have a big problem."

"Nothin' I can't handle," he said, but I could see sweat forming along his hairline. I could tell he wasn't an idiot, and he knew the numbers weren't stacking up for him.

"You got your butt in a big crack," I said. "There may be a moratorium on executions in this state, but the death penalty is still on the books. From what you've already said, we know you're on the hook for Arlen Drake and Bobby Sladen. How many other counts do you have buried under those bell peppers and tomatoes? There's only one way out of this that doesn't end with you strapped to a gurney, Doug."

"Don't call me that!" he shouted. "You don't know me. We ain't buddies. You don't get off calling me by my Christian name."

"All right then," I said. "But facts are facts. The police know about you. No matter what happens here, that doesn't go away."

He rubbed at his thick beard and scratched his elbow as he stared at me.

"Well, fuck," he said. "Looks like this is the Alamo. Ain't goin' back to prison, dude. If I go all Dillinger with the cops, I reckon that's as good a way to punch out as any." He leered at Libby. "No reason I got to go out with a dry dick, though."

He grabbed Libby by the hair and dragged her screaming across the singlewide toward a low-back easy chair. I started to rush him, but he swung the shotgun barrel around and caught me on the other side of my head. The barrel split the skin, and blood trickled across my cheek as I collapsed back on the sofa, dazed.

Petrie bent Libby over the back of the chair and stuck his hand in the waistband of her pants. He yanked hard, and the synthetic fabric ripped. He yanked again and pulled her pants down to the middle of her thighs.

"Fuck you, asshole!" Libby shouted. "Soon as my hands are free, I'm gonna show you how it feels to have your balls ripped out through your throat!"

Petrie planted his foot in the small of her back to keep her pinned against the back of the chair. He kept the shotgun trained on me as he fumbled with the button to his cutoff jeans. Libby struggled and squirmed, trying to get out from under Petrie's boot.

I wiped at the blood that was dripping into my eye as the fog of getting shotgun-whipped began to lift. The odds were overwhelmingly on the side of me taking a buckshot load to the chest if I jumped him. If I didn't try, though, the chances of winding up on the wrong side of the winter cabbage were one hundred percent.

I tried the tape around my wrists. It wouldn't budge. Whatever I was going to do, I'd have to do it without my hands.

I watched Petrie carefully, looking for an opening. He was dividing his attention between two critical activities, and sooner or later he'd get distracted.

He had his pants down now, exposing a hairy, pimple-scarred butt.

"Now, you just relax," he told her. "It'll be worse if'n you tense up."

Libby sobbed a couple of times as she stared at the floor, her waist bent over the back of the chair, and she struggled to stand up. Each time she pushed back against the chair, Petrie yanked at her hair and twisted. Keeping the shotgun pointed in my direction, Petrie moved in close. I waited for him to turn his head, the best chance I'd probably get.

Libby beat me to it. As Petrie tried to press against her, she grabbed his junk with both bound hands. Her freshly manicured half-inch acrylic nails dug deep into the tender flesh, drawing blood.

Then she twisted her wrists.

Petrie screeched in pain and dropped the shotgun as he tried to push away, but she hung on like a snapping turtle, squeezing and jabbing and slicing into his skin as Petrie beat on her back with his fists.

"What are you waiting for?" she shouted.

I was on my feet in an instant. I kicked the shotgun, which skittered across the vinyl floor into the kitchen. Then I pivoted and kicked Petrie hard in the kidneys. He howled in pain and fury, let go of Libby's hair, and grabbed at his back. He fell backward and Libby pushed away from the chair. She fell on top of him. He struggled to push her off, which gave me the opportunity to kick the side of his head a few times until he collapsed, groaning, and passed out.

Sirens wailed in the distance.

"Kinda breezy," Libby said, nodding at her pants gathered around her thighs. "A little help before the cops break in here?"

Using some contortions that would leave me with muscle stingers for a week, I went back-to-back with her and helped pull her pants back up. As soon as her legs were free, she kicked Petrie in the balls as hard as she could.

"Ouch," I said.

"Nobody bends Libby Cordelia Hackney over a chair without permission," she said. "Might give him another kick just for shits and giggles."

"I think he's done," I said, as the Petaluma police cruisers pulled into the dirt road leading to the transmitter shack.

FIFTY-ONE

When the uniformed Petaluma officers stepped into the trailer, Libby and I sat calmly on the sofa, our hands still tied behind us. The shotgun was halfway under the kitchen table. Doug Petrie snored peacefully on the floor, his cutoffs around his ankles. My Glock was still in the freezer.

"Hi, guys," I said. "No rush. We took care of it."

After determining we weren't a threat, they cut the duct tape binding our wrists. I retrieved my Glock from the freezer and handed it to the lead officer for safekeeping.

Fender waltzed in a quarter hour later. The uniformed officers had already separated Libby and me. She was in the bedroom, and I was still in the living room. The officers had cuffed Petrie but had otherwise left him undisturbed until the crime scene guys showed up. It was incredibly undignified, but the guy had planned to put me under a cabbage patch, so fuck him.

"You're going to need cadaver dogs and a ground-penetrating radar," I told Fender.

"I'm coming in late in this conversation. Why don't we start over?"

"Libby cracked the case. Bobby Sladen hired Doug Petrie and Jeff Lineberger to murder Arlen Drake. They walked right into Drake's house, because why wouldn't they? They worked for him, after all. Drake never suspected a thing until Petrie slugged him and taped his wrists together. Lineberger did the shooting. Sladen offered them a hundred grand apiece for the job, but he welshed on the deal and Petrie killed him when they fought about it. Planted Sladen under his vegetable garden. From what he said, Bobby might have a lot of company. I think Doug Petrie is a world-class sick puppy who has been killing people for a long time."

"Thank God," Fender said. "I only have to worry about the Drake case. All this other shit is Petaluma's problem."

"Why'd you send the police in the first place?"

"I followed up on your suspicions. Calling me before you drove up here was the smartest thing you could have done. I did some more sifting after you told me Petrie had been seen with Bobby. Petrie's phone records included calls to and from Bobby Sladen's phone. A couple of calls took place on the day of the murder, and the spacing suggests Petrie called before and after he and Lineberger killed Drake. I figured you and Libby could use some help."

"You should pick up Lineberger at the station. It goes off the air in an hour, at sundown. If he hears anything about Petrie being arrested, he'll be in the wind."

"On it," he said. He stepped outside for a few minutes to talk it over with the Petaluma boys. Two of them climbed into a cruiser and headed back out to the highway.

By the time he reentered the mobile home, Libby had joined me on the sofa.

"Start from the beginning," he told us. "Leave nothing out."

We were there for several more hours.

The news trucks arrived shortly after dark. By then, cadaver dogs had gone absolutely nuts sniffing around Doug Petrie's vegetable garden.

Petrie was transported to the local hospital for observation. I might have kicked him a little harder than I intended. I wasn't sorry. He'd have aching balls for weeks, with no idea how they got that way, and they'd be covered with scabs from acrylic nail scratches and punctures as well. Libby expressed not a shred of remorse for that either.

The medics performed a quick mental status exam to assure Petrie hadn't given me brain damage, and then one of them patched the shotgun barrel laceration on my head. Had to shave a patch of my hair to do it.

"I won't be able to pose for GQ for weeks," I said.

The medic said, "I didn't know they had a senior edition."

That stung more than Petrie's shotgun butt.

"This is going to be a shitshow," Fender said, watching the crime scene crew set up the LED lights around the property. "We borrowed a ground penetrating radar. How many bodies do you reckon he has stashed in there?"

"Too many."

A car turned off the highway and raised clouds of dust as it made its way to the crime scene. It parked and Tim Simms stepped out. He walked directly to me, the only person he immediately recognized. I introduced him to Inspector Fender.

"I was at home. Heard the dead air. Jeff didn't answer at the station, so I drove over to see if he was okay. The police had him under arrest! What in hell is going on here?"

"You might want to sit down," I said, pointing to the bench on the mobile home stoop.

Fender laid out the entire story, at least the part we knew, as best he could.

"So Bobby's dead?" Simms asked.

"According to Petrie," I said. "He's buried in the vegetable garden, maybe with a lot of other people. The cadaver dogs indicated it's a mass grave. They'll be days clearing the site."

"Don't know what that means for me," Simms said. "I reckon the station's going off the air for a few days. I need a new first engineer, and I suppose I'll be running the board myself until I can hire a new guy. Hell, I don't even know if there *is* a station anymore. Both owners are dead."

"Um," I said. "I'm afraid the bad news isn't over. Before he died, Bobby made a deal with Boyd Demarest, a white nationalist gangster in San Francisco. Once the insurance paid off and Bobby was the sole owner, he planned to sign the place over to Demarest to settle his debt. Demarest plans to sell it to some crank televangelist in Utah."

"You know," Fender said. "Since Bobby had Arlen Drake murdered for the insurance money and to get the station solely in his name, and Boyd Demarest planned to take it from him in a bust-out, that sort of makes Demarest an accomplice. He might not get the station after all."

"Sounds like a hard case to make," I said.

"Maybe not. I'll talk it over with the DA. I have friends at the FBI now as well. This is the kind of situation they drool over."

"Give Agent Diaz a call," I said. "This could be your first case. As for the station, Mr. Simms, I don't know. Without an owner of record, the FCC might shut it down while things are sorted out. Either that, or someone needs to find Bobby's next of kin."

"That doesn't work either," Fender said. "Bobby can't own the entire station, since he murdered Drake to acquire it. He isn't allowed to profit from a murder he committed. He still owns only fifty-one percent."

"Sounds like this little piece of shit station is going to keep the lawyers busy for months," Simms said.

"Years, maybe," I said. "I'd call the FCC right away, try to work out a deal to keep it on the air in the interim."

"Or maybe it's time to walk away clean," he said. "My dad did it. Maybe there's a place for a seasoned broadcast management veteran like me under some new call letters." He held out his hand. "I appreciate you and Ms. Hackney and the police for solving Arlen's murder. He was a good man, and he was always aces to me. Probably why I held out this long." He looked around. "Not so sure this is the right place for me anymore, though.'

We shook hands, and he returned to his car. I thought I saw an unexpected little spring in his step.

FIFTY-TWO

Heidi and I walked into Luigi's Pizza at Pier 39 and were seated immediately. We always ordered a large pizza each when we visited there. I like a great garbage pie, piled with every topping there is, right down to the anchovies and lots of them. Heidi is more restrained, and she often commits the cardinal sin of ordering pineapple on hers. We don't worry about not finishing, because both of us have refrigerators and leftover pizza is frequently even tastier than fresh. I added a pitcher of Anchor Steam to the order, and we were set.

It had been six weeks since Libby and I had kicked the living shit out of Doug Petrie and uncovered what had become something of a media frenzy. Forensic recovery experts had worked in teams around the clock for days, removing human remains from Petrie's vegetable garden. When my aching head had finally cleared enough to think, I realized he had the perfect killing field. The transmitter shack and Petrie's single-wide were a quarter mile off the road, out in the boonies. The shack was solid concrete block, and the door was inch-thick steel. A captive could be held in there screaming for days, if necessary, and nobody would ever hear a peep.

Petrie had clammed up as soon as he was arrested, and he hadn't said a word to the police. He wasn't destitute, but neither could he afford a private defense attorney. I'd mentioned it to Wilson Varnadore, since it promised to be such a high-profile trial, but he said Petrie had tried to rape and murder his client Libby Hackney, so it probably wasn't a great fit. After that, I kind of lost interest. The guy had tried to turn me into fertilizer, after all.

"How many bodies now?" Heidi asked, as she pulled the first slice of her pizza off the pan, glistening strings of mozzarella hanging from it. She expertly swept them to the top of the slice with her fork and took a bite. She immediately opened her mouth and waved air inside. "Hot. Hot!"

"Why I always wait," I said. "They've identified remains of seventeen bodies so far. DNA tests are still out on several more."

"At least some families are getting closure."

"Some of them have been waiting a long time. It looks like he's been at it almost since he took the job at the station. Maybe before that, in the Navy, as well."

She shuddered. "What a monster."

"They walk amongst us," I said.

Libby Cordelia Hackney breezed through the door, scoped out the room, and found me. She wended her way between the tables to get to us.

"Got hung up. Possible new case." She pointed at Heidi. "Who's this?"

I made the introductions.

"Wow," Libby said, as she took Heidi's hand and gave her the head-to-toe. "Hoochie Mama! She's a catch, Gold."

She grabbed a slice of my garbage pie and poured some beer into the glass I'd ordered for her.

"Nice people ask first," I said.

"I'll give you a slice of mine. Where's the waiter?"

She ordered her own pie, a North Beach Special, and asked for another pitcher.

"Been running my ass ragged," she said, after another chug of the Anchor Steam. "Phone's been ringing off the hook. Turns out people take notice when you shut down a serial killer."

I knew what she meant. As the newly appointed Captain of Major Crimes, Dexter Spears tried to take all the credit for Petrie's apprehension, but someone—I suspected Fender—tipped off someone else at the *Chronicle* that two local private cops actually took him down. The next day, Libby and I were both pictured on the front page of the local section, albeit below the fold.

Most of it was about how Libby had caught the real murderer in a case in which she had been accused and jailed. It was a compelling yarn. A couple of movie companies were sniffing around for rights to the story a day or so after it was printed.

The article gave me a few inches of play as well, including a brief description of some of my more notorious cases over the years.

T'was enough. Did serve. My phone was ringing when I unlocked my office door the next day, and it hadn't stopped ringing. I was already referring overflow clients to Jack Delroy at Full Moon, because I can only juggle so many cases at one time.

When I told Heidi that I thought Fender had outed me, she asked if he would get into any trouble for it with Spears.

"Leon can tell Spears where to shove it and how far," I said. "This time next month, he'll be going through orientation at Quantico. He was selected for the FBI."

We talked a little more about the Drake murder and Petrie until we all agreed that it wasn't doing anything for our appetites.

"So," I told Libby after asking the server for some take-home boxes. "Here's the deal. As Heidi has pointed out—"

"Repeatedly," Heidi said.

"—More than once," I agreed. "Anyway, business is good right now. Really good. For you, too, it seems. That's great, but as I've told you before, you need some serious seasoning. You've got the chops. No doubt about it. You need someone to show you the hard knots. How to stay out of jail, for instance."

"What are you suggesting?" Libby said. "You want to adopt me?"

"Kind of," Heidi said. "Between you and me, he can use some help."

"Time and tide," I said. "Waits for nobody. Taking a couple of shotgun butts to the head cleared shit up for me. I still have a few good years left, but the mileage is starting to show. I'm gonna do like Jack Delroy and back away from the knuckles and know-how cases."

"Fuck that shit," Libby said. "Sorry, Hooch."

"Don't mind me," Heidi said. "My ancestors invented Anglo-Saxon epithets."

I caught a smirk at the corner of her mouth. She was amused.

"The action's on the street, man. I've seen you in heavy metal mode," Libby told me. "You've still got some piss and vinegar left."

"Vinegar's what happens when the wine grows old. As for piss, I'm doing a lot more of that as well, mostly at night. What I'm saying is, I get hurt easier and I don't heal as quickly as I used to. It's time to stop rolling in the dirt with bad guys. There's plenty of work out there that doesn't involve potential brain damage. Fraud. Embezzlement. Errant spouses. Security systems. Missing persons."

"This whole shitshow started with a missing person case."

"True enough. Fortunately, most of them don't turn out this way. I'm ready to leave the dangerous stuff to younger guys. And you. So that's it. I'm backing off the rough-and-tumble stuff."

"Whatever, Boomer. More work for me."

"I'm not a…" I stopped and took a breath. "Look, Heidi and I have been talking. We both think it's time to bring a little youth into the program. I was wondering if you'd consider joining forces. We hang out a shingle together. Partners. Gold and Hackney, Discreet Investigations. You help me, I help you."

"Your office is kinda cramped," she said. "And it smells like fish when the wind on the bay changes."

"Fair enough. We don't have to work under the same roof. Keep your own office. We'll hang out a shingle at both places. Having two offices is kind of cool anyway. Makes us look like a franchise. We can work independently, but if I need backup, I'll call you. If you need backup, call me. If we both need backup, we call Sonny."

"Who's Sonny?" Libby asked.

"Oh, you're going to *love* Sonny," Heidi said.

"Between us, we can put together a decent operation, and I'll turn you into a top-flight detective. One of the best," I said. "So, what do you say?"

She drained her mug of beer. The server dropped off the take-out boxes. She tapped her fingertips on the top of her box after stowing the rest of her pizza.

"I've been thinking, too," she said. "We were good together out in Petrie's trailer. I don't want any grief about pulling the honeypot game, though. That shit pays the rent."

"And you don't call me *Boomer*," I said. "I'm really not, you know, by at least a year or so. So, what do you say?"

"Was this some sort of audition?" Libby asked, looking back and forth at Heidi and me.

"The trailer was the audition. As Heidi has pointed out, however, I'm not allowed to take on a new investigator until Mama approves."

"So," Libby said to Heidi. "What's the verdict, Hooch?"

Heidi glanced at me. "What is this *Hooch?*"

"American slang," I said. "It means hot sexy lady. You have to admit, she has a good eye."

"I see," Heidi said. "This might be a bigger job than you anticipate."

"I'm up to it," I told her.

"I never doubted it. All right, then." She took Libby's hand. "Mama approves."

Libby smiled as I held out my hand and said, "Congratulations. You made the team."

THE END

ABOUT THE AUTHOR

Retired clinical/forensic psychologist and college professor Richard Helms is the author of twenty-seven published novels. He is the recipient of the Killer Nashville Silver Falchion Award (twice); the Mystery Readers International Macavity Award; the Short Mystery Fiction Society Derringer Award (twice); the International Thriller Writers Thriller Award; and the Private Eye Writers of America Shamus Award (twice). His story "See Humble and Die" was featured in Houghton-Mifflin-Harcourt's *Best American Mystery Stories of 2020*, edited by Otto Penzler and C.J. Box, and his story "The Twenty-Fourth Canterbury" appears in the 2026 edition, edited by Penzler and Tess Gerritsen. His short stories have appeared frequently in *Ellery Queen Mystery Magazine*, *Alfred Hitchcock Mystery Magazine*, *Black Cat Mystery Magazine*, *Mystery Weekly*, and various anthologies and collections. *Great White* his is twenty-seventh novel. A former member of the Mystery Writers of America Board of Directors and president of MWA's Southeast Region, Richard Helms was presented with the SEMWA Magnolia Award in 2017 for his service to the chapter. Richard Helms and his wife Elaine live in Charlotte, North Carolina.

www.ingramcontent.com/pod-product-compliance
Lightning Source LLC
LaVergne TN
LVHW090549110826
845146LV00001B/80

* 9 7 9 8 9 9 0 0 4 1 2 3 3 *